Saraph

Saraph

A Novel
by

Todd S. Bindig

gatekeeper press™

Columbus, Ohio

Saraph

Published by Gatekeeper Press
2167 Stringtown Rd, Suite 109
Columbus, OH 43123-2989
www.GatekeeperPress.com

The editorial work for this book is entirely the product of the author. Gatekeeper Press did not participate in and is not responsible for any aspect of this element.

Library of Congress Control Number: 2021935744

ISBN (hardcover): 9781662912115
ISBN (paperback): 9781662912122

Contents

Prologue

"No One Cared about the Bread"

1940

The Spitfire growled and coughed as it came to rest on the misty British airfield; a fierce beast of the sky, now wounded and exhausted. She had thundered and soared and fought bravely but was now in great need of care and rest. No more would be asked of her; not this day at least.

Pilot Officer Robert Worthington slipped down from the wing of the Spitfire. He could feel his entire body trembling as he steadied himself and tried to slow his breathing. Robert was a promising young pilot, from a landed family, fresh out of school. Were it not for the Blitz, he would be in his first year at Oxford. But all of that seemed so far away now.

He saw the men, running across the airfield to see to the Spitfire. He walked, attempting to gain his composure, to meet his Squadron Leader and give his mission report. And there, striding towards him, was Squadron Leader Sharpps. Crisp and proper, Squadron Leader Martin Sharpps was everything the Royal Air Force could have hoped for in an Officer. All of his men looked up to him and respected him. Pilot Officer Worthington was no exception. He would have done almost anything for his Senior Officer's approval; he certainly did not want to be seen sniveling like a school-boy who'd lost a cricket match, no matter the validity of the cause of his distress.

"I say! Worthington!" called Squadron Leader Sharpps. "Let's get you inside, out of this bloody fog." Sharpps clapped his hand on the young Officer's shoulder and said quietly: "Steady on, Robert. You're home now."

The two men walked across the damp grass of the airfield to the Great House that was serving as Headquarters for their unit. When they reached the study that served as Sharpps's office, he called out: "Corporal Thomas!"

A RAF enlisted man, with ginger hair, who looked to be too young to shave, appeared and stood at attention. Saluting, he said smartly, "Here sir!"

Squadron Leader Sharpps smiled and returned his salute. "Excellent. Corporal, would you be so good as to find Pilot Officer Worthington something to eat, and bring him a pint as well?"

The Corporal smiled: "Very good, Sir."

"Right. Off you go." Sharpps pulled out a chair beside his desk and gestured to the young Pilot Officer, "Have a seat, Lad," as he sat down himself.

Pilot Officer Worthington sat down, saying: "Thank you, Sir." His hands were still shaking and he wasn't entirely certain that they would ever stop. "I suppose that you'll be wanting a full report."

Squadron Leader Sharpps smiled, but there was a seriousness behind his eyes; a grave concern that went beyond a patrol where only one plane returned. "No, Robert. You shall not be giving a full report to me about this mission, at this time. Two men arrived from some Ultra-Secret Intelligence Office of His Majesty's Government. They inquired about your patrol and if it had yet returned. They stated that if anyone survived the patrol – which they made emphatically clear that they sincerely doubted would be the case – that man, or men, was to speak first to them. Now, I don't know what's going on, but those two are rather odd. You must tell them the truth, Pilot Officer Worthington, but be careful how you say it. You've clearly had one hell of a fight, but keep your wits about you lad. There's something about the taste of these two – if you get my meaning – that's not exactly … well, you'll see what I mean in a moment."

"Sir?" Corporal Thomas had returned.

"Yes, Thomas, come in," replied Sharpps.

The Corporal came in carrying a plate with a heel of bread and a piece of white cheese in one hand and a pint of red ale in the other. He set them down in front of Pilot Officer Worthington and addressed Squadron Leader Sharpps: "Will there be anything else, Sir?"

"No. Thank you, Corporal. Please inform Sergeant Harris that Pilot Officer Worthington is ready for our guests to speak with him now."

Robert's hands were still shaking, but he was able to take a long drink of his red ale as the Corporal left the room. "Sir," he said quietly, "Do you think that I'm in any trouble?"

Squadron Leader Sharpps took a breath and quietly answered. "I don't know what's going on, Robert. I certainly hope you're not in any trouble. But – to put it plainly – I wasn't on that patrol and don't know what they are here to ask you about. Frankly, it's not every day when odd men from Secret Government Offices arrive to ask one of my men about a mission, which we all thought was going to be a routine little jaunt, but ended up with a single survivor. What I do know, my lad, is that you need to stay calm and cooperate with these men."

"Ahem." Sergeant Harris, standing at the door, cleared his throat. "Sir. The Gentlemen."

The Sergeant stepped aside, letting in two men. Robert's first thought, as he and Squadron Leader Sharpps stood to greet them, was that Sharpps was quite right: these men were in no way what he had expected to see as representatives of an Ultra-Secret Government Office. The first was an older man, about five-foot-two or three, with short cropped grey hair, a full grey beard and moustache, and round spectacles. He was not what Robert would have called fat, but he was certainly stout. He was wearing a tweed coat with leather elbows. His companion appeared to be considerably younger. "About my age," thought Robert. The second man was taller, about six feet tall, and quite thin. He was clean shaven, but his hair was a rumpled, mousey brown and probably two months grown past when it ought to have been trimmed. He was dressed like Robert would imagine an upper-classman at Oxford would look, if he cared nothing for proper dress and if he slept in his clothes.

"Gentlemen," said Squadron Leader Sharpps, "This is the man about which you were inquiring: Pilot Officer Robert Worthington. He has been instructed to give you his complete cooperation. If you should be in need of anything, ring that bell there," gesturing to a rope behind the desk, "and someone will be right with you."

The first man answered with a crisp Oxford accent, "Very good, Sir. Thank you. May I use your desk?"

Squadron Leader Sharpps replied, stepping away from the desk and towards the door, "Of course. Would you like me to have a chair brought in for your … counterpart?"

The first man replied, not looking for any sign of agreement from the second man, "No. no. That won't be necessary."

"Very well then," said Squadron Leader Sharpps, "I shall leave you to your business." And with that, both he and Sergeant Harris left the room and shut the door.

The bearded, spectacled man, sat down at the squadron leader's desk. The tall, lean man, smoothly and silently walked and stood slightly behind the older man and to his left. The tall man made piercing eye contact with Robert. Then, in a graceful motion, not breaking eye contact, he bent, reaching forward, and picked up Robert's piece of cheese. He straightened, and brought the cheese to his mouth, slowly taking a very small bite, never breaking eye contact. Robert, left standing awkwardly by his chair, only now realized that he still had his pint glass of red ale in his hand.

"Have a seat Pilot Officer Worthington," said the seated man. "Come, don't let our little talk disturb your … snack."

Robert felt the heat and color rise to his face. He sat, taking another sip of ale as he did. "Thank you, Sir," he said, setting his half-finished drink on the desk.

"Where are my manners," chuckled the older man. "Of course, we know who you are. Allow me to make our introduction. My name is Professor Jones and this is my associate, Mr. Smith. We work for a department of His Majesty's Government that handles, shall we say, extremely sensitive matters." He smiled broadly.

Robert's head was spinning and his hands had positively not stopped shaking, but he was certain of at least one thing: these men's names were definitely not Jones and Smith. "It's a pleasure to meet you," said Robert, his manners taking over.

"Charmed," said Mr. Smith, dryly. His eyes burned a crystal-blue fire, starring into Robert's. He took another very small bite of Robert's piece of cheese.

"We'd like to discuss your patrol, your last patrol, the one from which you just arrived home," began Professor Jones. "Tell us," he said slowly, "what happened up there?"

Robert took a deep breath. His eye caught the glass of red ale, seductively, flirtatiously beckoning him. He took it in his shaking hand and drank. Setting the glass down, he starred past the two men from His Majesty's Government and began speaking.

"It was a standard patrol. Nothing unusual. We didn't expect to meet any Germans; they haven't been bombing up here in a while, certainly not at this time of day. The fog and clouds were thick over the sea, and Fitzpatrick – he was Senior on this one – said we should climb above the clouds and have a look around. But, we never expected to see anything."

"But you did see something, above the clouds and the mist." stated Professor Jones, in more of a matter-of-fact way than as an actual question.

"Yes," answered the young Pilot Officer. "We came upon them – almost crashing into them – as we came out of the clouds. Germans. Lots of Germans. I never got a count, things happened too fast. I do know that they had Messerschmitt bombers. But it was those bloody Focke-Wulfs that tore us up. I never got a count, but there were more of them than there were of us. We tried to fight them, but it was no use. In seconds, I was the only Spitfire left. I tried to escape, by diving back into the mist, but … that's …" He was shaking badly and the tears were freely rolling down his cheeks.

"But, what?" asked the professor whose-name-was-definitely-not-Jones. "What happened then?"

Robert tried to pull himself together, but his ability so to do was rapidly slipping away. "Sir. All my friends were gone. I was terrified. Desperate. I had to run. I'm not a coward. I'm not!"

"We know you're not a coward, Lad," said the professor, reassuringly. "Now finish your nice ale and tell us what happened next."

Robert swallowed the last of his ale, and desperately wanted another. He looked from one man to the other and felt like a small, scared child. "I can't."

"Why can't you?" asked the bearded man behind the desk. "Don't you know what happened? One minute you were in a fire-fight, desperately out-matched, and then you were safely back home. What happened in between?" He leaned back in his chair and steepled his fingers above his chest.

Robert wanted, more than anything, to get up and run from the room. It was only the thought of Squadron Leader Sharpps that kept him in his seat. "I... I... You won't believe me. You'll think that I'm mad."

"Pilot Officer Worthington," the professor said softly, but with an undeniable firmness, "what did you see?"

Robert broke. "A dragon. I saw a bloody dragon. It was huge and dark and incredibly fast. It roared out of the clouds past me and the whole world was burning. It tore one of the bombers in two with its powerful legs. Its tail hurdled fighters from the sky. The Germans tried to fight, but it was as if their bullets could do nothing to it. And everything was burning. It was like the clouds were made of fire. All the German planes were falling into the sea, burning as they fell. And I pushed my Spitfire as hard as I could to get away. I was certain that I would die; falling and burning and screaming from the sky. But it let me go. It paid absolutely no attention to me at all. It was like I wasn't even there. Or," he paused. He had not thought of it until that very moment. "Or perhaps it was ... it was almost like ... it was almost like it was fighting for us."

"Well," said Professor Jones, as calmly as if he had just been read Mother Goose, "that is certainly a very interesting story. Now. You, my lad, are never, ever going to tell that story again. Not to anyone, ever in your life. Would you like to know why you are never going tell that story again? You are never going to tell that story again because people will think that you are a lunatic. Won't they think that he is a lunatic, Mr. Smith?"

"A raving lunatic, Professor Jones," answered Smith dryly, popping the last bit of the cheese, which he had been slowly eating throughout the entire conversation, into his mouth.

"And we wouldn't want people to think young Robert is a lunatic, would we Mr. Smith?"

"We would certainly not want that at all, Professor Jones."

"Why, they might lock the poor lad up."

"Right you are, Professor Jones. They'd throw away the key."

"And all sorts of unfortunate things happen in asylums, don't they, Mr. Smith?"

"Terribly unfortunate things, Professor Jones."

"And we wouldn't want that, would we, Robert?" The Professor's eyes burned into the young Pilot Officer like dragon-fire. "So, I'll tell you what you're going to do, my lad. You're going to forget that story you just told and try a new one."

Robert took a breath and started again, only this time, when he turned his Spitfire and dove into the clouds and mists, the Germans either lost him or paid him no mind; who's to say?

"That's much better, Robert," said the man calling himself 'Professor Jones'.

"Much better, indeed," said the man whom Professor Jones had introduced as 'Mr. Smith' and who had eaten Robert's piece of cheese – not that Robert had anything resembling an appetite anymore.

"Why don't you go give that nice, second report to your Squadron Leader – Sharpps is it?" said Professor Jones, calmly smiling. "Give him that report, have another pint of that lovely red ale and then take a nice rest."

Pilot Officer Robert Worthington stood up, saying nothing, and walked to the door. He opened it, not looking back, walked out, and closed the door behind him.

Neither of the men from His Majesty's Government moved or spoke for a few moments. "Well, then" said Professor Jones, turning to Mr. Smith and standing. "That went rather well, I'd say."

"Quite well, indeed, Professor Jones."

"Oh, you can bloody-well stop it with that; the lad is gone."

"What?" asked Mr. Smith.

"That sinister, spooky tone," said Professor Jones, now chuckling. "And why ever did you eat that poor boy's cheese?"

"What? I was being menacing; being scary," said Mr. Smith. "And we didn't have time for breakfast, after all. I'm bloody hungry."

"Well was it at least a good cheese?" asked Professor Jones, with mock interest.

"Actually, it was quite nice. Mature and salty with a rather lovely bite to it," answered Mr. Smith.

"You are quite ridiculous, Mr. Smith."

"What?"

"Right. Let's go. Our work here is done. He'll never tell that story again."

. . . . . .

The two odd men from an Ultra-Secret Office of His Majesty's Government left shortly after that, with few words to anyone. Squadron Leader Sharpps interviewed Pilot Officer Worthington and, after hearing his story, reassured him that he was no coward to run – all the same, he could take as much time as he needed before going up again. Martin Sharpps was a very good Squadron Leader, after all.

Pilot Officer Robert Worthington never got in a plane again – piloted by himself or anyone else. His hands never did stop shaking. He did, however, come to develop a great taste for red ale.

One other strange thing: there was never another German bombing run in that part of England.

Part I

---

or

"Before"

Chapter 1

"Boys will be Brothers"

1978

The sound in his ears was unintelligible, high-pitched, yipping – it made him think of what a pack of small dogs would sound like – as the older boy's fist repeatedly slammed into his face. He was desperately writhing to try to get out of the grasp of the other two boys and fight back, but the skinny boy with light-auburn hair and ice-blue eyes was no match for the three older boys. He could feel the warm blood running from his nose and the repeated thumping of the other boy's fists, but he was surprised that it didn't really hurt as much as he imagined that it would have when the fight began.

The high-pitched yipping of the other children watching the fight was louder and louder. From the back of the crowd, another boy – small, skinny, ginger-haired, with blue eyes and sunburnt cheeks – came charging forward. Without the "battle-cry" typical of young boys, the ginger-haired boy leapt upon one of the older boys, with his fists flailing.

The older boys distracted, their hold on the first boy momentarily loosened, but that second was all he needed. His small, skinny arm wiggled free and a youthful fist-of-fury exploded forth into the face of the biggest of the boys – the one who had been pommeling him until a second ago. The older boy's nose erupted into a geyser of crimson. He cried out and stumbled back.

The older boy who had been leapt upon and pommeled by the small, ginger ball-of-fury had managed to free himself and was fighting back. He was bigger and stronger, but the ginger boy was shockingly fast. He managed to strike and dodge and strike again, but eventually the bigger boy knocked him to the ground and fell upon him. The ginger boy writhed to get free, but the larger boy's weight was sufficient to hold him long enough to land damaging, bloodying blows.

The booming voice of the first teacher on the scene – an extremely tall, bald, and over-weight gym teacher named Mr. Sanderson – startled the third of the older boys – who was currently the only participant of the battle left unscathed – and the third, older boy began to try to run away. Unfortunately for him, he ran directly into Mrs. Whitmer – an elderly art teacher who was also running to break up the fight – and they both fell to the ground.

In the blink of an eye, three other teachers were on the scene and the crowd had scattered. The boys were separated and the fight was over. Mr. Sanderson towered over everyone. He bent down and helped Mrs. Whitmer to her feet. "You boys are all going to Principal Hornsby's office to explain yourselves! Until then, not a damn word out of any of you!"

Mr. Sanderson's beefy hands grabbed hold of the skinny arms of the two smaller boys and he marched across the playground to Principal Hornsby's office, calling out: "Tina. John. You two bring those others and put them in the conference room. And don't let them have the chance to talk about their story either!"

When Mr. Sanderson and the two smaller, younger boys reached Principal Hornsby's office, his secretary, Miss Andrews – a pretty, black-haired, young woman in her mid-twenties – stood up at her desk and put her hand to her mouth as she gasped, "oh my goodness! Boys!"

"Nah, Kim," said Mr. Sanderson, "It looks like these ones were the good-guys." He gestured to two chairs for the boys to sit down and then pointed to the three older boys being lead into the conference room. "It was those three that I saw whaling on these two."

Miss Andrews appeared to be on the verge of tears. Mr. Sanderson said: "Alright. Kim, call Mrs. Schultz to clean the boys up and then call the mothers in. I'm going to talk to Steve." With that the enormous gym teacher walked to Principal Hornsby's door and went in without knocking.

Miss Andrews sat down and picked up her phone. "Nurse Schultz? Yes. Please come to Principal Hornsby's office. There has been a fight. Yes. Yes, bring First-Aid supplies and ice. Thank you!"

The boy with the light-auburn hair and ice-blue eyes turned to the ginger-haired boy. "Thank you."

The ginger boy smiled a crooked smile and said: "You're welcome."

"My name is Dave," said the first boy, with the light-auburn hair.

"I'm Chris," said the second boy, with the ginger hair and the crooked smile.

They both smiled – blood trickling from noses and scrapes – and shook hands.

. . . . . .

Mary Shepherd, Dave's mother – a five-foot-four, extraordinarily beautiful woman with long, light-blonde, wavy hair, which fell down her back and over her shoulders, and who had the same ice-blue eyes as her son – walked into the school office just as Nurse Schultz was finishing with the two boys. Both nose-bleeds had been stopped, scrapes – both on faces and knuckles – had been cleaned and bandaged, and each of the boys was holding an ice-pack to his cheek. "David," she said with her eyes flashing in anger and her arms crossed, looking directly at her son. "At least you had the intelligence to do this on a day I had off from work. If I had to leave the hospital for this nonsense, you'd be in real trouble."

"Yes, Mama," said Dave, looking at the floor. He knew that she was right. His mother was a nurse at the local hospital and though he didn't know exactly what she did, he knew her job was very important. If she had to leave work to come to the school, he knew he'd be in real trouble.

"Good thing, too, that your father never minds when your little sister stays at the store with him."

"Yes, Mama."

She couldn't understand it. Dave was a good boy and had never been in any trouble before. Even now, she couldn't help but smile at her sweet-little-boy. However, when the school secretary called her to tell her that her first-grade son had been in a fight – fifteen minutes after she got home from picking up her daughter, his sister, from her half-day kindergarten – she had been furious.

However, now that she was here – seeing her son sitting next to another little boy who appeared to be Dave's best-friend – she was more confused than angry. It was then that another woman walked into the school office.

Maggie Hanley was Chris' mother. She was five-foot-two, with brown hair in a short pony-tail. She had green eyes with dark circles under them. She was extremely thin and her skin was ghostly pale. She wore a waitress' uniform from a local diner and she looked utterly exhausted.

She looked first at Mary, then Nurse Schultz and lastly at Chris. She sighed, and in a soft, quiet voice said: "Hi, Chris."

Chris smiled his crooked smile but then looked at the floor and said: "Hi, Mom." But then quickly looked up again and asked brightly, "how's work today?"

"Busy. But at least the lunch rush was pretty much over when they called," she said with a small smile.

Mary turned to the other mother, smiled warmly, and extended her hand, "Hello. My name is Mary Shepherd. I'm Dave's mother"

Maggie smiled shyly and took her hand, "I'm Maggie Hanley. My son is Chris. Pleased to meet you."

"I wish it was under better circumstances. Apparently, our boys had a bit of a fight," said Mary, turning to Dave and frowning.

A deep voice interrupted her. "That's not exactly true, Ma'am. At least not the way that you think."

The women turned to see the man speaking. Mr. Sanderson filled the door to the principal's office. "I'm Frank Sanderson, the gym teacher. Why don't you ladies and your two young men join me to discuss this business with Mr. Hornsby?"

The two mothers walked to their sons, took their hands as the boys stood, and followed the large man with the deep voice into the principal's office.

Mrs. Schultz – a stocky, no-nonsense, RN in her late-fifties, with her grey hair in a tight bun and her white cap securely bobby-pinned – said nothing, but collected her supplies and calmly walked to the conference room where the older boys' mothers were arriving. "Boys will be boys," she thought as she began cleaning the blood off the oldest boy's nose.

. . . . . .

"Have a seat, ladies," said the principal. Two wooden chairs with ornately carved arm-rests had been placed in front of the large desk, facing it. Mary and Maggie looked at each other and sat down. The two boys stood with Mr. Sanderson, who placed his hands – more gently than menacing – on their shoulders.

The man sitting behind the desk was a small, thin, weasel-like man with glasses that had lenses too big for his narrow face, and thinning, greying hair that desperately needed washing. He smiled with crooked teeth and said, in a squeaky voice: "I'm Mr. Hornsby, the principal of our fine school. I assume that you are Mrs. Hanley and Mrs. Shepherd."

The women smiled and nodded politely.

"Mr. Sanderson, would you be so good as to tell these lovely ladies what you were telling me, with regard to their boys?" Mr. Hornsby smiled as the women turned to the gym teacher standing on their left. The principal stared at Dave's mother, in an extremely inappropriate way, until he realized that Dave was, in turn, staring at him – his young brow frowning angrily at the principal. Mr. Hornsby's eyes then quickly looked to the gym teacher as the big man began speaking.

"I was on the playground with some other teachers after lunch. Because we have a small school, at lunch and recess we have all the kids together, first to fourth grade – not the kindergarteners, they go home for the day at the start of lunch. I've never thought this was a good idea – the different grades together – but"

"Hrmph!" Mr. Hornsby loudly cleared his throat.

"As I was saying," continued Mr. Sanderson. "I was on the playground and I heard some commotion. It was clear that there was a fight. I came running, as fast as I could to break it up. Mrs. Whitmer was running from the other direction. As I came closer, I saw three older boys – fourth-graders – beating up your boys. Well, that's not right, really. It would be better to say that they were trying to beat up your boys; your sons were giving 'em hell. I broke up the fight. One of the older boys knocked Mrs. Whitmer down, trying to get away – poor old lady, she had to go home to lie down. But anyway, don't be hard on the boys. They were out-numbered by bigger kids. And they didn't start the fight anyway."

It was then that Dave spoke up. "Excuse me, Mr. Sanderson."

"Yes, Dave."

"I'm sorry, Sir. But, what you said just now isn't the truth."

Mr. Sanderson was calm and still. "Ok, Dave. Tell us what happened."

Dave stared at the floor and slowly said: "They didn't start the fight. I did."

Mary took a deep breath and looked intently at her son.

"I heard those older boys talking about Vietnam. The biggest one said that everyone who had come home should have been sent to jail because they were all baby-killers. So, I ran, jumped up and punched him in his stupid face!"

Mary sighed and said, "David," sounding more sad than angry.

Principal Hornsby spoke: "Young man. Vietnam has been over for almost as long as you have been alive. This is very inappropriate behavior. He should not have said that, but you can't hit another student because he makes you angry."

"My Dad fought in Vietnam and my Mama was a nurse there! They aren't that thing those boys said!" yelled Dave, tears welling up in his eyes.

Mary shook her head and said quietly: "David. Quiet down, Son."

"And after I hit him, he threw me down and the others held me while he hit me," Dave continued, more quietly. "I tried to fight them, but they held me down until Chris came and fought one of them. I got my hand free and hit the big one in the nose. He bled a lot." Dave was smiling proudly now but tears were still in his eyes.

Then Chris spoke up: "That's right. I saw the fight happening and heard someone say what happened to make it start. So, I ran to help. I jumped on one of them and fought him, as hard as I could."

Maggie was crying softly, her face in her hands and shaking her head. "Oh, Chris."

"I had to, Mom!" Chris's eyes were now filling with tears, as well. "Daddy died over there!" The tears were streaming down his face and his words were broken and staggered. "And any way … Dave was … fighting three of them … all alone!" His words drifted off into a storm of tears.

Dave reached out and put his hand on Chris' shoulder, both to comfort and again thank his new best-friend. Mary, opened her purse and handed Maggie a small, unopened packet of tissues. Maggie took it, whispered "thank you," and dried her sad, tired eyes.

Mr. Hornsby opened his mouth to speak, but the big gym teacher interrupted him. "Mrs. Shepherd. Mrs. Hanley. I think that you should be very proud of your boys; I know I am. I know you can't tell by looking at me now but I fought with the Marine Corps in Vietnam, back in the early days. I served my country proudly and with honor, as did the men I served with. Now, I think that those other boys ought to get a week's suspension for beating on much smaller kids. I also, personally, think that they should have to write an apology letter to the Legion Post for what they said about us Vets. And, I think that if anyone else thinks differently about those things," he paused, looking hard at the principal, whose mouth was hanging open in shock, "we're gonna have a very serious disagreement; if ya know what I mean."

Mr. Hornsby abruptly closed his mouth. He took a slow breath as the two mothers turned to look at him; all eyes now staring at him intently. Then, slowly, he spoke with a voice that seemed both quieter and squeakier than before. "David and Christopher are excused. Mrs. Shepherd and Mrs. Hanley, you may take your sons home and they are not required to return to school until they have healed from their injuries. Mr. Sanderson and I shall finish our discussion with the other boys. And, I assure you ladies that your sons will return to a safe school."

Mary smiled and looked at Maggie. "Maggie, may I talk to you outside, when we leave?"

Maggie gave a small smile in return and said, quietly, "That would be nice."

Mary and Maggie stood together. They walked over to their sons and took the boys' hands.

Mary looked up and smiled at the big gym teacher. "Thank you, Mr. Sanderson, for everything." She then turned to the principal, who looked even smaller and more weasel-like than before. "Good day, Mr. Hornsby."

Turning to her new friend, she said, "Shall we go, Maggie."

Maggie Hanley smiled and responded, "Indeed," with a quiet giggle.

The two women walked out the door that Mr. Sanderson was holding open for them, holding hands with their sons, all of them now smiling. Mr. Sanderson shut the door behind them and turned to the principal, crossing his arms and smiling broadly. He leaned slightly forward and –more quietly than anyone that day had heard him speak – he said: "What's the plan, Steve?"

Steven Hornsby, gulped, realized his mouth was as dry as a desert, and smiled awkwardly up at the gym teacher who now seemed even more enormous than he had ever before appeared.

. . . .

The two women had, ironically, parked right next to each-other. Neither car was brand new, but Mary's sky-blue Chevy Station Wagon had less rust than Maggie's faded yellow Chevette.

Mary smiled warmly at Maggie. She liked her. She knew next to nothing about the woman but had an immediate affection for her and her son. "Maggie, would you like to follow us home and have dinner at our house tonight? You can meet my husband, John, and our little girl, Abigail, and the young warriors can spend some time getting to know each other better. It might be really fun."

Maggie smiled at Mary. She wasn't used to people being kind to her and hadn't socially spoken or interacted with another adult since Chris and she had moved to the area, so she hesitated for a moment. But, there was something in Mary's beautiful, ice-blue eyes. It was a degree of absolute sincerity that Maggie hadn't seen since her Danny – her husband and Chris' father – had left for the war. He looked at her like that when he promised that he would love her forever: "no matter how it goes over there – I'll always love you and our baby."

"That does sound really nice. Sure. After all," said Maggie, "my super-cool boss said that if I had to go to the school, I didn't need to come back for the rest of my shift." Maggie smiled. She said it like her boss had been doing her a favor, but the tone in which he had said it that afternoon had revealed that it was meant to be a punishment.

"Alright!" said Mary, getting into the Station Wagon with Dave in the front seat, next to her. "You can just follow us there."

Maggie smiled. "Indeed," she said with a tiny giggle.

As Maggie was getting into the Chevette with Chris, Mary rolled down her window. "Hey! I meant to ask you when we left the office and you said that, what's the story with the 'indeed' thing?"

Maggie smiled. "My husband used to say it and make a silly face, raising one eye-brow. Usually, he said it when something hard or sad was happening; but also just whenever, to be fun. I like to say it sometimes. It always makes me laugh a little."

Mary laughed, "That's great! But be careful, that might catch on."

Maggie laughed, "Indeed!"

The two women and their sons drove out of the school parking lot. Maggie smiled. She couldn't shake the feeling that things were going to get at least a little better. And she drove, following the sky-blue Station Wagon.

· · · · · ·

Maggie Hanley had lived in Western Maine for close to a decade, so the twisting drive through the hills and forests was nothing new or surprising. What did surprise her was how far they were driving. "They really live way out here!" she thought to herself.

When they finally came to the turn-off that was, she assumed, the Shepherds' drive way, she knew that she would have missed it had she not been following Mary. There was nothing to mark the turn. It looked, at first, like Mary was driving off the road, into the forest. Instead, as she followed, she found herself driving down a long, twisting way that seemed to be some sort of access-road through the forest. They drove down the twisting and turning road for a bit over two miles, and Maggie was really starting to wonder how much further this road would go when, just as they came out of a turn that came up a steep slope, they arrived.

To call it a 'house' would be a vast understatement. Maggie had never been in a mansion before, but that's what she would call this place. It was at least 3 stories and spread out widely. The design looked like pictures she had seen in a National Geographic magazine of a Viking "great hall," with swirling wood carved in the shape of animals and knot-work. It had the feel of a cabin, but it was much too large and ornate for that term to apply. They pulled up in a large gravel parking area, which could hold several cars. It was situated between the front door of the house and a large wooden deck that stretched out into a lake.

The lake was large, but not so large that she couldn't see the other side clearly. Its waters were a beautiful blue and they gently lapped against the shore. Forest surrounded the lake and all she could see, all around, were forested hills. Around the house was a large green lawn, and there seemed to be a gap in the trees, behind the house, so she guessed the lawn went all the way around the house. There wasn't really a beach, but it looked like the large wooden deck would be perfect for both gaining access to the water and for resting and relaxing. In fact, she saw what she guessed was a pit for a campfire with some chairs and a picnic table on the far-side of the deck.

They all got out of their cars and Mary smiled and waved at Maggie. "Sorry it's such a long and winding drive. How about the boys go play on the deck and we can go inside and talk. John will be home soon and we can figure dinner out then," she said.

Maggie smiled. "Sounds good. Chris, have fun with Dave but be safe."

"Ok, Mom"

Dave pulled Chris' shirt sleeve. "Come on! Maybe, if we're real quiet, we can see some fish!" said Dave excitedly.

The two boys ran over to the large deck and then slowed down and crept out to the edge.

Mary led Maggie to the large wooden front door and they went inside. Maggie was awe-struck by what she saw. The entry room was huge and was open up two, or maybe three, stories. Before them was a large stone staircase that split half-way up, going to the right and to the left, with a mezzanine balcony behind it, linking the stairs at the top, and hallways going off in both directions. Large open halls led to the right and to the left, below the staircase. Off to her right were comfortable-looking chairs and a couch around a large fire-place. The décor was very far from late-1970's modern; it was more like what she would have called 'medieval'. There were large tapestries featuring dragons and unicorns, faeries and princesses. There were several wall sconces, all with tall candles. Behind her, over the front door, was a large, beautiful, stained glass window, featuring a red dragon in flight against a blue sky.

"Come on, we'll wait in the kitchen," said Mary.

Maggie followed and hoped she didn't look as awe-struck as she felt.

They walked down the hall to the right, past the fire-place, and into a large kitchen. The large, well-furnished kitchen had an island in the center with some stools around it. Further, there were some steps down, spanning across a large arched entry and opening into a large sitting room with full, comfortable looking couches and chairs around a coffee table, next to another large fire-place. Along one wall were glass French-doors that looked out to the large deck and the lake. A stretch of green grass separated the doors and the deck with a slate, flagstone path leading the way from one to the other and ending near the fire-pit and chairs on the deck. The ceiling of the kitchen wasn't as high as the entry room, but it was impressive nonetheless. Some pots, pans and cooking utensils hung from a rack suspended over the island in the center of the kitchen. The ceiling stayed constant as it stretched from the kitchen to the sitting room, and opened with a sky-light above the coffee table. The décor in the sitting room was the same as the entry room.

Mary led Maggie to the sitting room and gestured to a couch and chair with their backs to the kitchen but with a full view of the deck and lake through the glass French-doors. There they could watch the boys at the edge of the deck, lying on their bellies next to each other, looking into the beautiful blue water, trying to see some fish. "Have a seat," said Mary smiling.

"You have a really beautiful house," said Maggie, sitting in the chair.

"Thank you," said Mary sitting on the couch closest to the chair. "It was built for my parents when they came here from Iceland after World War Two. I don't know the details, but I guess my father did some

work for the British and American governments and because of it, we
got this house, the lake and a lot of land all around it."

"Wow!" said Maggie. "Whatever he did must have been a really
big deal!"

"I don't actually know," said Mary. "He never would talk about
it, not at all. And my father was not the sort of man you pressured into
talking. I'm pretty sure that my mother didn't know either, at least not
any details. Either way, she never told me anything about it."

"Do you have a lot of brothers or sisters?" asked Maggie.

"No. Just me," said Mary. "I always thought that was weird,
because we're Catholic. And, you know, all the other families at church
were sort of big. But my mother said that was the way it always was with
'our Family': one, rarely two children. She said that's all our people get.
Imagine my surprise when I got pregnant with Abigail less than a year
after I had Dave." She laughed. "Want to hear God laugh? Tell him your
plans."

"Yeah," said Maggie looking down. But then, quickly, she asked,
"So, how did you meet your husband?"

Mary smiled brightly. "I met my John in Vietnam. I was a Navy
nurse at Da Nang, and John was a Force Recon Marine who was sent
to us after he was pretty seriously wounded during the Tet Offensive
in January of '68. I was one of the nurses who took care of him. I
really thought that he was amazingly sweet and fell for him right away.
He healed well and quickly. He had to stay at the hospital until they
could send him home and we started dating. Well, like I said, we fell in
love really fast. He was going back home, and because of his injuries,
would be honorably discharged from the Marine Corps – this was really
upsetting to him, because that's all he ever wanted to do. Also, he didn't
really have any place to go. So, I told him to come and live in Maine, near
here, of course. The thing was, I had to finish my service in the Navy,
and so, we were going to have a distance relationship, a weird one, with
the girl off at war and the boy waiting at home. Well, I know it sounds
crazy because we had only known each other for two months, but he
asked me to marry him. I said yes, of course, but I wanted him to ask
my father before we made plans. He said that was the right thing to do
and was excited to meet my parents – he had no idea what he was in
for." She laughed.

"Anyway, he came back home and got a room in one of the towns near here, I forget which now, and worked at the bar that was downstairs from his room, doing pretty much anything – bouncing, cooking, cleaning, tending bar, whatever they needed. He had saved all his money while he was in the Marines and he got by on very little, so he saved more while he did that job. He wrote to me, literally every day, and I wrote back when I could. I was transferred to a Navy Hospital in Virginia in the end of '68, which was better. Also, we figured out how to see each other whenever I got R&R, which was really nice."

"I finally got out of the Navy in the fall of 1970. I had also saved a lot of money. Aside from what we had spent seeing each other on my R&Rs, we were doing alright. I hadn't seen my parents since I left for Vietnam in late 1967 – they never travelled and really kept to themselves – and I wanted to save my time to see John. They knew about him from my letters home, but didn't meet him 'til I came home. We got married in 1971 and I had Dave about a year later."

"So, you guys moved in with your parents, here, when you got married?" asked Maggie.

"Actually, before we got married. I stayed in my old room and John moved into the bedroom that became ours after we were married – on the opposite side of the house, my parents' room in between." Mary laughed, "Catholic, and all that, you know."

"My father died the same day that Dave was born – that was really sad – and my mother died about a month later – she really missed my father – so the house and everything was left to us."

"And you're still a nurse?" asked Maggie.

"Sure am," answered Mary. "I'm a RN at that little hospital about three miles from the boys' school. We have a small ER, we also have a labor and delivery / maternity floor, with another floor with a few in-patient beds. We don't do anything too serious; if the patient is really sick we transport them to Augusta or Portland. I work three days a week."

"What does your husband, John, do?" asked Maggie.

"He runs a 'Campin' Store'," Mary said the words in a deep voice and laughed. "We're not far from Mt. Blue State Park. The store is between here and there. I'm sure he'll tell you about it; he loves his job."

"That's a good thing," smiled Maggie.

. . . .

Dave and Chris had been happily looking at the little fish at the end of the deck for some time when they heard, first, the approaching engine, and then, the crunch of the gravel under the tires as the black Chevy Pick-up pulled up to the house. Dave turned to Chris, "That's my Dad and Abigail! You should meet them!"

The two boys jumped up and ran to the truck, which had now come to a stop. John was busy un-buckling Abigail's seat belt. He lifted his daughter to the ground and turned to meet the boys running across the gravel.

"Well. Dave, you've found a friend," said John Shepherd. Dave's father was six feet tall, with shoulder-length wavy black hair, a full, thick, black beard, and deep-blue eyes. He was in impressive physical shape – very strong and fast – and had a deep, rolling voice with a Texas drawl he had never lost, though he had left Texas about fifteen years ago. There was something almost wolf-like to the way he moved and especially the way he looked when he spoke to you – often looking out of the corner of his eye, tilting his head as he spoke. If you paid very close attention, you would notice that he walked with a very slight limp, from an old injury to his left leg.

Chris stepped forward and extended his hand. "I'm Chris Hanley," he said. And then he proudly added, "Dave and I are best-friends!"

John bent and shook the young boy's hand and smiled warmly. "Hello, Chris. I'm John Shepherd. It's very nice to meet you."

Abigail stepped forward. "Hi. I'm Abigail Shepherd. I'm Dave's sister and I'm 5." She was an adorable little girl; the miniature image of her mother. She had long light-blonde hair that was wavy when it was down, but today was in two braids that fell over her shoulders. She had the same ice-blue eyes as her mother and brother, and rosy cheeks.

Chris looked at Abigail and smiled his crooked smile. "Hi Abigail. You are the prettiest girl I have ever seen."

Abigail giggled. "Thank you."

John grabbed his old ruck-sack from the truck. "Why don't you kids go play for a bit. Chris, you stayin' for supper?"

Chris answered, "I think so. My mom is inside talking to your wife."

"Great," said John, still smiling. "Y'all run along and play now," as he walked into the house.

He knew right where they would be, so he set his ruck-sack down right inside the door, slipped off his hiking boots and walked to the kitchen in his sock-feet. He walked over to the refrigerator. "Hi, Baby," he said causally, without looking as he opened the refrigerator door. "I'm getting' a beer, you want anything?"

"Hi. John," said Mary from the couch. "This is our new friend Maggie Hanley, she's Chris' mom."

Maggie started to stand, but Mary shook her head and she sat back down. John's head looked up over the refrigerator door and he smiled, "Hello, Ma'am. I'm John. Can I get you ladies something to drink? Tea, coffee, beer, wine?"

Maggie looked to Mary. Mary said, "Wine sounds nice. Do you like wine, Maggie?"

Maggie smiled, "I don't usually have wine much, but I remember that I liked one that was sweet and light-yellow color."

John called out, "I got two like that. One's called Black Tower and the other's called Blue Nun. Both are cold."

Maggie squinted slightly and then said, "I think Black Tower sounds familiar. It might be the one I had before and liked."

Mary laughed. "Black Tower it is, then."

John removed the cork from the cold bottle and set it on the counter-top. He walked over to the cupboard and removed two wine glasses. He then walked back to the refrigerator and took out a bottle of ice-cold Busch beer and popped off the bottle-cap. He poured the wine into the glasses and took the drinks into the sitting-room. He set the glasses of wine on the coffee table, bent down and gently kissed Mary's lips and sat down next to her with his beer in his hand. He took a long drink and gestured with the bottle at the glass French-doors. "Looks like the kids are gettin' on well."

The three children were running and laughing on the lawn. "Yes," said Mary. "So, Chris was in the fight too; he helped Dave. Three fourth-graders. Dave started it because the older boys said something stupid about the war."

"The war? Vietnam? Why the hell are little kids talkin' about 'Nam on the playground?"

"Probably their parents," answered Mary.

"That's been over for years now. Time to move on, not fight about it. Certainly not little kids. What the bigger kids say to set Dave off?"

"I believe the term 'baby-killer' was used."

"Well then." John took another drink of his beer. "And you say Chris jumped in to help Dave against the bigger kids?"

"Yes," answered Mary.

"Brave kid."

"His Daddy died in Vietnam," said Maggie, quietly.

"And he also said he couldn't just leave Dave alone against three bigger kids," said Mary.

John said nothing. A moment passed. He nodded and finished his beer. He then stood up, walked to the refrigerator, opened another bottle of beer and returned to his seat, setting it on the coffee table. "You have a fine boy, Ma'am. He was very polite when he met me and he's damn brave for a little kid."

"Thank you," she smiled. "You don't have to call me ma'am though; Maggie's fine."

"Well," said Mary taking a sip of her wine. "Have a drink and tell us your story." She caressed John's hand. He looked into her ice-blue eyes and she said, "I was just telling her how we met."

John smiled.

"Okay," said Maggie. And she slowly began the story.

. . . .

"I met Danny Hanley at a foster-home we both lived in as teenagers. My mom died when I was very little – I barely remember her – and I never knew my father or anything about his story. Danny's parents were a different story, but it ended the same way. By the time we were teenagers, we had been transferred all over the area around the suburbs of Albany, New York and finally ended up at the same foster-home with a nice, older couple. There were two other girls and one other boy, but Danny and I spent all the time we could together. We were inseparable."

"By the time we were eighteen, we decided to take the little money we had saved, get married and move away from New York. I don't remember why we chose Portland, Maine but that's where we went. We had a horrible time with money and were barely getting by. I was a waitress, like I still am, but he couldn't seem to find anything. He was big, strong, smart, and worked hard – when he could find work – but he couldn't find anything. I'll never forget the day when work found him."

"He was sitting at the counter in the diner where I was working. The boss was actually really cool about it and would let him a have free coffee and something small for lunch. He said that he would give Danny a job, if anything opened up, but no one ever quit – probably because he was such a nice boss."

"Anyway, Danny was sitting at the counter when the Marine Corps recruiter walked in and sat down at a stool a little way down the counter from Danny. I was his waitress. He seemed very nice and extremely polite. He ordered a black coffee and just sat there drinking it. Danny was drinking his coffee and looking at a newspaper, the want-ads. After about twenty minutes. The recruiter spoke up. 'Hey buddy. I can't help but notice that you're looking for a job.'"

"Danny looked up. 'I'm sorry. Are you talking to me?'"

"'I sure am,' answered the recruiter. 'You looking for work?'"

"I'm not sure why he answered; it was probably the desperation of not being able to find a job for six months. Danny answered: 'Actually, yeah. I'm looking for a job.'"

"The Marine Corps recruiter smiled. 'Well this is your lucky day, buddy. The Marines are hiring strong young men like you. Good pay. Job security.'"

"Danny shook his head. 'I don't want to go to Vietnam.'"

"The recruiter smiled. 'Not every Marine goes to Vietnam. There are lots of jobs in the Corps.'"

"So, to make a long story short, Danny left with the Marine Corps recruiter. After a couple of days, Danny was certain that this was the answer. He said that after his training, we could live in a little house next to the base and he could set up his contract to go wherever we wanted to go because he had volunteered, instead of being drafted. I don't know if that recruiter lied to him or if he just convinced himself because he was so desperate, but he was absolutely convinced that it would work."

"He went through the selection process and was cleared to go to Paris Island. I got pregnant, probably the night before he left. I sent him the letter telling him right before he graduated, because I didn't want him to have something else to worry about in Basic Training. My boss paid for me to take a bus down to see his graduation. It was at his graduation when I found out that he was going to be in the Infantry, rather than the job he had originally wanted. He seemed okay with this, but I was never certain if he was tricked or made a choice."

"I went back to Maine and he had his specialized training for the Infantry. I wrote to him a lot, he wrote to me about once a week. He sounded different – not like a scared and desperate kid, but like a brave and driven man. He said, over and over, how much he loved me and our baby and how important it was that he was able to take care of us."

"I got to spend one more night with him before he left for Vietnam. I remember how many times he wiped my tears away and said, 'it's only a year, and then we have forever together.'"

"Chris was born two months after Danny left. I wrote to him every day and sent him as many pictures of the baby and me as I could get my boss or the girls at work to take. Danny wrote to me once in a while, more often than I would have thought he could have the time to write. He didn't tell me a lot about the actual war, but I could tell he was really tired and the war was taking its toll. When he got near the end of his tour-of-duty, he started to sound a little brighter and more hopeful. I remember the last letter he sent me and how he talked about how he only had a few more days until he could come home."

"My boss let me bring Chris to work and he could nap in the back room or roll around in his play-pen. He was really little and wasn't walking or even really crawling yet. I was pouring a lady's coffee when the Priest and the man in a Marine dress-uniform came into the diner. They asked my boss if I was there, and I came over. The Priest said that they had tried to find me at my apartment, twice. The landlady sent them here. I wasn't sure what was happening, but the serious, talk-too-gentle way they had was scaring me. The man in the uniform handed me a letter and told me that he regretted to inform me that my husband had been killed in action, fighting in Vietnam."

"The Priest was saying something. My boss was saying something. Sally, one of the other girls, was crying. The world started spinning and went dark."

"I woke up in the back room of the diner. Sally was holding Chris. Both of them were crying. My boss was talking to the Priest and Tommy, the cook – who was fat, old enough to be my father, and had a Navy tattoo on his left forearm – was wiping my face with a cool, wet towel."

"I looked at Tommy and said, plainly – like I was telling him how a customer wanted her eggs – 'My Danny is dead.'"

"I went to the military funeral and remember almost nothing about it other than them handing me the folded flag and them shooting the guns, which made Chris cry."

"When they sent me Danny's life insurance money and the rest of his pay – he had been sending all of his money home the whole time – I bought a car and Chris and I moved up here. I couldn't be there anymore. I loved the people at work, and even my boss and Tommy cried when I left, but I had to go."

"And that's how Chris and I got up here."

. . . .

Tears were streaming, silently, down Mary's cheeks. Maggie had the thin line of a single tear down her right cheek. John did not move, but starred out the window like he was looking a thousand miles away. His bottle of beer, now warm, was still full on the coffee table. The kids were laughing and running in the yard.

John stood up slowly and picked up his bottle of beer. "I'll fix somethin' to eat. Won't be good like what Mary makes, but I'll make somethin'. I'll bring the bottle of wine out for you ladies so you don't have to get up."

The first thing John did was take a piece of "extra-mature" British cheese – which he knew was Mary's favorite – out of the refrigerator and sliced it into crumbly slices on a pretty china plate. Then he took the rest of the bottle of Dark Tower and brought them both to the coffee table by his wife and their new friend.

Neither of them had moved or spoken. Mary was softly sniffing. John left and returned with a box of tissues.

John went back to the kitchen. He opened the freezer and took a bag of frozen French fries, pouring them on a cookie sheet. He set the oven and put them in, setting a timer as he closed the door. He then opened the refrigerator and closed it. "I got no damn clue what I'm doin'," he thought to himself. He quickly drank his warm beer, which he had set by the refrigerator when he got Mary's "very nice cheese". He set the empty bottle next to the other, next to the sink. He went back to the refrigerator and took out the package of sliced roast beef. He made a bunch of roast beef sandwiches on some seeded rye bread. He stacked them on a plate in the middle of the island. Then he got three plastic kids' plates and set them around the island. He put another regular plate there as well. He set two regular plates to the side and got the ketchup out of the refrigerator. The timer buzzed and he took the fries out of the oven. He placed some fries on each of the plates on the island and a sandwich from the stack on each plate as well. He poured a cup of cherry juice at each of the kids' places. He opened another bottle of beer, set in on the table, and walked into the sitting room.

"I made some roast beef sandwiches on the rye bread, with some French fries. I figured you ladies would like to eat in here. I'll take care of the kids. After they are done, I'll set them up in the play room and we can talk some more."

Mary smiled at her husband.

Maggie quietly said: "Thank you."

John asked: "Would you ladies like sandwiches and some fries? I even got some ketchup."

Mary laughed.

Maggie said, "thank you. That would be very nice." And she smiled at John.

. . . . . .

John called the children in to eat. They sat down at the island and said Grace. The kids were excited about sandwiches and fries. "Mama always makes us have vegetables and stuff like that," Dave told Chris.

"Tonight's an exception," John explained with a smile.

The children and John ate while they told him about their game: they were magical knights, fighting evil goblins. "I'm a princess who is also a knight," explained Abigail, matter-of-factly.

After they finished, John had them help bring their dishes to the sink and took them to a large play room. "Now y'all can play in here for a while, but after you're done, we got to put all the toys away."

They said they understood and happily began playing.

John walked back to the kitchen. He could hear the two women in the next room, quietly talking. He quickly washed his and the children's dishes. While he did, he thought about Maggie's story. "That lady has had a horrible time," he thought. "There's got to be somethin' we can do to help her, at least a little bit." John finished, picked up his half-full beer from dinner and walked into the sitting room.

Mary turned and smiled a beautiful smile at John. "Thank you for the sandwiches, they were lovely."

Maggie had her glass of wine in her hand. "Yes, thank you very much."

"Well, you're welcome. Sorry we didn't offer you somethin' fancy; Mary's a fantastic cook."

"This was great," said Maggie. "And that cheese was amazing!"

"It's my favorite!" said Mary. "My father discovered it when he was stationed in England, during the war. I guess one of the men he worked with ate it all the time. It's surprising it's possible, but I'm so glad that we can get it out here. It's such a nice cheese."

John sat down.

Maggie gave a small smile. "I'm so glad we met you. You've been so nice to me. Really, you two are the only not-work adults I've talked to in years. And I'm so glad that Chris and Dave are getting along so well. Chris is really going to need a friend and, who knows, if we know you long enough, they might listen to your recommendations about where he'll end up. It's not like there's anyone else they could ask."

Mary's face turned serious. "What are you talking about, Maggie."

"Foster care. The courts often listen to family friends when they place children. I don't want Chris to have the same troubles that I grew-up with. He deserves so much more."

"Maggie. You can't seriously be thinking about giving-up that wonderful boy to a foster home." Said Mary, now becoming visibly upset.

"I hate the idea, Mary. But I don't really have a choice."

"Why ever not? There are always choices. Maggie, there's always a way," said Mary. "You're a young woman. It's not like you're dying!"

Maggie set down her wine glass and took a breath. "Yeah … I am."

"Oh my God!" said Mary. She put her hands to her face. John put his arm around her and looked at Maggie.

"I shouldn't have said anything," said Maggie, looking down.

"Now that's enough of that talk," said John. She looked up, expecting him to look angry or upset. But his eyes were gentle, calm and resolute.

"You're safe here," he said calmly. "Tell us what's going on and, I swear to you, we will help as much as we can. Know one thing though, that boy is not goin' to a foster-home while I'm alive."

Maggie smiled and began slowly: "There isn't really a lot to say. I have a cancer in my blood and there's nothing that they can do about it. I work as much as I can, but it is getting harder and harder. I'm just really tired. The good part is that my doctor said that it won't hurt; I'll just keep getting more tired and eventually I won't wake up. I'm at peace about it, except for what will happen with Chris."

Mary was quietly crying while John's hand gently rubbed her back. "Maggie," said John quietly, "we're going to help you. We're going to take you and Chris in as part of our family and we're going to care for you. Before you say somethin' like 'no' or 'it's too much', you need to know a few things about my life so you'll understand why we are goin' to do this."

. . . . . .

"I don't know my birthday. I was found in a field in Texas, by a couple of shepherds who were walkin' around and watching their sheep in the middle of the night. I was wrapped up in a World War Two standard-issue USMC wool blanket with a note pinned to it. They found me when I started cryin' from the cold. The shepherds took me to a near-by convent and gave me to the nuns."

"I guess the letter said somethin' like: 'Take care of my little boy. His name is John. With his daddy gone, I can't go on. If you don't find him in time, he'll join us in heaven.' Not a lot to go on."

"The nuns took me in. They kept my first name John, both from the letter and because John was the 'Disciple whom Jesus loved' – they told me that Jesus must love me or I wouldn't have been found in time. They gave me the last name Shepherd, because they thought it was appropriate, as I had been 'lookin' after the sheep.' They had no other information, so they listed my birthday as December twenty-fourth; it was Christmas Eve when the shepherds found me."

"I don't know why I was raised at the convent instead of the local orphanage, but I do know that the Mother Superior insisted on it – she wasn't the sort of lady that backed down in an argument. So, I had a lot of mamas. They were strict, but extremely loving. And I was very well educated; I still even remember some of my Latin."

"Well, as it got closer to my eighteenth 'birthday,' the Mother Superior told me I had to go make my own way. She asked what I wanted to do. I told her that I always thought that my daddy had been a Marine, so I should go do that too. She blessed me, told me to go with God, and not to forget my prayers. She drove me to the recruiter's office and sat with me while he talked. I truly don't know what she, or the other Sisters, thought about it, but they supported my choice and I joined the Corps."

"Started Infantry. Did very well and loved it. Went Force Recon. And in '66, our unit went to Vietnam. I'm not goin' to talk about that, for a lot of reasons, but I guess you know why and how I left."

"I was blessed to meet the sweetest, most beautiful, kind and loving woman, and I guess that Mary told you that story so I'll skip ahead, 'cause I doubt that she told you about the day I met her parents."

"It was a cool fall day. We pulled up to the house and Mary told me not to be afraid and that she loved me. I thought that was funny, because I've seen some horrible things; nothin' here was gonna be scary. Boy, was I wrong."

"Her mother came out to meet us. Mary looks just like her, just a little taller. She was very quiet but smiled a lot. I was introduced and was as polite as I could possibly be. She had a heavy Icelandic accent, but I knew they were from there so I wasn't surprised. Then Mary's father came out the front door."

"Now, I'm not exaggeratin' when I say he was the biggest man I have ever seen. He was easily over seven feet tall, and carved outta stone. Quite honestly, this man was pure muscle and as big as a grizzly bear. His hair was long, past his shoulders and half-way down his chest and he had a long, full beard that went down just as far. He was only wearin' blue jeans with a big black belt and tucked into big, black boots that came nearly up to his knees. His chest hair was thick enough to shear like a sheep. And all the hair on his head, beard and chest was white as snow. He had Mary and the kids' ice-blue eyes, and his eyebrows were white and bushy. Across his forehead was a deep scowl."

"I don't think I've ever met a man, before or after, who made me afraid. But when I saw him, I was terrified right down to my bones."

"I walked forward and extended my hand, 'Hello, Mr. Vinterlogen, Sir. My name is John Shepherd.'"

"He eyed me suspiciously for a moment. Then he took my hand, which was tiny in his, shook it and said, while staring deep enough into my eyes to see my soul, 'Come, John Shepherd, ve go into voods to talk. Girls vill vait inside house.' His voice was like a low rollin' thunder."

"I think I said, 'yes, Sir' and we walked past the deck, across the yard and down a trail in the forest, me followin' him."

"There are two benches down that trail a bit, positioned at an angle so you can look at some one while you talk to them, but also so you can look through the trees and get a view of the lake. It's real nice, we'll show you sometime. Anyway, he sat on one bench and gestured to the other. I sat down. He looked at me with his furrowed brow and spoke. 'So, you vant marry my little girl and come to ask Fater's permission, yes?'"

"'Yes, Sir.'"

"'You vere varrior? Marine in Wietnam for almost two years?'"

"'Yes, Sir.'"

"'Now you vork in bar?'"

"'Yes, Sir.'"

"'Little girl, Mary, say you vant do sometin' else. Tat you bot save lots of gold. Tat she vork too. True, yes?"

"'Yes, Sir.' And I told him my idea for the Campin' Store."

"'Hmmm. Goot plan. But I tink you do not have the gold for house and store togeter.'"

"'Not yet, Sir. I will work hard, Sir. We will get by with very little and one day …'"

"The giant interrupted. 'Nah, Nah, Nah. Tis is no goot plan. Too much vork for too much time. I have new plan. You get your tings and move here, I give you goot room. Little girl, Mary, get her tings and she moves into her old room. Ve go to church and get Priest so you get married – I know you goot Catolic boy. Vhen married she can come to your room to stay, and you make baby, but not before. Not before!' his eyes were very stern as he paused a moment. "Now, you leave tis bar. You not have time for tis vork. You need to make tis Campin' Store. I give you te gold for everytin' you need to make store vork. Also, I tink you need a new pick-up truck to get to store and to home. I give you the gold for tat too. I tink tis is goot plan. You tink so?'"

"I did my very best to appear calm. 'Yes, Sir! This is the best and most generous plan! Thank you, Sir!'"

"'You be goot husband to my little girl. And do not forget tis when you see oters who need your help. And one more ting.'"

"'Yes, Sir?'"

"'Tell my little girl tat her fater is not te dragon she tinks he is.' And he smiled. The scowl almost disappeared. Almost."

. . . . . .

John was sitting in the corner of the couch with a foot on the coffee table. Mary had moved so she was resting her head on his shoulder, and she was curled up on the couch. They were both facing

Maggie, who was sitting comfortably in her chair, had just finished her wine, and was listening intently to John's story.

"So, you see, Maggie," said John, "my life has been amazin'ly blessed. I was found. My up-bringin' was amazin', I survived things I should not have survived, I have Mary, and Mary's father literally gave me everythin' I could have ever asked for, in one brief conversation, within moments of having met me. And, I have two healthy, smart, loving, strong, and brave kids. I am truly a blessed man. How can I look at myself in the mirror if I don't share that blessin' with you?"

"We want you to come and live with us," said Mary. "I want you to be the sister I never had. I want to take care of you. You won't have to work at the diner anymore; you can help me with the kids. And I want to take care of your health, at least as much as we can, for as long as we can. And when we can't anymore," she took a slow breath, "we will take care of Chris; as a member of the family. Please say yes."

Maggie was quiet. She looked into Mary's eyes for a long time. Then, she looked at John for a moment. She looked at the floor and was both laughing and crying, at the same time. She looked up at them and dried her eyes. Then, she quietly asked: "Are you serious about this?"

In unison, John and Mary replied: "Absolutely."

"You can stay here tonight and we'll move all your stuff here tomorrow," said John.

"Dave has a bunk bed, so he and Chris can share a room, if they like," said Mary. "And you can have a room right down the hall from the boys and Abigail; we're on the other side of the house."

Maggie laughed. "Tonight?"

"Why not? The rooms are ready," said Mary.

"You are seriously going to take me and my son into your home and treat us as family after a day?"

"That's pretty consistent with our story," answered Mary.

Maggie thought about it for a minute and answered: "Yeah, I guess that's true." She shifted in her chair. "And when I die ... when I die, you'll adopt Chris?"

"We can get a lawyer for you and you can put it in a Will; if that's what you want us to do," said John.

"You would do that?" Maggie asked.

"Of course," answered Mary.

Maggie paused. She sat in the chair quietly staring at the floor. Then, she looked up and smiled. "Thank you so much. I love you. I'll be your sister."

The two women stood and warmly embraced. John finished his warm beer and sat quietly. Then he said, "We should tell the kids the good news."

Maggie paused. "I have one question before we tell them. Mary, was your father really that big?"

John and Mary both laughed. "He was ridiculously huge," laughed Mary.

. . . .

The next morning, Dave woke up early. Chris was still asleep in the bottom bunk. Dave did not wake him. He got dressed quietly and walked down to the kitchen.

His mother was in the kitchen making pancake batter. She smiled, as he entered. "Good morning, sweet boy!"

"'Mornin', Mama."

"You're up early. How are you feeling?"

"I'm pretty sore, from yesterday, but I'm okay." Dave's face was bruised from the fight.

"Poor baby. You don't have to go to school today and Dad and I took off work, so we can help them move in."

"Ok. That'll be fun," Dave replied.

"Well, what do you want to do until breakfast is ready and everyone wakes up?"

"Can I go out to the deck and look at the fish?"

"Sure." She smiled warmly.

Dave walked out to the deck, sat down, and looked out at the water. After a few moments, he noticed something moving in the bushes near the side of the deck. He looked and a small kitten walked out of the bushes and over to his side. She was a tabby with light grey and black striped fur and a white chest and chin. Her fur was medium length and very fluffy. She had grey-blue eyes. She rubbed up against Dave's hip and purred loudly.

Dave picked the kitten up, held her in his lap and stroked the back of her head. She continued to purr loudly and turned and started licking his hand.

John had just finished his Tai Chi routine in the side yard and walked over to Dave on the deck. "Somebody made another friend."

"I love this kitten. Can I keep her?"

"How do you know it's a girl kitten?" asked John, with a smile.

"Because she's a girl," said Dave, with matter-of-fact certainty.

"Well, let's show her to Mama and we'll see what she thinks."

Dave stood up, still holding the kitten, and they walked back into the house, through the French-doors.

Mary smiled. "Who's this?"

Dave smiled proudly, "She loves me! Can I keep her?"

"Wherever did that little kitty come from? Where's her mama?"

"I don't know. But she's here now and she is the best cat ever!" said Dave excitedly.

"Well you'll have to name her then," said Mary, with pretended seriousness.

"What is the name of that cat-lady from the Egypt stories?"

"Do you mean Bast?" asked Mary with a smile.

"It was like that, but prettier."

"Bastet?"

"That's it!" said Dave happily. He lifted the kitten and looked into her grey-blue eyes. "You are Bastet!" The kitten continued to purr loudly.

"Now hold on," said John. "We need to decide if she is an indoor or outdoor cat."

"John. She's a cat. They pretty much go where they want."

"Ok. Then we need to get her a litter-box and a food dish. And, eventually, we'll need to get her spayed."

The kitten abruptly looked at John and hissed. Mary and John looked at each other in surprise and then laughed.

"Ok, then," laughed John.

Mary softly pet the kitten in her son's arms. "I don't think we'll be bothering with that sort of thing with you, m'Lady," she said to the kitten, who resumed purring and cuddling Dave. "I've never seen any other cats out here, after all. But we do need to get you some shots."

"I want her to have a pretty collar too," said Dave. "I think it should be red, with a small, gold tag that says her name, Bastet, so she know how important she is."

"Sounds good," said John.

"Our family just keeps growing," laughed Mary.

. . . .

Maggie and Chris became part of the family. Probably because of the love and care she received, Maggie lived for another year – considerably longer than the doctor had predicted. When she died, and everyone had time to stop crying, John and Mary adopted Chris. Out of the family's respect for his mother and father, Chris kept his last name.

A short time later, to everyone's surprise, Mary became pregnant and had another baby girl, whom they named Christina. Dave and Chris were both nine and Abigail was seven. "This has to be a first in my family's history – giving birth to three children," Mary said when their little girl was born.

Dave and Chris were constant companions. The reputation they got for fearlessness – from a playground fight in the first grade – followed them all through school. While still very young, they got the idea that they wanted to become Navy SEALs.

Chapter 2

or

"Let's get a Steak"

1993

The two Petty Officers Third Class, were in civilian clothes: jeans, t-shirts and running sneakers, with their military ID's on lanyards around their necks. They both had at least two day's growth of beard and their hair was at least three months grown past military regulation. If they had been anything other than Navy SEALs, none of this would have been tolerated. But, if they had been anything other than Navy SEALs, they wouldn't have been walking down this hallway, and certainly not to the room which they were headed.

Dave Shepherd said to his brother Chris Hanley, "These briefings are always exhausting."

Chris replied: "Indeed. They should just drop the charade, stop trying to sell it, and simply tell us what we need to get done so we can get about the business of doing it."

"I don't really mind them telling us why it's important, but come on, let's get on with it!" said Dave, impatiently.

They had completed Basic Underwater Demolition/SEAL and SEAL Qualification Training, finished their probationary time with their Team, and been Bona Fide, Trident-wearing SEALs with their Team for almost a year. But, they were still the "new guys." At twenty-one years old, they were in the "world-class-warrior" club, but had only really been on a hand-full of operations. Nothing revealed this more than their eagerness to get past the planning stages of the mission and right into the action.

They approached the two older, bigger, and taller Marine MPs, who were standing guard on either side of a closed door, and, in unison, raised their ID badges to eye level. The Marine on the right reached out and opened the door for them.

"Thanks," said Dave.

"Keep up the good work," added Chris with a crooked smile.

Dave and Chris walked into the dimly-lit room and sat at the table next to each other, facing the projection screen. Two Officers in service uniforms were standing by the screen and quietly talking with a man in khaki pants and a light-blue dress shirt with the collar open and sleeves rolled up. He had gel in his stylish hair and wore designer glasses.

"That's the Intel-guy," thought Dave to himself.

The other Team members were drifting in and sitting around the table. They all were dressed similarly to Dave and Chris and they all looked equally enthusiastic to be there.

Roughly fifteen minutes after the briefing was supposed to begin, the Senior Officer, Commander Goldstein, walked to the back of the room and stood in the corner, while the Junior Officer, Lieutenant Junior Grade Walker, called the meeting to order. "Good morning, Gentlemen. I'm sure that you're all very busy, so we'll get right down to business. This is Mr. Smith, he is an Agent with Central Intelligence and is here to present a tentative mission for this Team."

When the Lieutenant said the agent's name, every man at the table either shifted in his seat or rolled his eyes. "Why can't these guys ever use real names?" thought Dave. "Yeah, I'm sure his name is 'Smith'."

The agent confidently smiled and said: "Hi guys. I've got a Classified and extremely important mission for you. This is your target," he placed a picture on the projector and it appeared on the screen.

The man in the picture was a very large – maybe six-six or taller, and well-muscled – dark-skinned, black man who was completely clean shaven – head and face – and wearing sunglasses and an open Hawaiian shirt. Dave immediately noticed an interesting detail: the man's teeth appeared to have been filed into points.

"He is located in western Zaire, about one hundred miles west of Kinshasa – the capitol city; at most, two hundred miles from the Atlantic coast. His original name is not known for sure, but he is called: 'Roi du Sang' – the 'King of Blood'."

"This target is a powerful war-lord, weapons smuggler, and sex-trafficker. He's an all-around bad-guy who enjoys slaughtering villages who have not sworn loyalty to him, and sometimes ones who have. He rapes their women with a voracious appetite and then sells the ones he thinks will make money, killing the rest. Another thing. It is said that he only attacks after the sun has set and that he drinks the blood of his enemies."

"So, he's a vampire," said Dave, out-loud.

"Shepherd?" responded Lieutenant Walker.

"He wants people to think that he's a vampire. Increased fear and intimidation," said Dave.

The agent smiled. "Yes. The stories told about him are like that, and the people, for miles and miles around him are thoroughly terrified."

"Ok, so let's get to the point, you want us to hit this guy," said Chief Petty Officer Russo, a seasoned operator in his late thirties, of almost pure Sicilian ancestry.

"We want this target terminated, yes," said the agent.

"Why this guy? There are plenty of guys like him all over Africa. Why him? And on a similar note, why us? That's not our typical area-of-operation; other Teams work that region." Russo crossed his arms and leaned back in his chair.

"I can answer the second one," said Lieutenant Walker. "The other Teams that this usually would be presented to are busy with various operations in Somalia and some operations that are related to some new terrorist organization that may have been involved with that thing that happened in New York City in February; Al Q-something. You're here, in Little Creek, so this mission went to your Team."

"As for 'why him'," said the agent, "There are other factors involved in this that are, frankly, above your pay-grade. He's the target. That's all you need to know."

"Lovely," said Russo.

"So, I have detailed Intelligence on the target's location and movements," said the agent.

"The idea was to present the mission to you all and see if we can get two men to look at the Intel and work out a plan," said Lieutenant Walker.

Dave raised his hand and spoke before he was called upon. "Chris and I would like an opportunity to have a look and to work out the plan."

Chris rolled his eyes and turned to Dave; frowning but saying nothing.

Lieutenant Walker looked to the back of the room, for guidance, but it was Chief Petty Officer Russo who spoke first. "No offense meant, but these two are still really new. Are we sure we want to ... I mean ... I sure don't want to do it ... but do we want the new-guys making the plan? Again, no offense."

Chris gave a quiet laugh. He would have never volunteered to plan the mission; certainly not yet. But, now that Russo said what he said, Chris knew that there would be no stopping Dave from going after it.

Dave did not move or speak. He could feel his temper rise and all sorts of responses came to his mind, but, he knew enough to shut up, at least for now. It was then that Commander Goldstein spoke up.

"I think that it is an excellent idea for fresh-eyes to be given a chance to show what they can do. Shepherd and Hanley will be given the materials and develop a mission plan. I want an entrance and an exit plan, as well as an action plan with details. Say ... by tomorrow evening, should be good. Of course the plan must be approved and the operators agree to engage, but this should be fine. Good initiative, Shepherd and Hanley! Let Lieutenant Walker know when you're finished, and he'll call the Team together for you to present the plan."

"Yes, sir," said Dave calmly.

"All right," said Lieutenant Walker. "You are all free to go. Shepherd and Hanley, you can come pick up the material from Agent Smith.

Everyone got up and Chris turned to Dave. "Well, this'll be fun," he said with his crooked smile.

.   .   .   .

Chris and Dave's room looked like a typical college dorm-room: non-descript beds, dressers, desks, closets, and a small bathroom. The biggest difference was that the beds were made, the walls were free of decorations and the room was clean. Chris' desk was clear, with the exception of a lamp and a framed picture of Abigail. Dave's desk had a similar lamp, but was covered with maps and intelligence reports, which he was presently reading, sitting in his desk chair.

Chris entered the room eating a crisp, red apple. "How's it goin'?"

Dave did not look up. "I might have something. His birthday is coming up."

"So?"

"His birthday is perfect. This 'King of Blood' has had a huge party, with all of his fighters, for his birthday, as long as they have been tracking him. And," Dave paused for effect, "it's always in the same place."

"Ok. So, a 'huge' party, given for the person we are trying to kill, is the place and time that you want to stage the operation? Don't you think that it will be a little too public?"

Dave smiled, "No. It'll be perfect." Dave swiveled in his chair to face Chris. "Hear me out. So, this party is for all our guy's men. They always converge at this village by a lake. The party starts at, of course, sundown – after all, he is a vampire. So, they get epically wasted and do all sorts of war-lord-guy party stuff with whores, and whomever happens to be stupid enough to not get out of Dodge for the night. But, these guys don't have the stamina to go all night. Think about it. Most of them are mal-nourished and pretty skinny. They have much less access to alcohol than an average American high school kid. That's why this party is such a big deal. So, they are going to burn out."

Chris nodded. "I'm listening."

"Ok. So, the sunset there is going to be at about six-thirty or seven, local time. If we insert and take the target around two or three, they all will either be snoring or, at the very least, unable to function. That gives us about three to four hours, before day-light, to get out of there."

Chris was quietly listening and thinking.

"Also, as Russo pointed out, there are many war-lords like this guy and we never do anything about them, so he'll never be expecting us. It should be pretty straight-forward."

"You want any help working out the details?" asked Chris.

"Nah. I think I got it."

"I'm not taking credit for it if I don't help," said Chris.

"Fine. You look at it when I'm done and we can fine tune it; you can be the editor."

"Ok," laughed Chris. "I'll write Gayle, then. She's loving college; says pre-law rocks. Looks like the Navy is going to pay for the whole thing – this and then Law school. With her grades, you'd think they would. She's pretty happy about it. After that, I'm going to bed."

"Cool," said Dave. "Tell her I said 'hi'."

"Don't stay up too late with this thing."

"That's so thoughtful of you!" said Dave with mock gratitude.

"Oh, I wasn't thinking about you. Your stupid light will keep me up." Chris laughed.

. . . .

There was a satellite image on the projector to serve as a detailed map of the area. Commander Goldstein, Lieutenant Junior Grade Walker, and Agent Smith were sitting at the table with the rest of the Team. Chris was standing next to Dave, trying not to look as uncomfortable as he felt. Dave had just finished explaining why the "King of Blood's" birthday party was the perfect night to execute the operation – an idea that initially met with the same response it got from Chris, but which ended with silent attention from the room.

"Here's how we do it," began Dave. "Six of us will HALO in, ready to fight, and have a single Zodiac, with paddles, dropped with us. Our LZ is this beach here." Dave pointed to the edge of the lake, near the village.

"Chris and I will take point and move into the village. One will quickly move to and cover the far right flank, one the far left and one position center, to cover retreat. The last will ready the Zodiac for exfiltration. Chris and I will silently procure the target. Chris will cover me while I engage. I will slash the target's throat with a kukri machete, drive a wooden stake through his heart and into the ground, complete the decapitation with the kukri machete, and impale the target's head on the other end of the stake."

Chief Petty Officer Russo laughed out-loud, most of the other Team members mumbled to each other, and Lieutenant Walker spoke.

"Why, exactly, are you chopping off his head and staking him to the ground?"

"Because he's a vampire; the people believe that he's a vampire. We need to kill the myth with the man or some other psycho will pretend to be the 'King of Blood' reborn, and it'll start all over," replied Dave.

"This should be a simple sniper mission," said Russo.

Dave smiled. "This target operates at night, in dense jungle. I don't think you're Carlos Hathcock, Chief … no offense," Dave paused for effect, and Chris couldn't hold back a small laugh. "And that's the quality of sniper we'd need if we wanted to do what you suggest."

Russo laughed. "That's fair."

Commander Goldstein spoke. "This is a bold plan. But everything would have to be perfect for it to work. What happens if they are still awake when you arrive?"

"We wait," replied Dave. "We should be able to find plenty of cover and wait until the right time. We really shouldn't have to fire a shot and no one should ever know that we were there or who killed him."

The Commander nodded. "Very well. How will you get out?"

"We'll take the Zodiac across the lake and down this river to here," he pointed to a spot on the satellite image. "It's about one-and-a-half to two miles down-stream from the village. Should take about forty-five minutes, if we are trying to be silent. This location is a helicopter LZ on the side of the river. The target keeps always one, but up to three, allegedly fully fueled, UH-1 Huey at this LZ, mostly for his smuggling – they are allegedly unarmed. So, we tactically-acquire one and fly it, low and full throttle, the approximate two-hundred miles to the coast and then fifty miles out to sea. We rig the Huey to keep flying in that direction and exit with the Zodiac. The Huey flies further out to sea until it runs out of fuel, crashes and sinks. Then we wait for a submarine to extract us. If everything goes the way it should, we will be in the sub and under-way by the time the sun rises and they find their 'King'."

The Commander was taking notes and looked up when Dave stopped speaking. "So, you will be in the air for about two hours at top speed. In theory, the UH-1 should be able to do that and crash far away from where you drop. We could definitely make sure a sub is there to pick you up. Obviously we would need Intel, immediately before the operation, to ensure everything is where you have planned that it will be."

"That won't be a problem," said Agent Smith.

"You do understand, Shepherd," said the Commander, looking sternly at Dave, "that we won't be able to get you out, at least not quickly or without great cost, if you fail and get caught."

"If that happens, Sir, we'll be dead before we're late."

"It's a bold plan, but an extremely dangerous one." The Commander paused and then spoke to the room. "Does anyone know how to fly a UH-1?"

Petty Officer First Class Luis Rivera – a five-foot-three Puerto Rican with a thin but athletic build, a shaved head and a goatee – raised his hand and said, "I can do that. I'll pilot the Huey and handle the Zodiac."

"Very well," said the Commander. "If three others agree to go, we can proceed with the approval process and then get all the technical details arranged."

Three other Team members immediately volunteered – Chief Petty Officer Russo was not one of them – and the room was dismissed. Agent Smith approached Dave and Chris as they were cleaning up. "This is a very good plan."

"Thanks," said Dave, not looking up.

"Seriously," said the agent, "it would appear that you have a full grasp of the importance of this operation and some of the ... special details that need to be addressed."

"Great," said Dave, still not looking up.

"Well," said the agent, "I will await the results with great interest." He then turned and walked out of the room, leaving only Chris and Dave.

Chris laughed. "Jesus. That's our Dave, always makin' friends wherever he goes."

"What?"

"Never mind," laughed Chris.

. . . .

1984

John Shepherd and Pete Filkowski were sitting on the deck, both facing the lake, with a small table between them. There were two cold, open bottles of Busch beer sitting on the table. John was leaning forward with his forearms on his knees, while Pete was leaning back in his chair, slowly puffing on his pipe. They were watching two twelve-year-old boys who were strongly swimming the distance to the landing at the other side of the lake.

"They're doing great, John," said Pete taking the pipe from his mouth and tending to the bowl. Pete was shorter than John at five foot-eight, more than ten years older, and in significantly less athletic condition – though he had become slightly stout, he was still very strong. His hair was cut short and bald at the top and both his hair and carefully trimmed beard were now grey. Pete, like John, had fought in Vietnam. But where John had fought in the north of South Vietnam as a Force Recon Marine, Pete had fought three tours as a SEAL in the Mekong Delta. They had met at an American Legion recruiting event – a picnic where the local Legion Post tried to recruit new members by giving the candidates lots of beer and showing them a good time. Though neither of them joined the Post, they became close friends. These days, Pete helped John out at the Campin' Store – though he refused to be paid, saying: "Keep the money; what else have I got to do? You want to pay me? Make sure there's always cold beer in the 'fridge when I come over," which John did.

"Pete, the particular trail they are runnin' around the lake is three miles and swimmin' across and back is definitely more than a mile. Sure, they're enthusiastic, but they're also twelve. Runnin' a lap around the lake, swimmin' across and back and then runnin' another lap around is a bit much."

"They're fine," said Pete, tapping out his pipe in the small glass ash-tray by his side and reaching for his pouch of Captain Black pipe tobacco. "You want some?"

"Maybe later," said John, carefully watching the boys swimming back.

"They are the ones who wanted to 'get ready for SEAL training'. And they are doing great. They run great. They swim great. They do their PT. They are coming along nicely with shooting. Their Kung Fu class looks great, though to be honest, if your Abigail was the same age as they are, she'd be kickin' their butts and when she catches up to them she just might." He took a drink of his beer and made a face. "You and this Cowboy Beer."

"It's cold and I like it," said John, not breaking his focus on the swimming boys. "Besides, it's free for you."

"Whatever you say, Jarhead." He laughed and drank some more.

Dave and Chris climbed out of the water, onto the deck, breathing heavily. They sat down, toweling off their feet and putting on sneakers and Dave looked up and said: "How was that? I told you we could do it, Dad!"

John sat back, relieved that the boys hadn't drowned. "That was strong swimmin'. You boys did great, but you two can take a break for a minute, or even stop for today."

"Can't stop or rest, Da," said Chris standing. "We're gonna be SEALs and SEALs never quit!"

"Hooyah!" yelled Pete, and the boys ran towards the trail.

John reached for his beer and took a long drink. "Ya know, sometimes you're a real pain in the ass."

Pete smiled, "Yup. Just call me hemorrhoid," and he lit his pipe.

Both men laughed. Then Pete spoke. "Seriously, John, I know that they're twelve, but if they continue to be serious about becoming SEALs, they need to start working like this, pretty much all the time. That training is no joke; toughest training in the world. Almost no one makes it and you can't even try unless you're in amazing shape. I know that I've let myself go, but back in the day ..."

"Yeah, I get it," said John. "I just don't want to push them so hard that they break."

"Looks to me like they're pushing themselves."

"I suppose you're right," said John taking another sip of beer.

"I'll tell you what, my friend," said Pete. "That is exactly the most important factor in them not just getting through the training, but for them succeeding as Navy SEALs."

The two men looked out at the lake and quietly sipped their cold beers. Then, behind them, they heard a giggle and the patter of small feet. They both turned. Behind them was a blonde, three-year-old girl running around with a small fluffy cat; it was unclear who was chasing whom.

Christina was a playful, sweet, good-natured little girl. John loved to watch her run and play. The cat, Bastet, was, strictly speaking, Dave's cat. He took care of her and she slept on his bed and followed him around, which is probably why she and Christina played together so often: Christi followed Dave around too. The cat never grew much bigger than when she was found as a kitten – still small, fluffy and playful – but there was something different about her, like she understood everything people said and everything that was going on.

In between giggles, Christi squeaked: "Hi Daddy! Hi Uncle Pete!"

"Hello, Baby," said John. "Now, don't get too wild and hurt that little kitty."

"I won't," and she ran off giggling, Bastet chasing after her.

"Cute kid," said Pete. "Takes after your wife."

"You know it," said John. "They're like twins." Then, changing the subject, "how long has it been."

"About … twenty three minutes," said John looking at his watch. "They should be coming out of the woods any minute now."

As he said it, first Dave, then, just behind, Chris emerged from the trail on the other side of the gravel parking area, running across and stopping on the deck. "There they are!" cried Pete. "Now jump in the water to cool off and catch your breath. Remember, a SEAL always wants to fight with one foot in the water."

"Yes, Sir!" the boys yelled, then ran and jumped off the end of the deck, landing in the cold water.

John sat up straighter. "That's them." He heard the engine of Mary's red Station Wagon, coming up the rise and around the turn. It emerged and rolled across the gravel to a stop.

"Come-on, boys! Dry off and help Mama with the groceries!" John got up and started walking towards the car. "You comin', Pete?"

"I suppose," said Pete, setting his pipe in the ash-tray and standing slowly.

John walked over to the car and the driver-side door, from which Mary was exiting. She smiled brightly, embraced her husband, and kissed him. "Hi, Sweetie!" she said brightly.

Abigail stepped out of the passenger-side of the car, in her Kung-Fu uniform, and she said, "Hi, Daddy!" Then turning to the boys, running toward them, "Hi, Chris! Hi, Dave!" Then waving to Pete, who was ambling across the gravel, "Hi, Uncle Pete!"

John opened the back of the Station Wagon and took two full bags. "Now boys, I know you're strong enough, but only take one at a time so nothin' falls out."

"Yes, Sir," they said in unison.

Pete came and took a bag, as did Abigail. Mary had walked inside with John and the two of them were starting to put away the spoils of her shopping. Mary always planned to shop for the week during Abigail's Kung Fu class, to minimize trips into town. The boys' class was during the week, after school. She dropped them off and continued home with Abigail – Christina buckled in, as her co-pilot, in the back – and John would pick them up after class, on his way home from the Campin' Store.

John was putting some things away in the refrigerator as Pete set down his bag. He handed him the bottle of beer that he had grabbed for him in anticipation. "Thanks," said Pete.

John looked at Abigail, who was setting down her bag, and he smiled. "Boys, please bring in the rest." Chris and Dave ran back out to the car. "How was class, Darlin'?" he asked his eldest girl.

"Good. I really want to catch up to the boys, but it's more important that my technique is perfect," she said. "Anyway, I really like Shifu. His daughter is a teenager and she helps with my class. She has a black sash and says that someday I will have one too, if I keep working as hard as I am!"

"I'm very proud of you, Darlin'," said John.

"I thought that we might grill something tonight, if you don't mind starting it up," said Mary to John, with a smile.

"Sure," said John. "What are you thinkin'?"

"I was thinking of either salmon or chicken," she said. As she finished speaking, Bastet scampered into the kitchen followed by Christina, who was still giggling.

Bastet, sat at Mary's feet, purring loudly, and Christina hugged Mary's leg.

John laughed and said, "I guess her Ladyship is happy with the choices."

"Which one?" asked Mary, laughing as well.

"The one with the fur and fancy red collar, who heard you from the yard and came to show her approval. Not the little angel who's your tiny twin."

The cat sat up straight and made a sound that was a blend of a purr and a meow: "Prrrow."

Dave and Chris walked in with the last of the bags. "And how did my fine, young warriors do today?" said Mary, smiling at them.

"We ran around the lake, then swam across and back, and then ran around the lake again," said Dave proudly.

"And we're not even that tired," chimed in Chris.

"Oh my goodness," said Mary. "That's really far."

"We have to work hard and never quit," said Dave.

"That's what SEALs do," added Chris.

"Well, Hooyah!" Pete said loudly.

"Hooyah!" yelled Christi, still hugging her mama's leg.

Everyone laughed and John walked out the French-doors to start the grill.

. . . .

1993

The constant hum and gentle vibration of the C-130 would have easily put Dave to sleep in any other circumstance. He lay in the webbing, next to Chris and the four other Navy SEALs. Everyone was quiet, lost in his own personal thought. Each had checked and rechecked his own, and everyone else's, parachute. All weapons and gear had been triple checked. All that was left to do now was wait.

Chris and Dave had done several HALO jumps, in training, but this was to be their first combat jump. Dave felt a bit nervous, so he went over the plan in his head; over and over again. Chris was more excited than nervous. So far, their missions had been relatively simple; mostly reconnaissance in Central American jungles, scouting out drug lords so the DEA could arrest them. This, however was a true combat black-op and the two young SEALs were well aware of the fact that this was the most dangerous thing that they had ever done.

Even though the four other SEALs were senior, the fact that Dave had the most important role in developing the plan meant that Dave would take a leadership role in the mission. No one had any problem with this situation as it was pretty typical of the way SEAL Teams generally operated. Dave knew that he needed to stay focused on his specific job in the mission, but he was also aware that, as the de facto Team Leader, he needed to keep everyone else's job in mind as well. Even though this was the cause of some worry to the young SEAL, at some level he knew that these men were all professionals, knew their jobs, and would execute them flawlessly.

"Two minutes to drop," the voice of the pilot spoke in their ear-pieces.

The six SEALs stood as one, secured their gear, and moved to the back of the C-130. They grouped up and waited for the Crew-Chief. The rear door of the C-130 began to lower and the clock at the side of the plane began to flash red numbers: 30, 29, 28 ...

Chris' voice came through the ear-pieces of the Team, a high-pitched singing voice: "It's the final countdown!" – a parody of the 1980's hair-metal song.

"Damn it, Chris!" said Dave, laughing. "Now that's going to be stuck in my head the whole way down."

All the SEALs quietly laughed as the Crew Chief counted down the last numbers with his fingers: 3, 2, 1. "Go! Go! Go!"

The SEALs dove from the C-130 and plummeted to the jungle below. Every time Dave fell through the sky he had a feeling that he couldn't really understand or describe. He felt very-much at home; like this was more natural for him than walking. His senses were sharpened, and he was amazingly calm; at peace.

After between a minute and a minute-and-a-half, they opened their parachutes with no problems. They were drifting through the sky, coming in over a small lake, approaching a beach. That's when Dave saw her.

A young, dark-skinned woman with hardly any clothes was emerging from the tree line and running to the beach. As the distance was rapidly closing, Dave could see that he would come in over her head and land right behind her. As he focused on that spot, he could see that a large, dark-skinned man was clumsily crashing through the brush, chasing the woman.

Dave's boots hit the ground and he moved faster than thought. In one lightning-fast motion he detached his parachute and raised his silenced Heckler and Koch MP5. There was already a round in the chamber. He flicked off the safety and fired a single shot. It hit the man directly between the eyes and he crashed to the ground dead. As the other SEALs touched down and detached their parachutes they all raised their silenced MP5's and scanned the tree-line. The woman behind them was frozen in terror and they could hear her rapid breathing. Neither Dave, nor any of the other SEALs could see, hear, smell or feel any movement or danger. "Clear," said Dave quietly, his laryngophone transmitting to the rest of the Team. Each SEAL, in turn, repeated, "Clear."

Dave turned to the half-naked woman. She was probably slightly older than he and it surprised him that she made no move to cover her nakedness. He had no idea if she understood English, but he spoke nonetheless. Quietly he said, "You're safe now; those men can't hurt you anymore. Run!" and he pointed east.

The woman stared at Dave, in terror, for a moment and then ran into the night.

The team moved quickly. Five SEALs faded silently into the jungle, while Petty Officer First Class Luis Rivera collected the detached parachutes, rapidly inflated the Zodiac, and assembled the paddles. He got the Zodiac in position to rapidly launch and knelt beside it facing the tree line, silenced MP5 at the ready.

The other SEALs could see fires, burning low, as they silently approached the village. There were no sounds other than those of the night jungle. As they came to the clearing, one SEAL went left, one right and the other knelt. These three would provide exfiltration cover or spring to the attack, if needed. Each was armed with a Heckler and Koch MP5 equipped with a silencer and a pistol of personal choice. The pistols Dave and Chris carried were identical Colt .45 1911's, which their father had given them as a gift after graduating from BUD/S. The .45's were cocked and locked. They each also carried a USMC KA-BAR fighting knife, in a reverse position – pommel down – on their left chest, for rapid draw. These were the second half of their graduation gift.

With MP5's at the ready, Dave and Chris crept silently through the village. They could hear snores, as well as the quiet breathing of sleep, along with the singing of night insects. It wasn't difficult to find the "King of Blood's" location; even though the fires had burnt down, his was still obviously the largest. Dave approached with Chris approximately fifteen to twenty feet behind.

Dave hadn't been sure what to expect at this point in the operation. However, as he rounded a hut and got a clear view of the "king's" fire, what he saw was the last thing he would have expected. Their target was quietly sitting on a large cut log – like a stool – next to the fire, and it appeared that he was waiting for them. Dave stepped into view and slowly walked forward, not entirely sure what he should do next. The large, dark man did not move until Chris also came into view and Dave was about seven feet away. Roi du Sang looked up and said, in low, rumbling, heavily accented English: "So, the dream was right. You are the Americans who think that they can kill Roi du Sang! HAHAHA!" He laughed quietly as he stood.

He was huge; definitely more than six feet, six inches tall. His muscled body looked like polished black steel, and, he was entirely naked. Dave realized, as the king laughed, that his teeth were not filed into points; they were naturally pointed and razor sharp, like a tiger.

Roi du Sang continued to speak: "You have come to kill Roi du Sang on the night of my celebration. Very well. You may try." He stretched his arms out, wide. "Shoot me with all your pathetic bullets, little Americans. And when you are done, I shall drink your blood."

Roi du Sang, standing naked, with his arms spread wide, looked up to the sky and gave a deep, rumbling laugh.

With a speed that surprised Chris, Dave flew into action with inhuman force and brutality. His hands released the MP5, which fell to his chest on its sling. As he sprung forward, his right hand smoothly grabbed the hilt of the Kukri machete – over his left shoulder – and he simultaneously drew the weapon and slashed – from left to right – cutting through his enemy's throat, all the way to the bone.

Roi du Sang's body convulsed, his hands automatically swung to hold his throat, and he dropped to his knees. Completing the throat-slash, Dave fluidly threw the Kukri, sticking it in the ground next to the kneeling "king" and drew a four-foot long, two-and-a-half inch diameter hardwood stake – which had been sharpened to a point at both ends – from over his right shoulder with his right hand. Dave brutally kicked his enemy in the center of the chest, causing him to fall, sprawling on his back. Then with a smooth, but unspeakably powerful movement, Dave brought the stake over his head and, with two hands brought it down, slamming it through his enemy's body, directly through his heart, then his spine, and out of his back into the earth. Letting go of the stake, Dave's right hand flew to the hilt of the Kukri, and in a fluid movement swung it around and powerfully completed the decapitation. He re-sheathed the kukri on his back and bent to pick up Roi du Sang's head. With two hands he grasped it, held it high and brought it down on the other end of the stake, impaling it there while the former "King of Blood's" body convulsed in its death-rattle.

Dave turned to face Chris and spoke quietly, his speech being transmitted to the Team via laryngophone: "Target terminated."

Chris whispered, "Indeed," still feeling slightly awed by what he had just seen. In under ten seconds, his brother had brutally slaughtered their target with a smoothness and grace that took his breath away. There was another thing that Chris immediately noticed: Dave didn't appear to be even slightly out of breath.

They moved silently, but with great speed. Chris and Dave passed through the tree line and the other SEALs wheeled in behind them, covering their retreat. As they passed through the jungle, there was no sound. They came out to the beach, and rapidly moved to the Zodiac. They launched out into the lake, Petty Officer First Class Luis Rivera steering the Zodiac, Chris and the other three SEALs paddling, swiftly, but as quietly as possible, and Dave in the bow, MP5 ready to engage any target that might appear.

They crossed the lake, much more quickly than they had expected. As they came to the point where the lake emptied into the river, a low rumble revealed the first of two unfortunate things that then presented themselves.

The first problem was that Intelligence had failed to mention the waterfall, and the nature of the river below. In the original plan, they had thought that the transition from the lake to the river was smooth, and that the river was a slow, gentle jungle stream. In reality, they were approaching a waterfall that dropped approximately twenty feet into a raging river. "Well, I guess that explains how we got across the lake so fast," thought Dave.

The second problem was that the village was no longer silent. They could hear a roar of yells and cries, and see lights from trucks, filtering through the trees. Somehow, Roi du Sang's people had been awoken, alerted, and were obviously looking for them.

The Team braced to go over the waterfall and Dave quietly whispered, "Damn it."

. . . .

Dave had assumed that the woman he saw was a victim, trying to escape a sexual assault. The reality was that this woman was a very skilled, extremely well paid, and profoundly loyal prostitute employed by Roi du Sang. The man that Dave had shot in the face was one of the "king's" highest ranking men who, in addition to being very drunk, was in the middle of an encounter with her that was moving to the beach for a better view of the stars and more privacy. Not only did this woman speak English – and a number of other languages – she immediately, correctly, assumed that the men who came from the sky were Americans, here to kill her employer, and possibly everyone else. Now, she didn't believe that Roi du Sang could be killed, but these men were going to be a problem, so she ran to get help.

When she ran, she went as directly and quickly as she could to a guard position that had been set up, a bit down a road that led to the village, as well as to the landing zone – a road of which Intelligence had been unaware. She knew that these men would be armed and sober. Even if she had to wake them, they were her best chance.

She quickly came upon three trucks, full of men armed with AK-47s. They were all sound asleep. She woke the man in charge, who smiled widely when he saw her. She quickly explained that she was not there for what he thought, but that the Americans were here.

The man-in-charge was now doubly aggravated – both because he had been forced to work during the party, and second because the woman was not there for a more enjoyable reason. He angrily woke his men – one driver, and ten men to a truck. He sent two trucks to the village and he took the third truck to the helicopter, just in case the damned American dogs tried to steal it.

As the trucks roared into the night. The woman stood at the crossroads. She took a breath, and silently hoped that she wasn't too late and that the men would capture or kill the Americans. Then she quietly began to walk down the road, back to the village. She made no outward sign that she was aware that she was nearly naked, or that she would care if she were aware.

. . . .

Navy SEALs are highly trained, highly motived operators. Most people would have lost control of the boat and drowned if they had fallen over a twenty-foot waterfall into a raging river. This Team did not. Currently, they were soaking wet and fighting to maintain control of the Zodiac, but they were skillfully directing it down the river. In the initial plan, Dave had calculated that it would take about forty-five minutes to get to the landing zone, quietly paddling through the darkness. Instead, after less than ten, the location was in sight. It took a great deal of strength to get to shore, but they were able to land the Zodiac.

Unlike the Intelligence report they received before they got on the C-130, there was one, not three, Huey UH-1 helicopter. Petty Officer First Class Luis Rivera, quickly began to inspect the helicopter, Dave and Chris moved to provide cover and the other three SEALs began pulling the Zodiac out of the water and partially deflating it. They would use the portable, waterproof, air compressor to re-inflate the boat when they got out to sea.

"I can't believe it, but it looks like we're in great shape here; the chopper's good and the tank is full," said Rivera, putting on the flight helmet.

"Great, let's get going," said Dave.

The rotors began to spin. Within a few moments, the SEALs were getting onboard, and putting on the earphones they would need to communicate. Chris pulled back and was climbing on board, and Dave was backing to the Huey. Rivera's, voice came through the ear-pieces of the Team members, "It looks like we're luckier than I thought."

That was exactly the moment when the headlights of a truck flashed from down a road, of which they had not been aware, and it barreled into the landing zone. "He had to say it," thought Dave, breaking into a run.

"Time to go!" yelled Rivera, as the skids of the Huey left the ground.

Dave leapt into the open door of the Huey. AK-47 fire erupted from the back of the truck. The Huey was, quickly rising; now eight feet off the ground. Chris and two other seals were firing from an open door, while the other SEAL was helping Dave up. The SEALs were firing their MP5s on full-automatic and seven of the ten men fell from the back of the truck to the ground. Dave pulled on a set of the earphones and yelled into the microphone: "Punch it, Rivera!"

The Huey roared. The blast of air knocked the men on the truck to their knees. One of them managed to continue to fire his AK-47, full-automatic, at the Huey. They could hear the bullets strike the side of the helicopter as it leapt over the tree tops. Rivera leveled the Huey and flew right above the trees, as fast as the helicopter would go. The five SEALs in the back, fastened seatbelts and pulled the side doors closed. Dave could tell by the way the helicopter shook that Rivera was pushing the Huey as hard as she could go.

The stolen helicopter flew through the night, over the jungles of Zaire, towards the Atlantic Ocean, just less than two hundred miles away. The five SEALs in the back sat, silently checking their weapons – making sure full magazines were engaged; locked and loaded with safeties on. As tempting as it was to relax, they all knew that this mission was far from over.

After about an hour-and-a-half, they crossed the coast and flew out to sea. They were flying exceptionally lower than regulations and continued at maximum speed. "Hey Dave," said Rivera, after they were well out of sight of land.

"Yeah?"

"We're about an hour early. Do you have the thing to signal them?"

"Yeah. How far out you think we can get before we have to bail?"

"We told them fifty, but they wanted us to get as far out as we could. Judging on what I see here, we can ditch at sixty-five, and it will be out of our sight when it goes down. Say, about another twenty minutes before I have to slow down."

"Sounds good, you need help rigging it?"

"Nah, I'll start when we slow down."

"Cool."

Dave sat back and waited. In about seventeen minutes, the Huey stopped shaking and the engine sounded less like a hurricane. The SEALs began securing their gear to enter the water. The Zodiac was partially inflated, to make it faster once they hit the water. The plan was that they would exit while the helicopter was still moving, which they had done many times before. The part that was different was that Rivera was going to exit from the pilot's door, which none of them had done before and which was extremely dangerous.

The time came and Chris and the other three SEALs rapidly exited the Huey, following the Zodiac. Dave signaled Rivera, who gave a thumbs up, and Dave leapt from the aircraft.

He hit the cold water of the Atlantic and immediately felt better. Dave absolutely hated the heat, every kind of heat; humid, dry, no difference. It always made him feel aggressive, like he could literally explode at any moment. The chill of the ocean water wiped that away, and as he surfaced, he smiled. Rivera, had successfully got out of the helicopter and was swimming to Dave. The helicopter continued to fly – far more slowly than it had been – off in relatively the same direction that it had been. They all swam to the now-fully-inflated Zodiac and got in. Dave took out the signal and activated it, and then they waited. None of them spoke as they drifted on the gentle ocean waves in the darkness.

. . . .

When they were all safely on the sub they secured all their weapons and gear, were taken to showers, given clean uniforms, and taken to a small, private kitchen area. They sat together and ate before heading to the rooms which had been reserved for them to get some sleep.

Dave was dipping a chicken nugget into some barbeque sauce and Chris was eating an orange. Rivera was the most senior of the

SEALs on this operation and he spoke first. "That was interesting for a bit there."

One of the other three SEALs spoke up, "might have been nice to know about that waterfall."

"Or the river," said another.

"The road was sort of a problem," said the third.

"Well," said Chris, "I saw every single piece of Intel we got and none of that was in there."

"It's usually like that," said Rivera. "Sometimes more, sometimes less, but there are always surprises; every single time." Then turning to Dave, "Speaking of the plan, you really chop that dude's head off?"

Chris answered: "He sure did. It was pretty intense."

Turning back to Chris, Rivera asked "Did he at least shoot him first?"

"He did not," answered Chris.

"Was he asleep?" asked Rivera.

"Nope," answered Chris. "He was sitting by the fire, waiting for us, buck-ass nude."

"Wait. He was what?" asked Rivera, laughing.

"Sitting by the fire, waiting for us ... naked," smiled Chris, with his crooked smile.

"Why was he naked?" laughed Rivera.

Dave stood. "Maybe he was hot," he said quietly, as he walked to the door. "I've got to get some sleep," he said, as he left the room.

Everyone was quite for a moment. Then Chris broke the silence. "Indeed. ... Africa is quite hot, you know."

The five SEALs burst into roars of laughter.

. . . .

Dave awoke suddenly. Sitting up, he was immediately aware of two things. First, he was not in the bedroom in the US Navy submarine. He was on the ground, in a cave, next to a small campfire. Second, he was not alone. On the other side of the fire was a young woman, sitting on a rock. She was small in stature – he estimated that she was maybe five feet tall, when standing – with a small, delicate bone-structure. She had ghostly pale skin and sparkling blue eyes. Her long, black hair was in a ponytail that fell over her left shoulder; he could tell that it was wavy when loose. She wore no make-up or jewelry of any kind. She was wearing black jeans and a black, eighties-style, concert t-shirt that said "Don't Fear the Reaper" in jagged red letters. He also noticed that she was barefoot. She stared at him intently with a small, delicate smile.

"Hi, Dave," she said with a soft, sweet voice.

"Hello," said Dave, standing up.

"Have a seat," she gestured to a rock.

Dave sat down. "I'm sorry, do I know you?"

"Mmmhmm," she nodded affirmatively, "but it might take you a minute to figure it out."

Dave was puzzled. He was pretty sure that he had never seen her before, but didn't want to be rude.

"Here," she said, "this might help. Now don't be afraid." She gently blew in his direction.

In less than a second, he felt her ice-cold breath on his face and every fiber of his being began to tingle. He felt cold, down to his bones. And then he knew. He knew. With all that he was, he knew that the woman, only three feet away from him, on the other side of the fire, in this strange cave … was Death.

"I told you not to be afraid, silly boy," she said sweetly, with a gentle smile.

"Why are you here? I mean … it can't possibly be my time yet," Dave stammered.

She tilted her head to the side. "You know. I get that all the time, and it is almost never true." She shook her head and laughed. Her laughter sounded like sparkling, sweet music. "But, don't worry, this time it is. You're right, it's not 'your time'," she said, miming quotation marks in the air with her fingers.

"Then why are you … why am I … here?"

"I wanted to see you in person."

"Why?"

"Because you're special." She smiled, scrunching her nose and squinting, as she said it.

"I'm what? Why am I … special?"

"Lots of reasons. I've watched you for what you would call a 'long time,' and you're special. You haven't noticed all the … different sorts of people and things that are always attracted to you … are always around you?"

"Ummm…"

"Let's see … well, your cat."

"My cat?"

"She doesn't seem a little different to you?"

"What? Bastet?"

"You really shouldn't say her name here; it'll really freak her out."

Dave was thoroughly confused. "I really don't understand."

"Ok. You didn't think your last mission was kinda weird?"

"The Africa thing? Wait. Was that guy really a vampire?"

"Sure was. And a pretty awful one too. They aren't always like that, you know. But this one was a truly evil monster. I was glad when you brought him to me. He can't hurt anyone anymore."

"So you think I'm special because I killed a vampire?"

"No, Dave," she smiled. Her smile was truly beautiful. "You're special because you're you; not because of anything that you do."

When she said that – maybe it was how she looked at him as she did – Dave felt like a very small child.

"Thank you," he said quietly.

"Awww, you're welcome."

"Can I ask a question?"

"Sure. You can ask me anything you'd like."

"Well. It's just. I don't know. I guess I'm surprised that you look like this; like a pretty girl."

She smiled, "you really think I'm pretty?"

Dave looked at the ground and could feel the heat from how brightly red he must be blushing.

She laughed brightly. "Well, that wasn't really a question, Dave. It's ok, though. I'll tell you. I can look like whatever I want to look like. I can appear all in white with sparkling, golden wings, or as 'The Grim Reaper," or as "Kali," or as whatever I feel like. Usually, I show up looking like what the one I'm coming for wants or needs. I don't technically have a body. I mean, I can use matter and make it however I like, but none of this is, strictly speaking, 'me'."

"Well, I like you like this. Certainly more than the other things you mentioned."

"I know. That's why I came like this," she smiled.

"So, are you … an angel?"

"Of course I am; what else did you think I would be? I am loyally in His service and shall be until the end. So many are so confused about me; so many misconceptions – usually about me being evil or delighting in causing suffering. I actually try to make things as easy as I can when I come. I'm not malicious or hurtful. I just take you where you're going next."

"Can I ask about that?"

"You can ask," she smiled. "But … I can't tell you anything about that. Don't worry, you'll find out when you're ready."

"Can I ask about other people; if they're ok?"

"No, that would not be appropriate." She paused and then said: "Think of it like this: it's very private and personal. It's like an intimate thing. I know that you wouldn't ask about other very intimate things that people do, right?"

Dave blushed again.

"Right. So, think of it like that."

Dave smiled at her. "You're really not scary at all."

"And yet, strangely, I start so many conversations with the words 'don't be afraid'," she laughed. "People are scared of the unknown. People are scared of change. People are scared of being apart from the people that they love. That's why people are scared of me. It's all that and the pain that often comes before, but that pain isn't me."

"So, is what I do bad? I mean … fighting and killing. Am I bad?" asked Dave, a bit shyly.

"Intent is always important. True intent, not what people talk themselves into or rationalize. There are some things that are always wrong and some things that are always right, but, most of the time, your true intent is what really matters. I've known you, as long as you have been. From the time that you were very small, you have had a desire to protect the innocent and the weak. Because of the way that your world is, sometimes that sort of thing will require fighting and killing. But, deep down, you are motivated by a very noble intent." She smiled. "Why do you ask that? Do you think that you are bad?"

"I don't know. But, I want to be the 'good-guy,' you know?"

"Things like that: 'I want to be the good-guy' ... you'd be surprised how rare that desire is. It's really ... special."

"What should I do, then – to be the 'good-guy' I mean?" asked Dave.

"Just be you," she said. She paused, gazing at him for a moment. "I'm really glad that we talked." She smiled sweetly. "If you ever want to talk again, just call me."

"How do I do that?"

"You call my name, silly."

"But, I don't know your name."

"Yes, you do. And even if you didn't, remember that intent is important."

"Thank you," said Dave, though he didn't know why he said it.

"You're welcome, Dave." She looked into his eyes for a moment, smiling the whole time. Then she said: "It's time for you to wake up now."

Dave closed his eyes for an instant. When he opened them, he was lying in the bed, in the room, in the US Navy submarine.

.   .   .   .

Standing in the same conference room where the first briefing was held, back in Little Creek, Virginia, Dave and the rest of the team, had just finished giving a mission report to Agent Smith, Commander Goldstein and an un-named Captain, who had joined them for the first time today. Lieutenant Junior Grade Walker and the other SEALs, who had been at the initial meeting, were not present.

They had included nearly every detail, with special emphasis on things like the waterfall, the river and the road, which were absent from the Intelligence. Dave, however, did not report anything about the target being a vampire. "That was only a dream," he told himself.

"And the teeth must have been some sort of optical illusion related to adrenaline." He didn't truly believe those things, deep down, but that's what he told himself. Besides, they would think that he was crazy if he had said that they had assassinated an actual vampire.

When they had finished, Agent Smith stood up, smiling. "Well. That was fantastic. Good working with you all; hope to do it again sometime." No one responded to him and he turned and left the room.

"Very well," said Commander Goldstein. "You men are dismissed. Petty Officer Shepherd, please stay behind for a word."

Chris looked at Dave and mouthed the words, "good luck". The five SEALs exited the room.

"Have a seat, David," said Commander Goldstein.

Dave pulled out a chair and sat down. He hadn't shaved since before this operation began, so he had a fairly substantial beard – a blend of the light auburn of his shaggy hair, with some black and darker red. He was wearing camouflage cargo shorts and a black t-shirt, with Teva sandals on his feet. Had he known a Captain with whom he was unfamiliar would be present, he might have put more effort into looking more professional … maybe.

"David, this is Captain Porter," said Commander Goldstein. "I'll let him give the details himself."

Captain Porter silently looked at Dave for a moment. Then he spoke. "Petty Officer Third Class David Shepherd. Born in Maine, 1972, to parents who were both veterans; Father a Force Recon Marine, Mother a Navy Nurse. Joined the US Navy, right out of high school, 1990, and, after Basic, went directly to BUD/S. Graduated very close to the top of your class and went on to SEAL Qualification Training. Did very well. Assigned to SEAL Team Four and had nothing but positive reports through probation and in regular duty. With only three years since leaving civilian life, you have successfully led an extremely bold, dangerous, and imaginative mission; with no casualties – not even a scratch on a single one of the men. Is this correct?"

"To the best of my knowledge, Yes, Sir."

"Excellent," said the Captain, with a smile. "Do you know who I am and why I'm here?"

"No, Sir."

"I am the current Commanding Officer of the Naval Special Warfare Development Group, officially referred to as DEVGRU, but most commonly known as SEAL Team Six. Do you know anything about Team Six?"

"I believe so, Sir."

"Outstanding. Then you know that we are the very best of the very best."

"That was my understanding, Sir."

"Alright. That brings me to you, David. Based on the recommendation of Commander Goldstein and a detailed review of your record, I would like to offer you a position on my Team. You will have to undergo extensive specialized training, at a number of schools, but once that is completed, you will receive a promotion, a considerable raise and begin a whole new type of career with the most elite branch of the most elite service in the world. What do you say?"

"I'm not sure, Sir," said Dave, truthfully.

The smile fell from both the Captain's and the Commander's face. "That is not the response that I am used to when I ask this question."

"Permission to speak freely, Sir."

"Of course! We're all SEALs here; you can always say what's on your mind."

"Ok," began Dave. "I haven't seen my parents since I graduated Basic Training and haven't been home since before that. I have a little time coming up soon, and I sort of was looking forward to going home for a small break. If I go with you, it sounds like it will be quite a while before I get home again. Also, I really like my current Team."

Commander Goldstein spoke up: "Is this about Chris?"

"Who is Chris?" asked the Captain.

"Petty Officer Third Class Chris Hanley. They are brothers and inseparable," answered the Commander.

"How did they get past the Sullivan Act?" asked the Captain.

"Well, they have different last names and they are not biologically related; Dave's family adopted Chris in the early 1980's. Therefore, it is not technically illegal. They went through all the training together and requested to be placed together here. They honestly work fantastically together – it's almost like they know what each other are thinking – so no one has a problem with it."

"So that's the problem?" asked the Captain, looking directly at Dave.

"Part of it, Yes," answered Dave.

"So you won't join SEAL Team Six if your brother can't join with you?"

"That's correct, Sir."

"Very well," the Captain responded with a smile. "If he can make it through the training, the offer extends to Chris as well. And as for the time off, would a month be enough time before you start the training?"

"A month would be very nice, Sir," said Dave, trying not to smile.

"Would you like to tell him, or shall we?"

"I can tell him, Sir. He'll say yes. I'm certain of it."

"Do you have any other special requests?"

"Sir, I know this is going to sound weird."

"Go on," said the Captain with a smile.

"I don't want to cut my hair anymore. I don't really have a particularly good reason. I just want to grow it out like my ancestors did. Also, I want to grow-out my beard as well."

The Officers laughed. Typically, Special Operators were given extensive allowance with this sort of thing but could be required to meet other standards when working with other units. "As long as you can look presentable when required and the hair doesn't get in the way of you doing your job, that's fine," said the Captain.

"Absolutely, Sir. I'll keep it tied back on duty."

"You don't have to worry about other units; I'll have my special permission in your file – I'll say it's a cultural requirement, just to piss off any of the PC crowd reading it. However, if this gets in the way and makes it so you can't do your job, I'll shave you bald, myself!"

All three men laughed and Dave said, "Understood, Sir."

"Very well," said Captain Porter. "You let Chris know the good news and call your parents. You should be able to be home next week, for about a month, and then it's time for more training at Dam Neck.

"Thank you, Sir."

"You boys should go off-base and get something good to celebrate, my treat. Just give Commander Goldstein the receipt."

"Thank you, Sir."

"You're dismissed."

Dave stood, saluted and left the room.

The two officers smiled. "You're gonna love those two," said Commander Goldstein, with complete sincerity.

. . . .

Dave and Chris were in their room and Dave had just told his brother about SEAL Team Six. "This is really, really awesome!" said Chris, excitedly.

"Pretty cool. Sounds like a lot more training and then all sorts of intensity," replied Dave.

"I gotta write Gayle!" said Chris.

"Why don't you just call her and see if she can be home some of the time that we are? It shouldn't be too difficult to figure out."

"Sweet!" said Chris.

"So, the Captain said that we should go off-base somewhere, get something good to eat and he'll pay," said Dave. "We definitely need to get some beers, but what else are you hungry for?"

"I don't know," said Chris with his crooked smile. "It's funny, but ever since that mission, I had one meal on my mind."

"What's that," said Dave.

"Hmmm, how about a steak?!"

Dave laughed at the pun. "Nice and rare and juicy?"

"Indeed! Bloody as hell!"

"Ok," said Dave laughing. "Let's get a steak."

Chapter 3

or

"Not sure yet"

2001

The sun was rising and the crisp, late-summer morning held nothing but promise. Mid-September was approaching and as the two young women rounded the last corner of their morning run they could both feel the optimism inherent to such a clear, new morning. The campus was slowly beginning to wake but, for the moment, all they could hear was the call of the occasional bird and the crunch of the gravel beneath their running sneakers.

Christina Shepherd and Sabrina Katzen had been roommates and best friends since freshman year at the University of Maine, Orono. They had initially been placed together because they were both in a special Navy ROTC program where the candidate, not the Navy, pays tuition and the commitment to the Navy afterwards is reduced to three years – giving them more freedom and more options. Additionally, they were both in the Nursing program. On the day they moved into the dorm they became fast friends; a friendship that had only grown since. They had excelled in their program and had a bright future before them. Now, they were twenty years old and in the beginning of their senior year; living off-campus in a small, but nice, apartment.

Christina – grown-up – looked nearly identical to her mother and her older sister, Abigail. All three women had the same long, wavy light blond hair and ice-blue eyes. Sabrina was just slightly taller than Christina – five-five, rather than five-four – and had long, wavy, dark auburn hair that she mostly wore in a high pony-tail. She had high cheek-bones, soft creamy skin, grey-blue eyes and wore cat's-eye glasses. Both women were in excellent, extremely athletic shape, and yet were beautifully curvaceous and feminine at the same time.

They reached their apartment and went inside. Last night they had stayed up late, studying for a quiz, scheduled for later this morning, in their eleven o'clock Pathophysiology class. Though they were both confident that they knew anything and everything that could possibly go wrong with the lungs, they were a little tired this morning. Their typical morning routine was to get up at six, take a three-mile morning run from about six-fifteen to six-forty-five, shower and get dressed, and then walk to morning Mass at Our Lady of Wisdom – the church in the Newman Center. Mass would begin at eight and afterward they would walk to the Student Union building and have a light breakfast – usually coffee with some fresh fruit or a bagel. Finally, they would either go to class or study until class.

Today, Christina took the first shower while Sabrina drank a glass of orange juice and sat, quietly looking out the window. For some reason, today, she could not stop thinking about her parents. She was the only child of two physicians who had owned a family-practice together, outside Augusta, Maine. They were older when they got married and were surprised when her mother had become pregnant with Sabrina – thinking that the time for children had passed. They had been loving parents who provided her with the best of everything: a loving home, an excellent education at an all-girls Catholic school, and anything she could want or need. She never felt entitled or spoiled; just loved and cared-for. They had died in a tragic car-crash, on the way home from visiting her at school, one weekend in the late fall of her freshman year.

Sabrina had been devastated by the death of her parents. Without her Faith, and Christina's support, she would not have come through the crisis well. However, Christina never left her side. On every break or vacation, Sabrina had been invited and gone home with her friend and been warmly received by the Shepherd family. Christina's parents were warm and loving people. Sabrina had met Christina's older sister, Abigail, and liked her very much. Abigail was now a top-preforming lawyer with the Navy's JAG corps and stationed in Norfolk, Virginia. Sabrina had not yet met Christina's two brothers, Dave and Chris, who were both Navy SEALs. She knew that Chris had been adopted and was, interestingly, also in a serious romantic relationship with Abigail, which was very much supported by the family. Sabrina also knew that, of her siblings, Christina was the closest with Dave – she absolutely adored him.

Sabrina felt very much welcome and comfortable at the Shepherds' beautiful home. Christina's parents had helped her – when things had settled down – to put everything in order. Sabrina had been the sole heir to everything of her parents'. However, she was heartbroken by their deaths and could not face going back to her childhood home. Christina's parents had helped her work with a lawyer, who had arranged to sell everything and use the funds for Sabrina's education and a stipend for living expenses. The sizable amount that remained was put in Trust for Sabrina, to which she would gain access at age twenty-five – shortly after her initial contract with the Navy would end, should she choose not to extend it.

The relationship she had with Christina was more like that of a sister than a friend. They were constant companions; supporting and bringing out the absolute best in each other. They went to Mass together every day, studied together, ran together, and were in an all-female Mixed Martial Arts class together. Neither had any interest in dating or partying, which led to many unsavory and completely untrue rumors, but neither of them paid attention to or cared what those sorts of people had to say. They had already requested to be stationed together at the Naval Medical Center at Portsmouth, Virginia, once they were commissioned. Given their extremely high standing in their program, they expected to have the request granted.

Sabrina finished her juice and set the glass in the kitchen sink. She couldn't understand why her thoughts were dwelling on her parents. It had been nearly three years since they had died and, while she would always both cherish their memory and pray for them, she didn't usually have this sort of persistent thought about them. She heard the bathroom door open followed by Christina's bedroom door closing. It was her turn in the shower.

She showered and dressed in blue jeans and a purple t-shirt. Brushed her hair and put it into a high ponytail. She slipped on her sandals and walked out into the kitchen/sitting area. Christina was waiting for her, having just finished a glass of orange juice.

"Ready to go?" asked Christina.

"All set," Sabrina said with a smile.

The two young women closed and locked the door and began to walk to the Newman Center. The sun was up and it was a bright and beautiful Tuesday morning. They both carried backpacks – slung over one shoulder – containing what books, notebooks and other supplies they would need before returning to their apartment that afternoon. Their apartment was right next to the campus, so it was only a short walk to Mass.

They were two of a very small group of students – mostly girls – who went to Mass every morning. They smiled and waved to a few of the other girls, but did not engage in conversation. Mass was over fairly quickly and they headed to the Student Union building to have breakfast.

They ordered two medium cups of coffee – with two creams and two sugars, in each – two bagels with cream cheese, and had a seat at one of the tables in the Student Union. It was 8:45.

"You know, it's really nice out today. Do you feel like moving to one of the tables outside?" asked Christina.

"Sure, that sounds great," replied Sabrina.

They stood and walked toward the door. As they passed by one of the large televisions, mounted to the ceiling, a breaking news alert message flashed across the screen and the program switched to a news anchor. "This just in: a plane has crashed into the side of the north tower of the World Trade Center in New York City."

The girls stopped and looked at the screen. Fire was coming from the side of the building. "That's terrible!" said Sabrina.

"Those poor people!" added Christina.

Without a word, they sat down at the nearest table. They watched the news, picked at their bagels, sipped their coffees, and silently prayed that the people, both in the plane and in the building, would, by some miracle, be ok.

A crowd was beginning to gather. As students passed by, the screen caught their attention and they stopped to watch and listen. There was now a live camera feed of the World Trade Center, with the reporter speaking, unseen. The students were either silently watching or mumbling quietly to each other. All that was replaced by a simultaneous, sudden gasp as a second plane crashed into the side of the south tower, in a ball of fire, at 9:03.

The girls looked at each other, filled with a terrible sense of dread. "That can't be a coincidence," said Sabrina.

"No," replied Christina, shaking her head. "There's no way that happened twice, in under twenty minutes, by accident."

"Christi, if someone did this on purpose, America is going to war," said Sabrina.

"Yeah. We sure are,' Christi replied.

The crowd in the Student Union was growing and growing. Everyone was riveted to the screen, watching the two burning towers and listening to the reporters discuss possible explanations. They reported that another plane crashed into the Pentagon at 9:37. Christi and Sabrina didn't move and could barely breathe. Then, at 9:59, the south tower fell.

A chorus of "Oh God!" sounded through the Student Union. Now tears were freely streaming from the majority of those watching. Countless lives had ended in a matter of seconds – in a crushing, fiery hell – and all they could do was to watch in absolute horror.

No one spoke, no one moved. The sounds from the television seemed far away, like a horrible, horrible dream. The smoke and the fire held everyone's attention. Another breaking report. A plane, full of people, crashed and burned in a field in Pennsylvania at 10:03. And, at 10:28, the second tower of the World Trade Center fell.

Christi and Sabrina were holding hands. Everything around them was a blur of confusion and horror. "Hey Christi," said Sabrina.

Christi turned to look at her best friend. "Yeah?"

"Let's go. Let's get out of here."

"Ok."

They got up and walked out of the Student Union building. The sun shone brightly and it was a pleasant, mild temperature. They quickly walked, hand in hand, towards their apartment; oblivious to anything and everything around them. They had watched thousands of people die and, at this moment, the trauma was so fresh and real and horrible that they just felt numb. There were so many questions about what had happened, and what would happen next, but there was one thing that, deep down, they both knew with complete certainty: they would never forget that sunny Tuesday morning. They would never forget September 11th 2001.

. . . . . .

Chief Petty Officer Dave Shepherd sat with Chief Petty Officer Chris Hanley, and some of their other Team members, at a table next to the bar, in one of the SEAL Team Six Team-Rooms, in Dam Neck, Virginia. They were staring at the television. No one had said a word since the first tower fell, about a half-hour ago. Now that the second tower fell, the reactions in the room were mixed.

"Well, this is going to be some serious business," said Dave, quietly to Chris.

"Indeed," said Chris, sternly frowning at the television screen.

The other SEALs were in small groups, and their voices blended. Some were behind the bar, pouring beers from one of the taps into their personal mugs that hung on the wall behind the bar. Petty Officer Second Class Jacob Levi, called out "Hey Chiefs, either of you need a beer?"

Levi was a relatively new member to the Team. He was five feet, six inches tall, with close cut dark hair, dark eyes and olive skin. He was originally from Rockland County, New York and took his Jewish heritage extremely seriously. Levi was smiling, but Dave could see that his teeth were clenched and his hands were shaking.

"Thanks, Jake," said Dave. "I think I'll have one in a little bit. I have to make a few calls. Why don't you pour yourself one before an Officer shows up to give us something stupid to do."

"Yeah, I'll skip mine for now, as well," said Chris.

"Ok," said Levi, downing his first beer in one gulp and pouring another.

Dave turned to Chris. "We've got to call them and tell them that everything's going to be ok."

"Sure," said Chris. "But, Dave, we don't know anything yet."

"I know," replied Dave "But they all know that we couldn't tell them anything, anyway, even if we knew. They really just need to hear our voices."

"To tell the truth, Dave, I sort of really need to hear Gayle's voice, right now," said Chris.

"Cool. You call Gayle and I'll call Christi. After that, we should probably both call Mama and Dad on speaker."

"Sounds good," said Chris.

"When we're done, we can go see the Captain and see if there's any information about what we're going to do next," said Dave.

The two brothers got up and walked out of the Team-Room, and back to their suite. Dave, walked into his room and Chris to his, both with their cell phones. Dave shut the door and called Christi.

. . . .

Christi and Sabrina arrived back at their apartment. Christi locked the door behind them and secured the chain. She wasn't sure why she did that, but it felt like something that she needed to do.

In the sitting area, there was a comfortable chair and love-seat around a small coffee table, facing a television. Christi sat in the chair and Sabrina sat on the love-seat, after setting their backpacks on the kitchen table. Christi drew breath slowly and was about to speak when she heard her cell-phone ring from her backpack. She jumped up. "I know it's Dave!" and she ran to her backpack to answer her phone. As she picked it up, the caller ID informed her that she was right.

"Dave!" she said excitedly as she answered the phone.

"Hi, Christi," said Dave on the other end of the line. "You ok, Kitten?" 'Kitten' had been Dave's pet-name for Christi when she was very small, largely because she always played with Bastet. As she got older, she sometimes told him not to call her that name, and he hadn't in years. But today, it just came out.

"I'm ok … physically," said Christi. "Sabrina and I saw the whole thing in the Student Union building."

"Is *she* ok?" Dave had never met Sabrina Katzen, but he knew that she had been through a lot and that she was practically a sister to Christi.

"She's pretty much the same as I am, right now."

"Where are you two?"

"We're in our apartment."

"Good. Stay there."

"Dave, what is happening?"

"Not sure yet."

"Who did this to us, Dave?"

"Not sure yet."

"Well, what are we going to do about it?"

"Not sure yet."

"Dave!" she was getting very upset. "You're a SEAL on Team Six! What are you going to do about someone killing all those people?!!!"

"Not sure yet," said Dave, calmly. "But I can tell you this: if it was up to me, I would bathe whoever did this in an ocean of fire."

Christi was trying to catch her breath.

"Hey, Christi," said Dave.

"What?"

"I love you, Kitten."

"I love you, too."

"Tell Sabrina that everything's going to be ok. I don't know what we're going to do yet, but you can rest assured that it'll be something really big."

"Ok."

"Chris and I are going to call Mama and Dad. Stick by the phone. I'll tell them to call you as soon as we get off."

"Ok," said Christi, wiping her eyes.

They got off the phone and Christi sat down with Sabrina.

"So, he doesn't know anything yet?" asked Sabrina.

"Nope, but it *did* just happen," answered Christi.

"What do you think is going to happen?" asked Sabrina.

"Did I ever tell you about when I was twelve and Dave, Chris and Gayle came home, right before Dave and Chris joined SEAL Team Six, when Dave explained why they do what they do?"

"I don't know."

Christi stood up and walked over to the mantle above the fake fireplace, where she and Sabrina had some framed pictures. She picked one of them up, brought it back and handed it to Sabrina. It was a photograph of man sitting in a chair by a lake, laughing. He was probably in his mid-twenties. He had long, light-auburn hair in a ponytail that fell over his shoulder and a full, but well-trimmed beard. He wore dark, black sun-glasses. He was shirtless, with thick chest-hair and was in impressively muscled physical condition. Christi spoke with an amazing conviction: "That's my brother. That's Dave. He loves me and our family and this country. I'll tell you what I *know* is going to happen. He's going to find the bastards that did this. He's going to find them! And when he does, he's going to kick their asses all the way to Hell!!!"

. . . .

1993

Abigail Shepherd parked her red Chevy Cavalier, next to her father's black Chevy Pick-up truck, on the gravel area in front of the Shepherd family home. It had taken her just over two hours to drive up from school – University of Maine, Portland – where she was a pre-law, honor student in Navy ROTC. She was home for the weekend because Chris and Dave soon would be home. She hadn't seen them in almost three years and was very excited, especially to see Chris.

It was true that Chris was her adopted brother, but, from the first moment they met – when she was five – there had been a sort of closeness between them. As they grew older, it developed from friendship, into romantic attraction. They had their first "date" when she was fourteen and he was sixteen. By the time he left for the Navy – she was sixteen, nearly seventeen – they were in a serious, committed relationship. Since then, it had been letters and phone-calls – a distance relationship – but they had both been true to each other. Now, at nineteen, a college freshman, she would finally get to see him in person again. 'Excited' didn't really even cover it.

She walked into the house and to the kitchen. Her mother and little sister, Christi, were busy putting the finishing touches on frosting a cake. It was in the shape of a sea-lion, balancing a ball on its nose. The ball was red, the sea-lion was blue, and there was a large yellow 6 in the center of the ball.

"You know that's a sea-lion, not a seal, right?" she asked.

Her mother and her twelve-year-old sister looked up. "It looks better this way," said Christi.

They all laughed and Mary Shepherd, her mother, smiled and said: "Welcome home, Gayle! I hope the drive wasn't too bad." Mary turned to the sink, quickly washing her hands, and came over to hug her oldest daughter.

Other than the fact that, Gayle was about two inches shorter than her mother, they could be twins. Mary never seemed to age. Gayle no longer looked like a little girl next to her mother: "That's Christi's job now," she thought to herself and laughed.

"Your Daddy and Uncle Pete went to pick up the boys at the Navy Air Base in Brunswick. You actually could have driven together."

"I know. But, I need my car to get back to school on Monday. While they're home, I'll come home every weekend. But, I can't miss any classes. I actually have some homework I need to do while I'm here. But, depending on when they have to leave, I can probably drive them back to Brunswick," said Gayle.

"You work so hard, Sweetheart. Daddy and I are so proud of you."

Gayle smiled. "Thanks Mama. Why are they picking them up at the Naval Air Base?"

"I guess their Commander or Captain or whatever Officer told them to hop a C-130 instead of buying a regular plane ticket. I guess SEALs do this all the time," said Mary.

"Nice," said Gayle.

"And how are you doing?" she said, turning to Christi.

Christi had finished washing her hands, but then realized that they had yet to feed Bastet this morning. The small, fluffy tabby with the bright red collar and grey-blue eyes, sat on a counter, intently staring at them. Now, Christi was mixing her food – some hard food, mixed in with a can of soft – and the cat jumped to the floor. "I'm sorry, m'Lady," said Christi, as she set down a gold colored food dish with the name 'Bastet' in script letters written on the side.

The cat said, "Prrrow," and began to eat, purring loudly.

Christi turned to Gayle, "Sorry, but I had to feed Bastet. I'm doing well. School is going great. Kung Fu class is great. And Dave comes home today!" She jumped up and down clapping her hands, excitedly.

Gayle laughed. "Kung Fu class, hmm? Keep working hard and someday you'll get that black sash, too. But, how's that biology class? It's really important for a nurse to know that stuff."

"Yup. Getting over one-hundred, with all the extra-credit. Definitely gonna be a nurse, like Mama!"

"That's good!" said Gayle. "Keep up the good work!"

Mary smiled, "Christi, would you help Gayle take her things up to her room, please?"

"Sure!" she said brightly. "Let's go!"

The girls brought in Gayle's things and Mary continued to prepare for the picnic that they would have on the deck to welcome the boys home. About an hour later, the cooler of beer was on the deck – with the chairs and small side tables – the roast beef sandwiches were stacked on a plate in the kitchen, and the bowls of chips were next to the "seal" cake. She had even set up the wood in the fire-pit for the inevitable campfire, later that evening.

Mary was putting the finishing touches on the deck when she heard the blue Chevy Lumina mini-van pull up. She turned and briskly walked to meet them. The side door slid open and Dave and Chris stepped out. They were both in amazing physical condition; well-muscled and strong. Dave was five foot-eight, had been growing-out his light auburn hair – it looked fluffy and bordering on un-kept – and had grown a full, but trimmed, beard. Chris had always been a bit taller, now five-ten, and his ginger hair was close-cut and stylish. He too had a beard, but his was considerably more closely trimmed as well as more stylish. They were dressed in camouflage cargo shorts, t-shirts, and Teva sandals. Both of them smiled brightly and moved to hug her.

"Hi Mama!" said Dave.

"Hi, Ma!" said Chris.

"My boys!" Mary hugged them and wiped away a joyful tear. "You both look so strong! Aren't you going to be cold in those shorts?" It was mid-October.

"We just came from Virginia, Ma," said Chris. "But you're right, I'll probably get changed in a bit."

"Not me," said Dave. "I'm finally starting to get comfortable. You know how I hate the heat."

John and Pete got out of the mini-van. "We can bring your things inside later. You boys still want to share your old room, or do you want different ones."

"I don't know, Da," said Chris. "I think we would break that bed."

Dave laughed, "Yeah. We should probably split up."

"No problem," said John. "We'll take your stuff up later."

Pete cleared his throat, "Come on, boys. I have a sneaking suspicion that there is something cold and almost-tasty in that cooler over there to welcome you home," and he began to amble to the deck.

John laughed, "You know, I wouldn't be offended if you brought your own favorite."

"Nah," said Pete. "I'm used to your Cowboy Beer now. You ruined me; no goin' back."

Gayle walked out of the front door wearing blue jeans, a grey University of Maine sweatshirt and sneakers. She smiled brightly. "Hi, Chris. Hi, Dave." Her eyes sparkled when she looked at Chris.

Chris and Dave both said hello and they each gave her a hug, Chris' lingered for considerably longer.

"Chris, would you like to go for a walk around the lake with me?" asked Gayle.

"They only just got here, Sweetheart," said Mary.

"Oh, it's ok Ma," said Chris. "We've been sitting for hours. Let's go!" He took Gayle's hand and they walked toward one of the longer trails and into the woods. Dave noticed that they were both blushing brightly and he gave a small laugh, under his breath.

"Come, on Mama," said Dave. "Let's go sit on the deck. I wouldn't want Uncle Pete to feel obligated to drink all the beer by himself."

"Don't you go worryin' about me, Dave," said Pete in mock-seriousness. "I can handle my duties on my own."

Everyone laughed. John and Pete walked to the deck and each took a bottle of beer out of the ice, opened them, took a sip, and sat down. "I'll bring out some chips," said Mary.

"You want a hand?" asked Dave.

"Thanks, but no," smiled Mary. "Go have a beer with your dad."

Dave smiled and walked across the gravel and on to the lawn. It had been about three years since he had been here and he was trying to soak it in. The sky here was very different, such a crisp blue. It reflected in the blue lake, rippling gently. The usually green forest was a wild blend of yellows, oranges, and reds. He breathed in deeply to smell the autumn air ...

The impact knocked the wind out of him. A tremendous force slammed into him from the back/left of his body, knocking him to the ground. He spun around. His twelve-year-old little sister, Christi, was sitting on top of him giggling uncontrollably over having welcomed her brother home by tackling him to the ground. In between the giggles she was able to yell: "Daddy! I snuck up on a Navy SEAL and took him down!"

"Hooyah!" yelled Pete, raising his bottle of beer in a toast. "What's the matter Dave? Going soft?"

Dave laughed. "Hi, Christi, how are you?" he asked, as Bastet bounded across the lawn and began licking Dave's right cheek.

Mary walked out of the French-doors, with a large bowl of potato chips in her hand and said: "Oh my goodness!"

"Sorry Mama," say Dave laughing. "Looks like they got me."

"Christina! Get off your brother this instant!" said Mary, laughing.

"Ok, Mama," said Christi, standing up and reaching for a chip.

Dave rolled to his side and stroked Bastet's fluffy head. "Hello, m'Lady. I've missed you." Bastet purred loudly and Dave stood up. Christi turned and smiled at Dave, crunching on a chip. He fluffed her hair and said, "I missed you too, Kitten."

Christi frowned. "Stop calling me that, Dave! I'm too old to be called 'Kitten'!"

Dave smiled, "I'm sorry. I'll try to remember. He took the bowl from Mary and gave her a small kiss on the cheek. "Thank you, Mama."

Dave walked over to the cooler and took a beer, sitting down. "I haven't seen one of these in a while."

"I find it impossible to believe that a SEAL hasn't seen a beer 'in a while'," said Pete, making quotes in the air with his fingers.

"I didn't say that," said Dave, laughing as he opened the bottle. "I said I hadn't seen one of these, you know, 'Cowboy Beers'."

All three men laughed as Dave took a drink. "Thanks for coming to get us, Dad."

"It was my pleasure, Son," said John, sipping his beer. "Ahhh, head for the mountains!" John quoted the advertising slogan for Busch from the eighties, and caused them all to laugh again.

About an hour later, everyone but Chris and Gayle were sitting on the deck, happily talking. Chris and Gayle walked out from the trail – having circled the lake – holding hands, smiling, and talking quietly to each other. They came up to the others and Chris said, "I'm going to change into some jeans instead of these shorts, if that's ok."

"I put your stuff into the room down the hall from your old one, door's open, you can't miss it," said John.

"Thanks," said Chris. "I'll be right back." He gave Gayle a small kiss on the cheek and went to the house. Gayle sat down, smiling.

Mary got up. "Now that you're back, I'll get the sandwiches."

"Would you like help?" asked Gayle.

"If you'd like," smiled Mary, and they went inside.

"So, you got any idea what training's gonna be like?" John asked Dave.

"Only vaguely. I know that there is a special Team Six course that takes something like three to six months, but it's more skill based than abusive pounding. We also have to travel to a ton of schools and learn all sorts of stuff. I think one of them is Marine Scout Sniper training, which will be pretty cool. Also, we do some stuff with the Israeli Defense Forces, the British SAS and some other foreign groups. They really want us to have every kind of special training that there is, so, it'll be a while before all that is done. That being said, I guess that we can operate with a Team once we clear that initial training."

"That sounds like a lot of serious business," said Pete. "Back when I did my stuff, there was no Team Six, and all we trained to do was kill Viet Cong."

"Yeah, I guess the Teams have changed a lot, from what the older guys say," said Dave.

Chris returned, sat down and got a bottle of beer. He opened it and took a drink.

"You two have a nice walk?" asked John.

"Indeed, quite nice," smiled Chris. "It's been a long time."

"Distance relationships are hard," said John. "I remember."

"Well, she's got school and I've got my job, so we don't have a lot of choice," said Chris. "Anyway, I know I'm not even slightly interested in even looking for anyone else; Gayle's the only girl for me."

"Glad to hear it," said John.

Mary and Gayle returned with the sandwiches and the "seal" cake. "That's great," laughed Dave.

"Thanks, Ma," said Chris.

They sat, said Grace, and ate. The conversation was causal and easy and the day passed nicely. As the sun set, it became cooler and everyone but Dave put on a light jacket, while Dave lit the campfire.

"Still only one match," Dave smiled proudly as they all pulled their chairs around the fire.

"I'll be impressed when you do it with no matches at all," smiled Christi.

Mary put her hand on John's knee and he nodded. "Boys, I want to talk about somethin'. You grew up wantin' to be SEALs and you made it; you are world class elite warriors. And we're all real proud of you both. Now, you are goin' to an even higher level. A level where war – usually secret war – is goin' to be a reality for you as long as you're there. Your mama and I were wonderin' about how you see your role; what you are thinkin' about all of this?"

Dave and Chris nodded. Dave opened a cold bottle of beer while Chris said: "We have actually been talking about this all week; from the time we accepted the offer until we got up here. The two of us are in complete agreement, but Dave explains it better, so I'll sit back and let him tell you our view."

Chris opened a cold bottle of beer, as did John and Pete. Pete lit his pipe and leaned back, giving it a few puffs. The smell of Captain Black pipe tobacco mingled with the cool fall air and the scent of the leaves was magical. The evening insects sang their song and Christi noticed the first of the bats, darting across the evening sky, as she sat cross-legged on the deck. She looked at Dave and listened intently as he spoke.

"When we were kids, I remember all the stories we were read, or that I later read myself. The Hobbit and The Lord of the Rings, The King Arthur stories, The Chronicles of Narnia, The Chronicles of Prydain, all the different so-called myths, legends, and Faerie stories from all the different lands. I loved these stories, but not just because they were fantasy adventures. To me they were real. Some of the most important things that guide my life are from these stories."

"From these stories, probably one of the most important ideas I got, if not *the* most important idea, is that those who have strength should – no, must – use that strength, not to dominate and oppress, but to defend and protect the most vulnerable, the innocent, the weak."

"There are some profoundly evil people in the world, who want nothing but to destroy. They don't bring others down to bring themselves up. They want to stay where they are and bring others even lower than they are. They want nothing more than to destroy. They are the servants of Chaos."

"Our Nation is supposed to be a light of hope and freedom to the world. Whether or not that is truly the current state of affairs, what is undeniably true is that we are, in fact, the strongest, most powerful military force in the world. This power must be used to do what is right."

"We chose this life to provide that sort of service. We are knights; warriors of righteousness. We fight for the good; to protect the innocent. We stand against evil and pursue it to the ends of the earth with the undying fire of righteous fury. We have worked to become the strongest, most effective warriors in this epic battle. So long as the mission and our cause are in accord, we will fight until we are victorious or we can no longer fight. But on the day that the mission does not uphold these noble values, we shall walk away and fight no more."

The shadows had grown and now night had come. The light from the fire flickered gently and its soft heat warmed all who were near it. The soft sound of the draw from Pete's pipe was a soothing, restful tone. The night insects' song was peaceful and serene. On the other end of the lake, a loon called out to her mate, who gently answered back. Christi looked intently at her brother, completely in awe of him. She felt absolutely safe, loved, and unassailable. Whatever there was in the world that could threaten her, whatever there was of which to be afraid, he would stand against it; he would hunt it to the ends of the earth if it ever dared to strike out. Nothing in this world, or any other, would harm her; not while he stood in her defense. She smiled and pet the small fluffy cat who had curled up next to her on the deck.

John and Mary were sitting next to each other, her hand draped gently on his thigh, both of them smiling at their son, with looks of utmost pride.

Chris and Gayle were sitting closely and holding hands. Chris turned to her and whispered in her ear "Told you he was good." She had a soft laugh and smiled.

Pete took a drink from his beer, a puff from his pipe and said: "That was poetry, Dave. Perfect, noble poetry." He sat back, and quietly puffed his pipe.

Dave said almost nothing more that night. He looked into the fire and quietly sipped his beer.

Christi quietly watched him and thought about what he had said. Slowly and gently she drifted off to sleep. She woke up the next morning with Bastet curled next to her on her pillow. She never asked, and no one ever told her, but she knew that her brother Dave – the brave and noble knight – had carried her to her room and tucked her into bed.

. . . .

2001

Christi paused for a moment. During the end of the story, Sabrina's eyes had not left the framed picture in her hands. Then Christi spoke again: "I never forgot what he said by the campfire that night. The weekend before I left for college, Dave, Chris and Abigail showed up and surprised us. We had a great time. We took a lot of pictures that day, but I especially liked that one. It always made me remember that there is at least one brave and noble man who is willing to stand and fight; willing to sacrifice everything – even his life – to protect me."

Sabrina looked up for a moment, smiled and looked back down at the picture. "Did he really say all that, or did you just make it all up?"

Christi laughed. "Trust me. When you meet my brother, you'll know rather quickly. No one could 'make up' David Shepherd."

Sabrina smiled. "You know, all morning – before it happened, that is – I was thinking about my parents. I'm not sure why, but that just adds to all of this. I just ... I don't know. I just really don't want to go outside, at least for a while."

Christi smiled sadly at her best friend, "I'm scared too, Sabrina. But it's going to be okay."

A small tear was creeping down Sabrina's beautiful cheek and she tried to smile.

"I'll tell you what," said Christi. "How about you keep that picture for a little while; keep it in your room. It always helped me feel a little braver, or at least helped me to fake it."

"Thanks," said Sabrina. "That's really nice of you."

She got up to take the picture to her room. "Hey Christi, you know something?"

"No. What?"

"Your brother's … ummm … kind of cute."

"Oh my Goodness!" Christi started laughing and couldn't seem to stop.

. . . .

Chief Petty Officer Dave Shepherd walked down the hallway and stopped in front of a door with a name plate that read: Captain Timothy Porter. He took a deep breath and knocked on the door. "Come." Said a deep voice from inside. Dave took another deep breath and opened the door.

Captain Porter was the Commanding Officer for SEAL Team Six. There were a few Officers in the chain-of-command between Dave and the Captain. Dave would have to be extremely careful what he said next if he was to avoid being accused of breaking the chain-of-command; a most egregious offence.

Dave gave the Captain a salute, which was returned. "Have a seat, Shepard." Dave sat in a chair facing the Captain's desk. "What can I do for you?"

"Permission to speak freely, sir?" asked Dave.

"Dave. You don't have to ask that and the salute wasn't necessary either. You know how I run my unit. You are always welcome in my office. Now, what's up?" said Captain Porter with a smile.

"Well. It's been a really bad day, Sir."

"I would certainly say so."

"I know it's very early on, but I was wondering if you could tell me the general idea of what we are planning to do."

The Captain leaned back in his chair. "Not sure yet, Dave. We're not even twelve hours into this yet. We have gotten no orders, not even for planning. We're not even sure that it's over yet, so everyone who makes those kind of decisions is in 'protection mode'. I can tell you what I think is going to happen. If I was to guess, an assessment will be made of the operational readiness of all Special Operation Groups. Once they decide on the target, we will do whatever special training is needed. If I were to guess, I would say that DEVGRU Teams will be utilized in direct actions on individual, high-value targets – we'll probably be going after their leaders, directly. Of course that's all speculation."

"That's what we thought, too," said Dave. "I don't think this is going to be over quickly. I think this is going to be an extremely long and drawn-out process and that there is going to be more and more involved, the deeper that we dig."

"My though as well," said the Captain.

"So, that will probably mean that we are going to be out in the field, taking care of whatever needs our attention, for quite some time," said Dave.

"I would imagine so," replied Captain Porter.

"That being the case, I was wondering if you would consider an idea that I have – with all due respect and with all due regard to the chain-of-command."

The Captain smiled. "You're not making any formal requests, we're just talking. There is no issue with the chain-of-command. As far as I'm concerned, my private conversations never need to be anyone's business."

"Thank you, Sir."

"What's your idea?"

"Well, Chris and I have been on the phone all afternoon, and I bet almost everyone on our Teams has been as well. I bet our experience is not unique: family and loved ones are scared for not only themselves, but for us as well. So, I was wondering, what are the chances – obviously this would be dependent of the requirements of whatever happens next – but, what are the chances that we, the Teams, could take a few days and go home for Christmas?" Dave gave a timid smile.

The Captain quietly thought about Dave's proposal, rocking in his chair. Then he spoke: "The boost to morale would be immeasurable. And the timing ... the timing is very good. We'll have to see what happens in Washington, they might want to take immediate action, in which case this won't happen. However, I could make an argument that you boys will begin intensive preparation for three months, get ... say ... two weeks leave, and then deploy with a vengeance. It might work. The President would certainly love the image of you guys at home by a Christmas tree; that would be just his sort of thing. I could probably manage to make sure he sees the plan at the same time the Joint Chiefs do; this situation is the sort of thing that they would bring me in for the planning and discussion phase. And we wouldn't even need a specific target or specific orders to begin the build-up; we could start with general stuff. I like your idea Dave, and think there is a strong possibility that it might work."

Dave smiled, "That would be great. Chris and I haven't been home for Christmas since '97, I think."

"Well, don't spread the good news just yet. A lot might happen between here and there. However, if it is possible, I'd love to send at least some of my Teams home for Christmas."

. . . .

It was Christmas Eve, 2001, and the snow was softly falling through the dark sky of the early evening. The Shepherd family house was happily busy. In the kitchen, Mary was preparing a platter – with excellent cheeses and crackers. Gayle, Christi and Sabrina were frosting the cookies they had baked earlier that day.

John was in the large family room – located down a short hall from the kitchen, towards the back center of the house. There was a huge, floor to ceiling, window that looked out on the spacious, snow-covered backyard and the beautifully frosted forest beyond. The room was the size of a small ballroom, had a very high ceiling and enough space to comfortably entertain more than fifty people, if the furniture was moved. It had the same medieval style décor as the rest of the house but had a discretely positioned entertainment center, conveniently concealable behind a tapestry of a large cerulean blue dragon, against a rich green forest background, which was currently tied to the side with a red sash.

Today was listed on all of John's identification as his birthday. However, he never chose to celebrate Christmas Eve as his birthday. This was for a number of reasons, but not the least of which was that today was the day that he was found. This illustrated one very important fact. Of all the days that his birthday could be, he knew with certainty that it was not this day. John felt that it was just easier to stick to Christmas celebrations and leave it alone. That having been said, the family always slipped in birthday cards and presents on Christmas morning.

John had made a fire in the large fire-place, strung the colored lights around their Christmas tree – which was in a corner of the room – and had placed boxes of ornaments by the ladder, next to the tree. It was their family tradition to decorate the tree on Christmas Eve. They would have snacks, decorate the tree, read stories, and watch Midnight Mass – televised from the Vatican by the Knights of Columbus – taking turns discretely wrapping presents.

Knit stockings – with each of their names – were hung near, rather than on, the fireplace for Santa Claus to fill when he visited that night. Sabrina had been delighted – the first year she spent Christmas in this house – to find that there was already a pretty red stocking with her name on it – in knit, golden, script letters – hanging with the others. Every year, when she and Christi arrived for Christmas break, it warmed her heart to see it hanging with the rest of the family. Dave and Chris had stocking that were also hung, even though they had never been able to get home for a Christmas when she had been there. There was a small stocking for Bastet, with her name and a picture of a crown. There was even a stocking for "Uncle Pete" – with a picture of a pipe on it – though he would not be by until the brunch on Christmas Day, after Christmas Morning Mass.

John was loading CD's into the entertainment center. It was an eclectic mix, ranging from Handel's Messiah to A Charlie Brown Christmas; from Traditional Hymns to John Denver and the Muppets. He even included Trans-Siberian Orchestra, just to see the range of reactions from the girls. He was lighting candles when he heard the bell for the front door.

John stopped what he was doing and walked down the hall to the door. They were not expecting anyone and no one ever drove down the long access road to the house uninvited or unannounced, especially not in the snow, or at night. Mary walked into the front room, from the kitchen, with the three girls behind her. "John?" she asked.

"I've got no idea," he replied.

John opened the huge, heavy wooden door, uncertain of what would be on the other-side; a sense of dread building inside him.

"Merry Christmas!" yelled Dave, Chris and Pete, in unison.

John threw the door wide and started laughing. Mary's hand's came to her face as tears of joy streamed down her cheeks. Christi and Gayle ran to the door. Christi ran up to hug Dave, and Gayle both kissed and hugged Chris. Sabrina stood by Mary and smiled a beautiful smile. Pete called out, from behind the boys, "You'd think they'd let an old man come in from the cold before all of this huggin' stuff, especially when he kept the secret and drove all the way to Brunswick to pick 'em up ... in the snow. But oh no, he shivers away."

Everyone laughed and they all came inside.

Abigail had always arranged her schedule to take leave for the two weeks surrounding Christmas to come home, just like she had always done at winter-break in college and then in Law School. She had initially worried that it would be difficult, but apparently most of the Officers at JAG did this, especially this year.

Dave and Chris were a very different story. No one had expected them. Not only because for the last several years they had not been able to come, for a number of different reasons that they could not discuss, but with everything happening in Afghanistan – the Battle of Tora Bora had just ended a week before – they were sure the boys would not be home. They had spoken on the phone, much more often since September, but things like "deployment" or "special days" were not discussed. They all assumed that the boys would call on Christmas Eve, like the last several years. This was a huge surprise.

When SEAL Team Six was informed that Army Delta Force and Army Special Forces had been tasked as part of the international Special Operations in Afghanistan, word had come down through the chain-of-command of a plan – virtually identical to the one Dave had suggested to Captain Porter – of intensive prep-training and then a two-week leave, followed by deployment in January. Dave had coordinated the flight – another C-130 – and Chris had contacted Uncle Pete. The utmost secrecy had been maintained and surprise had been gloriously achieved.

Mary hugged Dave and Chris and continued to cry tears of joy while John clapped his hand on Pete's shoulder. "How long ya know about this ya sneaky bastard?" he asked laughing.

"SEALs never tell." As Pete laughed, his laugh turned into a cough.

"Don't sound good, Pete. Maybe cuttin' back on the pipe might be a good idea," said John.

"Nah! It's just cold outside, is all," said Pete.

Everyone moved inside. Dave almost tripped over Bastet as she brushed his legs and purred. He laughed as he picked the small fluffy cat up and held her. "I missed you, Bastet! You have to be the best cat in history!" He looked in the cat's grey-blue eyes. She was at least twenty-three years old; older than Christi. Yet she still looked and acted like a kitten. It wasn't possible, but here she was.

Bastet purred loudly but, after a moment, wiggled to be let down. Dave set her down gently and she darted down the hall to the family room. Chris was busy speaking quietly to Gayle, their arms still around each other. Dave was straightening back up when he heard Christi's voice. "Dave, I'd like you to meet my friend, Sabrina."

Dave turned. The first thing that he noticed were Sabrina's eyes – a beautiful grey-blue that Dave immediately thought reminded him of the Ocean – which looked intently into his own. She wore her cat's-eye, red framed glasses, which accentuated her high cheek-bones, and her dark auburn hair was in a high pony-tail, tied with a small red ribbon in a small, pretty bow. She was wearing a grey University of Maine, Nursing t-shirt and flannel pajama pants. She looked athletic and yet beautifully, femininely curvaceous. Dave was mesmerized. A feeling that he had never before felt rushed and surged through his body. He felt himself slowly draw a deep breath and then he spoke quietly, at almost a whisper: "Hi."

She smiled brightly. "Hi, Dave."

Dave was frozen by her beauty. Their eyes were locked together and neither of them moved. Christi laughed.

"Alright. Alright," said Pete, walking forward. "Can we get out of the front room and have a little snack?"

Mary laughed. "You know where the beer is, Uncle Pete. Girls, can you please help me bring the snacks into the family room?"

Christi and Gayle followed their mother. Sabrina remained motionless, eyes still locked with Dave. Christi pulled her sleeve. "Sabrina, come on," she whispered.

Sabrina smiled and her eyes darted to the floor. "Sorry." She turned and walked with Christi. When they got to the kitchen, but were still far enough from the others not to be heard, Sabrina took Christi's arm and whispered, "The picture doesn't do him justice."

"What?" Christi whispered back.

"His eyes ... they're so ...."

Christi started to giggle, "Oh my God. You *like* him."

Sabrina didn't answer, but her cheeks flushed pink. She quickly turned and briskly walked to the island.

"Are you alright, Sweetheart?" asked Mary.

"Mmhmm," Sabrina nodded, picking up a plate with slices of different cheeses and then briskly walked into the family room.

Christi virtually bounced to the island, now giggling out-loud. Mary smiled and said, "They are *really* cute."

Gayle had a look of confusion. Christi, laughed, "Oh, Gayle didn't notice because she was cuddling with Chris."

Gayle blushed and said, "What? I'm just glad to see him. What happened?"

"It looks like we might have a little romantic attraction starting," said Mary.

"Dave and Sabrina?" said Gayle. "Oh, I can't wait until Chris notices! This is going to be so much fun."

"Now you girls be good," laughed Mary. They picked up the snack trays and walked into the family room.

They entered into a beautiful, bright room. Music from A Charlie Brown Christmas was softly playing; a high voice singing "Christmas time is here; happiness and cheer...". The candles glowed and the overhead lights had been turned down to a gentle dimness. There was a gentle light outside, above the window, delicately illuminating the falling snow on the lawn and the frosted trees of the forest beyond. Pete had got a bottle of beer and was standing next to the fire, looking at the flames. John and Chris were standing by the tree, beginning to take out some ornaments and placing them on the branches. Dave and Sabrina were standing close together, next to the beautifully decorated table, quietly talking, each with a small piece of cheese in one hand.

Christi, Gayle and Mary brought their trays to the table and set them down. They overheard Sabrina say, "It's just such a good cheese. Every time I taste it, I'm always surprised. The crunchy little salty bits are amazing."

"Yeah, Mama's cheese is the best," said Dave quietly. They were still looking at each other like they were in a dream.

Christi giggled and Gayle walked over to Chris. Mary said: "Would anyone care for some wine or anything else?"

Dave looked into Sabrina's eyes and was nearly lost again, but caught himself and said, "Would you like a glass of wine, Sabrina?"

She smiled beautifully, "Yes. That would be very nice."

"What kind do you like?" Dave asked.

"Mmmm, why don't you pick," she answered.

"I'll go with Mama and get us something."

Chris over-heard the end of the conversation and quickly turned to Gayle, whispering: "Dave is drinking wine instead of beer, what's going on?"

Gayle smiled and her eyes danced, knowingly. "Maybe he wants to look cultured for a pretty girl."

Chris' mouth dropped open. "We *must* watch this."

"Oh, be good!" laughed Gayle quietly.

Dave followed Mary to the kitchen. "Well, you seem to be getting along with Sabrina quiet well," she said.

"Yeah. She's really nice ... and so beautiful!" said Dave, his cheeks a rosy pink.

Mary smiled, "She's a wonderful girl. We are blessed that she and Christi met. She's practically a part of the family now; we all love her."

Dave smiled brightly, "What kind of wine should I get for her?"

"Well, she doesn't have it often and when she does, she usually has something white and sweet, but maybe bring out something different tonight, just to see if she likes it. How about this Pinot Noir," Mary said as she drew a bottle from the wine rack.

"Ok, I'll have a glass too," said Dave.

"You really *are* trying to impress her," laughed Mary.

She was so glad to see her boys home. When they had arrived, she had been filled with so much joy to see them; to see that they were well and safe. They had obviously made a lot of effort, not only to surprise them, but even in how they dressed – it was more dressed-up than she had seen them in years. They both wore khaki pants and a dress shirt. Chris's shirt was a light blue and he wore a thin red tie. Dave's shirt was black and looked like silk or satin, unbuttoned at the collar – two buttons down, just revealing some chest hair. Chris's ginger hair was close-trimmed and well styled. Dave's light auburn hair was in a pony-tail and his beard was more closely trimmed and neat than the last time she had seen him. They had made an effort to look nice when they arrived home.

Dave had returned to the family room with the wine. Gayle, Chris and Christi came in to get drinks. "Hi, Ma!" said Chris brightly, as he opened the refrigerator. He took out two bottles of Busch beer and a bottle of Black Tower wine. He handed the wine to Gayle who opened it and poured Christi and herself a glass. Mary had already poured a glass of the Pinot Noir for herself.

"It looks like we're all set," smiled Mary "Let's go trim the tree."

They all walked into the family room. Pete had left the fireplace, had walked over to the tree and was talking with John. Chris walked over to join them and handed John a bottle of beer. "Here you go, Da. There was only this Cowboy Beer, but I figured that you wouldn't mind."

John gestured to himself – he was wearing faded blue jeans and a flannel shirt with rolled up sleeves. "I am what I am, Son." Chris, Pete and John all laughed.

"Well, with you and Dave all dressed up, I feel like we are really under-dressed," said Christi. She, Gayle and Mary were all dressed similarly to Sabrina, with t-shirts and flannel pajama pants.

"Nah," said Chris loosening his thin, 1980's style tie, unbuttoning the top button on his shirt and smiling his crooked smile. "We're over-dressed. Christmas Eve is always laid-back and informal, right?"

"I guess," said Christi, smiling.

Dave and Sabrina were standing by the cheese, sipping wine and softly talking to each other. "How do you like the wine?" asked Dave.

"It's not what I'm used to, but it is nice … especially with your mother's amazing cheese!" Sabrina said, smiling.

John set his beer down. "Alright. Tree time."

They all gathered together by the tree and began hanging the ornaments. John climbed the ladder and placed the star on the top of the tree. The tree was about ten to twelve feet high, so they had to use the ladder to hang ornaments on the higher branches. They all laughed and talked as they decorated and there was a warm gentle feeling to the room. After they finished, they stepped back, and finished their drinks, quietly looking at the Christmas tree.

They quietly talked in small groups, had snacks, and sipped wine and beer. It was a very pleasant evening.

"Hey, Chris!" called Dave.

"'S-up?" said Chris.

"Sabrina was telling me that she and Christi are probably going to be stationed in Portsmouth by this summer. That means that they'll be about 10 minutes away from Gayle, up in Norfolk, and both of their locations are just over a half-an-hour away from us." Dave sounded like he was trying hard not to sound too excited.

"That's cool," said Chris with a perplexed look.

"What that means is that, when you and I are at base, we can all get together sometimes!" Now Dave sounded as excited as a small boy … on Christmas Eve. Sabrina was also smiling brightly and her eyes were sparkling.

"Indeed," Chris laughed. He and Gayle had gotten together for dinner, or a day at Virginia Beach, as often as they could – but, not as often as they wanted. However, Dave almost never joined them. Ever since they started dating, back in high school, Dave had been resistant to join them when they went out, saying that they needed their privacy and that he didn't want to be a "third wheel". Now, it would appear, he had a reason to come.

"It's time for stories," said Mary.

Christi smiled and set a small plate with a cookie and a small piece of carrot on the small table next to the tree. "For Santa," she said with a smile.

"I think that I'm gonna pass the torch with the stories, this year," said John. "Dave, you're the oldest by a couple months. You get to do the reading."

"Of course, as the father, you will still be reading the Bible story," said Mary with a smile.

"Of course, Darlin'," said John with a smile. He knew that it wasn't only because he was the father, but that Mary thought the story was also an appropriate connection to his "birthday."

John picked up the Bible from the table with the other books. "From the Gospel according to St. Luke, Chapter two, verses one through nineteen. And in those days ..."

As John read, everyone was quiet. After he finished everyone finished the last of their drinks and snacks and gathered by the fire place. Dave sat in the center of the large soft couch. Mary sat in the puffy chair on his left side. John and Pete stood together on the side of the fireplace near Mary's chair, and Chris and Gayle stood together on the other side of the fireplace. Christi and Sabrina sat on the couch, snuggled in, with their legs curled up on the couch and their heads against Dave's shoulders, on either side of him – Christi on his left, Sabrina on his right – exactly as they had for the past three years when John read the Christmas stories.

Dave felt a warmth and excitement in his chest and abdomen. It wasn't from the wine. It wasn't from the fire. It wasn't from being the one to read the stories. It wasn't even from the anticipation of Christmas. Dave could feel Sabrina's cheek, softly pressing into his shoulder. Dave had spent the entire evening talking with Sabrina and he was the happiest he could ever remember being to be sitting so closely to her now.

Dave began with Dr. Seuss. "Every Who down in Whoville liked Christmas a lot ..."

Dave read for well over an hour. As he finished one favorite Christmas story, Christi would hand him another. As he read, the others quietly listened, while they looked and smiled at the new couple on the couch.

By the time Dave had finished The Grinch, Christi had moved, unnoticed, from the center of the couch, next to Dave, to the end of the couch, closer to her mother. This was interestingly prompted by Bastet tugging on her pant-leg. Bastet was now curled up with Christi, softly purring.

Chris and Gayle stood, holding each other with her head against his chest for a while, but then quietly went to the other side of the family room to wrap presents. "They are absolutely adorable," said Gayle.

"Indeed," said Chris, with a smile. "This is a whole new side of Dave that I've never seen."

John and Pete had quietly gone outside so that Pete could puff on his pipe. "Thanks, for bringin' them up here, Pete, it means a lot."

"I'll tell you what, John," said Pete smiling and puffing his pipe. "I wouldn't have missed seeing those two meet for the world."

"You got that right, brother," said John, taking a sip of beer.

As he continued to read, slowly and very naturally, Dave's arm moved around Sabrina and her head moved from his shoulder to his chest. He was holding her and she was cuddling closely. She was never sure if it had been the warmth of the fire, or Dave's soft voice, or the way she felt, cuddled next to him with his strong arm around her, but Sabrina slowly drifted off to the most peaceful sleep that she could ever recall having as Dave read. Mary smiled, watching her son, and felt so happy that she wouldn't have been surprised if she was actually glowing.

After Dave finished the last of the stories, Christi got up and joined Gayle and Chris, wrapping presents. Mary whispered to Dave: "Would you like me to wake her so you can get up?"

"No thanks," whispered Dave. "I'm all good."

"I can imagine," said Mary with a smile. "I'll get you a beer and some snacks for while you sit here with her."

"Thanks, Mama."

Mary got up, got the beer, some cheese and a few crackers. She handed Dave the beer and set the dish of snacks next to him. She then went and joined the others.

Dave sat on the couch, holding Sabrina, for the rest of the evening. He watched the fire flicker in the fireplace and listened to her soft breathing. He too drifted off to sleep, sometime before midnight Mass.

After the Mass had ended, Chris gave Gayle a kiss goodnight and they both went off to their separate rooms.

Pete walked up to the guest room that they always had ready for him. Pete liked beer, no matter how much he made fun of John's favorite, and from time to time he stayed the night, rather than driving the long, winding road back home.

Christi gently woke Sabrina, who got up without waking Dave, and they walked to their room. Sabrina blushed and felt a bit embarrassed about falling asleep with Dave, but after Christi said that everything was perfectly fine, she smiled brightly. "Christi, I really, *really* like your brother!"

"Oh, he really, *really* likes you too!" Christi said in reply.

"You really think so?" asked Sabrina shyly.

"Um … Oh my God, yes!" answered Christi, giggling quietly.

Mary, gently woke Dave. He opened his eyes, the fire had died down and only a few candles were still burning. "Where's Sabrina?" he asked.

"Christi just took her off to bed a moment ago," she smiled. "You really like her, huh?"

"Yeah, Mama," said Dave. "She's the sweetest, nicest, most beautiful girl I have ever met."

"Well, you make a sweet couple. Now go to bed so Santa can come. You can sit with Sabrina at Mass in the morning."

Dave walked to his room. He lay in bed awake for a while, but eventually he drifted back to sleep. All his thoughts and dreams were of Sabrina.

. . . .

Everyone got up, bright and early, to open presents. The stockings had been filled by Santa and the tree was surrounded by brightly colored packages. They happily exchanged gifts and then got ready for Mass.

Dave and Sabrina, initially exchanged shy smiles, neither sure if the other was entirely comfortable with how close they had gotten the night before. But, before long they were sitting close together, smiling and talking quietly to each other.

John, Mary and Pete got into John's black Chevy Pick-up and Gayle drove everyone else in Mary's silver Chevy Venture mini-van. Chris sat in the front passenger seat, Christi sat in the middle row, and Dave and Sabrina sat in the back. They were holding hands.

All the ladies wore pretty dresses and the men were in the nicest clothes they had. The nicest things Chris and Dave had with them were what they wore the night before, but Mary had said that was fine and that they looked nice.

Everyone noticed, but no one commented, that Dave and Sabrina sat closely together in the pew and that they were holding hands.

The Mass had few people, as most had gone the night before. The colors were striking, the music beautiful and Father Mike's homily focused on Hope and Peace.

They went home and all worked together in the kitchen to make a large and appetizing brunch. There was food, and laughter. There was more wine and beer. They sang songs and told stories. It was a wonderful day.

Dave and Sabrina were close throughout the entire day, almost always holding hands, smiling and laughing. Before bed, Sabrina gave Dave a close, warm, and lingering hug and smiled brightly. "Thanks for a really nice day, Dave. I'll see you tomorrow."

"Thanks for the best Christmas ever, Sabrina. Goodnight."

The next two weeks flew by. Chris and Gayle spent lots of time alone together, but Dave and Sabrina always brought Christi along with them. Once, John asked Mary why she thought they always asked Christi to come along.

"They are caring, smart and moral kids, John. Caring in that Christi is Sabrina's best friend, and she is very close with Dave – they don't want her to get lonely or to feel left-out. Smart in that they are in a new relationship. They are obviously intensely attracted to each other and, I think, very much in love. Bringing Christi along means that things won't go too far and they can avoid feeling bad about doing something, in the heat of the moment, which they will later regret."

When the time came for the break to end, Chris arranged to take a commercial flight back to Virginia with Gayle, and then she would drive him to Dam Neck, so they could spend a bit more time together. Christi and Sabrina would drive Dave to Brunswick for his flight, on their way back to school. Mary cried when they all left, and John made the boys promise not to be heroes.

Christi drove her blue Chevy Cavalier and Sabrina and Dave sat, closely together, in the back, holding hands. When they got to the Air Base, Sabrina got out with Dave and Christi yelled from the open window, "Be safe Dave, but don't forget to kick those bastards' asses!"

Dave had his bag over his shoulder and they walked, hand-in-hand towards the gate. Dave turned to face Sabrina. She smiled at him and wiped the single tear from her eye. "Hey," he said pulling her close, "everything's going to be ok."

She nodded and laughed a little. "I'll call and write you as often as I can," said Dave. He paused and then said: "Sabrina." She looked deeply into his eyes. "I love you."

"I love you, too, Dave," said Sabrina, smiling brightly.

Then, in front of the Naval Air Base, on a cold, January day, Dave and Sabrina had their first kiss. They held each other closely and kissed sweetly, gently, and lovingly.

Christi watched from the car, as Dave turned and walked through the gate. Sabrina walked back to the car and sat in the front passenger seat. Both of them took a deep breath, said a silent prayer that both Dave and Chris would be safe in Afghanistan, and then Christi began to drive.

"Christi," said Sabrina. "He loves me."

Christi laughed. "He sure does."

"And Christi ... I really love him, too."

Chapter 4

or

"Life's a beach."

2004

Dave turned the black Chevy Cavalier into the parking lot of Sharky's Pub. It was a smaller, out of the way restaurant, very far from the crowded main haunts of Virginia Beach. Though Sharky's was right on the beach, it was generally pretty quiet and subdued. That's why Dave liked this place. Also, it was off-season – and a cool, cloudy day at that – so there would be no tourists to worry about.

Chris was sitting in the front passenger seat. "So, all you know is that she is bringing him?"

"No," said Dave. "It's like I told you: he's a Navy doctor – his rank is Commander, I think – who Christi met at the hospital, but they don't actually work together. I think they have 'sort-of' been dating casually for about two or three months. He's Gayle's age. Sabrina says that he's nice, but she also says that Christi told her that it isn't particularly serious."

"Why are we just meeting him now?" asked Chris.

"Well, we just got home Tuesday and today is Saturday," said Dave. "It's the first day they have had off since we got back to the States. This is literally the first chance they could get down here."

"Indeed. You have a point," said Chris.

"You should really relax," said Dave. "I am also burning up to meet Christi's first boyfriend, but from what Sabrina says, this isn't that big of a deal."

"He better not be a pretentious ass," said Chris. "You know how doctors can be."

"Oh yeah," said Dave, sarcastically, "and SEALs are never arrogant pricks. I mean, every time we see Marcinko on TV, he strikes me as having the humility of a saint and the manners of royalty." They both laughed.

When they saw Gayle's silver Chevy Trailblazer turn into the parking lot, Dave and Chris got out to meet them. The SUV had hardly come to a stop when Sabrina jumped out of the front passenger door, ran over to Dave, threw her arms around his neck and kissed him affectionately. Dave wrapped his arms around her waist and held her as closely as possible as they kissed. They paused and she looked into his eyes, while running the fingers of her right hand through his beard, "Welcome home, Sweetie! I really missed you!"

"I missed you too, Sabrina!" said Dave, and he kissed her some more.

Gayle got out of the driver's door and walked over to Chris. They embraced and kissed, though more briefly than Dave and Sabrina. "Welcome back, Sailor," said Gayle.

"Ready for duty, Ma'am," said Chris with his crooked smile.

Gayle laughed and said: "Behave."

The fact that Dave and Chris were enlisted – both Chief Petty Officers – and Sabrina and Gayle were officers – Sabrina a Lieutenant Junior Grade and Gayle a newly-promoted Commander – had been discussed by Superior Officers with reference to the Navy's Fraternization policies. But, since the individuals involved were not remotely under the same Command – and also since the couples were discrete, never meeting in uniform or on base – their relationships were not viewed as inappropriate.

Christi got out of the back of the Trailblazer with a tall, handsome man. He was just over six feet tall. He wore khaki pants and a blue dress-shirt open at the collar, with rolled up sleeves. His brown hair was short and expertly styled and he had a meticulously trimmed goatee. He had a thin but athletic build and dark blue eyes. They walked, first to Dave and Sabrina, who pivoted, but Dave's left hand was still around Sabrina's waist and her right hand was draped on Dave's left shoulder. Christi smiled, "Welcome back! Dave, this is Shawn Zielinski."

Shawn extended his right hand and smiled – Dave thought to himself "I have never seen whiter teeth!" They shook hands, "It's nice to finally meet you, Dave. Christi talks about you all the time."

"It's nice to meet you as well," said Dave.

Shawn and Chris shook hands and exchanged pleasantries as well. "So, what do you all say we go get our usual table? I believe that it's my turn. Come on," said Dave. The five of them had been meeting at Sharky's, as often as they could, for the past two years – since Dave and Chris got back from their first deployment to Afghanistan. Early on they had devised a system for rotating who paid, so there would be no fighting about it. Today, it was Dave's turn.

They walked into Sharky's pub. Inside, there was more room than one would have expected, looking at the exterior of the building. The lights were dim. There was a bar near the back, next to double-doors that lead to the kitchen. There were some booths and a few round tables, surrounded by chairs. To the left were doors to the bathrooms and to the right was a medium sized dance-floor and an old fashioned jukebox. The décor was what one might expect at a beach-side pub: some nets on the ceiling by the bar, with plastic crabs in them, and a painted mural of a smiling shark on the wall by the jukebox. It wasn't fancy, but it wasn't a dive either.

It was a little after five and the pub was empty, other than the bar-tender – a clean-shaven, well-muscled man with shoulder-length, shaggy, dirty-blond hair and brown eyes – who stood behind the bar, reading a book.

"Hi, Steve," said Dave. "You mind if we get our usual table?"

"Glad to see y'all are back," said Steve, with a southern drawl. "Suzy'll be right out. Have a seat."

Dave walked over to a round table and pulled out a chair for Sabrina, who smiled and sat down. Dave sat next to her, to her right. Chris and Gayle walked to the table and Gayle, pulled out the chair to Dave's right. Chris sat down, and looked at Dave, with his crooked smile. He said, "I love it when she treats me like a lady," and laughed. Gayle sat down to Chris' right and smiled at Dave, rapidly batting her eyes at him, like a cartoon character. Dave gave her a mock frown and turned to Sabrina, giving her a quick kiss on the cheek. Sabrina beamed her beautiful smile.

Christi looked at Shawn, "please don't pull out my chair," and she sat down to Sabrina's left. Shawn smiled and sat between Christi and Gayle, directly across the table from Dave.

Dave and Chris always tried to sit so that they could see the door. The reason that they always picked this table, and sat in the same chairs, was that it afforded them a view of the door, the bar, and most of the seating area. To their back was an empty corner. The girls were aware of the seating preference, but never said anything about it.

Suzy, a waitress, came over to the table with laminated menus, set them down and brightly said, "Hi y'all! Welcome to Sharky's! Can I get y'all something to drink while you decide what yer havin'?" She was in her late thirties, with brown hair and brown eyes, and spoke with the same southern drawl as Steve.

Sabrina looked at the back of the menu. "This looks yummy. I'd like a strawberry daiquiri, please."

"Oh, I'll have one too!" said Christi.

"I would like a glass of sweet white wine. Whatever you and Steve think is the best you have right now." said Gayle

"We got a Moscato that's real nice," smiled Suzy.

"That sounds perfect," smiled Gayle.

"Think I'll have a bottle of the Samuel Adams Boston Lager," said Shawn

Suzy turned to Dave and Chris, "and for you boys?"

"I'll have a pint of what's on tap: Budweiser, Yuengling, whatever. Tell Steve anything that's cold and not 'light'," said Dave.

"Same for me," said Chris.

"Two pints of Yuengling Lager, it is," said Suzy and she walked to the bar.

They all looked at the menu. The selection was heavy on seafood, but there was a rib steak, fried chicken-in-a-basket, a regular hamburger, and a "veggie-burger," in addition to some appetizers and sides.

Suzy came back with the drinks and took their order. Sabrina, Christi and Gayle all ordered the veggie-burger with cheese – they had split one to try it, the last time that they were here, and had loved it – Shawn ordered garlic-butter baked salmon fillet, and both Dave and Chris ordered medium-rare steaks.

They all took a drink and Shawn said: "So, Christi tells me that you guys just got home."

Dave answered, "Yeah, on Tuesday."

"She said that you were over there for six months," said Shawn.

"About that," answered Chris. "This time."

"I can imagine that they send you there a lot, being with the Teams."

"Yeah," said Dave. "We're with SEAL Team Six, so we have a lot of different assignments. Almost all of it is stuff we can't discuss, but it was in the news that we helped with Operation Anaconda in '02 and that our guys got Jessica Lynch out in '03, though that one wasn't specifically us."

"That's impressive!" said Shawn.

"Mostly it's just hot," said Dave.

"So, you work in the Medical Center with Christi and Sabrina?" said Chris, quickly changing the subject.

"Yes and no," answered Shawn. "We all work there, but I work on a different floor and in a different department than they do."

"What do you do?" asked Dave.

"I work with out-patient General Medicine, while they are on an in-patient, med-surg floor," answered Shawn.

"How did you two meet?" asked Chris.

"Well, actually, we met in the cafeteria. I was getting lunch. I was walking with my tray to find a seat, when my phone rang. I reached out to set my tray on the nearest table and answer my phone. I really wasn't paying close attention, because it wasn't an empty table – Christi and Sabrina were sitting there. Well, as I answered my phone, I quickly became aware that my tray wasn't all the way on the table, as it fell to the floor. I tried to catch it and dropped my phone. I also missed the tray and I'm sure that I looked ridiculous."

"He did," said Christi. "He looked absolutely ridiculous. Well, in the process of flailing around, he knocked my coffee over and it spilled in my lap. I jumped up and probably said some not-polite things."

"She was pretty upset," laughed Shawn. "I apologized, profusely. Then, I did something that I still can't believe I did, under those circumstances. I asked her if I could make it up to her by buying her a coffee after work."

"Well," said Christi, "I normally would have just said no, but for some reason I said: 'no, but you can buy me a beer, as long as my friend can come and you buy her one too.'"

"The rest is history," said Shawn.

The food arrived and everything was excellent. A few people had gradually drifted into the pub, as they were speaking and eating, and now it was about half full. The music that had been quietly playing in the background, was now slightly louder to compete with the talking and laughing.

"So, you said that you and Christi wanted to tell us about some plans you were making," Dave said to Sabrina, taking her hand.

Sabrina smiled. "Yes. Well, as you know, our service requirement to the Navy is up in about a year from now. We decided that we'd like to have that be it and return to civilian life. Things are very different than they were when we decided on this path, back in senior year of high school. We've talked about it a lot, and we don't plan to continue."

"Oh," said Dave. "What do you plan to do after that?"

"We actually have been talking about this with your mother," said Sabrina.

"With Mama?" asked Dave. "What did she say?"

"She wants us to come and work with her," smiled Christi. "She thinks that we should both move back home and we could all work together at her hospital."

"Oh," said Dave. He had really loved being able to see Sabrina whenever they were back to Dam Neck. If she moved to Maine, that time would be extremely decreased.

Two couples had begun slow dancing. Completely disengaging with the conversation, Dave squeezed Sabrina's hand, softly. "Will you dance with me?"

"Sure," she said softly.

They got up and the rest of the table was momentarily quiet and watched them walk over to the dance floor. A new song began as Dave put his arms around Sabrina's waist and she wrapped her arms around his neck. They looked into each other's eyes and slowly began to sway with the music. It was an old song by The Eagles. "All alone at the end of the evening, when the bright lights have faded to blue ..."

Dave started to think about everything he wanted in life, everything he had planned – for this night and all the time after. The more time he spent with Sabrina, the more time he wanted with her. He struggled with the time they were apart, and now the thought of that time apart only increasing was beginning to fill him with a feeling of despair. He held her as close as he could, looking into her eyes. The song continued: "but the dreams I've seen lately, keep on turnin' out, and burnin' out, and turnin' out the same …"

Sabrina smiled her beautiful smile. "Dave," she said softly.

"What is it?" he asked quietly.

"This is a really stupid song," she said in her gentle, loving voice.

Dave laughed out-loud. "I love you so much, Sabrina."

"I love you too, Dave," she smiled. And they gently kissed, as they danced to the rest of the song.

When the song ended, Dave and Sabrina walked back to the table, hand-in-hand. Shawn had gone to the bathroom. Christi stood up and announced, "I have to pee."

Sabrina softly squeezed Dave's hand, "I'll be right back."

Gayle also stood up and the three girls walked to the bathroom together. Dave sat down. "They really do always travel in packs," laughed Chris. Dave said nothing and finished his beer.

"So, what you missed while you were dancing is that Gayle is also considering leaving the Navy when her time is up in '06, even though she is a superstar at JAG and is getting promoted up the chain at record speed. And, if she does, she also plans to move back home. She's thinking about trying to get a job with the DA's office. It looks like soon it might just be us down here."

"Great," said Dave.

"Well, I don't like it either," said Chris. "But, you don't have to get all 'now I'm gonna sit here and brood about it for the rest of the night'; they're *here* now."

"Sorry, I have a lot on my mind," said Dave.

"No, you have Sabrina on your mind," said Chris with a laugh. "Look. She's got over a year left, and we'll probably be here for at least a few months. You should spend as much time with her as you can. I'll cover for you, just like you have for me. You'll never be more than an hour from base and you have a cell phone for me to reach you if you absolutely need to get back. There is no reason for you to get upset about it now."

"It's not really just that," said Dave.

"Well, what's the problem?"

"It's not a problem and I can't say just yet."

"Ok, fine," said Chris.

Shawn returned to the table and sat down. "Where did they all go?"

"They went to the bathroom," answered Chris. "So, where are you from? What's your story?"

"I'm from a suburb, near Syracuse, NY. I was an only child and my parents split-up earlier than I can remember. I spent time with both of them, though I lived with my mother. She's a RN, which is probably why I got interested in medicine. I did the whole school then medical school then residency thing, but didn't really have a future plan. So, when the Navy recruited me and made an offer to take care of school debt in exchange for six years, I said yes. They put me in this out-patient clinic at the hospital and everything was pretty chill. Then 9/11 happened. I tried to get re-assigned, first for Afghanistan and then for Iraq, but they kept me here. I guess lots of MD's were volunteering to go, but no one wanted to do a calm, state-side job, so I got stuck where I was. I really wish that I could do more – you know, get out there, in the world. Who knows, when my six years is up, maybe an opportunity will present itself."

"So, how serious are you and Christi?" asked Chris.

"I don't know. We've been kind-of dating for about three months, but it feels more like we're friends than anything else. I mean, we haven't even kissed. I know that you're her brothers, but you wouldn't have to worry about me, even if it were serious. I'm a 'good-Catholic-boy' and I believe in being a gentleman. So, we would be moving slowly anyway."

As Shawn finished the sentence, Sabrina sat down by Dave and slid her arm around his waist. He turned to face her and she kissed him. "Hi, Sweetie," she said, as the other girls sat down.

Christi turned to Dave and casually said, "So, Dave, off the record, what can you guys tell us about Iraq, having just come from there?"

"It's hot there," smiled Dave.

Christi laughed, "That isn't what I meant."

"Well, without going into detail," Dave began, "there are only a few things we could say, but not much more than you hear on the news. For instance, our Team is 'sort-of' in Iraq, but we can't really discuss the other places we went. We're not a normal unit; not even a normal SEAL unit. For example, if you watched the news while we were away, you know about the Battle of Fallujah. Ok, so, SEALs were involved doing things like sniper over-watch and special missions, but those are regular SEAL Teams who are stationed over there. We are more mobile; we carry out a mission and then we leave and go somewhere else. That being said, we had some work related to Fallujah, but, most of the stuff we do you will probably never hear about."

"That's not really what I mean, either," said Christi. "I'm just asking how you think it's going."

"Like I told you, mostly it's hot," said Dave. "I really hate the Middle East – just about everything about it – and the heat just makes it even more ridiculous. I feel horrible for the regular military who are out-there all the time. I can't imagine doing their jobs. With us, we have a target, we move, it's done, we leave. Those guys are pretty stationary by comparison and everyone is a potential threat."

Chris spoke, saying: "I feel like you're asking if we are winning. If that's the question, the answer depends on what you mean. We are obliterating our targets and killing lots of bad-guys, but I don't think that's the same as winning. To win a 'War on Terror,' we have to do more than kill the terrorists. What we have to do is find a way to eliminate the reason people become terrorists, which if you have an idea how to do that, tell me because I don't have a single clue."

Dave spoke again: "Here's the way that I look at it. The people that we are fighting will want to kill us and our people wherever we are. We need to fight them over there so we don't have to fight them over here. I, personally, couldn't care less about Iraq, or Afghanistan, or any of the other places we get sent. I care about protecting us; *our* people. If we do what we do over there, they won't be placing IED's, or blowing up buildings over here because they will be busy with us over there."

Christi nodded.

"So, that's what girls talk about when you go to the bathroom in groups; the war?" asked Chris, with his crooked smile.

Everyone laughed. Christi said, "No. It's just you're just back from there and I was curious."

Dave turned to Sabrina, and said, while holding her hand, "Are you curious?"

"No, not really" she said smiling. "You're home and safe. That's all I really need to know about it, other than what you tell me already," and she gave him a quick, soft kiss.

Dave smiled and nodded. Then he said, addressing the table, "I'm going to go get another pint from Steve, anyone want anything?"

While Dave and Sabrina had been dancing, Suzy had stopped by and the others had ordered more drinks. So now, only Dave and Sabrina had empty glasses. "Another strawberry daiquiri would be very nice. Thanks." Sabrina smiled.

Dave gave her a quick kiss. "I'll be right back," and he walked to the bar.

When Dave got up to the bar Steve turned to him and smiled, "What's up, Dave?"

"Can I get another pint and a strawberry daiquiri for Sabrina?"

"Sure thing, my friend. Hey, and Dave, we're all real glad that you and Chris are back home safe."

"Thanks, Steve," said Dave, as Steve turned to get the drinks.

Dave had not really noticed the odd little man sitting on the bar stool next to him, until the man spoke. "Yeah Dave, so glad you're back." His voice was sing-song and squeaky. His hair was just less than shoulder-length, dirty, un-kept and brown. His clothes were also dirty and un-kept. His eyes sparkled, bright green and Dave wasn't sure but he thought that maybe the little man had pointed ears.

"I'm sorry," said Dave. "Have we met?"

"You don't know me, but I sure know you." The little man laughed.

Dave thought the man might be a mentally ill, homeless person. "Ok, buddy," he said, as Steve returned with the drinks. "You have a good night. Hey Steve, can you put another drink for this guy on my tab?"

"Sure," said Steve, as Dave walked back to the table with his drinks.

"Bye-bye, Dave," said the odd, little man, laughing. "One more cup of rum, please, Steve."

Steve gave the little man a sideways glance. "Listen, just some friendly advice: you probably want to leave that guy and his friends alone. He's a world-class warrior and so is one of the other guys. I strongly suggest that you do not mess with them."

The little man finished his glass of rum, and tapped the empty glass on the bar as he laughed. "You think you know him, but I know more than you. I'm not messing, I'm drinking … and watching."

Steve poured the rum. "Just don't make a problem."

"Nope, no problems. She'd never allow it." He laughed, quickly drank the rum and hopped down from the stool. "Bye-bye, Steve."

Steve glanced down the bar as the little man was finishing his drink, but at his last words he turned back. The little man was gone. He had not seen him walk away and the door to the pub had not opened, but the man was gone. "That was a weird little guy," he said to himself.

Dave had returned to the table and handed Sabrina her drink. She smiled at him and sipped the icy pink drink, as he sat down. "Yummy! Thank you."

Dave smiled back and took a long drink of beer. Chris spoke up, "So, Shawn was saying that he likes hiking and camping. He'd probably like Maine then."

Dave nodded. Shawn spoke, saying: "Yeah, I've never been but I used to go to the Adirondacks a lot and I spent a few weeks, a couple of times, out west in the Rockies."

"You'd love our parents' place then," said Gayle, sipping her wine. "It's more like hills than mountains, but the forest and lake are beautiful."

"And you can't beat the sky at night," said Chris.

Dave gently took Sabrina's hand, "will you come for a walk with me and sit on the beach with me for a few minutes, before it gets too dark?"

Sabrina smiled, "Sure, Sweetie." She turned to Christi and said, "We'll be back in a little while."

Dave and Sabrina, hand-in-hand, walked to the door. Gayle turned to Chris, "Is something going on? Dave is really quiet tonight."

"Yeah," said Christi, "what's up?"

"I'm not really sure," said Chris. "He got more broody than usual when you said that you two are going back home, probably because the only thing that he thinks about anymore is spending time with Sabrina. Seriously, you should see him when we're over there. He switches gears on a mission, but when we're not taking care of business, he's Broody McBrooderson."

They all laughed. "But there's something else tonight. He's been quiet and withdrawn, more than usual, since we set up this date. On Wednesday he even vanished for hours and wouldn't say where he went. Something's up, but he won't tell me."

"Sorry, Shawn," laughed Christi, "Dave isn't always like this."

"I was worried that it was me," said Shawn.

"No," said Chris. "It's something else."

Christi suddenly sat up straight and clapped her hands to her mouth. "I think I got it …"

. . . .

Dave and Sabrina walked across the parking lot and to Dave's car. He opened the trunk and took out a blanket. They walked over to where the sand of the beach began and slipped off their sandals. Hand-in-hand, they walked out on to the beach.

The wind from the Ocean tossed both their pony-tails. It was a gentle, but constant breeze. Dave looked at Sabrina. The wind pressed her soft sundress against her body, emphasizing her smooth feminine curves. "My God, you're so beautiful, Sabrina," he said.

She smiled at him, "Thank you, Dave."

They walked towards the rolling sand dunes, and found a private place to lay the blanket, somewhat sheltered from the wind. They sat down next to each other. Then, laying back and holding each other closely, they kissed, long and affectionately.

Dave then propped himself up on one elbow. "I really want to talk to you about something, Sabrina."

"Is everything ok? You've been a little quiet today?"

"I'm ok," he replied. "I've just been thinking about a lot of things."

"Ok, what's going on?"

"Well, we've been together for about two-and-a-half years. I love you so thoroughly and completely; with every fiber of who I am. When I'm with you, I'm happier than I ever imagined that I could be and when we are apart, all I do is think about you."

"Oh Dave," she reached out and gently caressed his cheek, "I love you, too."

"There's so much I want to say about so many things, but there's something that I want to ask you, first."

"What is it, Sweetie?" she asked, looking deep into his ice-blue eyes.

Dave pivoted his waist and sat up. He reached down and then brought up his hand. He was holding a small box. "Sabrina Katzen, will you marry me?"

Sabrina started laughing and threw her arms around his neck, pulling him to the ground and kissing him with a degree of passion neither of them had yet known. "Yes! Yes! Yes! I love you, David Shepherd!" And she kissed him again, her hands in his hair.

After a few moments, Dave laughed. "What?" she said softly, out of breath.

"Don't you want to see the ring?"

"Oh … yes!" she said smiling.

Dave reached for the box, which had been dropped at the other end of the blanket when Sabrina had begun kissing him. He opened it and handed to her. It was a white, sparkling opal, set on a silver band with knot-work-like twists where the opal met the silver. She breathed in, and took the ring, only then realizing that she was trembling. She put it on and said, "Oh Dave, it's so beautiful!"

"I knew that an opal was your favorite and that you prefer silver to gold," said Dave smiling shyly.

"I love you, so much!" and she pulled him to her, kissing him again.

The intensity of their kiss was far beyond what it had ever been before. Dave was filled with amazingly intense emotions and felt like he could just melt in Sabrina's arms. His love for her was so deep and complete, and his attraction and desire for her was so consuming, that he could feel it overwhelming him. Dave had never wanted anything more than he wanted Sabrina in this moment, but he didn't want to push things further than she wanted them to go. Dave reluctantly pulled away, a bit. "We should probably go for a walk to talk about the rest."

"We don't have to go for a walk," said Sabrina, in a soft, almost whispered voice; lightly biting her lower lip and looking deeply into his eyes. "We could … stay here for a while." Sabrina's cheeks were flushed, she was slightly out of breath, and the way she looked into Dave's eyes made it perfectly clear to him that she was feeling exactly the same things that he was.

Dave took a breath and smiled. "We can stay here as long as you want us to." He pulled her close again, but before he could kiss her, she spoke.

"I love you, so much!" Sabrina said with a smile. Then she caressed his cheek, looked deeply into his eyes, and gently said "We really *will* be glad we waited … when it's our wedding night."

"I Love you, Sabrina! You're right … we really should wait," said Dave, and they kissed passionately once more.

When they sat up, Sabrina laughed. "I sort of messed up your hair, but I'll fix it before we go back." She stroked his cheek, gently. They were both flushed and out of breath. Neither of them had ever dated anyone else, and this was the most passionately heated they had ever gotten. They both held traditional Catholic values about relationships, but it was harder than they had ever thought it would have been to adhere to them right now.

"You know," said Sabrina, "we really don't have to go anywhere else to talk. It's nice here. What else do you want to talk about?"

"Well," said Dave, catching his breath, "Mostly it's about where we go from here. We can see each other as much as possible until I get deployed again or you leave for Maine. I'm not sure what you had planned, but now that we're engaged, I'm sure that Mama and Dad will insist that you move into their house."

"She already wants us to; Christi and me. I said, yes. I thought it would be a sure way to see you as much as possible," she smiled.

"Oh, good," said Dave. "So, I was thinking that we could get married right after you leave the Navy. That way, when I'm here, we can have a little place, off-base. And when I have to go, you can stay with my parents and work up there."

"That sounds really good," she smiled. "I'm sure that the hospital will let me work something like that out."

"There's one other thing," said Dave.

"What is it, Sweetie?" she asked, running a hand down his chest.

He paused for a moment. "I have a very dangerous job. If you ask me not to, I won't re-enlist when the time comes."

"Oh, baby," she said smiling. "I know. I know all of that. I worry about you when you're gone and I pray for you every single day. I know why you do what you're doing and I don't think that I should be the one to tell you to stop. There will be a right time for you to stop and when it is that time, that's what you'll do. Until then, we'll make the best of it. I'll always love you and I'll always be yours. Everything in the world changes but always know that, no matter what happens, I will always love you."

They fell into each other's arms again and kissed for several minutes more. Then they got up, Sabrina fixed Dave's hair and he fixed hers — less successfully than she had his. They folded the blanket and walked, hand-in-hand, back to Sharky's Pub, in the gathering darkness. They slipped on their sandals and Dave put the blanket back in the car. Then, they went back inside.

They walked to the table and sat down. The other four had been laughing when they came in, but stopped as Dave and Sabrina sat down.

"So," said Christi to Sabrina, smiling brightly. "Did you have a nice time with your boyfriend?"

"No, I did not." said Sabrina, trying to sound very serious. They all froze, with trepidation over what she would say next. "I had a wonderful time with my fiancée!" She thrust her left hand to the center of the table, laughing as she displayed the ring."

Christi's voice went up at least an octave as she clapped her hands and cried out, loudly, "Oh my God, I knew it!!!"

Gayle laughed and said, "Congratulations!"

Shawn laughed, "I certainly picked the right night to come out with you guys."

Chris clapped his hand on Dave's shoulder, "So, that's where you went on Wednesday, you sneaky bastard. Well, you two were gone so long that we felt we needed to finish your drinks." He yelled loudly to the bar: "Hey Steve! We're gonna need another round! My brother just got engaged!"

There was a cheer from the entire Pub and a chorus of "congratulations" shouted. Suzy brought a tray of drinks and wished Dave and Sabrina "Good Luck!"

Dave and Sabrina held hands and quietly smiled. Chris said, "Congratulations, my brother. You had me worried, but now I know why. Oh, and if you think that I'm going to let you pay tonight, you are out of your mind."

"Thanks, Chris," said Dave.

From a dim corner, on the other side of the room, an odd little man with pointed ears and sparkling green eyes, watched unnoticed as they celebrated the good news. He sat very still and smiled. He spoke quietly, but excitedly, to himself. "Oh yes, this is very good news! What a glorious day this is, indeed! Her Grace will want to know this, oh yes she will. And I shall have rum! Yes, yes! Her Grace will reward me! Time to go. Bye-bye Sharky." And then he vanished into thin air.

. . . .

Dave and Sabrina happily told John and Mary Shepherd their good news and both of Dave's parents were ecstatically over-joyed. They made plans with the happy couple to have the wedding in their local church and then what would serve as the reception at their home afterwards. Dave and Sabrina would spend their first night as a married couple in a very private section of the house and the next day drive down to Scarborough – about two hours away – for a two-week honeymoon. They set the date for mid-summer of 2005.

Mary used to quiet often say: "If you want to hear God laugh, tell him your plans." Unfortunately, this was again the case. In response to the beginning of the second Battle of Fallujah, Dave and Chris' Team was re-deployed to Iraq, only two months after arriving home. No one was happy about it, but the fighting in Iraq was at a high-point. They tentatively changed the date of the wedding to October 2005, hoping Dave and Chris would safely be home by then.

．　．　．　．　．　．

2005

Dave and Chris knocked at a the door that was serving as Commander Fredrickson's office, deep within a fortified building in the "Green Zone," Baghdad, Iraq. "Come in."

Dave and Chris entered. They were dressed in desert camo fatigues, and other than Dave's pony tail, they were virtually indistinguishable from the other three SEALs in the Commander's office. Commander Fredrickson was a light-skinned black man who was about six feet tall, he had closely trimmed hair and a thick moustache. He was the Commanding Officer of the squadron of which Dave and Chris' Team was a part. There were no other Officers present at the meeting, but there was a man in civilian clothes who was obviously an Intelligence Agent of some sort. He had close cropped, styled hair and looked like a tourist.

Commander Fredrickson's deep voice welcomed them to the meeting. "Shepherd. Hanley. Welcome to the meeting. You're just in time."

"Good morning, Sir." They said in unison, sitting at the table.

"Alright Gentlemen, we have a weird one who is not on the radar of the regular military. This guy is a behind-the-scenes influencer: a puppet-master. Agent Smith."

The Intelligence Agent tossed a picture on the table. "This is Alzalam Alqadim. The grainy picture showed an older, bearded, Arabic man with a turban. We're pretty sure that's not his name …"

"Like we're pretty sure Smith's not yours?" said Chris. Everyone, including Agent Smith, laughed.

"Yes, well," continued Smith, "Alzalam Alqadim loosely translates to 'the one who came before,' so it probably isn't his given name. Anyway, we know very little about this target. We know that he is very high on the food-chain. We know that most of the 'top targets' SOCOM is tracking are somehow manipulated by him, but we don't know why or how. We know that he wasn't in Sadaam's government and it is said that Sadaam was afraid of him, but Sadaam never took any action against him and we don't know why. Our best informants are terrified of him and describe him as some sort of sorcerer or demon and they say that he can't be killed."

"We didn't initially want to use US personnel to hit this target, so we sent two separate mercenary hit teams – all Arabs. We lost both teams. After the second attempt – after the Second Battle of Fallujah – we know that he moved to a new location, here." He pointed to a spot on satellite photo of an area Northeast of Baghdad, in Nebai.

"What kind of security are we looking at?" asked Dave.

"We know that he has two very burly bodyguards. Other than that, nothing," answered Agent Smith.

"So, what the hell happened to the Merc teams?" asked Chris.

"We don't know. He was in Fallujah and both attempts were during the Second Battle, so anything could have happened," answered Agent Smith.

"That's comforting," said a SEAL at the table who had, so far remained silent. Petty Officer Second Class Diego Wagner, was five-ten, with close cropped, curly, dirty-blond hair, a closely cropped dark beard, and brown eyes. He had been born and raised in California but his mother was Guatemalan and his father was German, so he was perfectly fluent in all three languages. He was also an impressive mixed-martial-arts practitioner. He was relatively new to SEAL Team Six, and Dave was sort of surprised that he had been included in this group.

"So, this is the plan, Gentlemen," stated Commander Fredrickson. "You'll drive to here. Davis and Ryan will position as snipers, on the rises, here and here," he said pointing. "You should have acceptable cover and clear lines of sight to the house." They were looking at a second, closer, more detailed satellite photo.

"There's pretty much nothing around the house and not a ton of cover. Shepherd, Hanley and Wagner, you'll approach on foot. Enter the house, terminate the target and exfil to here."

"You men have been specially selected for this assignment for individual qualities. Select weapons of choice, but silence is strongly preferred. There's not a lot around this house, but he's not without some neighbors. Do not engage any of them. Hit the target tonight at midnight. Any questions?"

There were none and they were dismissed. More specific instruction would be delivered to each man, later that afternoon.

On typical missions, the Team involved does almost all the specific planning, but recently, Dave and Chris had begun to notice that they were being selected for special missions, with other guys from other Teams, for bizarre targets, where they had little-to-no say in the planning process. Thus far, these sorts of missions had gone smoothly, but they always made Dave uncomfortable.

Diego was walking along with Dave and Chris, and Davis and Ryan went off in another direction. "Does this seem a little weird to you guys?" asked Diego.

Chris and Dave both liked Diego. He was a nice guy, had good ideas, and was really good with hand-to-hand combat. Also, he was extremely well read; a quality that always caught Dave and Chris' attention in a positive way.

"Indeed," said Chris. "They are telling us almost nothing."

"Other than that two teams of Mercs were wiped out going after this target," said Dave.

"I thought we were supposed to have more of a role in planning," said Diego.

"This has been happening, more and more, to us with these 'specially selected' missions. I was kind-of surprised they pulled you in, because you are new to the Team, but maybe you were selected because they expect hand-to-hand stuff. They do want it as quiet as possible," said Dave.

"How different are these 'special' missions than the regular stuff we do?" asked Diego.

"The targets are different. Sometimes the locations are in strange places," answered Dave.

"And by 'different', Dave means that we are going after people who Intel tells us are … well, weird. Like when he told us that this target is a wizard, or whatever he said," clarified Chris.

"You don't think that's real, do you?" asked Diego.

"I don't know, we've seen some pretty weird stuff over the years," laughed Chris.

"Just make sure you select a couple bladed weapons to carry; because of the silence factor. For example, I have carried a Kukri machete since a mission in '93." said Dave.

"I remember that one. That was weird too. He was that vampire guy," said Chris.

"Wait. Did you just say you guys took out an actual vampire?" asked Diego, laughing.

"The local people said that he was a vampire and he played along," said Dave. "But these 'special missions' are like that … and they're weird. People do weird things to scare people. Just stay focused on the job and you'll be fine."

The three SEALs went back to their Team area and prepared their weapons and equipment for the mission. Dave and Chris still carried the .45s and KA-BARs their father had given them. Dave prepared his Kukri. Diego carried a Sig Sauer P226 and a SEAL Pup combat knife. All three of them prepared their specially modified M4 Carbines, with suppressors. All weapons were cleaned, sharpened and thoroughly prepared. Rounds were loaded into magazines. Grenades were acquired, both frags and flash-bangs – silence was preferred, but getting home alive was more important.

When they finished, they went to get something to eat and then went off to try to get some sleep. Dave took a moment to write Sabrina an E-mail, telling her that he loved her, missed her, and that he looked forward to calling her on Sunday. He always wrote her an E-mail before and after a mission. He never told her about the mission and he hoped that she never guessed or worried, however, she did both: she always knew and then prayed and worried until he wrote again. They spoke on the phone every Sunday. She never told him that she worried and he tried his best not to give her a reason to worry – staying as positive and non-specific as possible about what he was doing. After the E-mail was sent, he lay down and went to sleep.

It was dark when Dave woke up. He joined Chris and Diego in the Team area. They geared-up and read the specific instruction that had been left for them, including the specific location and keys for the van they would use to get to the location.

They met Davis and Ryan at the van – it was an old, beat-up, dusty, dark-colored van. There were no seats in the back, so the two snipers and Diego sat on the floor. Chris drove and Dave sat in the passenger seat. They drove to the target area, the snipers got into position and they all waited until midnight.

The house had been quiet and dark the whole time they waited silently in the shadows. At midnight, just as they were about to move, they noticed a flickering light through one of the windows. Diego looked at Chris and Chris shrugged. Dave motioned for the three of them to move and they quickly advanced on the house. When they reached the door, Dave tried the doorknob. It was not locked.

Dave stood up, kicked in the door and rapidly advanced into the small dark house. Chris and Diego moved in behind him, closely enough to be his shadow. Chris swept right and Diego swept left. The entire small house appeared to be a single room, or at least the majority of it was. As they entered, they had a clear view of everything there. But nothing could have prepared them for what they saw.

In the center of the room was a small fire on the dirt floor – that was the flickering they had seen. Standing behind the fire, facing them was their target: Alzalam Alqadim. He wore a dark colored robe, his arms raised in the air over the fire, and he was chanting in a guttural language that the SEALs could not understand – but, they were certain that it wasn't Arabic. His eyes were rolled back in his head and he was swaying as he continued chanting. Kneeling beside him were two large figures that appeared to be some sort of cross between a hyena and a very large man. As the SEALs entered the room, the hyena-men yelped and exploded into attack. The SEALs had no time to think; they burst into violent action.

Chris and Diego's modified M4's burst into fully automatic fire, directed into the chest areas of the charging hyena-men. They staggered and stumbled as the bullets tore through their bodies, now more falling forward than leaping.

Dave let go of his M4 and it fell to his chest. He charged at Alzalam Alqadim, his right hand moving to the kukri over his left shoulder. The small fire was between Dave and his target, but he charged forward, heedless of the flames. As Dave charged, Alzalam Alqudim's voice grew loud and his eyes moved to stare at the approaching SEAL. When Dave stepped into the flames, they were no longer small, but burst into a raging inferno; engulfing him completely and blazing through the ceiling, like a pillar of fire. Dave passed through the flames and brutally slashed from left to right, completely decapitating the old man in the dark robe.

The hyena-men stumbled and fell. Chris and Diego rapidly switched magazines and resumed firing, full-auto, in to the chests of the hyena-men. The roaring flames had burst through and kindled the ceiling and were now rapidly engulfing the small house.

Dave quickly sheathed his kukri, and grabbed Alzalam Alqadim's severed head, throwing it into the raging inferno in the center of the room. He then dropped to one knee, drew his KA-BAR and plunged it into Alzalam Alqadim's chest. He tore open the chest cavity and saw a still beating heart. He cut out the heart and threw it in the flames. As he did this, two things happened. First, the fury of the fire lessened. And second, the body of Alzalam Alqadim turned instantly to dust.

Dave yelled to Chris and Diego: "Cut out the hearts and throw them in the fire!"

Neither of the SEALs hesitated for a moment. They drew their knives and tore open the chests of the bullet riddled hyena-men. To their shock, though the chests of the hyena-men were shredded, their hearts were intact and beating. They quickly cut out the hearts and threw them in the fire. Like their master, the bodies of the hyena-men instantly turned to dust when their hearts were engulfed in flames.

The entire building was now on fire. "Time to go!" yelled Dave over the roar. The three SEALs ran from the building and toward the hidden, waiting van. As they reached it, the burning house collapsed behind them.

Davis and Ryan tossed their rifles in the back of the van and leapt into the front seat. Dave, Chris and Diego got in the back and the van sped away to safety.

As they caught their breath, Ryan looked back from the passenger seat. "You guys ok? We couldn't see anything going on inside, but when that pillar of fire went through the roof, we got kind of worried."

"Yeah," said Dave, catching his breath. "That was certainly different."

The two SEALs in the front, drove, now more slowly, so as to not attract attention, while the other three sat in the back, quietly. After a while Chris whispered, "how'd you know to do it like that?"

Dave shrugged, "I just knew."

"Dude," said Diego, "what the hell just happened?"

"I honestly don't know," whispered Dave. "What I do know is that none of us are going to say a single word about hyena-monsters or magical old men; in the report or anywhere else."

Diego nodded.

Chris had been examining his singed clothing and the several small burns on his skin. He glanced over and noticed that Diego was in the same shape. As he looked at Dave, something struck him as very strange. Though his clothes were singed, he did not have the slightest visible burn on his skin, and not one of the hairs on his pony-tail or beard were even slightly scorched. "Hey Dave," he whispered. "You ok?"

"Yeah, just really hot."

"I bet. That fire totally blew up and engulfed you. How are you not ... dead ... or at least a wicked burn trauma that we needed to med-evac?"

"I don't know," said Dave. "The fire must have been an illusion of some kind."

"Then how did the whole house go up?" asked Diego, now also noticing that Dave was completely unhurt. "And how did we get burned?"

"Again," said Dave, "I don't know, but we're not going to report it and we're not going to talk about it. Ok?"

Chris and Diego nodded and they all drove into the night.

The next day they gave a report to Commander Fredrickson and Agent Smith. They reported only that they engaged and terminated all three targets and that a lantern was accidently knocked over, causing a fire that burned down the house.

"Was there anything else?" asked Agent Smith. "Anything ... unusual."

Dave answered: "No, nothing unusual."

Agent Smith gave them a serious look. "And you're absolutely certain that they are dead?"

"Indeed," answered Chris, "They are very, very dead."

"Very good work, men!" said Commander Fredrickson. "You deserve a rest."

"Sir, permission to speak freely?" asked Dave.

"Sure, Shepherd, what can I do for you?"

"Sir, my fiancée is going to ask me, when I call her tomorrow. Do you have any word on when we will be returning to the States? We are planning to get married in October."

"That's right. Congratulations, Shepherd!" Commander Fredrickson said. "Nothing is written in stone at this point, but the plan is that we will be home at that point and I signed an approval for your requested leave. Hanley's as well. They haven't come back down to me yet, but I see no reason that you can't reassure her that everything will be ok."

"Thank you, Sir."

The Commander dismissed them all and Agent Smith watched them leave. Commander Fredrickson turned to Agent Smith, "Why all the weird questions, Agent?"

"No reason," he said smiling. "I'll let you know if anything else comes up."

. . . .

Dave was sitting in his room, on his bed, looking at a framed picture of Sabrina, which he was gently holding in his hands. There was a knock at the door. "Come in," he said.

Chris and Diego walked into the room. "Is that your fiancée?" asked Diego.

Dave showed him the picture, "Yeah."

"She's really pretty."

"Thanks."

Chris' face looked more serious than Dave had remembered seeing in quite a while. "Dave. We need to talk about what just happened."

"Which part?" laughed Dave.

"Well, let's start with the chanting wizard and the hyena-monsters and go from there," said Chris.

"Ok. I don't think that he was a wizard; I think it was a trick. And I don't think that they were hyena-monsters; they were probably guys in suits to scare us long enough so that they could kill us and protect their boss."

"That was real fur. I touched it," said Diego. "And you told us to cut their hearts out and throw them in the fire. You don't 'think' anything like what you're saying happened; you absolutely know what's going on."

"No, I really don't," said Dave. "In a fight, I operate on instinct. I don't think about it; I just go. So, at a sub-conscious level, sure maybe I know things. But consciously, I have no idea what's going on."

"It would explain why he's so fast," said Chris to Diego.

"I guess," said Diego.

"All I know is that I'm really tired of being hot all the damn time," said Dave. "And, right now, I kinda, sorta, really, truly miss Sabrina and want to go home."

. . . .

It was a cool, crisp beautiful, mid-October day in 2005 and Dave sat with Chris in the rectory of St. Joseph's parish. They had been back home for a week and would both be on leave for another three. Dave didn't know why he felt nervous but he had never felt a higher level of anxiety in his life than at this very moment.

When they got home, he had spent nearly every waking minute with Sabrina. They put the finishing touches on every detail of their wedding. It was going to be an intimate event. They were planning to have a traditional Catholic wedding. They decided to have a minimal Wedding Party, with Chris as Dave's Best-Man and Christi as Sabrina's Maid-of-Honor. They felt silly having a Wedding Party at all, but also felt it would be hurtful not to name their best-friends as such. The only other guests were John and Mary Shepherd, Abigail, Shawn – as Christi's guest – and "Uncle Pete". They had no other relatives and, though they had various acquaintances from work, none rose to a level of friendship that Dave and Sabrina felt comfortable including.

Dave had not seen Sabrina's dress and knew only that it was white. He had been told that his mother and sisters had gone with Sabrina to pick out the dress and there had been an interesting interchange with the woman in the dress shop. Apparently, the woman had strongly suggested that Sabrina would look "very beautiful" in a number of different color choices: red, blue, green. Sabrina reportedly said something along the lines of: "I can proudly wear a white dress on my wedding day and I'm not looking at anything but a white dress."

Dave had laughed when his mother told him the story. She told him that he should be proud to have a wife that held her purity in such high regard. Dave smiled and told her that he was proud of everything about Sabrina. To which his mother had replied, "That's my boy."

There was extensive discussion as to what Dave would wear. The initial wedding date was in the summer, so if Dave would have worn his Dress Uniform, it would have been white. Dave and Sabrina had discussed this privately and at some length. Both of them had liked the idea of Dave also dressing in white, as a symbol of purity. However, Dave was not excited about wearing his Dress Uniform, feeling that it was ostentatious. When Sabrina explored this idea further, Dave admitted that he didn't feel comfortable displaying his medals. "Everyone here knows what I do. I don't need to make a show about it." Sabrina told him that she was okay with whatever choice made him more comfortable.

When the date got changed to the fall, it would have been inappropriate for Dave to wear a white uniform; it would have been proper for him to wear his Dress Blues. That made the decision for him: it would be civilian clothes. However, when they went to the store to look at suits, Dave and Sabrina quickly agreed that Dave would absolutely not be wearing a white suit. Currently, Dave was wearing a black suit, a white shirt and a dark red, paisley tie; all of which Sabrina helped him to pick out.

Christi would be wearing a beautiful crimson-red gown, as Maid-of-Honor. Chris also did not wear his uniform – first because he also preferred not wearing it and second, as he put it: "there is no damn way that the Best-Man should be wearing his Dress Uniform if the Groom won't be wearing his." He was dressed similarly to Dave, but his tie was the same crimson-red as Christi's dress.

The reception, after, was planned to be a nice dinner party at the Shepherd family home. John and Mary had offered, and Dave and Sabrina had happily accepted. Everyone had helped, to some degree, in making the house ready and preparing the food. The guests would be the same as the Wedding Ceremony itself, plus Father Mike and one amazingly long-lived cat, who showed no signs of age, still looked and acted like a kitten, and was named after an Egyptian goddess.

John and Mary had also shown the couple a very private section of the house, a side-wing off of the end of the west wing of the house, which stretched north towards the forest and away from the lake. They were then told that they could have this wing of the house, "for as long as you want it to be your home." Dave and Sabrina were very grateful and loved the large, out-of-the-way bedroom that would be the first that they would share.

Back in Virginia, a few miles from Dam Neck, Dave had rented a small, private house – walking distance from a very secluded and private section of Virginia Beach, not too far from Sharky's Pub. When Dave would be stationed at Dam Neck, that's where they would be living. When he was sent over-seas, Sabrina would live back at the Shepherd's house in Maine, both so she wouldn't get lonely and so she could continue to work at her job as a RN with Mary and Christi. Whenever possible, Dave would also stay in Maine.

The nice little house in Virginia was two stories high. It had a kitchen, living room, bathroom, and their bedroom down-stairs. It also had a little bedroom upstairs – "Just in case," smiled Sabrina, shyly.

Dave and Sabrina had talked about having children. Both of them wanted a baby, but were aware that, historically, Dave's family was almost never able to have more than one child. "The three I had were unheard of," said Mary. "No one knows why, but it has always been like that in my family: we only get one, or sometimes two." Sabrina had smiled and said, "What was that you always say about wanting to hear God laugh?"

Father Mike walked into the room. He smiled, "It's time."

Chris clapped Dave on the shoulder and sang in a high, nasal voice: "It's the final countdown!" and smiled his crooked smile, as Dave glared at him.

"Damn it, Chris! If that song gets stuck in my head again ..."

The three of them walked into the Sanctuary of the church and stood at the front. Dave took a deep breath. The song was not stuck in his head.

.　.　.　.　.　.　.

Christi had finished her walk down the aisle. The organ changed and started to slowly play Pachelbel's Canon. Everyone stood. And there she was.

Sabrina slowly walked down the aisle to Dave, her beautiful grey-blue eyes looking straight at his and smiling her beautiful smile. Her long, dark auburn hair draped over her shoulders and was done up beautifully with a wreath of tiny red roses and baby's breath. Also, she held a small, lovely bouquet of larger red roses and baby's breath. Her white silken gown was more beautiful than any princess could have wished. The elegant cut of her dress gently hugged her beautiful feminine curves and her neck-line was a perfectly pure, low-sweeping cut. Her sleeves were half-way down her arms and her skirt reached her ankles. She was beautiful beyond mortal description.

As she walked forward, Dave could feel tears of joy trickle down his cheeks. She only smiled more brightly. Regal, beautiful, and elegant, she walked to him, and took his hand.

Looking back, Dave could remember almost nothing of the ceremony. They knelt, they stood, and they spoke the traditional Catholic vows. All he could remember, with anything like clarity, was her: his perfect Sabrina.

She did not break eye-contact when she slipped the white-gold ring on Dave's finger. "With this ring, I thee wed." And when Father Mike pronounced them "man and wife," they kissed with a passionate love that burned like a thousand suns.

They walked out of the church, arms locked, to "the Ode to Joy," from Beethoven's ninth symphony. They hugged everyone as they left, took some pictures, and drove back in a white limousine, which Uncle Pete had absolutely insisted they take home, and for which he paid. Later, they sometimes wondered how the driver had maneuvered the limousine down the access road to the house, but at the time, they were lost in each other's arms; kissing in a loving and passionate embrace.

The reception was beautiful; held in the family room from their first Christmas Eve together. There initially was soft, classical music playing. They had wine and a "very-nice" cheese which was a favorite of all. Father Mike gave a beautiful prayer and a poetic blessing. They had a buffet-style dinner, with many delicious selections.

During dinner, both Chris and Christi gave brief, heartfelt speeches. Christi's initially made people laugh about the reaction that Dave and Sabrina had when they first met – she likened it to the "never before, never again" scene with Kermit the Frog and Miss Piggy in the original Muppet Movie. But, she gradually shifted to talking about Dave and Sabrina falling asleep together on the couch, by the fire. She spoke with such sincere love, when she ended, that more than one person was moved to tears. She said: "I knew – right then, deep in my heart – that my best friend and my big brother would be together forever. And the only time I have been happier than I was at that moment is right now; seeing you two together like this."

Chris spoke eloquently about family and love and brotherhood. Spoke of the selfless, unconditional love modeled by John and Mary, and how this "made everyone here better people." He briefly made a "Broody McBrooderson" joke about how Dave was whenever he was apart from Sabrina, but then added: "That being said, I don't think that there is a single SEAL in the Navy who doesn't know that Dave is profoundly and thoroughly in love with Sabrina." He then toasted their long and happy life together.

After the dinner, John changed the music to a slow-dance mixed CD he had spent weeks putting together. Dave and Sabrina held each other closely and, looking deep into each other's eyes, had their first dance as a married couple. Later when they were asked the name of the song they had danced to at their wedding, they could only ever remember that it was not by The Eagles and both of them would laugh.

There were other slow dances, and a few more lively dances – one particularly memorable dance involved the girls dominating the floor to the Beastie Boys' "Intergalactic" while Dave sat and watched Sabrina as she was beautifully dancing and laughing with his sisters. He smiled and laughed as well. They danced together to a couple more slow songs and everyone, but Uncle Pete and Father Mike, joined them.

After a while, Mary brought out a beautiful wedding cake, which she had made and decorated with Christi and Gayle. Dave and Sabrina, lovingly and delicately, fed each other a small piece of cake. The music was slower now and the evening was coming to an end.

Dave and Sabrina thanked everyone for a lovely day. They took the time to talk with each and every person there. This is how they discovered that Gayle had made the decision to not leave, but rather to stay in the Navy, for now. If she stayed with JAG, she would be in Virginia whenever Chris was home, and they would have a lot more time together.

Dave and Sabrina said good night, and Mary hugged them very tightly, saying that she was so happy to have such a wonderful daughter-in-law.

The newly married couple walked, hand and hand, to the northwest wing of the house and to their bedroom. The curtains had been drawn and several candles were lit, casting a gentle glow through the room. The covers had been turned down and Sabrina's wedding bouquet was in a vase by the side of the bed. They closed and locked the door. They held each other closely and kissed, lovingly and gently. They looked into each other's eyes and told each other, "I love you!" and kissed again.

And what happened after that ... is absolutely none of your business.

Chapter 5

or

"... and then"

Dave and Sabrina Shepherd were lying – facing the lake, with their backs to the house – on the new, double chaise lounge, on the deck of the Shepherd family home. It was a surprisingly warm mid-November late-morning, but they were still wrapped in a soft blanket. Dave was wearing shorts and a t-shirt with his hair down and lying on his back with his arm around Sabrina. He was sound asleep. Sabrina was wearing yoga pants and a University of Maine sweatshirt. She cuddled closely to Dave with her head on his shoulder and her hand on his chest. She was not asleep but was quietly listening to the sounds of the soft lapping of the water and her husband's gentle breathing.

When they had returned from their honeymoon, Dave had requested a short extension of his leave. They were thoroughly shocked when he was granted leave until after the new year – Commander Fredrickson and Captain Porter said to consider it a wedding gift. Dave was also pleasantly surprised when they notified him that he had been promoted to the rank of Senior Chief Petty Officer. This would mean that, upon going back, Dave would have an increased administrative and command role and less of a direct operational role. Sabrina was ecstatic about this, though Dave had mixed feelings. He had been an operator for almost fifteen years and though he was getting older, he was far from too old for the field.

Chris and Gayle had not extended their leave and had both gone back to Virginia a few weeks after the wedding. Christi had not stopped working full-time at the hospital. She lived at the Shepherds' house – in her original bedroom – and worked day-shifts. Shawn had returned to Virginia, right after the wedding, and continued to work at the Navy Medical Center's out-patient clinic. He and Christi spoke on the phone, occasionally, and exchanged E-mails usually weekly, but often more than a month would pass with no contact between them. John worked at the Campin' Store, almost every day, and Mary worked part-time at the hospital. What this meant was that Dave and Sabrina had a lot of time alone together.

They had developed a morning routine. Sabrina always woke up early. When she woke she would lie quietly beside Dave until about seven o'clock. She would then gently wake him and after some time of cuddling closely they would go for a morning run together on one of the trails through the forest and around the lake. Sabrina would then take a shower while Dave would do Tai Chi or some other exercises, and then return to their room. When Sabrina came out of the shower, Dave would take his own. There were several bathrooms in the house, but Dave and Sabrina liked to stick to using the one attached to their bedroom. While Dave showered, Sabrina would lie on their bed and read her Bible. Sabrina had gone to daily Mass through high school, all through college, and sporadically while she was in Virginia. It was now a little difficult to get to St. Joseph's every day, so, she had substituted reading her Bible. However, when Dave eventually deployed again, she was sure that she would be back at daily Mass.

After Dave got out of the shower, they would have a light breakfast in the kitchen. Dave would make their coffee – hers with two creams and two sugars and his black – and she would toast bagels, or fry eggs, or cut fruit, or some combination thereof. They would sit together, eat, and talk. Sometimes John or Mary would be around and join them, but mostly Dave and Sabrina had the house to themselves all morning and afternoon.

This morning, after breakfast, they had taken a nice walk on one of the longer trails around the lake; holding hands and listening to the sounds of mid-late autumn. Sabrina had initially been a little chilly, but the walk had warmed her. When they got back to the deck, they had laid down on the new chair, which John and Mary had bought for them while they were on their honeymoon. They kissed and cuddled in the soft blanket for a long while. Eventually, Dave fell asleep and Sabrina happily held him. They had been like this for about an hour.

Sabrina heard an engine and the crunch of the gravel under the tires of Mary's Chevy Venture pulling up to the house. Then she heard the sound of feet walking onto the deck. "Hello?" said Mary, quietly.

Sabrina moved gently, so as not to wake Dave, and got up. She walked across the deck to where Mary was standing. "Sorry," said Mary smiling. "I didn't want to walk over and ... interrupt anything. I know that you didn't expect anyone to be home until this afternoon."

Sabrina blushed and smiled. "We were just having a rest after taking a walk and Dave fell asleep. I stayed with him so he wouldn't wake up."

"He woke up," said Dave, walking over to join them. "Hi, Mama."

They all sat in the chairs by the fire-pit. "I got out of work early because we are slow today. I wanted to stop by and let you know what I found out for you, and then, I was going to bring Dad some lunch and spend the rest of the day with him at the Campin' Store, to give you two alone time."

Dave and Sabrina held hands and smiled.

"So, I spoke with administration about your Per Diem status and they are willing to accommodate anything that you need. They said you can pick up any shifts, whenever you want. They love you and think you have done great work since you got here. So, you can sign up for full-time when Dave is over-seas, and work as many or as few hours as you like when he's in the country."

"That's great," said Sabrina, happily. "Thanks for finding that out for us. I think that I'm probably going to stay home for now and when we find out where Dave is going in January, I'll let them know what's going on. They're not sure if he will be headed to Virginia or overseas, when he goes back. So, if it's Virginia I'll be going down there, but if not, I'll stay here and work."

"Well, that sounds good to me," said Mary standing up. "I'm going to get John some treats and leave you two alone." She smiled and walked to the house.

Sabrina smiled and stood, still holding Dave's hand. "I'm sorry that you woke up; you looked so peaceful."

Dave stood, "I love cuddling like that with you."

"Mmm," smiled Sabrina. She led him back to the chaise lounge and they lay back down. She cuddled up to him and kissed him, gently running her fingers through his beard. "Now ... what *ever* shall we do for the rest of the day?" she asked coyly, looking deeply into Dave's eyes.

Dave smiled, pulled her close, and passionately kissed her.

. . . .

Shortly before Christmas, they got word that Dave was to report to Dam Neck, Virginia – in the beginning of January – where he would help train his Team until the end of May. They would then be deployed to a worsening situation in Iraq. The forces that were fighting the US-led Coalition were now beginning to fight each other as well. SEAL Team Six had a constant presence in the region and was now rotating squadrons. Dave and Chris' Team would go at the end of May/ beginning of June.

Chris and Gayle came up to join them all for Christmas and the whole family had a lovely time. Wine was poured and songs were sung. Christi insisted that Dave read the stories saying, in answer to Dave's objection, "No, I'm not too old, Mr. Grinch!"

Sabrina cuddled closely with Dave as he read. This time she did not fall asleep by the fire. The following day was bright and beautiful. Mary cooked a prime-rib roast and everyone found it to be delightful.

The travel plan was that Dave and Sabrina would drive the black Cavalier down to Virginia. They would move into the little house they had rented and try to have as close to a normal life as possible. Dave had been assured that he should be home every night and off on weekends, while in Virginia. Sabrina would be a happy housewife and was looking forward to the amount of reading on which she could catch up when she had free time. "Neil Gaiman has a book about a little girl and a cat that I have been trying to find the time to read for years. I'll start with that one."

The drive down the Atlantic coast from the Shepherds' house to Dam Neck Virginia was just over thirteen hours, so Dave and Sabrina planned to stop and spend the night in West Haven, Connecticut – just less than halfway – and then to finish the drive the next day.

They pulled into a motel parking lot at about three in the afternoon. They checked in and went to their room. They cuddled together on the bed and paged through a directory of restaurants. The selection was expansive and diverse. They found a few places that looked promising, and then cuddled and watched nature shows on cable TV until it was time for dinner.

At about five o'clock, they went to Duffy's Tavern. It was a wonderful Irish Pub and the hostess that met them at the door was very friendly. They had a seat at a booth – off to the side, in a quiet corner – and ordered a few drinks. Dave ordered a pint of Guinness and Sabrina ordered a Sea Breeze Cocktail. For dinner, Sabrina ordered the vegetarian shepherd's pie. She giggled as she ordered it: "I just have to! I'm a Shepherd now, you know." Dave smiled and ordered the fish-'n-chips.

They enjoyed their dinner, and talked pleasantly about some ideas Sabrina had for their little house. "We need to get nice curtains and maybe some throw-rugs. I wonder if the land-lady will let me paint."

"I'm sure that she will. It'll only make the house nicer."

"Oh, that'll be fun! Christi and I painted our apartment, back at school, and we had a great time."

After dinner, they drove down to the Sandy Point Bird Sanctuary and walked along the cold, abandoned beach, holding hands. Sabrina wore a cute ladies fitted, navy blue, wool pea coat and matching purple fleece beanie hat, scarf and gloves – they came as a set, which Dave had given to her as a Christmas present. Dave wore a boxier men's pea coat, with no hat, scarf or gloves. Sabrina's coat was buttoned up and she still felt cold from the wind. Dave wore his coat open and was actually a bit too warm with it on. They walked only briefly and when Dave noticed that Sabrina was shivering from the wind, he stopped, embraced and kissed her, and smiled saying, "Let's go back to our room and I'll cuddle you until you are warm."

Sabrina smiled, with her teeth chattering, and said, "Ok ... I love you, Sweetie!"

The next day they stayed in the room until checkout time; cuddling and watching more nature shows. They stopped at a diner for a quick breakfast and then drove the rest of the way down the coast to their new little house in Dam Neck. When they arrived, they no longer needed their winter coats, but Sabrina still would not be comfortable without a sweater, or a lighter jacket.

They arrived at their little house at about six in the evening and called Chris and Gayle to see if they wanted to meet for a late dinner.

They planned to meet at Sharky's Pub for a light evening snack and a few drinks at about seven-thirty.

Dave and Sabrina brought their clothes and things into the house, and together, quickly cleaned the dust of the kitchen and made their bed. "I can smell the Ocean," said Sabrina.

"Yeah," said Dave. "The beach is about a five-minute walk from here. It's a pretty secluded beach too; the tourist don't come down here. I thought you'd like it when I picked it out."

"It's really nice," she said, smiling and pulling him close to her.

. . . .

When they arrived at Sharky's Pub, it was pretty much empty and Chris and Gayle were already sitting at a booth. They walked over and sat down, "Sorry that we're a little late," said Sabrina. "We wanted to finish cleaning up the kitchen and the bedroom before we left."

"It's ok," said Gayle. "We actually only got here about five minutes ago.

"How was the drive down?" asked Chris.

"It was long, but we spent last night in Connecticut, and that was nice," said Dave. "Is the menu the same?"

"Pretty much," said Chris, "They added chicken-wings, the kind from Buffalo, New York. They're spicy and good."

"Nice. Let's split some of those," said Dave.

"Do you feel like splitting one of those veggie-burgers with me?" Sabrina asked Gayle. "I don't really want to eat a whole one, but half would be good."

"Yeah, those are really tasty!" said Gayle.

Steve came out from behind the bar, welcomed them back and took their order. He quickly brought Chis and Dave each a pint, Sabrina a strawberry daiquiri, and Gayle a glass of moscato.

While they waited for the food to arrive, Dave asked, "So, what's been going on down here since October; it's been almost three months since I've been here."

"Mostly training and reports. Iraq is a total mess right now. Mostly our regular troops are trying to keep them from killing each other, while at the same time trying not to get killed themselves," answered Chris.

"Great. Something to look forward to," said Dave.

"Well, at least you have a little more control, now that you're Senior Chief," said Chris with his crooked smile.

"More control of paperwork, you mean," said Dave.

"I wouldn't worry about that," said Chris. "The Senior Chiefs and Master Chiefs on the other Teams are getting more field-time than they want right now. I told you, it's a mess."

The food came and they chatted causally. They didn't stay long and agreed to meet again at Sharky's in the near future.

Dave and Sabrina drove home and went inside. "I love that we come home together after dates, now," said Sabrina. "It's really nice to not have to say good-bye. I know it sounds weird, but little things like that, about being married, just make me smile."

Dave locked the front door. "I really like that too. I used to get completely miserable when we had to be apart, but now," he pulled her close, "I get my sweet girl, right here with me."

She laughed and kissed him passionately; her arms around his neck. "I'm going to really miss this when you're over there."

"Me too," said Dave, "But that's not until the end of spring. Now, we can make our little house a home, and do all sorts of things. I love you, Sabrina. I really want to make you feel like the happiest, most loved girl in the world!"

She kissed him again. "Good, because I love you too."

They walked, hand-in-hand, to their bedroom, closed the door, and turned off the light.

. . . .

2006

It was a pleasantly warm Wednesday in late May. There were soft, puffy clouds floating through the bright blue sky and a gentle, cool breeze was blowing in off the Atlantic Ocean. Dave and Sabrina were alone on the beach, lying together on a blanket near the sand dunes. Sabrina thought that the Ocean was still a little too cold for swimming, so they had not worn swimsuits. Instead, Dave was wearing shorts and a t-shirt and Sabrina was wearing shorts and a tank-top. She had also brought along her sweatshirt, just in case she got chilly. Both wore their dark sun-glasses.

Before they came to the beach, they had packed a cooler with some ice, a few beers and wine coolers, and some other snacks. They then took their time, slowly rubbing sunblock into each other's skin. They walked, hand-in-hand, to the beach and found a nice spot for their blanket.

They had taken a long walk on the beach, their feet in the chilly water. They didn't talk much today. They would often stop and kiss or embrace, and their hands were constantly entwined. But they didn't say much, because there wasn't much to say. Tomorrow Dave would take Sabrina to the airport for her flight to Portland where Christi would meet her to drive her back to their other home. Then, Dave would be leaving again for Iraq. Neither of them wanted him to go.

They had now been married for seven months, and in that time, they were nearly constant companions. For the first three months they had literally been within arm's reach of each other, practically every moment of every day. For the last four months, Dave had waited until the last possible moment to go to work, nearly always came home for lunch, and did not stay at work one second longer than he was absolutely required. Every single night, since their first night together, they had fallen asleep in each other's arms and every morning they had met the new day together. They were an extremely close and intimate couple and the idea of being apart for almost six months was close to unbearable.

Now they were lying together on an empty beach, listening to the waves. Dave's arm was around her and she was cuddled close to him, with her head on his shoulder and her hand on his chest. They had not touched their cooler even though they had been on the beach for more than two hours.

Sabrina lifted herself up to look at Dave. "Do you feel like going back?"

"Sure. But you usually love the beach."

"I know. It's just that … I kinda just want to go home," she said with a hint of sadness in her soft voice.

"Ok, Baby. We can do whatever you want," Dave said with a smile.

They sat up and folded their blanket. Dave carried the cooler and Sabrina carried the blanket. They held hands and walked back to their little house.

When they got home, Dave set down the cooler and locked the door. Sabrina walked into their bedroom. And softly said, "Dave ... come here."

Dave walked into the bedroom and she closed the door behind him. He turned to face her. She placed both her hands on his chest, and gently pushed him back onto their bed. She looked intently into his eyes and said: "I will love you forever, David Shepherd."

. . . .

They did not leave the house, answer a phone, or turn on the radio for the rest of the day. That evening they made a pizza together, in their small kitchen. There were frequent kisses, caresses and embraces; all with soft words of affection. That night, they lit candles in their bedroom and were still kissing, in each other's arms, long after the last candle flickered out.

The next morning, they woke up together and gently cuddled instead of making breakfast. They got dressed and Dave carried Sabrina's bags to the car. Sabrina wanted to take a short walk on the beach together before they drove up to Norfolk.

Holding hands, they walked slowly down the beach. Sabrina was glad that at least she would not be alone while Dave was away; Christi still lived at the Shepherds' house. They would drive to work together and her job would keep her busy. But still ... "It really feels like such a long time that you'll be away," she said, stopping and embracing Dave.

"I know." He said.

Her head was against his chest and she could hear his heart beating. "I mean, we've been apart this long before. But this feels ... different ... because we're married."

She moved her head to kiss him and realized that Dave was quietly crying. "Oh Baby," she said as she caressed his cheek, "I love you so much."

They lovingly kissed and she wiped his tears from his cheeks. Dave laughed, "Isn't this usually the other way around?"

"Not for us," she smiled and kissed him again.

They turned around and walked back to the car. It took them just over a half-an-hour to get to the airport. They held hands the entire way. Dave carried Sabrina's larger bag, and she had her carry-on over her shoulder. They checked her bag and went to the security screener. Generally, this is where they would have had to say goodbye. However, Dave showed his military ID, with the Trident of the Navy SEALs on it, and the man at the check-point did not stop him, but instead wanted to shake his hand and say, "Thank you for your service!"

Dave and Sabrina walked to her gate, sat together and waited. When boarding was announced for her flight, they waited as long as they could. They embraced closely and Sabrina gave Dave a long and passionate kiss. "You come safely back home to me, David Shepherd!"

"I Love you, Sabrina," replied Dave, and they kissed again.

Dave stood by the window and waited until he lost sight of his wife's plane, climbing into the sky. Then he slowly walked back to the car, looking down, with his hands in his pockets, speaking to no one.

He drove back to Dam Neck to join his Team, making their final preparations before they left for the long flight to Iraq. Chris walked over to him, as he entered the room, clapping his hand on his shoulder. "Hey! You made it!"

Dave said nothing and began to pack the contents of his locker in a duffle bag. Chris frowned, "Dave … are you ok?"

Dave didn't look up. "No … I'm not ok."

.   .   .   .

Dave and Sabrina would talk on the phone about three times a week, depending on what was happening. They worked out a system where Dave would call Sabrina shortly after she got home from work, around four in the afternoon Maine-time. Iraq is seven hours ahead, so this was eleven o'clock at night for Dave. Also, video-calls had just become possible, so they tried to have one of those on some Sundays. He also tried to write her at least a short E-mail every day.

One night, about three weeks after Dave arrived in Iraq, he was missing Sabrina especially badly, so he called her. While she sounded happy to hear him, she also sounded distracted. About five-minutes into their conversation, Sabrina interrupted Dave in the middle of a sentence.

"Dave, I really have to tell you something, but I don't want it to make you lose focus and get hurt."

"Ok, Sabrina. What is it?"

"Umm, Dave ... I'm pregnant."

Dave's mouth hung open and his head was spinning.

"Dave? Are you still there?"

"Yes, yes. Oh my God, Sabrina! We're really going to have a baby?!"

"We sure are!" she laughed.

"That's so amazing! When did you find out?"

"I took the test yesterday. I haven't told anyone because I wanted you to know first."

"I love you so much, Sabrina!"

"I love you too, Dave! You're going to be a Daddy!"

Dave was smiling widely, "When are you due?"

"In the middle of February, if I calculated it right. That means ... we did this right before you left," she said with a small giggle.

"Oh my sweetest girl, I love you so much! We're having a baby!"

They talked like that for about another twenty minutes and then said good night. Dave decided to wait until morning to tell Chris. He lay in his bed, holding one of his framed pictures of Sabrina and gazing at her grey-blue eyes. He wanted, so much to hold her and to fall asleep in her loving arms. But he gently kissed the glass of the picture and whispered: "Goodnight my sweet angel, I love you!" He set the picture back at his bedside, turned out the light and went to sleep.

. . . .

"This feels like a huge mistake," said Dave after hearing the plan.

"Do you have a more specific objection, Senior Chief?" asked Commander Fredrickson.

"So, we will be splitting up into five groups of three, inserting at several points all over Ramadi, and then sort-of-simultaneously hitting several targets. However, we have minimal Intel and virtually no immediate support. What happens when we walk into a bomb factory, or a hornet's nest of insurgents? It feels like a mistake."

"Actually, that's the entire point," answered Fredrickson. "All of the targets are potentially the sort of situation that you are describing. And that's when you call the Marines, who are standing by, and direct them to destroy the target."

"For some of these targets, their estimated response time is more than fifteen minutes," said Dave.

"That's correct."

"Well that's a pretty long time to wait, if the situation goes wrong," said Dave. "Also, are the Marines able to respond to multiple targets at once? Because that could easily be needed."

"This is a Recon/Assault mission. I'm not sure to what you are objecting," said Commander Fredrickson.

"I don't like that we are only going in with three, with no over-watch, and almost no Intel. If we even fixed one of those problems, I would feel a lot better," said Dave.

"Well, we don't have the resources to do that," said the Commander. "Now, set up the group assignments. You are going tonight."

"Yes, Sir," said Dave.

. . . .

"So, this will be our target," said Dave. He had assigned and briefed the other four groups, who had gone off to gather weapons and prepare to get to their locations after nightfall, and was now talking to the group that he would be leading. He had selected the most difficult target for his own team – it would have the longest potential response time from the Marines and had the least reliable intelligence report.

Chris and Petty Officer First Class Diego Wagner were listening carefully. "It's sort of a converted warehouse, near the Euphrates, on the western outskirts of the city. We know almost nothing about the building, other than it isn't just an open space; there are wooden walls inside, separating the space into some rooms. That's about everything we have on that."

"Dave," said Chris, "they keep giving us these missions with no Intel. Sooner or later, someone is going to get hurt."

"So, they're also not real clear about what we are supposed to do," said Dave. "The way I understand it is that it is mostly Recon of the target, however, we may need to engage. If the target has a large force, we call the Marines in and they take care of it. If it is a bomb factory, we call EOD."

"Sounds like they want us to be getting the Intel that they should already have," said Diego.

"That's my impression," said Dave.

"Well, our target is pretty big," said Diego. "There could be a whole lot of bad-guys in there."

"So if there are, we'll call the Marines, wait until they get there, and then let them do what they do best," said Dave. "We'll get there around eleven tonight. You'll love the beat-up old car we're taking."

"This is exhausting," said Chris.

"I've got a bad feeling about this," said Diego

"Relax," said Dave, "maybe it will be nothing."

. . . .

It was a hot, mid-August night and Chris drove the beat-up car through the streets of Ramadi, towards their target. Dave was reviewing the details for a final time. "We enter through the north door, closest to the river. We sweep south, report any problems, and then we get out."

"Sounds fun," said Chris, sarcastically.

They backed the car into an alley about a block to the west of the target. They got out of the car and silently moved through the shadows to the north end of the target. As they had planned, there was an unlocked door on the north end of an old warehouse. The building was larger than they had expected but appeared to be quiet. They entered the building and began to systematically move through. The wooden partitions created almost a maze in the darkness, but as they got close to what appeared to be the middle of the building, everything changed.

They could see light ahead and heard men speaking – in what was probably Arabic. They were more careful now, moving slowly forward. When they got close to the open space, they saw that they would need to move – out of the shadows and behind a stack of wooden crates – in order to see what was happening behind the crates.

They silently moved as one, into position behind the crates. Dave peeked through the gaps in the stack and saw what he had absolutely hoped that he wouldn't see tonight. There was large truck with its back gate open and about ten men were just finishing loading what appeared to Dave to be heavy explosives on to the truck. The men each had an AK-47 slung across his back.

Dave slid back down and activated his laryngophone, speaking quietly: "Six. This is Ghost-one. We have multiple, armed targets with heavy explosives. Request immediate Support Team."

As the words, "Confirm. Ghost-one requests Support Team. On the way," came through their ear-pieces, full-automatic fire and shouts erupted from above them, to their backs.

The three SEALs spun around to engage. Above them, in the darkness, was a cat-walk they had not seen, nor of which had they been informed in the pre-mission Intelligence report. On the cat-walk, three insurgents, armed with AK-47s, had been watching their comrades load the truck full of explosives. They had not initially noticed when the three SEALs had moved into position, but after a few moments, the youngest of the three insurgents saw them, pulled on the most senior of the three's sleeve and pointed at the SEALs. The older man raised his rifle and yelled a warning to the others as he opened fire. The other two insurgents on the cat-walk then began shouting and shooting as well.

The SEALs returned fire as they scrambled to get something between themselves and the rain of bullets from above. There was some space between the wooden crates. That was the only cover that they had, as poor as it was, so that's where they went. As they were moving, Diego got hit by an insurgent's bullet, in his left shoulder. He spun and fell, stumbling back into the crates. Chris pulled him behind cover. Dave was returning fire with his suppressed, modified M4 carbine. As usual, Dave was firing single shots rather than three-round bursts or full-automatic. He quickly spotted his targets. He gave three, quick squeezes to his trigger. With surgical precision he placed a single round in the center of the chest of each of the three insurgents on the cat-walk, sending them falling backwards, into darkness.

Dave, communicating through laryngophone, said: "Six. Six. This is Ghost-one. We are taking fire and have a man down."

Diego was barely conscious and Chris held a field bandage on his wound. "Can you hold this?" Diego nodded and Chris joined Dave.

The men by the truck were yelling and running. Some of them were firing towards the crates but didn't seem to know where the SEALs were. Two men were opening the large door at the south wall of the warehouse. There were also shouts, in Arabic, coming from the north end of the warehouse.

"If they get that truck out of here, all of this was for nothing and a lot of people will die," said Dave to Chris.

"Indeed," said Chris. "You got a plan?"

"Yeah," said Dave. "None of them have seen us, so they don't know how many we have. They also don't know how many the cat-walk guys got. The way I see it, we have two choices. We stay here and hope we can hold them off until the Marines come and also hope the Marines can get that truck before they get where they're going. Or, you stay under cover and protect Diego, while I get that truck and hope they all come after me."

"Why don't I get the truck and you stay with Diego?" asked Chris.

"Because I'm faster in a fight and it's my plan," said Dave.

"Fine," said Chris. "Don't die."

Dave switched out his partial magazine for full one, flicked his M4's selector to three-round burst, got in position to move, took a deep breath, and burst into action.

Dave ran towards the truck, firing as he went. The two insurgents in front of him fell before they knew he was there. He twisted to the right, still at a full run and dropped two of the three at the back of the truck, as they were bringing up their AK's. The third insurgent screamed and fired wildly at Dave but none of his bullets even came close. Three of Dave's bullets tore through the insurgent's chest and he fell.

The engine of the truck rumbled to life. Dave pivoted to his left as he neared the truck's driver-side door and poured rounds into the two insurgents in that direction. They had their AK's pointed at him but were not firing. Dave squeezed the trigger in rapid succession and they fell to the floor.

Dave had reached the truck now and leapt to the sideboard. He tore open the door, as the truck began to move. With brutal speed and strength, he pulled the insurgent from behind the wheel and sent him clattering to the floor. Dave slid behind the wheel and slammed his foot to the floor. The engine of the truck roared and it rocketed out of the south warehouse door and into the hot Ramadi night.

He glanced in his rearview mirror and saw insurgents swarming from the warehouse – there were many, at least twenty, but probably more. They were running after the truck. While the truck was in the warehouse, they had not fired at Dave when he was near it, for fear of setting off the explosives. But now that he was on the street, they were wildly spraying bullets at the truck, hoping that the explosives would detonate; killing what they thought was their last attacker and destroying any evidence.

Dave drove the truck as fast as possible and violently swerved to the right and to the left. He was headed towards the Euphrates River. Not far from the location of their target, combat engineers had constructed a bridge to aid in moving troops through Ramadi. Speeding away from the warehouse, in a truck packed with heavy explosives, Dave had a plan.

He could hear the gun-fire and saw in his mirrors that two cars were in pursuit, both with insurgents firing AK-47's from the windows as they drove. The truck was performing shockingly well and Dave was able to stay ahead of his pursuers. The bridge was now in sight. It was a low – yet high enough to let patrol boats pass beneath – temporary, metal structure. He would have to time everything exactly right if this was going to work.

He slammed the gas pedal to the floor, trying to get up as much speed as possible. He roared across the metal bridge until he reached the center of the Euphrates. In one rapid motion, he violently turned the wheel, sending the truck off the bridge. As the truck flew through the air, Dave leapt from the door, into the water below. When he hit the water, he swam, below the surface, under the bridge, and to the other side. He climbed up a support beam to the bridge and, as quickly and quietly as possible, made his way along the side of the bridge to land.

As Dave was making his escape along the other side of the bridge, the two cars of insurgents had come to a stop in the middle of the bridge, where the truck had plunged into the water. The truck was rapidly sinking and they were firing at it and the water around it. Their hope was to kill the driver if he managed to swim away, or failing that, to blow-up the truck. They were so fully occupied with their task that they did not see the Marines, who had arrived at either side of the bridge. They only became aware when the Marines opened fire. The fight was over in seconds.

The Marines also arrived at the warehouse and made short work of the insurgents. Chris and Diego had never been discovered by the insurgents and Diego was quickly taken to a medical facility for treatment of his wound. Dave had hitched a ride with some Marines and was just now arriving back at the warehouse.

Chris was speaking with a Marine Lieutenant and Dave walked over to join them. Chris turned and laughed. "And why are you all wet?"

"I needed to take a quick swim," smiled Dave. "You know how I feel about this damn heat."

They gave each other a quick, brotherly hug and Chris introduced Dave to the Marine Officer. "L.T., this is Senior Chief Dave Shepherd."

Dave shook the young Lieutenant's hand. "Glad you guys finally made it," said Dave.

"Sorry that it took us a minute," said the young Lieutenant. "They had us staged hell-and-gone from here. But we drove-it-like-we-stole-it and we got here."

"Yeah," laughed Dave. "Me too."

. . . .

When Dave and Chris returned, they got cleaned up and had a few hours to eat and fill each other in about the parts of the story they missed. They then went to give report to Commander Fredrickson.

Before they began, they found out that Diego was doing well and should be back with the Team in a few weeks. They also found out that the truck and explosives were being recovered by EOD and that Intel was sweeping the warehouse for information. "Now before you tell me what I'm certain will be an amazing story about how that truck ended up in that river, I have to tell you, you did an excellent job. It looks like something very big was about to go down very soon and you boys stopped it cold."

Chris told most of the story of what happened and Dave filled in the parts that Chris hadn't seen. The Commander sat and listened, with body-language of clear awe.

"Senior Chief Shepherd, why did you not wait for the Marines to arrive?"

"Well," said Dave, "first, we didn't know when they would arrive. Second, that truck was probably going to kill a lot of innocent people and, frankly Sir, there was no way that I was going to let that happen. And third, I figured they would chase me and this would keep Chris and Diego safe … or at least, safer."

"It didn't cross your mind that the odds were that you'd never even get close to that truck?"

"No, Sir," said Dave, "I only thought about those other things."

"Well," said Commander Fredrickson, "I'm going to have a discussion with Captain Porter about it, but I will be recommending that you be awarded a medal for this action."

"That's really not necessary, Sir."

"I believe that it is. The Navy should recognize and thank such heroism."

"I'm not a hero, Sir," said Dave. "But if the Navy wants to thank me for doing my job, I can think of two much better ways."

"Go on," said the Commander.

"Well, for the Teams, we would really appreciate better Intel so that guys like Diego don't get shot in the future. As for me, personally, I'd really love to go home to see my wife for our first Wedding Anniversary. She's pregnant and I really miss her."

"Remind me, when is your Anniversary?"

"October, Sir."

"I can do my best to make that happen. But, I'm also putting you up for a medal."

. . . . . .

Later that day, Dave and Chris were sitting at the bar in their Team lounge, both quietly sipping a cold beer. Chris turned to Dave and said, "You know, if Sabrina saw you do that, back there, she would have been pretty angry."

"We don't ever talk about the specifics of my job for a lot of reasons," said Dave. "And she wouldn't have been angry, but she would have been upset. She worries about me enough."

"To qualify for any medal that I think they would put you up for here, you have to do something in the presence of great danger and at great personal risk," said Chris. "That's what you did. You know a lot of other guys who would do what you did?"

"For the reasons I did it? I certainly hope that every member of our Team would."

"Well, most wouldn't. Certainly not with a pregnant wife at home," said Chris.

"Then they shouldn't be one of us," said Dave.

"Dave, you broke cover, ran about twenty to thirty yards to a truck filled with heavy explosives, killing, what, seven insurgents – who were all trying to kill you, by the way – on the way there. You then acquired said truck and drove it through Ramadi, with insurgents shooting at you and trying to blow you up. And then you drove the truck off a bridge into the Euphrates. All of this to save people whom you do not know, and probably most of whom hate us. That doesn't register as a big deal to you? Personally, I think they should award you the Navy Cross!"

"Are you saying that you wouldn't have done it?"

"No, I probably would have tried, if you let me. Probably. However, I don't know that I would have made it, and I'm very sure that I wouldn't have driven the truck into the river – again, why?"

"Well, first of all, I was hot and, secondly, that's the only place I could think to put it where it wouldn't kill a ton of people if it went off," said Dave.

"That's what I mean, Dave. It didn't cross your mind that, in doing that, it might blow up and kill *you*?"

"It did cross my mind, actually. That's why I swam as fast as I could and then got out of the water and away from it."

"This thing was a huge deal and you need to recognize it!"

"Chris, I did my job. We made it out and innocent people didn't die. End of story."

"Dave, there are people who care about you and really need you to come home safe; that needs to be the end of the story."

Dave finished his beer. "Let's hope that it will be."

. . . .

Dave walked through the security area of the Portland International Jetport. He was wearing shorts, a t-shirt and Teva sandals, with a medium-sized duffle bag over his shoulder. As he crossed the last barrier, he could see where they were waiting. Sabrina came running to him, threw her arms around his neck and kissed him passionately.

He had thought about surprising her, but then he figured that it would be better to let her know he was coming, so she could take off from work. He was now extremely glad that he had let her know; he had never been welcomed like this when he arrived in an airport before. They held each other close, kissing for a long time. Christi walked over, tapped her brother on the shoulder and said, "It's good to have you back, Dave, but the two of you are attracting some attention."

Dave and Sabrina looked around, without breaking their embrace. All the people in the near vicinity – waiting, arriving, leaving, or working – were watching them and were now beginning to clap and cheer. Both of their faces turned a deep crimson and Sabrina whispered, "Let's go."

The clapping continued as the couple and Christi walked to the door. Christi led the way and Dave and Sabrina followed her, holding hands. "You check any bags?" asked Christi.

"Nope, just what I'm carrying," answered Dave.

"Cool. Mama and Daddy will meet us at home, after work," said Christi.

They walked to Christi's blue Chevy Cavalier. Dave and Sabrina got in the back and Christi started driving. The couple held hands and Sabrina lay her head on Dave's shoulder, "It's so nice that they let you come home for our Anniversary."

"Yeah," said Christi. "How'd you pull that off?"

"It's kind of a long story," said Dave, letting go of Sabrina's hand and putting his arm around her. "But, I'll explain it at dinner. You look great," he said to Sabrina, placing his other hand on her small baby-tummy.

"Thanks," she smiled, sitting up a bit and snuggling into Dave's embrace. "I feel a lot better than I did. I'm really glad that you're home." She smiled brightly.

"Me too," said Dave as he pulled her in more closely and kissed her lovingly."

. . . .

It was about three o'clock when they arrived home. Christi went off to her room, saying: "Everyone should be here in about two hours." Then she smiled, looking back over her shoulder as she walked away – glancing at the medium-sized duffle bag slung over Dave's shoulder – "it should give you two enough time to … unpack." She walked away giggling.

Sabrina turned and kissed Dave, softly on the cheek. "Well, you heard her. Let's go unpack your stuff." And she led him by the hand, down the hall to their room.

. . . .

John and Mary had brought home pizza from town. They were all sitting around the table in the family room, eating dinner.

John took a drink from his bottle of ice-cold Busch beer. "Pete apologized that he couldn't make it tonight. He said he had an appointment with his doctor this afternoon but would catch up with you later this week, before you go back."

"Nice," said Dave, "but those plans might be a little different than what I first thought."

Sabrina looked at her husband and put her hand on his knee. Before today, it had been over four months since she had seen him in person. His long hair looked lighter from the Iraqi sun, his beard was much bushier than it had been when he had left, and he looked more tired than she ever remembered seeing him.

"They have changed our rotation schedule, probably because a lot of the guys are burning-out. They are trying something new: four months overseas, four months in Virginia and four months off. But, they haven't set up what Teams are in which cycle or how it is going to work. I told my Commander and Captain that I really need to be home when the baby comes, and they said that could happen wherever my rotation is. So, that's good."

Sabrina squeezed his knee and said, smiling, "I'm really glad. I'm not sure how I could do it without you."

"I guess 'paternity-leave' is something that they are trying out," said Dave. "So, they said I can have time off for when you delivery and a bit after. Also, there's something else that you all need to know about."

They all sat up a bit and listened intently. "Something happened over there that I haven't told any of you anything about. I was involved in a mission – Chris was there too – where I did some things that they are kind of making a big deal about."

"You alright, Son?" asked John, with a furrowed brow.

"Yeah, I'm fine," said Dave. "Well, without the details, I stopped some bad guys from doing some bad things and my Commander was impressed with how I did it. It probably would have gone nowhere but, after they examined the Intel they got from the site, it turns out that these particular bad-guys were very, very bad and were planning to use the explosives involved to blow-up a hospital and kill a lot of innocent people. Therefore, as my Captain later explained, my actions that day are an even bigger deal. So, in December, they are going to fly you guys down to Washington to meet the President and he is going to have a picture taken of us when he gives me a medal."

"Dave, that's a very big deal," said Mary. "What medal is it?"

"It's the Navy Cross," said Dave taking a drink and making eye-contact with no one.

Everyone spoke at once, but Dave said nothing and continued to stare at the table and drink his beer. After two minutes, Dave spoke: "It's funny. I always realize how much I have actually missed the Cowboy Beer when I have it again for the first time after coming home."

Everyone got quiet. "I'm glad that you like it," said John with a smile.

"So, the President is going to love a photo-op with a SEAL who has a pregnant wife. That'll be … interesting," said Dave

"It sounds like you don't want to go," said Christi.

"Because I don't," said Dave. "I don't want to go to Washington DC. I don't want to get my picture taken with … any government official. And … I don't want the Navy Cross for doing my job."

Sabrina smiled and moved her hand from Dave's knee to around his waist, pulling him closer. Then John spoke: "That medal ain't for you Dave. It's for us. It's tellin' your family that the country is proud of you; that they think that you're a hero. That's why they still would award it if you had died doin' what you did to get it. So, you ain't saying that you're any better than your brothers over there. And it ain't you callin' yourself a hero. It's them sayin' that about you, specifically to us."

Dave looked up and smiled at his father. "Thanks Dad."

"Don't thank me," laughed John, taking a sip of his beer. "I'm the one who always tells you not to do the stupid crap that would get you one of these things."

They all laughed.

. . . .

Dave and Sabrina spent a lovely week celebrating their first Wedding Anniversary together. They had a very nice dinner at a restaurant in Farmington, took some long walks in the forest, looking at the autumn leaves, and they spent lots of time alone together.

Dave's Team was now set to be rotated back to Dam Neck, in the beginning of November. The plan was that Dave would stay in Maine until they got back and then join them – Sabrina would be coming along. The Navy Cross ceremony would be held a week before Christmas. The entire family, as well as Uncle Pete, would be there. At Dave's request, it would be a very small event. He argued that, because of the special nature of his job, if any photos were made public or the media was involved in any way, the enemy could more easily target him and his Team – the President, and senior Navy staff agreed.

The President was exactly like Dave had imagined that he would be: serious, yet jovial. He was impressed that Dave's entire family had served or were serving in the US military. He also made reference to John being from Texas, as often as possible.

Dave received the Navy Cross and afterwards they all had a nice dinner with the President, First-Lady, several high-ranking Naval Officers, as well as Captain Porter and Commander Fredrickson. Dave had neatly trimmed his beard, but refused to cut his hair. He was surprised that no mention was made about his pony-tail, but then remembered that they all would have read his file and that Captain Porter had made a special note about his hair when he started with SEAL Team Six.

After the ceremony, Dave, Sabrina and the rest of the family returned to Maine for Sabrina to have their baby. Chris and Gayle only stayed through Christmas and then went back to Virginia. Dave would be off until April of 2007, when he would begin the new rotation: training at Dam Neck for four months, deployment for four months, and "down-time" for four months. It was repeatedly emphasized that the "four month" time-line was set up to be fluid and could change, if need arose.

The baby's due-date was Valentine's Day, but she was born just less than a week early. Dave was by Sabrina's side throughout and, after a relatively smooth labor, their little girl – Anastasia – was born. She was just over seven pounds, had the same dark auburn hair as her mother and the same ice-blue eyes as her father. She was a good-natured baby: healthy, cuddly and full of life. She was Baptized at St. Joseph's by Father Mike and, of course, Chris and Christi were her God-Parents.

The plan remained that Sabrina and the baby would live in the little house in Virginia with Dave, when he was at Dam Neck, and would come back to the house in Maine when he was away. Sabrina decided that it would be easier – for now – for her to take a long leave from the hospital. Officially, she was listed as Per Diem, but she had no plan to pick-up any shifts for the foreseeable future.

When Anastasia was born, Dave had been in the Navy for just over sixteen years. One night, after the baby went to bed, He and Sabrina had a long talk about the future. They decided, together, that, for now, Dave would continue being a SEAL but that he would accept more administrative duties, as they were offered, and only volunteer for field operations if there were special reasons for him so to do. And that is how things proceeded, for about the next two years.

. . . .

2009

Lieutenant Commander Brad James was a short, thin, and pale Officer, with a head that might have once been shaven, but was now simply bald. None of the men under his command could believe that he had once completed SEAL training, let alone become a member of SEAL Team Six, but he was now the Commanding Officer of Dave and Chris' Squadron.

Captain Porter had retired in December of 2008 and was replaced, as the Commanding Officer of Team Six, by a tall Officer, originally from Boston, Massachusetts, with close cropped brown hair and brown eyes that never remained still. Most of the men with whom Dave or Chris spoke privately believed that Captain Patrick O'Hara was more of a political appointment than one made for tactical or strategic prowess.

Commander Fredrickson had been promoted to act as Captain O'Hara's Executive Officer, and this gave Dave and Chris some relief; they had a good relationship with this Officer and generally held him in high regard. They had hoped that he would have been Captain Porter's replacement, but Executive Officer was pretty close.

It was May. Dave and Chris were supposed to be stationed in Dam Neck for two-and-a-half more months but, when they were called to a "special meeting," they knew that was about to change. They had come into a conference room and were seated with two SEALs from another Squadron, about whom they only knew names and ranks: Petty Officers Second Class Owens and Barnes. They had all been selected for a "special assignment."

"This one comes from the Top, Gentlemen," began Lieutenant Commander James. "You have been specially selected for a mission of the highest priority. Our new Commander-in-Chief has decided to change the focus of our energies and increase our involvement in Afghanistan; crushing the Taliban and killing Osama Bin Laden. You will be the first mission towards this great goal."

Dave felt nauseous. "Great," he thought to himself, "a politically motivated mission/series of missions. What could possibly go wrong with that?"

"Make no mistake," said the Lieutenant Commander, "This will be a very challenging mission. But it is the first step to killing Bin Laden and destroying his command structure."

The mission described to them was complex. They would HALO into a mountain region north-east of Kabul, at night. They would then travel, by foot, for two days, into enemy controlled territory. Upon reaching the Taliban encampment of their target, they would set up a sniper position and terminate the target as soon as he presented himself. They would then travel, by foot, down the Panjshin Valley to the closest possible safe landing zone. The safety of the landing zone would be determined by satellite imagery and they would be extracted, by helicopter, if and only if the area was deemed "clear."

"Under no condition are you to be taken prisoner," stated the Lieutenant Commander.

"Begging you pardon, Sir," said Chris, "but what if something happens. If we can't get emergency extraction, what do we do?"

"You figure it out, Chief," responded the Lieutenant Commander. "You are supposed to be the best of the best. Act like it! The enemy is not to get ahold of you, dead or alive. This Administration is not going to have another 'Blackhawk Down' incident. Is that clear."

"Yes, Sir," the four SEALs responded in unison.

.   .   .   .

They would depart early the next morning and the plan was that they would be home in less than a week. Dave and Chris quietly gathered gear. Chris left to call Gayle and Dave went back to the little house.

When Dave got home, Sabrina had left him a note that she and Anastasia were down at the beach. Dave got changed and walked down to meet them. It was cloudy and a cool breeze blew off the Atlantic Ocean. Dave walked across the beach, towards his wife and two-year-old daughter. They were the only ones out today. They were sitting together in the sand and Sabrina was smiling and talking softly to Anastasia while the little girl was using a small, very pink shovel to dig sand into an equally pink bucket. They were both intent on the digging of the sand, so they didn't notice Dave until he said, "How are my girls?"

Sabrina was startled but Anastasia jumped up yelling, "Daddy home!"

He picked her up and kissed her little face. "Tickle," she laughed. She always made a point of letting him know that his beard tickled when he kissed her.

Sabrina stood up and kissed Dave as well. "Are we out here that late, or did you get home early?" she asked.

"I'm early," he said. "I found out today that I have to leave tomorrow, for about a week. A special ... thing."

"Oh," said Sabrina, looking down. She always told herself that she would never *tell* Dave how much hated it when he got sent off to fight, but she could not altogether hide the nature of her feelings; her sadness at his leaving always found a way to break through her best efforts to hold it inside.

"Hey," said Dave, setting down Anastasia and holding Sabrina. "Why don't we make a quick dinner, read some stories, put Stasia down a little early and just spend as much time together as we can before I go."

"Ok," Sabrina smiled sadly.

. . . .

The next morning, Sabrina woke before Dave's alarm and turned it off. She lay with him, listening to his soft breathing and said a prayer for his safe return. Then she cuddled close to him and woke him gently.

It was still dark when she kissed him goodbye and he left, saying "I love you, Sabrina. Take care of our baby. I'll miss you."

Sabrina smiled, "I love you and I'll miss you too, Dave." She kissed him again and he walked down the path from their small front porch.

As Sabrina turned and walked back into the little house, a dark, cold wave of fear washed over her. Dave had been going into the field less and less, but she still hated it when he left and couldn't help but worry until he safely returned. For some reason she could not understand, this time she actually felt afraid. She crossed herself, praying: "God please watch over him and protect him. Please bring him safely back home to me."

. . . .

The HALO jump had gone smoothly and the SEALs had moved swiftly and silently over the rocky terrain of northeast Afghanistan. It was an incredibly difficult journey. They were as silent and as hidden as possible. They were in known enemy territory, so any person they saw was a potential threat. They were nearly constantly moving and slept only minimally. Even then, there was always one of them awake and watching for danger.

In a day and a half, they had reached their target. They established a good sniper position and waited. Owens and Barnes would take turns holding the sniper position while Dave and Chris would guard and made small patrols, looking for any signs of enemy approach. They were to take the first clear shot that presented itself, send a short burst on the satellite-phone to inform Command of their success, and then get out, as quickly as possible.

The Taliban forces were obviously confident of their control of the area and thus safety. They had posted no guards and only a few carried their AK-47's. The area was remote and the only easy way in or out was the path that the SEALs would take to escape. Dave had never liked this escape-plan for that very reason; it was too obvious and thus too dangerous.

The sun set and it wasn't long before their target presented himself. He was an Afghani Chieftain, with an AK-47 slung over his shoulder. "Senior Chief," whispered Barnes, "I got him. Permission to take the shot?"

"Granted," said Dave.

The crack of the rifle echoed through the night sky, but the target had fallen dead to the ground before the men in the encampment heard the shot. The SEALs scrambled from their position and moved swiftly and silently down the path of their planned exit. As they moved, Dave sent the short burst: "Target terminated."

. . . .

Dave's message was received and quickly passed up the Chain of Command. Before the Evening News was close to airing, the Press Secretary of the President of the United States announced that an elite Navy SEAL Sniper Team had assassinated a crucial Chieftain in Osama Bin Laden's Afghan Command structure, "brining us closer to taking down his Terrorist network." This information was immediately aired on every major News network.

This is how, within hours of the Team successfully terminating their target, every Taliban stronghold knew that this Chieftain had been shot by a SEAL Team, in an incredibly secluded location, with only one easy path of escape.

. . . .

Dave looked, out of the darkness, at the desolate Afghani terrain and words Tennyson wrote about one-hundred and fifty years earlier were the only thing that came to his mind: "…Cannon to right of them, cannon to left of them, cannon in front of them … all in the valley of death …"

The cool night air was a welcome change from the heat of the day, but night was fading. The Team only had a few short hours before the cover of darkness – hiding their extraction – was gone. Ahead of them – in this "valley of death" – that darkness was the only cover they had. Dave slowly drew in the cool air and calmly exhaled.

Chris silently moved to Dave's side and whispered: "so … what are we doing?"

Dave smiled, "We have to get through this valley. The good news is that this is a classic kill-box, we have no cover whatsoever, and it's way worse than it looked in the briefing."

"Well, we'd better get through it fast then," said Chris with a crooked smile.

Dave responded quietly and without emotion: "Right. Let's go."

They had traveled for just over a day since they had terminated the target. Now that they had come to this open, valley position, they would move in teams of two. The first two would run approximately one hundred yards and then crouch down, covering the next team, both in front and behind. The second team would run, past the first team, on for approximately one hundred yards, and then they would crouch and provide cover. The plan was that they would do this for roughly three to five miles. At that point, they would find an appropriate landing zone, call for a helicopter and wait for a reply. They had been told that their extraction was a priority, so if it was clear, they shouldn't have to wait for long.

Owens and Barnes ran. Dave thought to himself, "When we get back, things have to change. These missions have been getting more and more ridiculous." The other team dropped to a kneeling position and Dave and Chris ran.

The rocky terrain was uncomfortable and difficult to run upon. Silence was impossible and as they passed close to the other team's position, Dave felt more and more that this was a terrible plan. Dave and Chris knelt, raised their modified M4 carbines to cover and tried to catch their breath as the other team began to run.

Dave thought to himself, "Tactically, this would have been an ideal mission for an air-strike. Could have taken out the whole camp. Only one reason to send us: makes it look more personal and increases the fear factor." The other team knelt and Dave and Chris ran.

They continued like that for two and a half miles. They were at a bend in the wide valley. About four hundred yards ahead, there was some cover and they could rest for a few minutes. Owens and Barnes passed Dave and Chris. Their breath was noticeably heavier than at the start and their feet fell heavily. They had been on the ground and moving over difficult terrain for more than three days, with almost no sleep and minimal food or water. "Even SEALs get tired," thought Dave.

They had completed each leg of the mission much faster than expected, which, Dave thought, "is good for us now, but when they come to expect it, that won't be awesome." The other team knelt and Dave and Chris ran.

As he moved forward, Dave noticed that it was harder and harder to avoid twisting his ankles. He had to consciously focus on keeping his eyes up and not looking down to avoid the bigger rocks. They passed the other team and continued on. They came to their position and stopped, kneeling and covering. "Two hundred yard 'til a rest," thought Dave.

Owens and Barnes ran. They looked tired. At each kneeling position, they had traded the heavy sniper rifle; in order to share the load. "That was smart," thought Dave. The other two SEALs seemed close; another team-within-a team, like Dave and Chris. As they passed close to their position, Dave thought that they should have a few cold beers when they get back and get to know each other a little better. "Other guys from the Teams do that. We should probably do it more," thought Dave.

Owens and Barnes slowed down and began to kneel, bringing up their M4's. Dave and Chris took a breath and began to rise from kneeling to run. And then, fully automatic AK-47 fire exploded from the cover that had formerly seemed so welcoming, as well as from the hillsides on both the right and the left. Owens and Barnes were hit by heavy fire and they both fell to the rocky earth.

Dave and Chris dropped to the ground and returned fire, to the right and to the left. Dave was rapidly selecting targets and firing three-round-bursts into them. The enemy fighters had initially hidden, but now they had abandoned cover and were firing wildly from standing positions. Dave dropped ten men in seconds, and quickly switched magazines.

Chris was to his back, also firing three-round-bursts. Both noticed that while the initial fire from the enemy had been a sudden wall of roaring death, now their fire was more sporadic as they changed magazines and yelled curses in Dari or Pashto; Dave and Chris couldn't be sure which language they were using.

Dave's mind frantically searched for a plan. There were at least one hundred enemy gunmen, probably closer to two-hundred. It's true that they were terrible shots – more zealots than warriors – and must also be exhausted, but it was now only Dave and Chris and they were in the open. Dave got an idea, it was a desperate plan but it was a plan nonetheless.

"Chris," he yelled between bursts – every trigger-pull a kill shot.

"Yeah," Chris yelled back, trying to focus on picking individual targets before squeezing the trigger.

"We've got to get out of here," yelled Dave.

"Ya think?!"

"Here's the plan, we run, just like we were – one runs, one covers – to that cover."

"You mean the cover where the guys who killed Owens and Barnes are?"

"Yeah. If we get in there, we might get them to shoot each other, and when they realize it, they'll pull back to regroup and we can get out."

"You are absolutely nuts, Dave!"

"Indeed," laughed Dave, changing magazines. "I'll run first."

"Fine," yelled Chris. "Don't die!"

Dave took a deep breath, tensed up and burst forward, at a full-speed run, firing his M4.

The rocks crunched under his boots and everything felt like it was in slow motion. He couldn't aim and maintain this speed on this terrain, so Dave just pointed his M4 in the general direction of the muzzle-flashes in front of him. He passed the bodies of Owens and Barnes, trying hard to focus on closing the distance to where he would stop to cover Chris, rather than thinking about how to get their dead Teammates out as well.

Chris started firing as Dave ran. He tried to push all the thoughts out of his head and provide at least some cover. He was amazed at how fast Dave was moving. "He's gonna make it," he thought … exactly as Dave was hit the first time.

Dave was almost a hundred yards away from cover when the first bullet hit him in the left thigh. It sent him spinning to the ground. Dave used his M4 to pull himself up to a semi-kneeling position and it felt like his entire lower-body was on fire. His head was swimming as he pulled the trigger, again and again. The second bullet hit him in the left shoulder and the third in the right, throwing him back, both of his arms to the sky.

Chris pulled himself up to run. He saw Dave's arms fly up as he was hit the second and the third time. Then, suddenly, there was a bright flash, an intense heat, and a sound that Chris would later describe as an unimaginable roar. Chris fell flat to the ground, wondering what could have caused that sort of explosion. Everything was hot and loud and he couldn't get his bearings. His ears were ringing. Chris struggled to pull himself up to try to return fire. He couldn't figure out what had happened or what was happening now, but he *was* sure of one thing. Dave was gone.

Part II

---

or

"After"

Chapter 1

or

"The Burning One"

Dave opened his eyes and sat up slowly. He was on the ground, in a cave, next to a small campfire. He knew this place; he'd been here before. She was sitting on the other side of the fire, just like before. She had the same ghostly pale skin and sparkling blue eyes. She had the same long, black hair in a ponytail that fell over her shoulder. And, she was wearing the same black jeans and the same black, eighties-style, concert t-shirt that said "Don't Fear the Reaper" in jagged red letters. She stared at him intently with the same small, delicate smile as the first time they met.

"Hello, Saraph," she said.

Dave slowly got up and sat on the same rock upon which he had sat the last time he was here. He looked at his leg and then at his shoulders, where the bullets had struck him. He had no signs of any injury and could feel no pain.

"Of course they're gone," she said, as if reading his mind.

"But, how is that possible?" he asked.

"I told you the last time," she smiled sweetly, "you're special."

"I'm dead … or dying. Aren't I?" Dave asked.

"Why would you think that?" she asked in a soft, gentle voice.

"Well you're here, for starters. Also, I got shot … repeatedly."

"Oh, my sweet Saraph," she smiled, "you are so confused."

"Umm, yes," said Dave, plainly.

"Ok. I'll try to help, but this is really something that you need to do yourself," she said gently. "What is the last thing that you remember, before you woke up here?"

"Running and fighting. Getting shot and falling."

"And then?" she asked.

"Nothing. I just woke up here. So, I'm dead?"

"Will you please stop saying that," she frowned, but not in an angry or intimidating way. "Of course you're not dead. I would have thought that you would have learned the last time that just because you're here with me doesn't mean that you're dead, or even mean that you are dying – which are entirely different things, by the way."

"Well, then why *am* I here?" he asked.

"You are sleeping. You will probably always sleep after, at least at the beginning, though the amount of time will vary. I'm here to keep you company. You're particularly vulnerable this time but all of the ones who would think to come for you are terrified of me. So, I thought I'd sit with you for a while," she answered.

"I'm vulnerable? To whom? The Taliban fighters?" asked Dave.

"No," she laughed brightly. "No, they are long gone. You really don't remember?"

"No," he answered. "So, why am I vulnerable?"

"Because it was the first time you did it and you aren't as strong as you'll soon be."

"Did what?"

"I told you that you have to do this yourself; I can't tell you," she smiled.

"I'm so confused," said Dave, "from what or whom are you protecting me?"

"Right now? Things like me but that aren't like me. They can be extremely … influential, and, right now, you have to figure out and decide things for yourself. Don't worry, once you remember things and decide what you want to do, you won't need me to protect you from them."

"So, none of this has to do with Afghanistan?" asked Dave.

"Not really, only in that it happened there."

"I'm really confused," said Dave, "Can't you tell me anything?"

"Listen, Saraph," she said, "I understand that what's happening to you right now is confusing. I can't imagine how hard it must be to understand. And I'm sorry that I can't do it for you; I really am. But if I told you everything, if I made you remember what you've forgotten, it wouldn't seem real to you when you woke up. All of this would just seem like a dream. Also, if I told you everything, I would influence you, even though I don't want to. You need to remember. You need to decide who you are and what you will do."

"How am I going to do that?"

"Start by remembering that which is the most important to you."

"That's easy: Sabrina. And our little girl, Anastasia. And our family. And doing what's right; protecting the innocent and the weak."

"Well," she smiled. "There you go. If you always remember that, everything else will figure itself out."

"How am I going to remember the things you say I forgot?" he asked.

"You will," she smiled. "Just relax and try not to block-out thoughts that seem a little … crazy. More things are possible than you can imagine. If you tell yourself something is impossible then you are not open to some new realities that you could not see before. Sometimes, something has always been there, but you can't see it until much later. Just stay open to possibilities that seem to be unbelievable. You know, things like talking with me." She laughed.

Dave laughed as well. "I'm just confused. I feel like something major has happened but that I can't quite figure out what it is. It's like trying to remember some dream after waking up."

"That's exactly right," she smiled. "The reason you forget those dreams is that they contain things that your conscious mind can't really grasp or understand in the context of the so-called real world. That's why you need to stay open to the magic that is alive in the world. And I don't mean 'dark magick,' I mean a very different kind of thing that exists but that human science could never possibly explain. Take 'Love' for example. Some have a very difficult time being open to magic like that, but – as you, of course, know – life is much more full and beautiful once you open yourself to it. That's all it will take, Saraph. Just be open."

"That's now the fourth time you've called me that word. What does it mean?"

"What? Saraph?" she smiled. "It's what things like me are going to call you now, unless you tell them not to."

"Things like you? You mean the things you are protecting me from?"

"No. No. They won't come near you now. I mean things that are like me, but who are considerably … smaller."

"Small angels?"

"They certainly aren't angels but they aren't humans or animals either. They are somewhere in between. They are all very different, but if you were to put them in one group the best term you would have for them is the 'Fae'."

"So Faeries are going to start talking to me, now?"

"Oh, that's far from the weirdest thing that you're going to have to get used to. And, anyway, they already have been talking to you, all of your life. You've been able to see them and hear them and interact with them, all along. You just didn't realize that others couldn't. The only difference is that, now, they are going to be actively making themselves known to you; you'll be talking to them all of the time."

"People are going to think that I'm crazy."

"Some might," she smiled, "but you'll be surprised at how many people can see them as well. And even if they initially can't, there are ways to make it so they can."

"I wish that there was more that you could tell me," he said.

"I know," she smiled, "but you'll be ok. There are … 'guides', or 'guardians' – or whatever they call themselves or think that they are doing – who are going to try to help you and to teach you. Just remember that the only person or thing that determines who or what you are is you. Remember what you said was the most important. Stay open. Don't be afraid. And if you need me, call my name. Now, sleep a little longer, Saraph. When you wake, remember. Just remember."

. . . .

Chief Petty Officer Chris Hanley was sitting at a table, in what was obviously an interrogation room, aboard the U.S.S. Theodore Roosevelt – a Nimitz-class nuclear powered aircraft carrier – somewhere in the Arabian Sea.

Sitting across from him, below the mirror that was obviously one-way glass, were two men who were obviously not Navy personnel. The first was a stout, older man who was about five-two, with short cropped grey hair, a full grey beard, and round, wire-rimmed glasses. He was wearing a tweed coat with leather elbows – which seemed an odd choice given the general heat, but the man did not appear to be uncomfortable. His companion appeared to be considerably younger. "Barely old enough to shave," thought Chris. He was taller, about six feet tall, and quite thin. He was clean shaven, but his hair was a rumpled, untrimmed, mousey brown. He wore a blue oxford shirt, with unbuttoned collar and rolled-up sleeves, and wrinkled khaki pants. It looked as if he might have slept in his clothes.

When the Seahawk had landed on the carrier's deck, they had taken Owens' and Barnes' bodies to the morgue and Dave – who was alive but completely unresponsive – to the Medical Department. Four Marine MP's had escorted Chris to a shower room, where he got cleaned-up and was given NWU's. "Gotta love the blueberry uniform," he thought to himself.

He was then escorted to this room, where he was met by a Captain, whom he did not know, wearing a Service Khaki uniform. The Captain directed Chris to sit down and briefly explained that he was to give a full account of the mission to men from an extremely Top Secret branch of Intelligence. He firmly stated that he was to omit nothing and give as many details as possible. His full cooperation was expected and required.

Chris had said nothing since the Seahawk had picked them up and continued to remain silent. Three men had then walked into the room – the two described above and another. The third man was quite different from the other two. He was about five-ten, with slicked black, hair. He was clean shaven, with hazel eyes and designer framed glasses. He also wore probably the most expensive suit that Chris had ever seen. He looked at Chris and spoke. "Chief Petty Officer Hanley, I am Mr. Ezekiel. I will leave with Captain Wilcox. You will tell your story to these men here, and I will discuss anything else with you at a later time." He and the Captain then left.

The other men did not give their names and Chris didn't ask. He began to tell the story in meticulous detail. The men quietly listened, but took no notes, which Chris thought was strange. He got to the explosion and stopped after he said, "Dave was gone."

The short grey-haired man with the glasses then spoke, with a crisp Oxford accent: "Hold for a moment, Chief Petty Officer Hanley … may I call you Chris?"

"Whatever," said Chris, flatly.

"Very well. Chris, I feel I've been remiss. We know your name, but you do not know ours. I am Professor Jones, and my colleague's name is Mr. Smith. We-"

Chris interrupted him, "No, it's not."

"I beg your pardon?"

"Mr. Smith. That's not his name. You might be 'Professor Jones,' but his name isn't Smith. Is there a reason that you Intel guys can never get creative?"

"Well, I uh," stammered Professor Jones.

"You're right," said the younger man in a Cockney accent, interrupting him. "My name in't Smith; never was. My name's Tim, actually. You can call me … Tim, if you like."

Chris smiled his crooked smile, "That's better."

Professor Jones spoke up, "Well, now that we are better acquainted and more relaxed, please tell us what happened next."

"Ok, I'll tell you. But there's no way that you'll believe me."

Professor Jones and Tim both slowly leaned forward. "Please," said Professor Jones, slowly and quietly, "you have no idea what we might believe. Tell us what happened to Senior Chief Petty Officer Shepherd."

"Dave," corrected Chris.

"What happened to Dave?" asked Professor Jones.

"Well … he was gone, but he wasn't. He wasn't because he … turned into a dragon."

The men sat back in their chairs, simultaneously, and Chris continued. "He was huge. Maybe twenty to thirty feet high, with a long tail and neck, strong hind-legs – like tree trunks, and his feet had talons - enormous bat-like wings where his arms had been, and horrifying fangs. He was roaring so loudly that I could feel the sound all the way to my bones, and he breathed a pillar of fire, high into the night sky."

"He leapt into the sky and flew, low and fast, at the enemy position in front of us. He incinerated them in seconds. He wheeled to the right and climbed higher into the sky. I could see the men on that hillside. Some were firing desperately in his direction, but most were running. It made no difference. Fire exploded from his mouth and hit the ground like a napalm strike. They were gone. He did the same thing to the other hillside. Then he flew higher and disappeared into the darkness. Over the next hour, maybe two, I would hear a roar echoing in the darkness and see light blaze somewhere off in the hills. Then, a while later, the same thing somewhere else. He was hunting them."

"I gathered Owens and Barnes. All I could smell was burning meat, as the fires flickered in the night. I sat alone in the darkness; I didn't know what else to do. Then, maybe an hour before sunrise, he came noiselessly out of the sky and landed on the ground in front of me. He looked at me for a moment and then lay on the ground. I realized that I wasn't really afraid. After about five minutes something weird happened. You know when you have a campfire and you touch a log that has been burning for a long time and the ash just falls away? It was sort of like that. The dragon sort of had ash fall away; there was a cloud of it. When the cloud cleared, there was Dave, laying on the ground in an almost-fetal position, not a scratch on him and completely naked. He was breathing and had a pulse, but he was completely unresponsive."

"I moved him over with the other guys and I called for extraction on the satellite phone. That was fun. They gave me all sorts of crap about still being too deep in enemy territory, but eventually they looked at satellite imagery to see if they could see any enemy troops. There were none. They went out three levels – I'm not sure what that radius is, but it's pretty far out. There was nothing, no movement of any kind. We had been in the middle of a hornet's nest, but now there was nothing. Dave had killed them all; every last one of them."

"You know the rest of the story: they picked us up and brought us here."

"Well, Chris," said Professor Jones, "That is an amazing story."

"This is the part where you tell me I'm crazy, or that I can't tell anyone, or something like that, right?" asked Chris, leaning back in his chair.

"No," said Professor Jones. "This is the part where Tim goes and gets us a snack. You must be starving. After that, we can talk about where we go from here."

Tim got up and walked to the door. He opened it, walked out and came back less than a minute later. He was carrying a tray with three pint glasses of beer, a plate of sliced cheese and a bowl of hard pretzels. He set the tray on the table and sat back down.

"Where'd you get all this? Were they just waiting with it, outside the door?" asked Chris.

"I think that you're going to have to get used to a lot of strange things over the next few weeks," said Professor Jones.

"Have a piece of cheese," smiled Tim, taking one himself.

Chris took a piece of cheese and took a small bite. His face reflected his surprise, "This is Ma's favorite cheese," he said.

"Yes," said Professor Jones, "it was her father's favorite as well. Tim discovered it, one misty morning in northern England and fell completely head-over-heals in love with it. Tim suggested it, to literally everyone, and when he tasted it, Vinterlogen also fell in love with it. He fell in love with it so much that he insisted we make certain that it was available when he moved to the United States. So, we pulled some strings and this cheese was always available to your family."

"Ok," said Chris, confused. "So you're saying that you made sure that we could always find Ma's favorite cheese? And, who is Vinterlogen?"

"Yes, of course," answered Professor Jones. "How else do you think an obscure Welsh cheese ended up in the second-least populated county in Maine?"

"It really is a very nice cheese, in't it?" said Tim.

"As for your other question, I shall go into much more detail in the days to come, but for now, Vinterlogen is your adopted mother's maiden-name. The Vinterlogen of whom I speak would have been your adopted grandfather – he died before you were born."

"But you said that Tim gave him the cheese."

"Yes."

"But that's not possible. Tim's just a kid and this Vinterlogen guy died before I was born."

Professor Jones smiled. "Very good. Now you are beginning to see. Not everything is as it appears to be, Chris. Take a sip of your beer."

Chris took a glass and drank. "Ok," he said, biting into a pretzel, "I can't wait to hear this one."

"Chris, you have seen many, many strange things over the years. You watched Dave kill a vampire in Africa. You, yourself, killed a werehyena, in the process of taking down an ancient dark-sorcerer in Iraq. This is not to mention how many other targets, with whom you have been involved, of whose 'special traits' you were not aware. And, last night, you watched your brother turn into a dragon and single-handedly annihilate a force of approximately two-to-three hundred men. Please, explain to me why you are skeptical about our having worked with your grandfather?"

"So, you worked with him?"

"Yes. At that time we were aiding in the British war effort," said Professor Jones.

"That was over sixty years ago," said Chris.

"That particular story was actually sixty-nine years ago," smiled Professor Jones.

"Well, since neither of you are that old, how's that work?" asked Chris.

"It's actually a rather long story, which we shall tell you both, once Dave wakes up. The short version is that we are here to help you and we have extensive experience in our particular jobs."

"I take it that you and, what's-his-name, Ezekiel, don't work for the US Government, then?" asked Chris.

"Mr. Ezekiel absolutely works for the US Government, but for an agency of which even you, with all your security clearance, would never have heard. We, strictly speaking, work *with* the government. Think of us as private contractors of sorts."

"So, the various 'Agent Smiths' we have encountered over the years? Who did they work for?"

"The ones to whom I believe you are referring worked for Mr. Ezekiel's organization, but were considerably below his pay-grade. Of course, some CIA men like to use that name as well, so with the less memorable missions, you would have been encountering them," said Professor Jones.

"You seem to know an awful lot about us."

"Well, that's our job, Chris," smiled Professor Jones. "More specifically, our job was to monitor Dave to see if or when he manifested. And then we move on to the next phase."

"Manifested?"

"Became a dragon," answered Tim.

"So you knew?" asked Chris.

"We had reasons to believe that it was a possibility," answered Professor Jones.

"What reasons? I've lived with Dave since I was six, and this literally came out of nowhere."

"That's because there are a number things of which you were not aware, but which we – being specialists – were always monitoring," answered Professor Jones.

"Specialists?" asked Chris. "What's your specialization?"

"Dragons … and other things like that," said Tim, smiling as he ate a piece of cheese.

"Dragons … plural?" asked Chris. "So, there are more?"

"There were other dragons, but we're fairly certain that Dave is the only one at the moment. But, we'll explain all of that in the next phase. It's easier if we just explain it once," said Professor Jones.

"What's 'the next phase'?"

"We wait for Dave to wake up. Then we see what he remembers. He needs to remember – and remember on his own – or we can't proceed. Once he does, we need to teach him to have more and better control. After that, we figure out where we go from there," answered Professor Jones.

"Where we go from there?" asked Chris.

"Well, the last dragon played a fairly significant role in the defeat of the Germans in World War Two," said Professor Jones.

"The last dragon fought in World War Two?"

"Yes," said Professor Jones, "and it was Dave's grandfather, Vinterlogen. Mr. Ezekiel is here because he wants to convince Dave to do the same and continue to serve the United States military, but in an … increased capacity. Your involvement would be as a member of Dave's support team."

"If he's a dragon, what support would he possibly need?" asked Chris.

"You saw him when he changed back. He's still sleeping now. Again, more shall be explained shortly, but, if he is doing this, he will absolutely need a dedicated support team," answered Professor Jones.

"I guess I don't get a choice then?" said Chris, folding his arms.

"Judging by your history together," said Professor Jones with a smile, "your enthusiastic participation was assumed."

Chris finished the rest of his almost-full glass of beer. "Great. So, now I'm going into combat zones with a dragon. And I suppose that the rest of the team will be gnomes," said Chris with his crooked smile.

"Nah," said Tim, "the gnomes absolutely hate the heat. There's no way that we'd get them to go to the Middle-East."

. . . .

Dave realized that he was flying. He looked down and could see the men firing at him and felt bullets impact his body. However, there was no pain and the bullets fell away. Their impact felt as light as gentle drops of rain.

The men were running and screaming as he breathed fire on them. There was no taste to it and he was surprised that, not only did he not feel the fire burn, he felt cooler after it left him. The fire absolutely incinerated all those who were before it. The unlucky ones were not directly before him, but on the edges of the path of his flame – they were screaming as they burned. He wheeled in the air, moved his powerful wings and climbed higher into the night sky. Then, with amazing speed, he swept over them again. There would be no survivors here.

He swept both sides of the valley and then he swiftly and silently climbed into the night sky. He drifted on the higher air current and looked at the earth below. He was hunting. His senses were unearthly; he could see, hear and smell everything. As he would see a group of fighters, he would swoop from the sky, silently at first but then roaring and spraying them with flames. Then he would climb back into the sky. He was hunting.

He could feel the dawn approaching. There were no more enemies left, so he returned to where it started. He landed and saw that there was a man before him. He was sitting next to two dead men. Dave knew him. "Chris," he thought. "Chris is my brother."

Dave lay down on the earth. He breathed slowly. So much had happened. He had known what he was doing as he did it and he felt in complete control of himself, but he didn't exactly feel like he was himself. He could feel his strength. He could feel his power. And being in flight felt amazingly natural. He was still Dave, but now he was also a dragon. He could feel himself falling asleep and, at some unconscious level, very deep inside, he knew that he was about to be in great danger. But still, he could feel himself drifting off. His eyes began to close and he thought to himself: "I'm still me, but now I'm also a dragon."

. . . . . .

Dave's eyes opened and he whispered the words, "I'm a dragon."

He was lying in a medical bed, in a dimly lit room. He had the stickers of a heart monitor on his chest – wires leading off the side of the bed – and a pulse-oximeter on his finger. He was wearing only a Navy hospital gown. He still felt tired, but knew that it was time to be awake.

He had been dreaming, but he knew that his dreams had been very much real. He had, in reality, had his second conversation with the Angel of Death, who had again appeared to him as a kind, attractive, young woman. That was real. And though he had dreamed he was a dragon, it was more accurate to say that he had remembered being the dragon than that he had dreamed it; he had only incidentally been asleep while he remembered it. He knew that this was real too. He had remembered.

Dave lay in bed for a few moments. He didn't know what to do. He felt an amazingly complex blend of emotions, all at once. The one thought that stood out, more than anything, was that he wanted to go home. He wanted to hold Sabrina and fall asleep in her arms. He wanted to wake to her gentle touch and soft kiss. He wanted to hear Anastasia giggle and watch her run and play with Bastet – the cat whose perpetual youth no longer amazed him. He wanted to see his parents, and sisters, and drink beer on the deck with Chris and Uncle Pete. He was tired of fighting and just wanted to go home. He felt the tears on his cheeks and wiped them away. He reached for the Nurses' call bell and pushed the red button.

After a few moments he heard feet outside the door. The handle turned and a man with ginger-hair and wearing blue NWU's walked in. Dave laughed out-loud. "You look great, Chris."

"Indeed. At least I'm not wearing a dress with my ass hangin' in the breeze," said Chris with his crooked smile, as he pulled a chair up by the side of the bed. "How are you feeling? You've been asleep for quite a while."

"How long?"

"A little over a day."

"Chris, I have to tell you something."

"Sure, what you got?"

"Chris, I'm a dragon. Or at least I can turn into one. I'm huge and I can fly and I breathe fire."

"Really? You sure?"

"I dreamed it, but I know it's real. You were in the dream too. I know it sounds weird to say about a dream, but I know that it's real."

"That's because it was," said Chris, slowly. "I was there when it happened. You turned into a dragon and you completely wiped them out. Then you came back, looked at me, went to sleep and turned back into you. It wasn't a dream, Dave. That craziness happened."

"What do we do now?" asked Dave.

Chris laughed. It was ironic because Dave usually had the plan. "Well, first you put on one of these lovely, blueberry uniforms and then I introduce you to a couple guys I met yesterday."

. . . . . .

Dave and Chris walked into a small conference room on board the USS Theodore Roosevelt. Chris shut the door and introduced Dave. "Dave this is Professor Jones and Tim."

"Hi," said Dave.

Professor Jones stood up and extended his hand, "it is a great pleasure to finally meet you, Senior Chief Petty Officer Shepherd."

Dave shook his hand, "You can just call me Dave."

Tim also shook Dave's hand and they all sat down. Professor Jones cleared his throat and began. "You have had an interesting career, Dave. I'm sure that you're aware that some of your past missions have been a bit ... unusual. Do you know how long we have been paying attention to your story?"

"No, I have no idea," said Dave.

"Well, Tim and I have been keeping an eye on you, more or less, since you were born. While, Mr. Ezekiel's department has paid attention to you since you so colorfully disposed of that vampire in the Congo."

"Who's Mr. Ezekiel?" asked Dave.

"Oh, he'll be by in a little while. He is a very important man who works for one of the most secret organizations in the American government. They have almost no rules or oversight and report directly to the President. Their activities focus on things and situations ... well, like you."

"Like me?"

"I'm sorry," said Professor Jones, "I was under the impression that you had remembered."

"Remembered what?" said Dave. "That I turned into a dragon?"

"Well, yes," smiled Professor Jones. "But it is more accurate to say that you *are* a dragon."

Dave looked down at the palms of his hands. He looked back up and said: "I don't think so, Professor."

"Don't worry, when we get to the training location I will explain everything in as much detail as you like. But for now ..."

"What do you mean, 'when we get to ...?'" asked Dave. "I don't recall agreeing to go anywhere. Actually, I was hoping that you would be discussing the details of my plans to go home."

"Dave, what are you doing?" asked Chris.

"Well, it looks like I have a pretty significant disability, doesn't it?" said Dave to Chris. "Can you imagine what would happen if I changed

… here? And what happens if I can't control it when I do change? It would be horrific beyond imagination."

"Which is why we need to teach you," said Professor Jones.

"Teach me to do what, exactly?"

"Teach you how to control the dragon," said Professor Jones.

"I thought you said that I was the dragon."

"You are, but it's more complicated than that. I promise I'll explain …"

"When we get there, I know. But what if I don't want to get there? What if I don't want any of this?"

"Dave?" said Chris.

"What Chris? What if I want to go home? Has anyone thought to take a second to ask me what I want? Do you have any idea what this is like for me? My entire life changed because of a Charlie-Fox mission! Did they happen to tell you that they announced what we did on live TV, while we were still on the ground?"

"Wait. What?!" asked Chris.

"Yup! Somebody needed the American people to think that he's 'Billy-Bad-Ass, goin' after the terrorists', so he sent out his Press Secretary to tell the world who we are, what we did, and, more importantly, where we did it. Of course they watch our news so they heard and then all came after us. Two of our guys died and we would have died too if … this … didn't happen!" Dave was starting to get extremely angry.

"Who told you that, David?" asked Professor Jones.

"Someone. It doesn't matter. But, it *happened* and now we know that it happened."

"David, what happened is not the point …"

"It is absolutely the point!" yelled Dave. "I'm not getting killed so the President can get better ratings!"

"Dave, calm down, bro," said Chris.

"No." responded Dave. "And why the hell aren't you more upset?"

"Because," said Chris, "that's the job. What was that poem you had on the wall in our room, when we were kids? It had that line that I never understood: 'Theirs not to reason why, theirs but to do and die.' Well, I get it now. We're not policy-makers. We're operational assets.

And sometimes, the mission is stupid. And sometimes, some of us don't make it home. You've always known that; that's always been what we are."

"Well, maybe I'm done. Maybe I don't want to be that anymore," said Dave.

"Excuse me, Dave?" said Tim.

Dave's head snapped towards the tall, thin, apparently young, man and he stared at him with an angry scowl.

"Right," said Tim. "We ... umm ... we understand. We would be scared too."

"Excuse me?"

"You're scared," said Tim with a shy smile. "It's totally normal. They are always scared."

"What are you talking about?" asked Dave.

"The dragons," Tim replied. "In the beginning, they are always scared. Who wouldn't be? It must feel like your whole life is totally changing, and that's partially correct. However, that's why we're here. We can help you make this more normal. Help you make your life, you know, sort of like it was."

"How's that work? What, I just walk up to my wife and say, 'Hey, Baby! I'm a fire-breathing monster now. Wanna cuddle?'"

"It's not like she isn't going to love you anymore, Dave," said Chris calmly.

"You know that?!" yelled Dave, tears beginning to stream down his face.

"Yeah, I do," said Chris. "Is that what this is about? Sabrina loves you more than anything. Do you see the way that she looks at you? Nothing in the world could change that, Dave. She might be confused, or scared, but she'll always love you."

"She'll be scared?" said Dave, wiping his eyes. "Yeah. Scared of me. And I really can't handle that, Chris. The fear in her eyes where there used to be love ... I just can't"

"That's what we're here for," said Tim. "Look, she won't have to be afraid when you are in complete control. Your grandfather came back from the war and lived with your grandmother and your mother, for decades, and never once had any problem keeping it under control."

"My grandfather?"

"Oh, sorry," said Tim. "I thought Chris told you. He was a dragon too."

"What?!" said Dave.

"I was planning to give you a detailed history at the training location," said Professor Jones. "But the short story is that, your grandfather was a dragon and he fought for the Allies, against the Germans, during World War Two, as a dragon."

"I guess I missed the day in history class where they told us about a dragon torching the Nazis," said Dave sarcastically.

"It isn't in the history books because we did our jobs. A large part of what we do is to make sure that your special gift is a secret. So actually, if you don't want your wife to know, she never needs to," said Professor Jones.

"That's not how we work, Professor," said Dave. "I don't keep secrets from my wife."

"So you described, in detail, the various decapitations and executions in which you were a primary participant?" asked Professor Jones.

"No," said Dave, "she didn't need to have that picture in her head, but she knows what I do."

"Well, I'm only saying that this could be like that," smiled Professor Jones. "Think of it as a nasty detail of your job, about which she needs know nothing."

"I don't think so," said Dave. "And who said anything about this being part of my job?"

"Well, after you learn how to have complete control of the dragon, it was assumed that you would continue to do your very important job," said Professor Jones.

"That's a pretty big assumption, Professor," said Dave crossing his arms. "What makes you think that I'm interested in that anymore, especially after the last mission?"

"Dave, stop it," said Chris.

"And further," continued Dave, "what makes you think that I'd ever use this, dragon-stuff, in the process? It's like I'm a living nuclear bomb. You think that I'm just going to unleash that wherever you tell me?"

"Dave," started Chris.

"And I don't know what the hell they did to you," said Dave turning to Chris, "but exactly why are you telling me to listen to them instead of taking my side?!"

"I'm on your side," said Chris. "That's why I think that you should get the training. You won't have to be scared when you know more about what this is and how to control it. After that, then you can talk about what comes next, but for now just let them help you."

Dave starred at the table. Everyone was quiet for a few moments.

"I'm not hiding this from Sabrina," said Dave quietly.

"And you don't have to," said Professor Jones. "As long as you don't go public, you can tell whomever you like … within reason."

"What's involved in the training?" asked Dave.

"Well," began the professor, "We'll start with a detailed history lesson and you can have your grandfather's book."

"He wrote a book?" asked Dave.

"Yes."

"Any reason why I'm just hearing about it now?" asked Dave. "This might have been nice to know before."

"Oh yes?" asked the professor. "It would be a good thing to tell a child or a young man that he may or may not have inherited the ability to turn into a dragon from his maternal grandfather – which has never happened before in history, by the way – and then give him a detailed account of what that is and how it works? This would be a good plan, you think?"

"What do you mean that it has never happened before?" asked Dave.

"We have no account of this being passed outside the male line. There are no accounts of a female having the trait, nor are there any accounts of a female passing on the trait. There are several cases when it skipped at least one generation, sometimes more, but it was always passed directly down the male line. When your grandfather had only a single daughter, we thought that he was the last dragon – as did he, by the way. We only followed you because he died the day you were born."

"Why does that matter?" asked Dave.

"Because, as far as we know, there is only one dragon at a time, now. The history is a bit unclear when – sometimes when the son is born, sometime shortly after, and sometimes the first time the son changes – but the father, or grandfather always dies, if he is not already dead before the boy is born," explained the professor.

"So, when he died the very day that you were born, we kept an eye on you, just in case. You displayed more and more characteristics – I'll explain them later – so we watched more closely. And ultimately, we proved to be correct in our suspicion that you would become what you now are: a dragon."

"Anyway, the training. Once you know the history we will then move to the 'control' portion of the program. You'll learn how to change at will, how to maintain focus, various skills and how to prepare to be safe when you change back."

"Be safe?" asked Dave.

"Yes," said the professor, "you are extremely vulnerable when you change back."

"Oh yeah," said Dave, "I remember. She told me that."

"Excuse me?" said the professor. "Who exactly told you what?"

"The Angel of Death. She told me that I was vulnerable."

Everyone froze. Chris was the first to speak, "Are you saying that you spoke to Death? Like, *the* Death, as in the actual Grim Reaper?"

"Yeah. But she wasn't like that; all dark and spooky, like a Halloween decoration. She looked like a sweet, pretty, young woman, but, the first time, she told me that she can look like anything she likes. She's an angel, you know."

"The first time?" asked Chris. "You spoke with Death more than once?"

"Twice." said Dave.

"This just gets weirder by the minute," said Chris.

"Did she tell you anything important?" asked Professor Jones.

"She told me lots of things that are important. She didn't tell me that I am a dragon; she said I had to remember for myself. I think that she told me about you though. I think she said that you were guides or guardians, or something like that."

"Fascinating," said Professor Jones. "Yes, we have used both of those terms at different times. Perhaps, at some point, you can tell us more about this dark lady."

"She wasn't dark, I mean she had black hair and wore black clothes, but she wasn't dark. She was nice and pretty and sweet and kind of funny sometimes," said Dave.

"Anyway," continued Professor Jones, "this vulnerable time is right after you change back. You need to be taken care of at this time."

"So," said Chris, "that's why I'm coming too; to learn what to do."

"Actually," said the professor, "the plan was to set up a five-man team, so we'll need three others."

"Why?" asked Dave.

"For your missions," answered Professor Jones.

"Right," said Dave. "I feel like I just told you, moments ago, that I don't know how comfortable I am with unleashing a dragon on whomever the government tells me."

"Why not?" asked a voice from behind them. They turned to see a clean-shaven man with slicked black hair, designer glasses, and an extremely expensive-looking suit. He walked over to the head of the table, pulled out a chair and sat down.

"Dave, this is Mr. Ezekiel," said Professor Jones. "Mr. Ezekiel, this is Senior Chief Petty Officer David Shepherd."

"No it's not," said Mr. Ezekiel with a smile. "This is Master Chief Petty Officer David Shepherd and this is Senior Chief Petty Officer Christopher Hanley; they've been promoted."

"They prefer to be called 'Dave' and 'Chris', said Tim.

"Do they?" asked Mr. Ezekiel. "Good to know. Ok … Dave … why not?"

"Excuse me?" asked Dave.

"Why don't you want to do your job, you know, your sworn duty to your country?" asked Mr. Ezekiel. "I mean, that's what you were saying when I came in, wasn't it. Or maybe I misheard you."

"Who the hell do you think you are?" asked Dave, feeling his anger build.

"Oh, I'm sorry. I'm Mr. Ezekiel, I thought that you were paying attention when I was introduced."

"Ok, Mr. Ezekiel," said Dave, "Maybe you missed my eighteen years of service to my country and maybe you missed the specifics of what I did in that service. That's fine, the professor can fill you in later. But don't imply that I am now, somehow, neglecting my duty."

"I wasn't implying anything," said Mr. Ezekiel with an arrogant smile. "I was asking you why you were talking about doing something so far out of character for such a distinguished Navy SEAL."

Chris spoke before Dave had a chance. "We were just discussing some of the specifics of the training, and what I believe my brother was trying to do was to explore some of the details of this situation and the safe-guards that you will, no doubt, be putting into place in order to prevent any negative issues or outcomes."

"Oh," said Mr. Ezekiel. "Well, in that case, I came just in time. Here's the basic plan. Dave, we'll start with you. You will still be listed with the SEALs, but will not be assigned to any existing Team. You won't be doing any regular missions any more. You will not be stationed at Dam Neck. After the training, you will go home until we need you. You will need to be available when we call you; we'll give you as much notice as we can. We'll send one of those 'black helicopters' that all the conspiracy nuts talk about and pick you up and then bring you back once you're done. Your financial compensation will be … extremely generous."

"Chris. Same plan. The only difference is that, if you insist, we can assign you to and allow you to operate with Team Six, as you are currently. However, if you do that, understand that we may need to pull you out of an operation to be sent on one of ours. Our missions take absolute priority."

"What would these missions be?" asked Dave.

"Well," said Mr. Ezekiel, "you're a dragon, Dave. You'd be sent to do pretty severe things to some really bad people. But everything will be Ultra-Top-Secret. Don't want the world to know that we have a dragon."

"What if it's a mission that I don't want to do?"

"We try to convince you," smiled Mr. Ezekiel, "we're good at that. But if we can't convince you, I don't think that there's anything that we can do to *make* you do anything that you don't want to do."

"So, if I say 'no'?"

"I try to convince you," smiled Mr. Ezekiel, "just like I said."

"What happens when I want to retire?" asked Dave.

"I'm not sure why you'd want to do that," smiled Mr. Ezekiel, "this is a pretty good deal. You live at home, with your nice family. You get paid amazingly well. And you occasionally get taken somewhere, for probably around twenty-four hours, to do something that will be incredibly easy … for you."

"But if I wanted to?"

"I try to convince you not to," smiled Mr. Ezekiel, "just like I said, before. It's like I told you, I can't think of anything that we can do to make a dragon do something that he has decided not to do. So, I can try to convince you, but I can't make you do anything that you don't want to do."

"What about the Team?"

"They'll get the same deal that Chris gets."

"Who else is on it?"

"Well, that's going to be tricky," said Mr. Ezekiel. "They have to be Team Six quality. And they have to have had some experience with … weird, supernatural stuff. There's no shortage of that happening, we just have to get guys who have seen it but are calm about it."

Chris spoke up. "You remember Diego Wagner?"

"Yeah," said Dave.

"He was on that thing with the Hyena-guys. He might work."

"Cool," said Dave.

"Alright," smiled Mr. Ezekiel, "it's actually better that he already knows you. We can approach him. I have a few ideas for the two other guys."

"So, what happens now?" asked Dave.

"Assuming that you say yes?" smiled Mr. Ezekiel, arrogantly. "In that case, you two go to Norway for training and the rest of the team will meet you there."

"How long is the training?" asked Dave.

"Well," said Professor Jones, "that depends almost entirely on you. It could be rather quickly completed, or it could take months. But again, there is no way to tell at this point."

"I need to call Sabrina, to let her know that I'm ok and that we will be having special training."

"Of course," smiled Professor Jones.

Dave turned to look at Chris, who smiled back with his crooked smile. "Alright, I'll do it. But you need to understand, the minute this gets stupid, I'm out."

"Come on, Professor, let's go set it up," said Mr. Ezekiel, standing.

Professor Jones stood, as well. "Tim, why don't you get these boys a few pints and some of that cheese you like so much?" And he left the room with Mr. Ezekiel.

Dave looked at Chris, quizzically. "Cheese?"

"Oh yeah," Chris laughed. "You're not going to believe this one."

"Aye," said Tim enthusiastically, "this cheese is amazing!"

. . . .

Dave hesitated before he picked up the phone. Sabrina was alone, with their daughter, Anastasia, in Virginia, thinking that he would be home in a few days. He needed to tell her that it would be longer, but he wanted to wait to tell her anything else until he was by her side. He knew that she would be glad to hear that he was safe and that the reason for his being away longer was training, rather than another mission, but he felt horrible telling her that he would be gone longer.

Dave took a deep breath and picked up the phone. "Hello?" came Sabrina's sweet voice over the phone.

"Hi, Baby," said Dave.

"Hi, Sweetie! How are you?"

"I'm safe. I'm actually on a ship, right now."

"Does that mean that you're on your way home?" she said, hopefully.

"Actually, that's why I'm calling. Chris and I are going to have to be gone a little while longer. They are sending us to Norway for some special training. But the good news is that, after that, my job is going to change; quite a bit, actually. I can't talk about it over the phone, but I'll be able to be home with you, a lot more often."

"Oh, that's good, at least." She paused, "Dave, do you know how soon you'll get back?"

"No, not really. They are not entirely sure how long the training will take."

"Ok. Well, there is something I have to tell you. I was hoping to be able to tell you when you got home, but it can't wait."

"What's wrong?" asked Dave.

"It's Uncle Pete. Dave … he died."

Dave was quiet for a minute. "What happened?"

"I guess that he was very sick for quite a while, but didn't tell anyone. He died peacefully, in his sleep. Dad went to pick him up for work on Tuesday, and when he didn't answer the door, he went in and found him in bed."

"Is Dad ok?" asked Dave.

"No, but Mama is taking good care of him."

"Can you get to the funeral?"

"Gayle said that she would take us if you two couldn't get back in time. She got that promotion – remember, she's a Captain now – so she had no trouble getting the time off. She'll pick us up and drive us home for the funeral."

"I feel terrible that we can't make it."

"Everyone will understand, you're on the other side of the planet, after all."

"I know, but I feel terrible anyway," said Dave.

"If you are going to be gone long, do you want me to stay in Maine?"

"Would you rather?"

"Yeah, it gets lonely without you here. Stasia is fun, but there's only so much you can talk about with a two-year-old," she laughed.

"You have such a pretty laugh; I really miss you," said Dave.

"I miss you too, Sweetie," she said.

"So, this new job, we get to move back home, for good."

"Really? No more Virginia?"

"Nope. It's a special unit, so they come pick me up and bring me back whenever they need me."

"That sounds really good."

"Yeah, that part is great, I'm not sure about the rest of it, but we'll see."

"So, do you want me to bring stuff home to Maine?"

"I guess. As much as you can without difficulty. We can take care of everything else when I get back. Maybe we can convince Mama or Christi to take care of Stasia for a few days and we can make a little vacation out of it?"

"That sounds really nice."

"I love you, Sabrina."

"I love you, too, Dave."

"As soon as I know anything about when I can get home, I'll let you know."

"Ok, I miss you."

"I miss you too, baby. Give our little angel a kiss for me."

"Ok, Sweetie."

"I love you. I'll talk with you soon."

"I love you, too. Be safe, Dave. 'Bye."

They hung up the phone and Dave took a breath. He said a silent prayer for his father's best friend, Uncle Pete. And then he got up and went to go meet Chris."

. . . .

Dave walked into the lounge area and saw that Chris was sitting at a table in the corner with two full glasses of beer. Dave walked over and sat down.

"Uncle Pete died," he said.

"Yeah, Gayle just told me. She said that she is going to take Sabrina and Anastasia home for the funeral."

"It sucks that we can't be there," said Dave.

"Yeah, I'm really gonna miss his sense of humor," said Chris.

"I'll call Dad later, if you want to join in," said Dave.

"Sounds good," said Chris. "So, what was all that before?"

"All what?"

"You know. All that about wanting to quit and that stuff."

"What? I want to go home. I'm tired of everything about this. When we started, I had all these noble, chivalry-style ideas that we were basically knights, defending the weak and innocent. Before we were in long enough to get burnt-out, 9/11 happened and it was all about righteous justice. But now, it just feels like we're pawns – very dangerous pawns – but pawns nonetheless."

"All this from one mission that went bad?"

"Went bad? We should be dead, Chris."

"Yeah, but we're not. Pull it together, everything's going to be fine."

"Why do you think things will be any different next time? We've gone from a Commander-in-Chief who, yes, was goofy but who absolutely loved us, to one who's probably technically smarter but it looks like he hates us and seems to think that our job is to make him look good. Why do you think that that sort of thing won't happen again?" asked Dave.

"Because you're a dragon," smiled Chris.

"Will you keep it down, please? Talking about my life with more strangers is the last thing in the world that I want to do right now," said Dave in a whisper.

"Sorry," whispered Chris.

"Anyway," said Dave, quietly, "You don't think that they will eventually parade me before the cameras?"

"No," said Chris. "Do you have any idea how scared people would be?"

"I guess you're right. Still I don't trust these people."

"Come on," said Chris. "Not even Tim?"

"Ok, Tim's alright. But, there's no way the other guy's real name is Professor Jones."

"You never know. Call him out on it. Tim was introduced as 'Mr. Smith,' so I called them out and he told me his real name."

"Or you just think that he did."

"When did you get this way?" laughed Chris.

"When they almost got us killed. I used to believe that they had our backs. Not now. I feel like the minute they see even the slightest benefit in it, they'll smoke us without a second's hesitation."

"But Dave, that's not these guys. Tim and Professor Jones seem to genuinely want to help you."

"Maybe. But that other guy – Ezekiel? He's bad news. First of all, he looks like the devil."

"You met the devil too?" asked Chris, with his crooked smile.

"Not funny," said Dave. "So, he's arrogant as hell. And that, 'I'll try to convince you,' and 'I can't make you,' crap reminded me of a bad recruiter trying to get some kid to enlist by saying he can 'travel the world and meet all sorts of interesting people'."

"You gotta admit that we've met some pretty interesting people," smiled Chris.

"Yeah, and then we killed them," said Dave dryly. "I'm just saying that I don't trust that guy for a second."

"Then why did you say yes to the whole thing?" asked Chris. "I bet that if you had agreed to the training and said that you would have considered the new Team, they would have agreed. You could have learned everything you need and then just quit."

"You think they'll ever let me 'just quit'?"

"I don't see how they can stop you."

"That's because you're not an evil bastard. You don't think that they'd hesitate to try to use people I care about as leverage? Please!"

"Then why'd you say yes, Dave?"

"Honestly? I said yes because I want to go home. I want to wake-up with Sabrina, every morning for the rest of my life. I want to see my little girl play with Bastet. I want to show her the little fish that live at the end of the deck. I want to go home."

"That's probably why Ezekiel led with that," said Chris. "He didn't have to have us 'working from home'. Frankly, I'm shocked that they let us."

"He probably did it so he knows exactly where everyone and everything we care about is. Who knows? I just know that when he said that, I knew the offer would never be made again, so I said yes."

"What are you going to do when they give us an assignment that you don't want to do?"

"I was actually thinking about that quite a bit. I'm not actually sure that they will use us very much at all," said Dave.

"Why not?"

"Well, think about it. They've had nuclear weapons for decades and haven't used them."

"Yeah, but that's because of the whole 'mutually assured destruction' thing; if we shoot them they shoot us. But, no one else has another ... 'you'."

"That's probably true. But if they can't afford to put me somewhere that I'm going to be seen, that kind of limits things."

"They said that your grandfather fought in World War Two."

"Yeah, but they didn't say what he did. I'm just sayin' that I'd be surprised if they had us doing a lot. So, we get to go home and we don't have very much to do. It doesn't sound terrible."

"But you just got through saying how much you don't trust Ezekiel."

"I don't. He's a weasel."

"So then why even listen to what he had to say, let alone say yes."

"It was the only way to get out of here. He's getting what he wants. I don't think he'll be a problem until he doesn't. And right now, what he wants gets me knowing how to keep my little secret a little secret and it gets me home."

"Yeah," said Chris. "But how long is it going to be before we actually get home? Professor Jones said that the training could take months."

"I don't see that happening," said Dave. "I'm extremely motivated to get home."

"So, you're going to cooperate with Professor Jones and not give him an attitude?"

"Of course," smiled Dave, "I was always a good student."

"No," said Chris with his crooked smile. "Gayle's the smart one, Christi's the cute, bubbly, fun one, and I'm the clever, wise-cracking one."

"So, what does that make me?" asked Dave, laughing.

"You? Oh, you're a bunch of things. You're the lovey-dovey, emotional one whenever you're near Sabrina or whenever she crosses your mind, which is roughly every thirty seconds or so. And you're Broody McBrooderson when she's not around. But, then again, there is something else."

"Yes?" said Dave.

"You are the most stubborn man I have ever met. So, yeah, maybe the combination of you being driven to get back to Sabrina and your stubbornness will get you through it quickly."

Dave laughed and took a long drink from his glass of beer. "I just hope that the training isn't stupid."

"At least you'll learn all the history stuff. I don't think that part is going to be for me and the other guys. But, it'll probably be very interesting."

"Maybe. I just want to get through it and get home."

"Well, at least try to pay attention. Some of it might be important."

"How much you want to bet that they make it up as they go?"

"Nah, I think the Professor and Tim are pretty decent guys. I doubt that they'll try to fake you out about anything," said Chris.

"I guess we'll see when we get there," said Dave.

"On the bright side, for you at least, we do know one thing for certain."

"Oh yeah," said Dave. "And what might that be?"

"Well, at least it won't be hot."

Chapter 2

or

"Here There be Dragons"

"The story begins in Ancient times, long before the Romans or the Athenians. It started here, in Scandinavia. There were many warrior clans, but the undisputedly greatest group in all of Scandinavia and northwest Europe were the Asgardians."

"Hold it, Professor," said Dave. "Asgardians? Like Thor and Odin?"

Dave, Tim and Professor Jones were sitting by a fireplace, in one of the side rooms in a very large cabin, in northern Norway. Chris was in another room reading – he had decided to let Dave give him the "cliff notes" of the history lesson – and the other members of the new Team would arrive tomorrow or the next day. Professor Jones had just begun telling Dave the history of the dragons.

"Yes," said Professor Jones, "Asgardians. Not exactly the ones you read about, but Asgardians nonetheless. Dave, it is important that you understand that the myths and faerie stories that you have read, all your life, are actually true. The specifics of the real stories are not exactly the same as what you read, but the essence of those stories is quite factually correct. There was a King, who used strong magic, named Odin and his huge and powerful son was named Thor. The other characters were more-or-less real as well. Ironically, Loki was the most exaggerated; actually more of a court jester than anything else. He featured prominently in the stories because he was the one telling the stories to the other warrior clans who survived to pass them on, eventually to us."

"The Asgardians were not gods, but they were quite gifted. Sort of like the Atlantians."

"Atlantis was real as well?" asked Dave.

"Yes," said Professor Jones. "They were also an Ancient people who were highly advanced. They shared many of their gifts with the peoples around the Mediterranean Sea: the Egyptians, the Greeks, the Phoenicians, and several others. Their arts and literature and technology changed that part of the world, forever. Alas, their civilization was lost. But that is a different story."

"The Asgardians were a northern people. While the Atlantians were gifted in arts, music, literature and science, the Asgardians were gifted in strength and fearlessness and magic. Their societies reflected their environments: the warm and mostly gentle Mediterranean, versus the cold, brutal north."

"So, there were obviously many different warrior clans of the north. They had their petty conflicts, but nothing particularly memorable. There was one group, however, who were amazingly powerful and brutal: the Jotnar – they were later called 'Frost Giants' by some. They lived in the furthest north and, in winter, would sweep down on the clans of Scandinavia and northwest Europe. Only the Asgardians could stand before them, and then barely."

"Their destruction grew and grew and Odin feared that eventually the Jotnar would wipe-out the other peoples of the north. Therefore, he called a great council of war, inviting all the warrior chiefs to bring their single greatest warrior with them to the meeting. The meeting was said to have been held in the Great Hall of Asgard – no one knows precisely where in Scandinavia this was located. It is also unknown the specific number of warrior chiefs there were, but all were invited and it is said that they all came."

"Odin had formed a plan. The Asgardians would sweep down upon the Jotnar, in one final battle to destroy them all. He called the battle Ragnarok. He, along with all of his strongest Wizards, would give a great gift of power to the greatest warriors in the clans. When the battle began they would be transformed into giant beasts. Their skin would become a stronger armor than any weapon could pierce. They would fly upon mighty wings, they would have talon-like claws on their feet, and fangs, and powerful tails. But most important of all, they would breathe a ravaging, withering fire of unspeakable heat: the warriors would become dragons. They would join the Asgardians in battle, and together they would annihilate the Jotnar."

"The plan was met with great cheers and shouts of agreement. However, one particularly strong warrior, asked about after the battle. He deeply loved his wife and wanted to go back home to her after their victory. Odin agreed to fashion the spell, such that the warriors would only temporarily become dragons, and would then transform back to men. Also, they would be able to again become dragons, if the need arose."

"The Asgardians and the men who would become dragons traveled north to the lands of the Jotnar, called Jotunheim. The other warrior clans gathered their men, away from Jotunheim, and waited, in case they would be sent for, to join the battle. It is said that it was Thor who actually challenged the Jotnar to the great, final battle and the whole of their strength amassed before the Asgardians."

"Heimdall, it is said, sounded his mighty horn and the great battle of Ragnarok began. Odin and his Wizards chanted great words of magic and the warriors were transformed, in bursts of fire, into dragons. The dragons took to the air and the Asgardians charged into battle. The truth of the stories, traditionally told describing the events of Ragnarok, is extremely doubtful. However, we do know that the Jotnar were considerably more numerous than the Asgardians had expected. The battle was an unspeakably brutal slaughter."

"Without the dragons, all would have been lost. Their fire was devastating to the Jotnar. But though their armor was strong, they were not impervious to harm. It is not known by what means, but the Jotnar were able to bring-down and kill the dragons."

"The specifics of the battle are not known, but it is said that it raged for nine days. The north had never seen such a brutal conflict, and such a one shall never here be seen again. Fires burned fallen bodies and melted shattered weapons. Blood stained the ground for as far as the eye could see. And after the nine days of battle, the last Jotunn fell. All of the Asgardians had died, battling the vastly numerically superior force, and with them, all but one of the dragons."

"It is said that, after two weeks had passed from the blowing of Heimdall's horn, a lone warrior walked out of the mist towards the gathered warrior clans. It was the warrior who had asked about returning home to his wife; he was the only survivor of Ragnarok. He told the tale of the battle to the gathered chieftains but the specifics of his tale have been lost to time. All we know is that, after Ragnarok, the days of Asgard had come to a bloody end and there were no more Asgardians thereafter. However, now there was a dragon in the world."

"That was in Ancient times. Since then, the dragon became a symbol of power in that part of the world. The dragon-gift, as it is sometimes called, was passed from father to son, sometimes skipping a generation, or even several generations, but always down the male line. There was never more than one dragon living, at any given time. No one knows why either of these facts are true, but, until you, they were."

"There are many stories and myths about dragons through the years. Almost none of them are true. For example, St. George and the dragon? Utter nonsense! No one has killed a dragon in combat since Ragnarok. When you are in the form of the dragon, we have not seen a weapon capable of killing you. In fact, the real end to any of the 'dragon-slaying' stories that even have a-toe-in-the-pool of reality is very different. It always had a warrior discovering that the dragon transforms back into a man and sleeps somewhere. The warrior sneaks in and kills the man in his sleep. He then takes credit for being a glorious dragon-slayer. Ridiculous!"

"So, I can't die?" asked Dave.

"We're not really sure how that works, actually," said Tim. "We know that there has never been a weapon that could harm you while in that form, and we know that the dragon-slayers all did their nasty business when the dragon was in that deep-sleeping state after becoming a man again. But we're not really sure what would happen to you right now."

"Well," said Dave, "when I got shot in Afghanistan I turned into the dragon. When I woke up, I was unhurt. So, maybe instead of dying, I would turn into the dragon again."

"It is important to recognize that we do not know that for certain," said Professor Jones. "It is not a hypothesis that we should test, either; if the outcome were different, we could not fix it."

"Yeah," said Dave. "I'm ok with leaving that alone. So, where do you two fit into this?"

"That is a very good question," said Professor Jones. "We work for Maeve, Queen of the Fae. All of the Fae, to varying degrees, like to keep to ourselves and have minimal interaction with humans. We are quite content for them to see us as characters in stories."

"You're Faeries?" asked Dave.

"Yes," said Tim, "what else would we be?"

"But I can see you."

"You've got 'The Sight'," said Tim, "of course you can see us. We can always tell when someone has 'The Sight'; you sort of glow."

"But other people see you too."

"Only when we let 'em," smiled Tim. "Unless they got 'The Sight' too, of course."

"More people do than you might think," said Professor Jones. "So, as I was saying, the Fae don't like attention, and any supernatural thing draws more attention to us. So, around the time that you call the 'Early Middle Ages', Her Grace thought that it was a good idea for Tim and I to start working with the dragons. Sort of as 'guides,' to help your kind not do stupid public things and as 'guardians,' to, shall we say, spin the story so no one believes that dragons are real."

"So, you two have been around, like this, since the Early Middle Ages?" asked Dave.

"Sure have," answered Tim.

"Ok, so what are your real names, then?" asked Dave.

"Mine's Tim, just like I told Chris."

"I actually *am* Jones," said the professor. "Though the 'professor' title is more honorary; I didn't attend University, strictly speaking."

"Ok," laughed Dave. "So, how many dragons have you worked with?"

"Lost count, over the years," said Tim, "But your Grandfather, Vinterlogen, he was by far the biggest dragon and we worked with him the longest."

"Really?" asked Dave.

"Vinterlogen was not his birth-name; that has long been forgotten. It became his name. In English, it means 'Winter's Law'. He used no other name until he met your grandmother. He then said that it was his surname, and carried on from there," began the professor.

"Vinterlogen was born in the 1470's, in a village in northern Norway, not far from here actually. Since you wouldn't know anything about Norwegian history, I'll give you some other events so you have an idea of what was going on then. This was during an English civil war, called the War of the Roses, about twenty years before 'Columbus sailed the ocean blue', and about ninety years before Shakespeare was born."

"So, he lived for five-hundred years?!" asked Dave in amazement.

"Yes," said Tim, "it was rather amazing for us as well. But he didn't get married until the late 1930's, his only child was a girl and he didn't have a grand-child until you. No one ever got close to killing him so … he was different than the other ones in all those ways."

"We never understood it, but we never questioned it either," said Professor Jones. "Your grandfather was a mighty warrior and the largest, most powerful dragon there has ever been. I have given you his book, so you can read details about his many exploits over the years, on your own."

"Now, you need to understand a few important facts about alliances."

"From the beginning, the dragons have had various alliances with various clans, kingdoms and nations. The absolutely most serious and continuous is with the Fae. The dragons and Fae began working together in the Early Middle Ages, as I explained before. The basic arrangement is that the Fae will assist the dragon in any way we can, and the dragon will be a defender of the Fae. Typically, though not always, the Queen has moved close to wherever the dragon lives and the vast majority of the Fae follow her, much like honeybees follow their queen."

"You keep talking about your Queen, but you never mention your King. Is there a reason?" asked Dave.

Professor Jones hurriedly looked at Tim, and shook his head anxiously. "We don't talk about that sort of thing, do we Tim?"

"Not at all, Professor Jones."

"It wouldn't be appropriate to discuss Her Grace's personal business."

"Quiet inappropriate indeed, Professor Jones."

Dave smiled at the change in their tone. Something about this topic made them very nervous, but Dave was content to leave it for now. "Well, will I ever meet your Queen?" he asked.

"Oh, I should think so," said the professor, "She lives in the forest surrounding your home in Maine."

"Anyway, there have been a few times that the dragon, especially your grandfather, acted in a way that one of the human governments, with which he was also working, felt was … shall we say … extreme. But in reality, he was acting to protect the Fae in some way or other. You see, the connection between the Fae and the dragon has always been extremely important … one might say that it is a priority to both parties. That's why we're here, with you, actually."

"As for the human rulers or governments, in the Ancient times, the dragon would make alliances with whichever given ruler he preferred. There was no hiding the dragon's involvement; they were out-in-the-open, as they say. This is where the dragon-shaped figure-heads on Viking ships came from and why 'here there be dragons' was written on the north of most maps. However, the historical accounts of these times were changed when they were eventually written down and we made sure that the true, historical, dragons vanished into the mists of mythology."

"During the Middle-Ages, the dragons became more covert and less directly involved. Oh, they were there, but their actions were explained away and, if there were witnesses who survived, any tales were seen as the crazy ravings of those who have seen too much battle and death."

"It was in these times that we began to assist, masquerading as secret government operatives of some sort of other, and facilitated the work of dragons with that of a military force. This is not always as easy as it would first appear. When dealing with a monarchy, personalities vary dramatically, as you might imagine. For example, King Henry VIII of England was absolutely impossible and a complete ass on top of it. Your grandfather wanted nothing to do with him."

"Also, there is the issue of the most prominent locations of the Fae. Our people are most populous in places like the hills, forests, and streams of Germania, Scandinavia, and what was at one time referred to, by some, as the 'British Isles' – though I strongly suggest that you do not make the serious mistake of using that term when speaking to her Grace, or any other of the Fae, for that matter. However, we are typically fairly concentrated in the more or less 'wilder' locations of these areas – think 'deepest, darkest woods', or someplace like that. When these areas were threatened, the dragon typically came to our aid and fought off the aggressor forces."

"So, various kingdoms were coming after you?" asked Dave.

"No, no, of course not. They were usually unaware of our existence," said the professor. "However, as war sweeps down upon an area, we, or things we value, would surely have been harmed. Thus, the dragon would either act independently – this was much easier and more common in the earlier days – or would become aligned with a specific government – this was considerably more complex, but more common in modern times. These actions would actually be to preserve us or the things we value, rather than a true alliance with the government in question."

"There were other factors in alliances, as well. For example, your grandfather stayed out of the religious wars. As I'm sure that you are aware, he was a strong Catholic. However, he did not see these wars as religious conflicts, but as opportunistic political power-grabs. So, he moved to Iceland and very much kept to himself, for literally Centuries. Her Grace agreed to only call on him for aid when the need was dire, and so, for a long time, he vanished."

"Though it was a major conflict, we strongly opposed his getting involved in what they called 'The Great War'. Despite all of the propaganda, on both sides, neither side had a clear 'moral-high-ground' nor had we, at that time, established any firm alliances with the member nations. Your grandfather agreed. It was not until what you call World War Two that he was to again become a major participant."

"Shortly before the outbreak of the war, he met and later married your grandmother. I, personally thought that would make him less likely to get involved as tensions rose. However, the more that she spoke of children, the more he cared about the events of the world."

"And then there was Hitler. In addition to other horrors attributed to him, Hitler had an obsession with the occult. He firmly believed in the Fae and had a secret department hunting us. Most of the Fae fled to Ireland, England, Scotland and Wales but there were still many left behind in northwest Europe. Queen Maeve, herself, came to your grandfather to beg – not ask, but beg – that he join the Allies and crush the Nazis. He quickly agreed, but the logistics of his involvement were incredibly complex."

"Troops would have to be involved to hold whatever he took, so liberating Hilter's Death-Camps would be impossible until there was an invasion of Europe. Also, a dragon is not a 'commando unit'; surgically precise. A dragon strikes with the utmost brutality; incinerating his foes. If he was to strike those Camps, it was more likely-than-not that he would end up killing the innocents he wanted to save, along with the guilty."

"The importance of air-power became the way in which your grandfather became involved. We negotiated his involvement with a secret office of the British government, shortly before the onset of the Battle of Britain. It was here that he became a devastating force. The dragon took squadron after squadron out of the sky over the English Channel. On days with significant cloud cover, he flew to intercept the German bombers and their fighter escorts; burning and tearing them from the sky, leaving no survivors. But it was in the darkness of night that he became the Reaper of the Luftwaffe.

"Sweeping into the battle, as the RAF attempted to drive the German planes away, he would hunt and kill the Luftwaffe. In the chaos of battle, he was mostly unseen, and the RAF pilots who did see him received a visit from a certain Professor Jones and Mr. Smith, who would convince them to say nothing about what they had seen."

"I was Mr. Smith," said Tim, with a smile. "I was really sinister and scary."

Dave laughed.

"Continuing on," said Professor Jones, scowling at Tim. "It went very well during the Battle of Britain. When the Americans came and we began the bombing of Europe, it was suggested that the dragon could fly with the planes, unseen, and reek devastation on enemy targets – he could get in low and hit specific targets, where our bombers were less precise."

"So, the Allied Command knew about the dragon?" asked Dave.

"Yes and no. The secret operatives knew. Some of the highest Commanders knew, but we never worked with anyone outside of the High-Command. Also, only a few ever met your grandfather in person, and none when he was the dragon."

"This generally went fairly well. However, there was one particularly bad incident. There is a German city called Dresden, which was effectively annihilated by the Allies. History has debated the morality of this attack, but not its' severity. It is listed as the most destructive air-raid of World War Two; including the atomic bombs dropped in Japan. The problem is that the real story is unknown to history."

"Hitler's SS Occult units were stationed there, near the end of the war. Somehow, they had found a last, hidden, community of Fae in the Black Forest – they had refused to leave their homes, believing that they would be safe if they remained hidden. The Nazis came upon them undetected, encircled them entirely, and – armed with flame-throwers – burnt all of them, and that entire section of the forest, to the ground. No one knows why they killed them, but it was done."

"No one knows how Queen Maeve found out, but her grief was great and quickly turned to rage. She came to your grandfather and told him what had been done, crying for vengeance. His vengeance was to be swift and horrible. Luckily, we were aware of his plan, though we could not dissuade him. We went to the High-Command and told them that if they did not send a bombing run to Dresden, there would be no way to disguise what would happen. So, that was what was done."

"There has never been a larger, or more powerful dragon than your grandfather. There was also no dragon attack that ever compared to Dresden. He came, silently through the night and fell upon them with the utmost fury. The SS Occult units were found and incinerated in moments; ironically dying in fire, the same way they had killed the Fae in the Black Forest. But then, he turned his wrath upon the city and the innocent burned with the guilty. He swept over the city – again and again and again – raining fire upon it and all within it. The Allied bombers could see the flames, miles out, and they assumed that they were a second, or even third wave. They dropped their pay-load and returned. No one ever told them otherwise."

"The next time I saw your grandfather, a week later, I asked him if he was satisfied by this destruction. I had never before, and would never again see the look that was in his eyes as he answered me. He told me that he would be satisfied when all of the Nazis burned for their crimes. I have never been more afraid."

"Thankfully, Hitler was dead in just over two months, and the War in Europe ended just over a week after that."

"The High-Command believed that your grandfather was profoundly influential in winning the air-war over first Britain and then Europe. Therefore, they wanted to reward him. He asked only for a cabin, some land with a lake, and some 'gold' – he had a habit of calling all money 'gold'. What he was given was the land and the house you grew up knowing as home. The financial award was never revealed. Also, he was given a guarantee that his home and land would be understood as belonging to him and all his future heirs, and outside of any government jurisdiction of any kind."

"Queen Maeve, and a sizable population of the Fae, moved to the streams, forests, hills and lake of this land and have dwelt there to this day."

"A year after the end of the War, your mother was born. Consistent with history, they had no other children. We believed, therefore, that he was the last dragon. And when he died, the day you were born, it was believed that the time of dragons had ended."

"But you said that you followed me and that things about me led you to believe that I might be a dragon," said Dave.

"Yes," said the professor. "The first thing was that Vinterlogen died the day that you were born and the second was that you were male. However, since the 'dragon-gift' had never been passed from a mother to a son, we had virtually no hope that it would come to you. However, as you aged, you displayed more and more traits consistent with the gift. You had a clear warrior spirit and an indomitable will. Your drive and focus set you in a league of your own. When you became a Navy SEAL, we took considerably more notice. When you killed the vampire, all of our attention was focused upon you; as was that of others."

"The American government learned quite a bit from the Nazis. Most famous would be the technology of rockets, leading to the space-program as well as the ballistic-missile for nuclear defense. However, there was one, very secret and special program that was developed, based on Hitler's pursuit of everything occult. We made a point of engaging this organization, from the beginning, and acting as liaisons of sorts. The idea was that we would not be taken off-guard, like we were with the Nazis, and also, frankly, that we would be able to control some of the information that they had about us."

"I'm not sure why, but they largely ignored the Queen's people. Perhaps they had no wish to look within their own boarders. Perhaps they did not see the Fae as a threat. And perhaps they were unaware of the extent of our people. Who knows? They were, however, tracking several, extremely hostile and powerful individuals and groups."

"In the early-Nineties, they decided to move on these targets, utilizing SEALs and Delta Force. Whether it was chance or fate, you were the first one to successfully eliminate one of their targets. This got you into SEAL Team Six and they have watched your every move, ever since – as have we."

"It was initially unclear how much they knew about the history of the dragons. The good news, as far as we were concerned, is that it was and is very little. We aren't sure whether they suspected that you were a dragon, or if they thought that you were just rather good at killing their targets. You have eliminated several nasties, over the years. You probably only know about the vampire and that business in Nebai, but there were many others that you terminated before they had a chance to manifest their individual supernatural nastiness and attempt to use it against you. It doesn't really matter which missions they were, and they didn't always have an agent show up for the briefing, but you can rest assured that if a mission felt weird or you had the hairs on the back of your neck raise, it was one of them."

"And these aren't the Fae?" asked Dave.

"No," said Tim. "We are the Queen's people. We are loyal to her and live by the laws she has given us. There are many different kinds of us, but that – the loyalty to her Grace – is the same for us all. These other things are very different. They sometimes live in small groups or sometimes rule humans – suspecting or otherwise – but mostly they work alone and are dark and manipulative."

"Those were the beings about which Mr. Ezekiel cared and upon which he focused," said Professor Jones. "Since you quite effectively killed a rather large number of them, he cared about you as well. However, when you became the dragon, he saw a whole new world blossom before him."

"Since you are currently attached to the US military as a high-value asset, he sees the value in continuing that attachment and utilizing you as a 'nuclear-option' of sorts. He is changing focus from eliminating supernatural threats to utilizing a very powerful one as a highly secret, highly effective, killing machine. He, and his organization, believes that you can hit targets no other force can hit, in a way no other force can hit them, and annihilate any evidence in the process. He's quite correct, by the way; you can do all these things. The only concern is that this is the most direct involvement that any government or agency has ever had in selecting targets for a dragon, including in World War Two."

"Then why are you helping him?" asked Dave.

"We're not," said the professor. "We're attempting to guide his hand. For reasons and by means that we do not know, and may never know, Mr. Ezekiel became aware of your transformation at exactly the same time that we did. Our only choices were to pursue you without him, and thus become his adversary, or to work with him and attempt to make sure things were handled … reasonably well."

"Thus far, things have been unproblematic. We are having our nice, informational session, currently. Then, we will do a 'meet-and-greet' tomorrow, with your team."

"How'd the process of selecting members go?" asked Dave.

"More quickly than I expected," answered Professor Jones. "I actually believed that it would have taken weeks or months, to be honest. However, it literally took minutes … perhaps hours. It would appear that Mr. Ezekiel has been scouting a 'special team' for quite some time. Chris was obviously going to join and your extensive experience together, not to mention the fact that he has seen you become the dragon, will help more than you imagine. Your friend, now Chief Petty Officer Diego Wagner, was contacted and told Mr. Ezekiel that he'd think about it. Then, Chris gave him a call … to explain some things. Diego called back immediately and accepted the position. The other two are younger Team Six members, whom I do not believe you have met. Both of them are Petty Officers First Class. One is named James Morrison and the other is Michael Zacchaeus. They have worked together quite a bit and have had two missions that involved supernatural targets. I'm not certain how much they know or what Mr. Ezekiel has told them, but apparently he spoke to them in person and they immediately accepted the positions."

"Well that's good news," said Dave. "The quicker they get here, the quicker I can go home."

"Maybe and maybe not," said the professor with a concerned expression. "If things are as they appear, the quickness of the recruiting is quite good. It means that we have experienced operators who are enthusiastic for a new assignment. However, there might be something else a-foot."

"Yes, you know Chris extremely well, and you trust him – as you should. Yes, you know Diego moderately well and I believe that you should trust him as well. These other two recruits are strangers, both to us and to you. However, Mr. Ezekiel went to them, in person, and they immediately accepted positions about which they, in theory, know almost nothing. As I said already, this might be a very good thing. But it also might be dangerous. I do not trust Mr. Ezekiel, not even remotely. I worry about his plans and schemes. But, we shall see. I am only saying that you ought to be wary."

"I'll try to remember," said Dave. "So, what happens after the Team assembles?"

"Well," said the professor, "more of that will depend on you than you think. We need you to have control of the transformation, both into and out of the dragon-form. For some, this was very easy. But for others, it took considerably more time than we had hoped."

"Once you have control over that, you'll need to work on being in control of what you do, while you are the dragon. You'll need to be able to select the correct target and not incinerate your Team members – or anyone else whom you do not intend, for that matter. You'll need to have controlled flight patterns – this might be easier for you as you have been in modern aircraft and have seen modern fighter jets maneuver. And, extremely importantly, the whole team will have to work on perfecting extraction. You will need to be able to find your Team, before you transform back, and then they will have to be able to get you out, safely – at least until you wake-up and can get yourself out."

"How does that 'sleeping-part' work?" asked Dave.

"That is a very good question," answered the professor. "We're not entirely sure. It seems as if it has more to do with your mind than your body. We think that it is like what happens when a computer 'restarts'. Your mind has to move from coping with being a dragon and return to its original 'settings', as it were. Think of it like what happens when you step off a boat, after a long time at sea. Your body/mind is still trying to compensate for the sea's movement, so you feel awkward. This is similar, but on a much larger scale. What we *do* know is that, typically, the more times that you make the transformation the easier it is both to go into and to come out of that state. The 'sleep' time also shortens with time, but that is extremely relative to the individual. The good news is that your first transformation – and what you did during it – went very well and your recovery time was actually rather quick."

"So, once all of the parts are in place, I shall contact Mr. Ezekiel. He will then come – I'm not certain if he will be coming alone, or bringing other members of his department – and your team will give a demonstration. If he is happy, we move forward. If he is not happy, there will be more training until he is."

"What does 'move forward' mean?" asked Dave.

"From what I understand," said the professor, "that's when you go home. My understanding was that Mr. Ezekiel would not be developing missions for you until he had some idea of when you and your Team would be ready – time sensitivity and all that sort of thing. So, the plan – to my knowledge – was then for you all to go wherever you have arranged to go and to do whatever it is that you do there. When Mr. Ezekiel has some task for you, you will be notified, they will come to pick you up, you will be transported to wherever you are going, complete the mission and be brought back home."

"Will you be staying with me, when I'm not … active?" asked Dave.

"Almost exclusively, no," answered Professor Jones. "We will stay in as close proximity to Mr. Ezekiel as we possibly can. The stated reason for this is that we will be more available to help him assess any given situation and then to offer advice on the best way to handle these situations."

"The unstated reason we will be staying as close as possible is that Mr. Ezekiel is an extremely dangerous man. He is in charge of an ultra-secret government office, with nearly limitless resources, and essentially no over-sight. Basically, he can do anything that he wants, so long as he stays within whatever vague limits the President has set. This is exactly like dealing with a dark, medieval, shadow-government, except with the unspeakable power of the strongest military in world history behind it."

"Dave, I want you to pay extremely close attention to what I say now. You need to be careful. Yes, I think that it is considerably safer to be working with Mr. Ezekiel than against him. However, you need to be conscious of how much power he actually has and what he can do with that power. This man will use whatever means necessary to achieve his goals. I think that you are not in a dangerous position … at the moment, but you could get in one, extremely quickly. We will be doing anything in our ability to keep you and everyone you love safe. But remember that the greatest possible danger is to embrace the illusion of safety and calm when danger is present. Be alert and aware."

"What should I be doing, if I think that there is a problem?" asked Dave.

"You tell us," smiled Tim. "We'll try to get it sorted."

"And if you can't?"

"Let's worry about that when it happens," said Professor Jones. "Hopefully, it never will. Just be careful."

They paused for a moment and Dave stared into the flames of the fireplace. Then a thought occurred to him. "The conversations that I have had with the Angel of Death, in the second one she called me by a strange name and said that 'things like her' – supernatural things – would call me that name. Now, it's true that those conversations felt like a dream, but I know that they are real. So, here's the question: why haven't you called me by that name?"

"What, Saraph?" asked Tim.

"Yeah."

"At first, there were too many people around and it would have been too difficult to explain," said Tim.

"But afterwards," said the professor, "we were being polite. You told us to call you Dave, so we have. This other name is special. To use it is to indicate a special connection. It says 'we know who you really are' and it lets you know who we are, in turn. To begin with, you were not particularly open to developing this sort of connection with us, though it appears that this has since changed. We can use the name, if you'd like, or we can continue to call you by the name of your birth."

"Whichever works for you is fine with me," said Dave. "I actually don't even know what the word means. She's pretty big on me finding things out for myself."

"Yes, I'd imagine so," said Professor Jones. "Most angels are. They usually deliver the message they have been given and not much else."

"So, what does it mean?" Dave, asked.

"The word 'Saraph' means 'the burning one' or 'the fiery one'. It is more common to see the plural: 'Seraphim', which is the highest choir of angels," said Professor Jones. "And before you ask, no you are not an angel, and no one with any sense would think that you were. The wife and child are a sure give-away that you cannot possibly be an angel."

Dave laughed. "Yeah, that and the ability to burn entire cities to the ground."

"Actually," said the professor, "that would be exactly why you might be mistaken for an angel. What do you think happened to Sodom and Gomorrah? Angels came and burned the cities to the ground. Angels, however, cannot reproduce and never get married. Anyway, you are not an angel."

"Do you have any other questions?"

"No," said Dave. "I don't suppose that I can call Sabrina."

"We are just below the Arctic Circle. There is no phone service, which you can use at this time," said Professor Jones. "Why don't you join Chris and have a few pints and something to eat. The others should be coming in by Seahawk tomorrow."

. . . .

Dave walked into the most central room of the large cabin. Sitting in a large, soft chair, next to a fireplace, with his feet up, was Chris. He had been reading a book, but had set in on the table next to him and was looking into the fire, quietly. Dave sat down in the opposite chair, put his feet up and quietly did the same, for some time.

Tim came out of the kitchen area with two pint glasses of beer and a tray with some bread, pretzels, cheese and mustard, for dipping.

He set it on the large coffee-table that was in front of them and left without saying anything.

Chris lifted his beer, without looking from the fire, and drank. Then he said "You learn a lot?"

"Yeah," said Dave, reaching for his drink.

"What do you think?"

Dave took a deep breath, a drink of his beer, and said, "I'm not sure. Some of the stuff they told me was … pretty crazy."

"Crazier than watching your brother turn into a dragon, while you're under serious enemy fire, in the middle of enemy-controlled territory?"

"What's goin' on?"

"I just had a lot of time to think, that's all," said Chris, taking another drink.

"What happened to 'that's the job'?"

"Nothing. Indeed, that *is* the job. Some of what you said before is starting to sink in. I still think that we made the right decision to come up here, but what comes next? I don't know."

"They got Diego … after you called him."

"I figured he'd come," said Chris.

"What'd you say to him?"

"Nothing." Chris paused, "Nothing other than that he'd understand more about the mission with the hyena-monsters if he came up here. I wasn't allowed to say anything about you."

Dave laughed, "I suppose they are planning some 'big reveal'."

"Who knows," sighed Chris. "Anyway, what'd you learn?"

"Well, they led with a story about Asgardians and Odin making warriors into dragons to battle the Frost Giants in Ragnarok. It kind of went from there. There was a bunch in there about faeries and their Queen. Some about conspiracies with governments, where dragons were involved. And apparently my grandfather, who fought in World War Two, was the reason that the Allies won the Battle of Britain, gained air-superiority over Europe, he also burned Dresden to the ground – because the Nazis killed some faeries, of course – and, oh yeah, he was five hundred years old. So, you know, the usual stuff you learn about family history, sitting next to a fire … next to the Arctic Circle."

Chris laughed heartily. "Just that? And I thought that it might be something weird."

They both drank, set their glasses down, and took some of the food. "I don't really know what to believe, though," said Dave.

"What do you mean, about the faeries and all that? I mean, it's weird, but I think we have been seeing weird things for years. And we abandoned anything resembling normal in Afghanistan. For a lot of reasons, actually."

"Other than the dragon," said Dave, "what reasons?"

"I told you, I've been thinking about what you said before," said Chris. "I never trusted politicians; none of them. But, telling the press what we did, where we did it, and who we are, while we were still in the field, is a whole new level of ridiculousness. I think you might have a point."

"Yeah?" said Dave. "Then this won't be a surprise. That Mr. Ezekiel? Well, the 'super-secret' department he runs is based on something Hitler started in the SS, where they track 'supernatural monsters' or things like that. Now, he wants to change his focus and use us — me really — to get things done that the military could 'never achieve'. The thing is, he has virtually unlimited resources, only vague direction from the President, himself, and virtually no oversight whatsoever. So, basically, he can do whatever he wants ... and he's both totally shady and extremely arrogant."

"Sounds like a great, new boss," said Chris, finishing his beer.

"Professor Jones said to be careful, but I'm not sure of what, or how we would go about being careful," said Dave.

"Maybe he meant to try not to make a problem," said Chris. "I mean we're giving the guy what he wants. There is no reason for him to do anything extreme."

"Unless he wants to kill me, instead of using me," said Dave. "It's what he did for years."

"That's a little paranoid, Dave. If he wanted to kill you, he could have easily done it while you were asleep, back on the ship."

"True, but I still really don't want to let my guard down, you know?"

"Indeed," said Chris. "So we need to have each other's back. I'm sure that we can trust Diego. What about the other guys?"

"Don't know," said Dave. "What worries me is that Jones isn't sure what to think either. Apparently, Ezekiel spoke to them personally and they signed right up."

"Well, that could be very good."

"Yeah … or very bad," said Dave. "We'll just have to meet them and see what we think."

"They tell you about the training?" asked Chris.

"Yeah," said Dave. "Sounds like I need to learn how to control the whole process. It really sounded like an 'all-me' thing. I imagine that the training for you guys is mostly about not freaking-out when a dragon shows up."

"How they gonna teach that?" asked Chris, with a laugh.

. . . .

Five men were standing near the beach at the inner-most point of the fjord. It was a cold, crisp late-morning and there was a thin layer of fresh, sparkling snow on the ground, which crunched under their boots as they walked.

They had been briefly introduced when Diego and the other two had joined Dave and Chris. James Morrison was a six foot-two, extremely muscular, very dark-skinned black man with a shaved head and a thick, spade-beard. Michael Zacchaeus – who went by 'Mike' – was also about six foot-two, but skinnier, with standard-military-regulation, buzzed hair, a clean shaven, pale face, wore glasses and had a southern accent. Professor Jones had sent them out, right after he had introduced himself and them.

Now, he and Tim – whom he had not introduced – walked down to the assembled SEALs. He pulled Dave aside and whispered in his ear, "You are absolutely certain? I could do this another way if you're not."

"No," whispered Dave, "you said this would be the most effective way, so, I'm sure. But here," he took off his heavy coat, "I sort of like this. Hold on to it for me." Dave was wearing "blueberry" NWU pants, a grey t-shirt, standard-issue boots, and his hair was in a pony-tail. A point of interest: Dave never wore his wedding ring while over-seas. When he left home, he would leave it with Sabrina – the logic being that if something were to happen she would always have it. When he returned home, they always had a special moment alone together, where she would slip the ring back on his finger.

Dave silently walked the one hundred yards down to the water's edge and stood with his back to the others. He had not slept last night. It was early evening when he and Chris had finished talking and he had spent all the time since reading most of his grandfather's book. He had a very clear idea of what he must, now, do. He took a deep breath and focused his mind.

"Gentlemen," began Professor Jones as Dave walked to the water's edge. "An example generally makes an explanation easier to understand. Please pay very close attention to Master Chief Petty Officer Shepherd. He will now give a brief presentation that will display to you all why you are here." The professor took a deep breath and said loudly, "Whenever you're ready, Mr. Shepherd!"

Dave took another deep breath, trying to remember every detail of what his grandfather had written about transformation and control. He closed his eyes and cleared his mind. He vividly pictured himself as the dragon and said to himself, "I am the dragon and the dragon is me." He concentrated on his center, imagining a great fire building within him. He could *actually* feel the heat quickly build. He raised his arms to the sky, tilted back his head, and inhaled deeply. Then, as he exhaled strongly, he pushed.

The men watched as Dave raised his arms to the sky and tilted back his head. "What do you think he's doin'?" said Mike to James. But before he could answer, it happened.

There was a flash of light and a wave of heat. A pillar of fire shot into the sky and a deafening roar echoed through the fjord. Where Dave had been standing was a dragon, with wings out-stretched, breathing fire into the sky. His scales were black, as were his wings, though there were some dark red highlights in them. Chris thought to himself: "He's bigger this time" – the dragon was well over fifty feet tall, not including his tail, with more than a sixty-foot wingspan. His huge head also had black horns with dark red highlights, which Chris had not before noticed.

The dragon turned his head, on his long neck and looked back at them. His enormous eyes were the same ice-blue as Dave's except that there was no white and instead of the round pupils of a man, his were the slits of a cat's eye. Diego, James and Mike instinctively took a few steps back and defensively raised their arms. The dragon turned back towards the sky, slightly bent his knees and then leapt into flight.

For his immense size, he was amazingly fast. His powerful wings surged through the air as he climbed up and up. Dave was conscious and aware that he was now the dragon. He remembered his first transformation and that, then, his awareness was more dream-like. This time all of his senses were crystal clear. He was the dragon and the dragon was him.

Soaring into the sky, his senses were amazingly acute. He could see every detail of every snowflake on the ground, far below. He could hear them drift through the sky. His sense of smell was amazing. Additionally, he could feel a strong intuitive sense of everything that was happening in the vicinity - from the fluctuation of the slightest currents of wind, to a squirrel scampering on a tree branch a half-mile away. He wheeled in his flight, turning over his back, left shoulder, back towards the fjord, far, far below. Plunging, with unearthly speed, he leveled and blasted fire across the icy water, sending up a thick mist of fog. He streaked over the group on the shore, then over the cabin and tightly wheeled to the right returning toward the water. He roared as he breathed a stream of flame along the shore as he passed them again, vanishing into the fog.

The men by the shore did not move. Diego, James and Michael were frozen in terror. Chris was in absolute awe. He had only briefly seen the dragon before, and then only in the dark; this was a whole new experience. Professor Jones stood calmly with no expression on his face. Tim stood, smiling brightly with joy gleaming in his eyes. After the dragon had vanished in the mist there was silence; only the crackling of the flames on the shore could be heard.

James turned his head to the professor and opened his mouth to speak. The dragon silently swooped out of the mist and landed, with almost no sound, before them. The three new Team members simultaneously crouched to the ground and cried out in abject terror. The dragon made no move indicating that he noticed the men, but rather gently lay down on the earth. Folding his wings and curling his tail and neck, he closed his eyes and, in less than a minute, he was asleep.

The "ashing" that Chris had earlier described happened in less than two minutes and when the cloud of ash cleared, Dave was laying on the ground, curled on his side in an almost-fetal position, asleep and naked. "Right," said Professor Jones. "Get him to his bed and then we can meet in the central room, by the fire, to discuss what just happened."

Chris and Tim walked over to Dave, picked him up under the knees and beneath the shoulders, and carried him back to the cabin. Professor Jones went before them and held the door open as they went in. Then he turned to the others. "Come on," he said, and he went inside.

Diego, James and Mike slowly stood up. They looked at each other and then at the swath of flame, burning brightly along the shore. None of them spoke. Then, they turned and walked back towards the cabin.

. . . .

"It just doesn't make any sense," said Mike. "I mean, it's not possible. Like, the physics are all wrong. Just start with the gainin' and loosin' of mass. Goin' from five-somethin' to fifty-somethin' in an instant; that is just not possible."

Chris walked into the central room, where he and Dave had talked the night before, and sat in one of the comfortable chairs that had been assembled in a semi-circle, with a break in the center of the arch, around the coffee table, by the fireplace.

James and Diego were nodding in agreement to what Mike had said, but stopped and turned as Professor Jones as Tim walked into the room and stood together in the break in the arch of chairs. Professor Jones spoke: "Now that you have seen what all of this is about, it will be much easier for me to explain what we are doing."

"You have all been selected because you have had operational experience with … supernatural elements. The degree to which you are aware of your past experiences varies, but you have had them nonetheless."

"This Team is an incredibly specialized unit. I'm not entirely certain exactly what Mr. Ezekiel has told you, but your job will be to act in support of missions where the dragon is to be deployed."

"Wait a minute," said James in a deep voice. "You need to explain what just happened in a little more detail."

"What would you like to know?" asked Professor Jones.

"How about you start with the dragon, and go from there," said James.

"Right," said Professor Jones. "Well, as you know from our introductions, his name is Master Chief Petty Officer David Shepherd – he'll probably tell you to call him Dave. He joined the Navy, right out of high school and the SEALs immediately after. He has been a SEAL for about eighteen years, in Team Six for sixteen of those. He is a highly distinguished and decorated operator, even being awarded the Navy Cross for some of his actions in Ramadi. His personal life is his business to tell, but if you have any questions about any of the details of his military service, you are welcome to read his dossier. Mr. Ezekiel has put one together on each of you – he thought it would make it easier for you to get to know each other more quickly."

"I wasn't asking about the man," said James. "I was asking about the actual dragon."

"Well," continued the professor, "The short version of the story is that he has the ability – a trait which he inherited – to turn into a dragon."

"I wanna know how that works," interrupted Mike, "because it ain't physically possible."

"Magic," said Tim, matter-of-factly.

"Excuse me?!!" said James, exasperated.

"It's magic," said Tim with a smile.

"Who the hell are you?" asked James, with more than a hint of anger.

"This is my associate, Mr. Smith," said Professor Jones. "Mr. Smith, would you be so good as to take care of those other matters we discussed earlier, while I finish in here?"

"Absolutely, Professor Jones," said Tim. He turned and left the room without another word.

"I can tell you what happened the first time," said Chris.

"Ok," said James. All turned to look at Chris, who had been quiet up to this point.

"We were on an Op in Afghanistan and we got ambushed. Our two other guys got killed, but when Dave got hit, instead of going down, he did what he did earlier. It was the same thing: a flash of light and heat, pillar of fire, roar, really big dragon – though, Professor, he was about double the size this time."

"Yes," said the professor, "that was to be expected. He knows what he is doing now so he is manifesting completely. I imagine that his senses were profoundly acute this time, as well. I would be surprised if he was ever bigger than this, now that he knows what he he's doing."

"Anyway," continued Chris, "he took off and killed all the bad-guys. Then he came back and did the same thing he did out there. After that, he slept for a little over a day."

"How do you know that it was the first time?" asked James.

"Because he's my brother. We've been together since my mother died and his family adopted me when I was six. He's never done this before that time," answered Chris.

"This is weird as hell," said James.

"Yes," answered Professor Jones, "but you have had unusual missions before, have you not?"

Mike answered, "We did have that thing with the spiders in that cave complex in Afghanistan, when Bob and Keith got killed."

"Yeah," said James, "but those were just animals. They were big, but not as big as we thought. It was all just an illusion because of the dark and our night-vision gear malfunctioning."

"All of your gear malfunctioned at the same time?" asked Professor Jones. "That seems an odd coincidence."

"So?" said James.

"Right. So then why were you convinced or told to never discuss that part of the mission and why was it conveniently left out of the report?"

"I wasn't told anything," said James, now defensive. "I just realized the truth; that's all."

Diego laughed. "Yeah. Just like I 'realized the truth' that the hyena-monsters Chris and I killed in Nebai were 'guys in costumes trying to scare us' even though we turned their bodies to dust only after we cut out their still-beating-hearts and threw them into a fire."

"That really happened?" asked Mike.

"Indeed," smiled Chris. "True story; Dave was there too. By the way, Diego, I think we've now figured out why that fire didn't hurt him."

Diego nodded.

"Did he turn into a dragon when he saw them?" ask James, sarcastically.

"No," answered Chris, un-phased. "I told you that it had only happened once before today."

"I don't buy it," said James.

"Did you not see the exact same thing that I did out there?" asked Diego. "Because I'm pretty open to believing all sorts of things after that."

"If you don't mind," said Professor Jones to James and Mike, "what did Mr. Ezekiel say to you two to convince you to come here?"

"He actually *did* mentioned the spider-cave and said that we had done a great job and showed discretion after," said Mike.

"Yeah," said James, "but he also said that we would be joining an ultra-secret, elite Team that would be operating on an entirely different level, for select missions."

"We got a promotion and a serious pay-raise," added Mike.

"On top of it, we would only have to complete this training, and then we could go back to our team and continue to operate there. If a special mission comes up, we get pulled. After, we get to go back. Sounded like a good deal," said James.

"Why, what did he tell you guys?" asked Mike.

"I got a similar story," said Diego, "but I haven't decided what I will be doing when I'm not active on this Team. Though, I'm pretty sure that I won't be going back to my old Team."

"I was with Dave when this all happened," said Chris, "I didn't need to be recruited; I go where he goes."

"I only ask," continued Professor Jones, "because I expected that you would be more open to ... the special features of our Team."

"Ok," said James, "but when Mike asked a totally legitimate question about how this works, the answer he got was 'magic'."

"That's because that is the correct answer to the question," answered Professor Jones, with a smile.

"Well, I believe in science," said James.

"Petty Officer First Class Morrison," answered Professor Jones, "science is not a religion. Science is a method of inquiry that yields a given body of knowledge. This knowledge changes over time as further inquiry or additional understanding increases or augments the body of information gained by this method. Science deals with things that are empirically verifiable, numerically quantifiable, and reliably repeatable. This means that there are a great many things that exist within the world – and which everyone agrees exist within the world – that are not within the scope of understanding that belongs to science."

"Give me one example," said James.

"Love," said Professor Jones.

Chris smiled. James had no reply.

"You see, James," said the professor, "there are a great many things in the world that no one truly understands. Most of those questions begin with the words 'why' or 'how'. What we do know for certain is that Dave has, twice now, turned into a dragon. This is a pattern and we are assuming – with very good reason – that it will continue to happen."

"What's the reason?" asked Mike.

"That's what happened with all his ancestors, throughout history, who also turned into dragons," answered Professor Jones.

"So, there were other dragons?" asked Mike in surprise.

"Yes, several," answered Professor Jones. "As I was saying, what we do know is that Dave is a dragon and that he has agreed to operate with this Team, at the behest of the United States government. It's actually not all that complicated."

"So, what's our role?" asked James.

"Exactly what Mr. Ezekiel said it would be," said Professor Jones. "You will be on an ultra-secret, elite Team, which will be operating on an entirely different level, for very select missions."

"Yeah," said James, "but what do we actually do?"

"The specifics will depend on the mission," said the professor, "but, generally speaking, you will insert with Dave, act in a supporting role while he does his dragon-business, and then get him – and the rest of you – out safely. However, one of your most important jobs will be to make absolutely certain that he is safe in the time immediately after he transforms back. As you have seen, when he returns to this form he … sleeps. At this time he is incredibly vulnerable. You will be keeping him safe and getting him out, until he awakens and can care for himself."

"So, my job is to carry the guy with the pony-tail out of combat zones, while he sleeps for, what did you say before … about a day?!"

"That's the job," said Chris plainly as he looked directly at James' eyes.

"Great," said James, looking down.

"Right," said Professor Jones. "So, once a mission is decided upon and you are brought in, you will be briefed and transported to the target area. The chain-of-command is quiet simple. Dave is both senior, as well as the dragon, so he will operate as the squad-leader while he is not in dragon-form or unconscious. If he is in one of those conditions, Chris will operate as squad-leader. This is both because he is next in rank, and because he has the most experience operating with Dave. Are there any other questions?"

"Yeah," said Diego, "I'm not clear on what additional training we need to do the job that you described. I'm pretty sure that I can do all of that now."

"Yes, I should hope so," smiled the professor. "Most of this training is supposed to be to help Dave have the control he needs to do what he will need to do. However, that being said, judging by this morning, he's probably already there. I'll need to talk to him when he wakes up, but I'm actually quite amazed. I've never seen or heard of one being this advanced, this quickly."

"He wants to go home," said Chris, simply.

"What?!" asked James, clearly exasperated.

"Dave wants to go home. He overwhelmingly wants to be with his wife, his daughter and his family. He is *extremely* focused on getting back to them, especially his wife."

"Well, that's great," said James. "We're working with a guy who's completely distracted by a girl back home?"

"Yes," said Chris. "And the longer that he's away from her the more broody he'll get – it's exhausting. But … that works a totally different way than you'd think when it comes to training or actual missions. It's like he flips a switch when we're in the field. He is so motivated to get back to her that he is capable of unbelievable things. We've operated together on nearly every mission over eighteen years, and I've seen him do things that you couldn't imagine. Through it all, I never felt in danger when I was working with him."

"Um … I got shot in that thing in Ramadi," said Diego. "I'm just sayin'."

"Indeed," Chris said with his crooked smile. "But that was a ridiculous situation and it wasn't Dave's fault you got hit. Though he definitely deserves the credit for us both getting out alive."

"True story," laughed Diego. "That was crazy."

"All I'm saying is that, while some guys start looking forward to going home and totally slack off – thus getting them or their Team-mates killed or injured – Dave is totally different. He gets hyper-focused on successfully finishing the job so he can go home – with honor – and be with her. So, I think that's why he is able to do all the things you want him to do, Professor. You talked to him yesterday, told him what he needed to do to get back to her, and he's doing it."

"Quite a plausible theory," said Professor Jones. "To finish answering Diego's question, the part of the training, not directly related to something that Dave has to do, absolutely has to do with all of you. We need to be sure that you can work comfortably together as a Team."

"We're SEALs," said James, "we work in Teams; that's what we do."

"Yes," said the professor, "that's absolutely correct. However, what you do not usually do is to do that work while operating with a dragon. To put it plainly, we need to be certain that you won't freak out … like some of you did earlier."

Chris laughed, but before anyone could say anything in reply, Professor Jones continued: "However, in your defense, you had not before seen a dragon, nor did you believe that they were things that existed in the world, outside of books or movies. I have high-hopes that you will successfully complete the next drill." He smiled.

"So, if there aren't any other questions, there are several drinks and snacks in the kitchen-area over there. I'm quite certain that you shall all find that we are fully stocked with your favorites, however obscure that they may be. You should spend this time building your ... Team-ness ... or whatever you want to call it. This evening, we shall procure anything that you may want for dinner and we can go from there. I'm going to check in on Dave."

The professor got up and left the room. Strangely, no one questioned whether or not his particular dinner request would be filled. The day had been sufficiently strange that now, almost anything seemed possible.

Everyone sat quietly for a few moments. James was the first to break the silence. He stood and said, "I'm going to get a beer, any of you want anything? I figure, if I'm going to be carrying a guy around all the time, I'd better get used to getting stuff."

Chris smiled his crooked smile and stood as well. "I'll give you a hand. Oh, and James, a support role is usually pretty important. There's nothing wrong with being a wing-man."

James smiled, "maybe you're right."

. . . .

Dave woke up about three hours after transforming back from the dragon. The professor was sitting quietly by his bedside when he woke. The professor was shocked that Dave had woken so quickly – the only other who had ever had such a short sleeping time had been his grandfather, and that was after Centuries.

"How are you feeling?" asked the professor.

"I'm fine," said Dave. "How did I do?"

"How do *you* think that you did?" asked the professor. "How difficult was the transformation? How were your senses? Could you think clearly? Did you hit what you meant to hit?"

"Yeah," said Dave. "I guess everything went fine. The transformation was easy, I did it just like what the book said to do and it just happened. I was never unaware and everything was clear. Everything else was good too."

"Excellent," said the professor. "I'm glad that the book helped so much; I had hoped that it would."

"What happens now," asked Dave.

"Well, if you feel up to it, I'd like to do a drill with the Team tomorrow to see if they can work more comfortably with you now that they have seen you and we have discussed it."

"How'd that go?"

"Not as well as I had hoped, but not as badly as I had feared. If they can keep it together tomorrow, I'll contact Mr. Ezekiel and after his evaluation we can move forward."

"And I can go home?" asked Dave.

"Yes," smiled the professor. "And then you can go home. Now. Why don't you get dressed and join your Team for some drinks. I'm sure that you'll have a lot to talk about."

. . . . . .

Dave was greeted, with varied degrees of warmth, when he joined the others. Everyone was pleasantly surprised that he was awake so soon. Chris handed him a bottle of dark, sweet Norwegian lager. They all drank together and the conversation stuck to light, casual topics, as they all got to know each other.

There was a lot of discussion about past missions, but no one asked Dave any questions about being a dragon. He was not surprised – among warriors, often there are things and details that are left unsaid. Dave figured that either they already knew everything that they wanted to know, they were too uncomfortable to ask, or they didn't care. He didn't feel particularly like talking, so any of those explanations was fine with him. He participated minimally in the conversation and drank a few bottles of beer. After a while, he walked over to the fireplace by himself with a fresh bottle, sat in one of the chairs and quietly looked into the flames.

The others watched him from the kitchen area, which was open and attached to the other room.

James turned to Chris and smiled. "I see what you mean about the brooding," he said quietly.

"This is nothing," replied Chris quietly, with his crooked smile. "He's only been away for just over a week."

The Team all laughed and went back to their drinks.

The next day they had an exercise where they all moved together to a location, Dave transformed into the dragon and destroyed a target, returned to them, transformed back and they successful got back to the cabin. The Team handled working with the dragon as if they had never done otherwise – though in discussion later, they all agreed that they would never really be completely comfortable with an actual dragon, though they could fake it for the mission.

The professor contacted Mr. Ezekiel via satellite phone and gave him the news that the Team was ready to be evaluated.

"Well what do you think of their performance?" asked Mr. Ezekiel.

"Frankly," said the professor, "I'm impressed beyond my ability to put it into words. Dave is preforming at a level profoundly beyond his experience, and the Team has worked together very well, in the field. I know that it's only been three days, but I think they're ready."

"Great!" said Mr. Ezekiel. "Send them back to wherever they're going."

"I'm sorry, I thought that you wanted to evaluate them in person," said Professor Jones.

"I trust your judgement," Mr. Ezekiel replied. "Besides, I absolutely hate the cold. I'm not coming up to the Arctic Circle. Nah, I can see the results after they do something real. Send them home." Mr. Ezekiel hung up the phone.

Professor Jones looked at the phone in his hand and then set it down. He sighed and said to the empty room, "I'm sure that they'll be thrilled." He smiled and left to tell the team.

Chapter 3

or

"Now We All Know"

Sabrina lay in Dave's arms, her head on his shoulder, casually twirling her fingers in his chest hair. Their sheets were soft and cool on their skin and the flickering light of the candle by their bedside cast a soft glow over the entirety of their bedroom. "Mmm, I really missed you," she said softly.

"I missed you, too," said Dave, squeezing her slightly more closely to him.

"Christi said that she would play with Stasia tomorrow, so we can sleep in. Mama and Dad said that they could stay home and talk about whatever you have on your mind, whenever you are ready, Mr. Mysterious," she smiled, lifting up slightly, pivoting and moving in his arms so that she could look into her husband's ice-blue eyes.

Dave's left arm was around Sabrina's shoulder but now slid to her lower-back and he moved his right hand to caress her cheek, "I'm not being mysterious. I just don't want to tell the story any more times than necessary. Chris will be there as well ... so you don't think I'm crazy."

"Oh, I don't think you're crazy," said Sabrina, sliding the hand that had been twirling his chest hair around his ribs and pressing her body into his. "I know it," she giggled softly.

Dave closed his eyes as he felt her soft, warm lips press into his.

. . . .

It was late morning when they finally were all sitting together in the room next to the kitchen. Dave and Sabrina had softly awoken, made coffee, and took a quiet walk around the lake, hand-in-hand. It was June now, so Dave preferred to take walks earlier in the day, before it got warm. They came back and sat down, joining the others.

Sabrina was snuggled next to Dave, on the couch and Mary, John, and Chris were seated in the other soft, comfortable chairs. Dave made tense eye-contact with Chris, who smiled back with his crooked smile and thought to himself, "This is going to be great."

Dave took a deep breath. His right arm was around Sabrina and he gave her a soft squeeze as he started speaking. "This is sort of a long story and it's really weird. If you want more details than I'm giving you, please ask. I guess I'll just start by getting right to the point." He took another deep breath. "I'm … a dragon."

Sabrina gave a short laugh. "You're a what?"

"A dragon, Darling," smiled Mary.

Dave's mouth hung open for a moment. "You don't sound surprised, Mama."

"That's because I'm not."

"What? You knew?" asked Dave.

"We weren't sure, but we suspected," said John.

Chris laughed loudly, "This is awesome!"

"Please wait a second," said Sabrina, sitting up a bit. "A dragon? You aren't speaking metaphorically about fighting skill or something like that; you mean a literal dragon?"

"Yes," said Dave quietly and shyly, "I can … turn into one."

"When did you find this out?"

"About a week ago, in Afghanistan, right before I called you from the ship," said Dave. "Please don't be angry at me."

"I'm not angry … I'm … I don't know," said Sabrina. "Is this really real?"

"Yes, Darling, it's really real," said Mary. "This is a trait that men in my family sometimes have. My father could do it as well."

"You knew about Grandfather?" asked Dave.

"Well of course we did, Dave. He told me all about it, when he thought that I was old enough to understand and he told your father after we were married; when I was pregnant with you, actually."

"Why didn't you tell me?" asked Dave.

"Because my father said that it wasn't possible for it to happen. If I had been a boy, yes. But not as it was. We didn't believe him but thought that it would be best not to tell you a crazy story until there was a good reason to tell it. I take it you already knew, Chris, when Dave told us all just now?"

Chris laughed, "Indeed! I saw it happen ... all three times."

"Chris," said Sabrina quietly, "my husband can ... turn into a dragon?"

"Yup," said Chris smiling, "But don't worry, he has complete control of it."

"What does that mean?" she asked.

"It means that it won't 'just happen'," said Dave. "I have to make it happen. And when I do, I'm still me; I'm in as much control of what I do as if I were doing it right now." He gently turned her to face him and looked into her grey-blue eyes. "I'm still me, Sabrina."

Sabrina felt confused and scared, but she smiled. "Ok. I love you, Dave, I'm just a little confused about this whole thing. I mean, how did it happen? What does it mean?"

"Well, how it started for my family is a long story that I'm not sure I believe. How it happened for me is sort of complicated. You see, I got shot-"

"What?!" cried Sabrina, moving back. "Where? Show me?"

Dave started to feel nervous. "It's ok, I'm fine. The wounds disappeared when I turned back from being the dragon."

"It's not ok!" said Sabrina raising her voice. Tears were gathering in her eyes and threatening to rush forth. "It's not 'ok' that you got shot!"

"Sabrina, I'm fine," said Dave. "Oh Baby, I love you." He wiped a tear from her cheek. "Everything is going to be ok."

Sabrina sat back, looking into Dave's eyes. "What does this all mean for us?"

"Other than my new job," said Dave as calmly as possible, "it shouldn't change anything at all for us." This is what he had feared, more than anything in his entire life. He was afraid that, upon finding out, Sabrina would be forever changed toward him. Right here, this very moment, was the moment of truth. Dave took a breath and waited to see what Sabrina would say next.

"So, you're still mine; still my husband and Anastasia's father? They're not going to make you leave us and never come back?" asked Sabrina.

"Of course I'm yours! There's nothing in this world or any other that could pull me away from you!"

"I know *that's* right." said Chris, quietly.

"Sabrina, the only thing this changes for us is that I'll be with you *more*, not less! For my new job, I live here with you and only leave briefly when I leave at all. And we never, ever have to talk about the dragon and you never, ever have to see it. Everything else can be exactly like it was before."

"Are you sure?" she asked.

"I never saw my father turn into a dragon, nor did my mother," smiled Mary. "And though he was a big man-"

"Huge," interrupted John. "The biggest and scariest man I have even seen."

"Not helpful, John!" said Mary scowling at her husband. She paused but then turned back to face Sabrina and smiled, saying: "His size, as a man, was not any different, the entire time my mother knew him. So, Dave won't change in the least, unless he gets fat from drinking too much beer. So – as I was saying – my father was very kind and gentle to me and my mother. He told me about many of his actions in the war, as a dragon, but at home, he was just … my father."

"So," said Dave, "nothing needs to change, for us … as long as you still want me."

"Of course I still want you," said Sabrina. "I'm just a little … confused … surprised … scared … I don't know. But, of course I love you!" She pulled close to him and they kissed.

"You two know, we're still here, right?" said John.

Dave and Sabrina looked into each other's eyes and smiled. "Yes, Dad," said Dave. "How could I forget?"

Sabrina cuddled up to Dave and held the arm he had around her, closely. Bastet jumped up on the couch, from nowhere, and curled up next to Sabrina, purring loudly. With the hand closest to the small, fluffy cat, Sabrina softly pet her behind her ears, while the other hand continued to hold closely onto Dave's arm.

"I know I'm changing the subject," Dave continued, "but, since I'm going to be home most of the time now, I was wondering if I could help-out at the Campin' Store, from time to time?"

"Well," said John, laughing, "I'll have to check your references, but I think that we can work something out."

"How do you want to tell your sisters?" asked Mary, getting back on topic.

"About the Campin' Store? I guess, I'll just tell them whenever it comes up; I don't think that they'll care all that much about it." Dave laughed.

Mary frowned.

"Sorry, Mama. I don't know, I don't want it to be weird."

"It'll only be weird if you don't tell them," said Mary.

"I mean, Christi's here, but Gayle is down in Virginia," began Dave.

"She's coming home," said Mary. "I'm sorry Chris, did she tell you?"

"Yeah," said Chris, "this morning. She's leaving the Navy."

"What?!" asked Dave. "She just made Captain a few months ago!"

"Yeah, in January," said Chris. "But, I guess things were getting sort of weird. Directives were coming down about prosecution, which she really didn't like, and after she was home for Uncle Pete's funeral, she decided that she wanted to come home for good and get a job with the DA's office in Farmington. They let her take early retirement and she should be home by the Fourth of July. It's one of the reasons I'm up here, instead of looking for a place in Norfolk."

"So, why don't you tell both of them, together, when we have the picnic on the Fourth?" said Mary.

"Ok, Mama," said Dave. "Is everything really ok?" he asked squeezing Sabrina softly.

"Mmhm," nodded Sabrina, cuddling in closer to him.

Bastet climbed up on Sabrina's lap and licked Dave's hand. "Prrrow!!!"

"Well, apparently her Ladyship agrees, so I think you're good," said John.

. . . .

Though Sabrina had said that everything was ok, Mary sensed that she was still working on understanding the new information she had received that morning. So, Mary took Christi and Anastasia to town for lunch and some errands and Chris went with John to the Campin' Store. Mary told Dave and Sabrina that they wouldn't be back until dinner and would bring pizza home, so they didn't need to worry about making anything.

Sensing what Mary was doing, the couple thanked her, gave their little girl a kiss, and waved as the vehicles pulled away. "I guess we have the rest of the day to ourselves," smiled Sabrina.

"Are you sure that you are ok?" asked Dave.

"I told you that I was," she said. "I mean, I don't understand any of this, but it isn't like you did anything or anything sounds like it will be all that different for us. So, yeah, I'm ok. Are you?"

"I guess," said Dave. "The biggest thing I have been thinking about is how you would react, so, I actually haven't really thought about how I feel about it at all. I guess that it doesn't really matter how I feel. It isn't like I can change anything about it."

Sabrina took his hand and led him into the house. "Are you hungry?"

"Not really. You?"

"No," said Sabrina. "You know what might be fun?"

"What?" asked Dave.

"How long has it been since we went swimming together? I don't mean swimming across the lake, or anything athletic. Just playing in the water together and then resting on the deck for a while."

"That sounds nice. It's not too warm out today though, won't you get cold?"

"If I do, we can get out and you can warm me up, on our chair in the sun."

"Ok," smiled Dave.

They went to their bedroom and got changed into swimsuits. They took towels and went out to the deck. Dave was right, it was a partly cloudy, cool day for early June. Sabrina went to the end of the deck and turned to Dave, smiling playfully. In that moment, he was once again struck by how utterly beautiful his wife was. The sun danced in her dark auburn hair and the smooth, feminine curves of her body took his breath away. "Now, don't push me in," she said coyly; tilting her head slightly to the side with a flirtatious, pretended shyness.

Dave smiled, "Ok." He ran across the deck and jumped into the cold lake.

The splash from Dave entering the lake sprayed cold droplets of water onto Sabrina. Her voice went higher than its usual register as she cried out, "David!" laughing and wincing from the cold.

"What?" he asked from the water, laughing. "I didn't push you in. The water jumped."

She playfully scrunched her nose at him and jumped into the water. She came up, laughing and wrapped her arms around Dave, holding him tightly. "Oh my God, it's so cold," she said breathlessly.

Dave laughed and spun her around in the water. "How are you not freezing?" she said, still laughing, but with her teeth chattering.

"I don't know," he said smiling. "The cold never really bothered me; I actually like it. You know that I usually don't wear a coat and I prefer shorts most of the time."

"Yeah, but this is ridiculous. I have to get out."

"Ok, let me help you." Dave helped lift Sabrina as she climbed on the deck. Both of them knew that she could get out without him, but there was something gentle and intimate about him helping her out of the water.

Dave quickly pulled himself out of the water, grabbed her towel and wrapped it around her; holding her shivering body tightly. "Ok," she said, with her teeth chattering. "Maybe swimming wasn't the best idea."

Dave was vigorously rubbing her arms and shoulders through the towel, to warm her up. "Nah, this is great."

"Let's lie in the sun," she said nodding her head toward the double chaise lounge, where Dave's towel had been laid out.

"Ok," said Dave.

They lay down together on Dave's towel and he held her, tightly wrapped in her towel, rubbing her back and arms to warm her. Sabrina's head was pushed tightly to his chest and she curled closely to his body. "You really got cold quickly," said Dave

"I can't believe that there isn't ice on that lake!" said Sabrina, still shivering.

"Well, it's really deep out there, so it stays cold for a long time. I don't think you've ever been in the water here before mid-July, have you?"

"Is the reason that you're always warm … the dragon?" said Sabrina softly, looking up to Dave's face.

"Maybe," he replied, "I don't really know."

Sabrina raised her hand to Dave's cheek, looked into his eyes, and said, "I'll never stop loving you."

Dave took a deep breath and felt a wave of emotion wash over him. Sabrina wiped a tear from his eye and smiled. They pulled each other close and kissed passionately.

. . . .

The sun was starting to go down. Dave and Sabrina had gone inside to change clothes and Sabrina wanted to take a shower. Mary had called and left a message that they would all be home later than planned. Dave went outside and started a fire in the fire-pit on the deck. After a few minutes, Sabrina walked out to join him. She was carrying a beer and a wine-cooler. She sat closely to Dave on a log bench and handed him the beer.

"Thanks," he said, smiling.

She snuggled up close next to him. She was wearing her black and white, horizontally striped, tank-top and light shorts.

"You're not going to be too cold?" Dave asked.

"Nope," she smiled and took a sip of her drink, "you warmed me all up. Besides, you made a nice fire."

"It *is* a very nice fire," said a soft female voice neither of them recognized.

Their backs were to the house so they instinctively turned to look in that direction. There was no one there. But, when they turned back to the fire, they saw her. Sitting across from them, with her back to the trees, was a small, apparently young, exotic-looking woman. She was probably just about five feet tall, if standing. She had long, curly, chestnut brown hair, with a wreath of late-spring's woodland flowers across her brow. She had pointed ears and pale-white skin. Her eyes were a bright, sparkling green and she smiled brightly at them. She wore a loosely draped, robe made of cloth that faded from green to brown, tied at the waist, but which barely covered her nakedness. "Hello," she said. "Do you mind if I join you?"

Dave and Sabrina looked at each other and then back at the small woman, "Sure," said Sabrina taking another drink.

"Well, don't let me interrupt you, you were talking about being 'all warmed up'," the small woman smiled playfully.

"Who are you?" asked Dave in a calm voice.

"I don't usually tell," she said. "But since it is you, Saraph, and your very lovely wife who are asking, I suppose it would be rude not to. I am Maeve."

"*The* Maeve?" asked Dave in disbelief. "The Queen of the Fae?"

Sabrina looked at Dave, moving her head quickly to him and then back to the small woman, "Faeries? Did you just say she's a Faerie? Well she can't be a faerie, Dave, she doesn't have wings." Sabrina had had about enough supernatural revelations for one day.

Maeve laughed. It sounded almost like a bright, sparkling brook in the spring-time. "Sweet One, just because you can't see them ..." she paused, arching her back so her robe fell away, exposing her bare breasts, "doesn't mean that their not there."

Dave quickly closed his eyes and moved his head down, and Sabrina turned towards him, rolling her eyes upward and whispering "Oh my God."

Maeve continued laughing playfully, "After this afternoon, I would have guessed that you two would be a little less shy than all this. My mistake; won't happen again. You can look now."

Dave and Sabrina blushed brightly at what the small woman said, but they slowly looked back in her direction. She was covered again and was smiling at them. When she saw how brightly they were blushing, she laughed again, "Oh relax! It's not like I was actually *watching* you while you were all ... snuggly together. And my people? They know better than to intrude, in any way, on your private moments. The details of your … cuddle-time are for the two of you alone, I'm just having a bit of fun, that's all."

"And to answer your questions, yes I am Maeve, Queen of the Fae. It's nice to finally meet you, in person, Saraph. The same for your lovely wife … Sabrina." The Queen smiled at her.

"As for the second question, yes, I have wings. But, you won't see them unless I'm using them. In which case, you'll probably see some other things too, which – judging by your reaction just now – might be a little bit more than you are comfortable with, so I'll just keep them where they are for now."

"Thanks," said Sabrina with a shy smile. "Dave, why does she keep calling you Saraph."

"That's what they all call me now, since … that change."

"They *all* call you? You talk to a lot of Faeries?" asked Sabrina.

"Not as many as you used to," smiled Maeve.

"That wasn't real," said Sabrina.

"What are you talking about?" asked Dave, intrigued.

"You know that I was an only child and I guess … shy. I didn't really have friends when I was little. Most of the time I liked to play in the woods behind my house. I had imaginary friends that were a little group of pixies, and there was also a pretty lady in the water – she was made of the water – in a little stream. We would play games and sing songs, it was a fun imaginary little world. When I had to start school, they said they would have to leave, but they also said that they could come back some day if I wanted them to."

Dave caressed her cheek, "you must have been the cutest, sweetest little girl."

Sabrina smiled back at him.

"Do you?" asked Maeve.

"Do I what?" Sabrina replied.

"Do you want them to come back?"

"That was a little girl's imaginary game."

"Ok, fine. Have it your way. Do you want to imagine them again?"

Sabrina gave a soft laugh. "Sure."

Maeve laughed. "I told you that she'd remember you and that she'd say yes. You can come out."

Dave and Sabrina's mouths dropped open as five pixies flew from the bushes, at the forest's edge. They were about six inches tall with something like dragon-fly wings. They were clothed in small forest leaves and their skin had a faint phosphorescent glow. Their voices were high-pitched and small. They flew rapidly and swirled around Dave and Sabrina. They spoke excitedly, all at once, and were hard to understand because of it. It seemed that they were very excited to see Sabrina – again – and equally excited to meet Dave. One of them lightly landed on Sabrina's knee and said, in a high voice, "You got so big, and Her Grace says you have a baby girl now!"

Sabrina's eyes were wide with wonder. "You're really real! There were so many times I missed you all, so much. Are you back to stay?"

"They can stay around as long as you want them here," said the Queen of the Fae, smiling. "However, I strongly suggest that you never tell them that it is alright for them to come into your bedroom – or they will be there when you wish they were not – and I will have a conversation with them about privacy – since you two enjoy alone time together and apparently like to have cuddly-time outside sometimes, as well. Oh and don't start blushing again," she laughed playfully. "You know, angels can see everything you do, *all* the time. We have to actually be there to see and I told my people, quite long ago, to respect your privacy."

Dave and Sabrina were blushing, but she was so happy to see her pixies, that Sabrina's embarrassment quickly passed. "How is this possible?" she asked.

"Which? The pixies or that you can see them?" asked Maeve.

"Both, I guess," smiled Sabrina.

"Well, the easy one is that you can see them – all of the Fae, actually – because you have 'The Sight'. You were born with it. By the way, so were your mother and your sisters, Saraph. Your sweet daughter and any other children that you have will certainly have it as well. You can see us and we can tell that you can see us. We are usually the ones who notice first, so it is easier to hide, or if we like, 'let you find us'."

"The other question is very complicated. The world is very big, and there are lots of things in it. You know about Him," Maeve gestured upward, "and His angels. You also know about him," Maeve gestured downward and made a sour face "and his ... whatever you want to call them. You know about humanity and all of the different sorts of animals and plants. Well, there are also other living things in the world that you don't really know about. Oh yes, there are tales and myths and legends, mostly true to varied degree, but most of humanity thinks that those are 'just stories' and that we don't exist. We like it that way, mostly because humans are pretty good at killing and destroying and we'd rather not get in the middle of that business."

"Anyway, all of the beings, of which I speak, were originally made by Him," gesturing up, "when He made everything else. For us, it was a lot like the animals; there wasn't really good or bad. It was only later, when corruption came, that some became very, very evil. The rest of us are under different sorts of rules than humanity, think of it like the animals. My people are under my rules, which mostly entail generally staying away from humans, trying to help the plants and the animals, and focusing on positive energy. Of course, they are sometimes playful and tricksy, but not out of malice."

"Anyway, that's how it's possible," smiled Maeve.

"Well," she said standing up, "It was a pleasure meeting such a sweet – and unexpectedly shy – couple. I just wanted to introduce myself. It sounds like your dinner will be here momentarily, so I'll leave you to it. Do you mind if I stop by in the future?"

"That would be very nice," said Sabrina politely.

"Wonderful!" smiled Maeve. "Come on, pixies, time to go." The Queen of the Fae turned and walked into the forest, with the pixies flying behind her.

Sabrina took a drink and turned her head to Dave. "This has been a weird day."

. . . .

Christi and Anastasia had begun a tradition, over the last month, of playing together when Stasia woke up on mornings, when Christi was off from work – "so Mama and Daddy can sleep in." They would sometimes have adventures in the forest and pick blackberries, sometimes play games on the lawn, and sometimes watch Stasia's favorite Veggie Tales, My Little Pony, or other fun DVDs. Bastet almost always joined them. These adventures were always capped off by Aunt Christi making a special fruit smoothie for the two of them to share – "Just for us!" – and a bowl of cream for Bastet – "Can you hear the kitty purr?"

Today, they were sitting on the deck, watching the little fish, but Bastet had not joined them. Christi was amazed how much they held not only Stasia's attention, but her own as well. It was the morning of the Fourth of July. It fell on a Saturday this year, and the whole family would be there. Gayle and Chris would probably not arrive until one or two. They were on the last leg of their drive up from Virginia, moving Gayle back home. She planned to live at the family home for now, but thought that, at some point, she would possibly look for a small house, closer to Farmington, where she would be starting a job as an Assistant District Attorney for Franklin County, sometime in the next couple weeks.

As had been the case for a long time now, Shawn would not be joining them. Christi and Shawn had grown apart. As time had passed, they spoke less and less until they only had an occasional E-mail, often more than six months apart. That spring he had applied for a position with the World Health Organization. Shawn had called Christi, in late May, to let her know that he had accepted a position – initially in Geneva, Switzerland – that eventually would have him traveling all over the world, "just like I have always wanted." The conversation never got heated, but in the end, Christi and Shawn quite mutually and amicably broke up, which was really only a formality. When Christi had told the rest of the family, she ended by saying that, far from being upset, she actually felt like a burden had been lifted.

Christi had taken care of Anastasia for a week, in mid-June while Dave and Sabrina had driven down to Virginia Beach. They had taken two days to drive down to their little house, spent two days there, packing the rest of their things, and drove back home over two days. Their Land-Lady had hated to see them go, but told them that she would have a nice place for them, if ever they wanted to take a vacation.

Christi checked the time on her watch, it was nearly ten so she guessed that Dave and Sabrina would probably be up and in the kitchen, if not now, soon. "Want to go make our smoothie?" she asked Stasia.

"With berries!" said the two-and-a-half year-old.

"Berries will be perfect!" said Christi. "The ones we picked yesterday should be good and frozen, so it'll be so yummy!"

They got up and walked to the French-doors.

. . . .

Dave and Sabrina had woken up, softly, together and had lay in each other's arms quietly talking for some time. They had been talking about some of the ideas they had for things that Anastasia might like with the picnic they were planning for later today. They both agreed that a little girl would probably not enjoy grown-ups talking and snacking.

Dave had suggested that they take a row-boat ride on the lake and Sabrina had thought that it was a great idea. Also, over the last month, the water in the lake had warmed up enough to be tolerable for a little swimming. "And you know she loves it when you make a fire," smiled Sabrina as she snuggled closely to him.

"Oh, that reminds me," said Dave suddenly. "You're never going to believe what I saw yesterday afternoon when you were putting Stasia down for her nap. I can't believe I forgot to tell you; I distinctly remember running over here to tell you."

"I have an idea why you might have forgotten," smiled Sabrina, seductively running a finger down her husband's chest.

"Umm," smiled Dave, "Well, you won't believe what I saw."

"What was it?"

"I went around the side of the house where Mama's garden is; I can't remember why. Anyway, she was working in the garden, but she had help." He paused. "She was working in the garden with some gnomes!"

"Come on," said Sabrina smiling. "Like … garden gnomes, Dave?"

"Exactly like that!" said Dave. "Maybe two-ish feet tall, grey beards, blue coats, and red pointy hats. Yup. Except that they were not garden gnomes, but real, live gnomes!"

"Really?"

"Oh, yeah! And Mama said that they have worked with her in the garden for as long as she can remember and that the only reason that I hadn't seen them before is because they didn't want me to, so they would hide whenever I or the others were around."

"And, you'll love this part," said Dave continuing excitedly. "They completely understand English, but they refuse to speak anything but

German. Mama says it is because they are stubborn about 'the old ways'."

Sabrina laughed but then quickly looked Dave in the eyes and with mock-seriousness said: "Are they going to take their shirts off too?"

"Sabrina, I told you I closed my eyes right away," said Dave, thinking that she was serious. "I only want to see you that way."

"Well, I should certainly hope so," said Sabrina playfully, moving quickly and tickling Dave's ribs. They both laughed and her tickles turned into a warm, gentle embrace as they began to kiss.

. . . .

Not far out on the lake, Dave was gently rowing the little boat with his back to the bow, while Sabrina sat on the back bench – her arm gently around Anastasia – with both of them facing Dave. All three of them were wearing life-jackets. Sabrina had said to their daughter, "It's always important to be safe on the water. See, even Daddy wears one."

"Ok, Mama," said Anastatsia, as she allowed Sabrina to adjust the floatation device.

Anastasia sat very still as the boat slowly moved through the water. She was smiling brightly – as she always did when they were in the boat – but both of her parents could tell that, as much as she liked taking rides in the little boat, she was still just a little bit afraid. However, the longer they were in the boat, the less nervous she appeared.

"Do you like the boat, Sweetie?" asked Dave.

"Mmhm," Anastasia nodded and smiled. She had her dark auburn hair in small pig-tails and was wearing a pink "My Little Pony" shirt her Aunt Christi had bought for her.

Sabrina gave her a small squeeze and said, "We can go swimming after your nap if you want and Daddy said that he'd make a campfire tonight."

Anastasia smiled brightly, but still did not move.

Dave finished the wide circle he was rowing in the lake – not too small to be a non-event but not so big to be tiring for Stasia. He pulled the boat next to the deck and helped first Sabrina and then his little girl out of the boat and onto the deck. Mary and John were setting food on the picnic table on the deck.

John walked over as Sabrina was helping Anastasia take off her life-jacket. "Did ya have a nice boat ride, Little Darlin'?"

"Yup," she replied. "Nice boat. Daddy make a fire tonight!"

John smiled. His black hair was now streaked with silver and his full beard was now nearly white, but he was still in good shape and his eyes still twinkled when he smiled. His friend Pete's funeral had been two days before Chris and Dave got back – about a month and a half ago. This was the first party-like event that they were having without him and John missed hearing his friend's voice make fun of his "Cowboy Beer."

Since he had met Pete, back in the late Sixties, his friend had smoked Captain Black pipe tobacco. John absolutely loved the smell of it, and would occasionally smoke a pipe-full from the pipe Pete bought him when Dave was born. It had never been a regular thing, and it wasn't now. However, Pete's old pipe was now resting in a place of honor on the mantle and John was sure that there would be the scent of Captain Black at the campfire tonight.

"Ok, Stasia, say good-night. Time for cuddle and then nap," said Sabrina, sweetly.

"Ok, Mama," said Anastasia. "Good-night!" and she ran after Sabrina who was walking to the French-doors.

Dave had tied up the boat and taken off his life-jacket. He was now drying a few drops of water off his dark-black sun glassed and then he bent to open the cooler. "You didn't tell Mama to get anythin' else, so I think it's only the Busch in there," said John. "There might be some other stuff in the kitchen, though."

"This is fine, Dad," he smiled. "Thanks."

Dave brought two bottles and they sat in two of the chairs on the deck, quietly looking out at the water.

Mary sat down in the chair next to John, after about twenty minutes. "She looks so cute in those pig-tails," she said.

"Christi must have given them to her this morning," said Dave.

"Those two have so much fun together. Christi loves her time with Stasia!" said Mary.

"It's really nice that she plays with her so much," said Dave.

"Well, you used to spend a ton of time with Christi, when she was little. Lots of times Chris and Gayle would go off together and you would stay back to play with your little sister and the cat. She absolutely adored you. It was really cute," smiled Mary.

"Yeah, but when you got older, and the Chris and Gayle were actually datin', but you just wanted to stay home with your little sister and the cat, I started to think that maybe you were never gonna get interested in girls." John gave a short laugh, "Guess you just needed to find the right one, 'cause you sure have been pretty darn interested in Sabrina – right from the first time you lay eyes on her."

Dave laughed, "Yeah, she's pretty awesome."

Sabrina's hands softly lay on his shoulders, from behind him and her dark auburn pony-tail fell across his chest as she kissed his cheek. "I love you too, Sweetie," she laughed softly.

She went to sit down in the chair, next to Dave, but as she did, Gayle's silver Trailblazer pulled up to the house.

"Everyone's home," smiled Mary. "Let's go say hi!"

They all got up and walked to meet them. Gayle gave Mary a big hug and then excitedly said, "We have to tell you something and we don't want to wait."

"Christi should be right over in the yard," said Mary. "Christi!" she called.

Christi walked around from the yard, followed by Bastet. "You're home!" she smiled brightly and ran up to Gayle, giving her warm hug.

Gayle took a deep breath and then said, "Chris finally asked me to marry him!" Then thrusting out her left hand to reveal a sparkling diamond solitaire set in gold, "and I said yes!"

Everyone laughed and hugged and gave congratulations, but only Sabrina, Christi and Mary seemed surprised. "John?" said Mary inquisitively.

"He did it the old-fashioned way; he asked my permission before he got on the plane to Virginia," smiled John.

Chris laughed, "Well, a sort of old-fashion. She is my adopted sister, so I felt I had to do something else as well. So, I asked Dave's permission too."

They all turned to see Dave beaming a huge smile.

Sabrina, hit his shoulder lightly, laughing: "You knew and you didn't tell me?"

"It wasn't my story to tell," smiled Dave, pulling her close and kissing her.

John spoke up and everyone got quiet. "Well, alright then," he smiled. "I'll start getting' the grill ready. Good thing that I picked out the best steaks, for those who like 'em." Sabrina, Christi and Gayle had fallen in love with veggie-burgers, back at Sharkys Pub, and since then, that's all they wanted at barbeques. "I kept it quiet but I knew that this Forth would merit somethin' extra special. Well ... now we all know."

. . . .

The sun had not yet set but the campfire glowed brightly. Anastasia was sitting on the log-bench between Dave and Sabrina. Dave was reading a bedtime story. Toad had made some cookies and he and Frog were learning about will-power. Toad was not happy about the lesson and was going home to make a cake. Then they sang a few songs: "The Itsy-Bitsy Spider," "Ba-Ba Black Sheep," and "Twinkle Twinkle Little Star". Then it was time for good-night kisses and Sabrina took her off to bed for prayers and one last song about a sleepy bunny.

Everyone got their drinks of choice and sat around the fire. John gently filled and lit his pipe. When Sabrina returned, she cuddled in next to Dave and sipped the wine-cooler he had opened for her. For the last time, Dave told the story of the dragon. Christi and Gayle took the information well and, strangely, didn't seem particularly surprised. Christi, in particular, seemed to want more information about the faeries than anything else and was ecstatic to learn that she had "The Sight". She revealed that, like Sabrina, she had also had "imaginary friends" she played with in the forest as a little girl, and she looked forward to seeing them again.

. . . .

Two weeks had passed since the Fourth of July. It was a quiet Saturday morning. Dave and Sabrina had woken gently together and took their time getting up. The house was quiet, and it seemed that everyone but Christi and Stasia – who were happily watching "My Little Pony" with Bastet – had slept in.

Sabrina was taking a shower and Dave walked out on the deck, his hair down and only wearing a pair of black shorts. He was quietly looking out over the water when he heard them. Three pixies were quickly flying towards him, from the forest. They hovered next to him and all spoke excitedly at once. Dave quietly said, "Shhh! Shhh! One at a time, please. I can't understand what you're saying when you all talk."

One of the pixies hovered in front of Dave's face. "Her Grace sends word for you, Saraph!" the pixie squeaked loudly.

"What does Her Grace say?" he asked smiling.

"They are coming!" said the pixie, sounding afraid.

"Who are coming?" asked Dave, his smile gone.

"The men in the black flying machine. They are coming, Saraph!"

"Give Her Grace my thanks for the warning and tell her to keep her people hidden until they are gone. You should go. Quickly!"

The pixies flew back into the forest and disappeared among the trees. Dave turned and walked back into the house.

Christi looked up as Dave entered the room. "You and Stasia should go to your room and stay there for a while," said Dave. "A helicopter is on the way here. I'm sure that they want to pick-up Chris and me for something. Stay inside and under no condition let them see either of you."

Christi looked slightly worried at Dave's serious tone but quickly got up and picked up Stasia. "Let's go, Sweetie, we can watch more ponies in a little while." She quickly left the room and Bastet followed her.

Dave quickly walked to Chris' room and knocked on the door. "Yeah?" said Chris' voice.

Dave opened the door and said, "They're coming. Get dressed."

"It was bound to happen eventually. I'll tell Gayle real quick and meet you out there," said Chris. "You good to go?"

"No," said Dave flatly, and he shut the door.

Dave next went to wake his parents, but they were already walking down the hall. John said, "Christi told us that they are coming."

"It's probably better if you all stay out of sight until they leave."

"Whatever, you want, Dave," said Mary.

Dave quickly went back to his and Sabrina's room. She was just coming out of the shower, with a towel wrapped around her as he closed the door behind him. "What convenient timing," she said with a coy smile.

"Dave hugged her and gave her a quick kiss. "What's wrong?" she said, sensing his tension.

"They are coming."

"Who?"

"A government helicopter is on the way. I'm sure they are coming to pick me and Chris up for some job."

"Are you going to be ok?" asked Sabrina.

"Yeah, but I don't want to go," said Dave. "Chris is getting ready and I told everyone else to stay out of sight. I don't want them to have any more information about you than they already have."

She pulled him close to her. "You shouldn't be gone long, right?"

"That's what they told us, but these sorts of people aren't really known for their honesty. After all, they told us that they would be giving us some notice and they didn't."

"If they didn't contact you, how do you know that they are coming?" asked Sabrina.

"The Queen sent some pixies to tell me. They were really freaked out."

Sabrina smiled. "Did the pixies tell you how long we have?"

"No."

"Then there's no time to waste," she said in a breathy-whisper, as her towel fell to the floor.

. . . .

Dave and Chris were both wearing camouflage cargo shorts, t-shirts, Teva sandals and dark sun glasses. Dave's hair was pulled back in a pony-tail and he had given his wedding ring to Sabrina for safe-keeping until they returned. They were sitting in chairs next to the house as the black helicopter touched down on the side yard. The rotors were not entirely silent, but they were surprised at how quiet they were by comparison to other helicopters.

The side door slid open and a man, dressed in black fatigues stepped out. "Master Chief Shepherd, Senior Chief Hanley, Mr. Ezekiel sends his regards. He and the rest of your Team will meet you at the plane. Would you please climb aboard?"

Dave and Chris said nothing, but got on the helicopter. The door closed behind them and all outside sound disappeared. There were no windows and the sound-proof interior was lit by a red light. Dave and Chris sat in chairs and fastened their seatbelts. The man who spoke before, sat in the row of chairs behind them and said: "We will reach the hangar in a few hours. You'll be briefed there."

Dave and Chris said nothing in reply. They knew that he would almost certainly not answer any questions they had, so they just didn't bother asking. They sat quietly for over an hour at which point, Dave turned to Chris and quietly asked, "So, did you guys make any plans?"

"We talked to Father Mike. We decided that it would be best to have the wedding next summer. We'll do it very similarly to how you did with the church and the reception at the house after, but there will be some people that we don't know, from Virginia, that Gayle wants to invite."

"You going to invite any of the guys?"

"Yeah, definitely Diego and I'm pretty sure I'll invite the other two guys. Maybe I'll track down Porter and Fredrickson, they were really cool to us."

"Gayle asked Christi and Sabrina to stand up with her. I want you as Best Man and I'll ask Diego to stand up as well. We really want Stasia to be the flower-girl.

"Of course I'll stand with you! And Stasia will be thrilled!"

"There's one other thing though."

"What?"

"Gayle wants the men standing up to wear the whites. And by 'the men' … that's including you," Chris laughed

"Really? What did you say?"

"Well," laughed Chris, "it doesn't really matter what I think about it. She out-ranks me."

"Come on!"

"Nope. That's what she wants. Don't worry, she's already enlisted Sabrina into the cause. Apparently, Sabrina has only seen you in your uniform once before – when you got the Navy Cross – and she may or may not have repeatedly used the word 'sexy' when she talked about it and enthusiastically agreed to convince you. I'm sure that she will be discussing it with you in detail at some point in the future and utilizing whatever means she needs to convince you of the merits of the case."

"Besides," laughed Chris, "Gayle easily convinced me that it was a good idea by pointing out how much fun I'd have telling you about it and watching you trying not to freak out about it. She was totally right."

. . . .

Dave and Chris walked across the floor of the hangar towards what appeared to be a strangely modified C-130, into which the rest of their team was loading gear. Mr. Ezekiel, in yet another expensive suit walked over to them, smiling, and extended his hand. Dave and Chris ignored the gesture. "Sure was nice of you to give us that notice you promised," said Dave sarcastically.

Mr. Ezekiel lowered his hand, but not his smile. "Didn't I? Oh, sorry about that. How'd you like the black helicopter all the crazy nut-jobs talk about?"

"It was a helicopter," said Dave.

"Yeah, and I guess they're not so crazy, since the helicopter actually exists," said Chris.

Mr. Ezekiel laughed. "Well, you want the briefing?"

"Sure," said Dave. "You want to tell us where we are?"

"Of course. You're in a C-130 hangar," said Mr. Ezekiel, walking towards an office in the rear of the building.

"I hate this guy," whispered Dave to Chris, as they followed.

"Oh yeah," replied Chris. "Absolutely."

They sat down in the office and Diego, James and Mike joined them around a table. Mr. Ezekiel pointed to a map. "Northeast Afghanistan, gentlemen. Mountains, caves, you've all been there before at one time or another. The President sent a surge of troops in May.

They've been doing very well, but we have a problem in this region. There are a couple cave complexes, most of them aren't a big deal, but there is one that's a nightmare. There's probably close to a battalion hidden away in there. They are extremely well armed and are repelling every advance that the Marines have made. We're pretty sure that we destroyed most of the exit caves, but there is one huge opening – he laid out a satellite photo – here, and two other large exits here and here. The whole thing is about a three mile diameter area."

"Now, the Marines are in a bit of a siege situation. We could wait them out – until they get desperate and try to charge – but there are a few problems with that plan. First of all, sieges are very slow, and boring, and we need results that we can show the American people. Second, these Marines are needed elsewhere."

"So, here's the plan. The Marines are going to be ordered to pull back to a distance where they can't see what you're doing. You're going to insert via HALO jump. Dave, you are going to fly first here, then here and then here" he pointed to the three cave openings. "The first one is big enough for you to go quite a way inside, actually, but the other two might be kind of tight and you can only get a little way down. So, at each cave, you are going to thoroughly incinerate everything as far back as you can reach and collapse the cave after you leave. Collapsing the cave will probably be easier with the smaller ones. Once you're done, you will fly to here," he pointed to a spot on the photo, "where your team will be waiting. You change back, they signal for a Seahawk – which will be waiting for you – to pick you up, and you fly back to Bagram, come back here, and we take you home."

"While Dave is doing his business, you gentlemen will HALO to this location, set up a defensive position, and – if you can avoid detection – all you need to do is wait for the dragon, radio the Seahawk, and keep Dave safe until they pick you up."

"What's the story about how all this happens to the cave, miraculously, right after the Marines pull back?" asked Dave.

"We're going with something along the lines of: 'We don't know. They must have had some accident with explosives while they were preparing to attack us,'" smiled Mr. Ezekiel.

"Dragon-fire is pretty severely intense," said Dave.

"They must have had some really strong stuff in there. Good thing it blew them up instead of us!" said Mr. Ezekiel.

"They're not going to blow up, they're going to burn. It's totally different," said Dave.

"Relax, Dave," said Mr. Ezekiel. "No one's going to send in a forensic team. The enemy is dead, that's all anyone is going to care about. They'll be relieved, not curious."

"Whatever you say," said Dave rolling his eyes and throwing up his hands.

"That's the universally correct answer!" said Mr. Ezekiel smiling. "You all should be saying that much more often."

. . . .

Mr. Ezekiel had said that all the C-130's that they would be using had some "special modifications," so, they would both fly faster and be considerably more fuel-efficient, getting them to the target – as well as home – much more quickly. They would be flying non-stop and dropping that night.

"How is a prop-plane flying faster and with more fuel-efficiency than a jet?" Mike had asked. "I hate to be the one throwing this around all the time but … it's not possible."

"Maybe things don't always work the way that you think they do and maybe things aren't always what they appear to be," Mr. Ezekiel had answered, smiling. "My office has access to technology that you've never even dreamt of being developed and it's been made to look like what we already have so it can be hidden in plain sight. So, don't worry about it. If everything goes the way it should, you'll be home before Monday."

Mike had grumbled to James, but the rest of them just quickly got changed into black fatigues and got on the plane. Early during the flight they checked their gear and weapons. All of them would be armed with M4's and a moderate amount of ammunition. No enemy contact was expected, so they were going in light, yet prepared enough for a mild defensive action.

The gear and the parachutes all seemed to be in order. Dave had discussed a plan with Chris, regarding clothing, "I don't want to be hanging out naked with all these people anymore. Can you get me dressed?"

"Sure," Chris had laughed. "I feel like there are too many jokes to pick from, so I'll just leave it."

The Team was alone in the back of the plane. "This is weird," said Diego. "I'm not cold and it's not loud. And how are all five crew members sitting up front?"

"Ezekiel said the plane was modified," said Chris. "It only *sort of* looks like a C-130. But I'm sure this is a whole different thing."

"Everything about this whole thing is weird," said James. "Our job is jumping out of the plane and waiting for a dragon to show up. Doesn't get a lot weirder."

"You'd be surprised," said Chris with his crooked smile. "You should ask Dave about the faeries he met."

"Chris," said Dave, irritated, "could you please shut up."

"You met faeries?" asked Diego.

"Can we please stay focused on the mission?" answered Dave.

The conversation pretty much ended there and they each went about doing their own thing. Mike Zacchaeus fell asleep in about fifteen minutes and Diego Wagner followed him about a half-hour later. Chris and James got into a quiet conversation about music and Dave sat, off by himself, lost in thought.

. . . .

When they were about forty-five minutes from the drop-zone, the Crew-Chief came back and told them to gear-up. Everything was prepared and about fifteen minutes before the drop, Chris took the Crew-Chief aside. "How much did they tell you about what we're doing?" he asked.

"It's a dark-black Op, so higher than Top Secret, and you'll HALO in. That's about it."

"Ok, so you're going to see some weird stuff and you really can't tell anyone about it," said Chris.

"Weirder than you guys jumping out of a perfectly good airplane at forty-thousand feet and dropping thirty-nine thousand of those feet before you open a 'chute?"

"Yeah," said Chris. "Weirder than that. You can't talk about it. In fact, you should do your best to forget about all of this."

"It's weird that there are two count downs. The first drop and then another a minute after. Are you going as two groups?"

"Something like that," answered Chris.

When the first countdown got to two minutes, the back door was lowered and Dave walked out from behind the bathroom screen. His hair was down, he was barefoot, and he was only wearing boxer shorts. He handed a bag containing his clothes to Chris who secured it to his gear. "You're absolutely certain that you can do this in free-fall?"

"Yeah," said Dave. "It's not like it's my first jump so it shouldn't be a problem."

"Boxers?" asked James smiling. "Bold."

"No tighty-whitey's for the Master Chief," said Chris. "Those big-boys gotta breathe!"

Dave shot a disapproving look at Chris as the team burst into laughter. "Sir," said the Crew-Chief. "What do you think that you're doing?"

"Just shut up and count, kid," said Chris.

The Crew-Chief counted, flashing his fingers: "Four. Three. Two. One. GO!GO!GO!"

At "GO!" Dave ran to the end to the lowered gate and leapt into the darkness. "That guy didn't have a parachute!" screamed the Crew-Chief.

"No," said Chris, "No, he did not. Now finish our damn countdown and forget that you ever saw us!"

. . . .

The Afghan fighters were in extremely good spirits. They had seen the Americans moving away and word was spreading amongst them that they had outlasted the invaders. They still manned the huge opening of the cave with a substantial and well-armed force but they believed that the worst of this particular fight was over. It was ironic, they thought, that there appeared to be a storm brewing – a flash that must be lightning and a distant sound that must be thunder – in the clouds that were in the direction of where the Americans had gone.

They believed that the dawn would come, and with it reason to rejoice. They had no warning whatsoever as death came upon them out of the night sky.

. . . .

Dave fell through the dark, Afghani sky. He closed his eyes and spread his arms: "I am the dragon and the dragon is me." There was the flash, the fire, and the roar. And then the dragon was sailing through the darkness.

Dave could clearly see the opening to the cave and the men with their weapons guarding it. There were flickering lights, from the small fires within, but he did not need any such light. He could see perfectly in complete darkness and could focus his eyes to see further away than any living thing. He silently swooped through the darkness, coming around, above and behind them so they would not see his approach. Then he fell upon them.

Out of the night, he swept into the opening of the cave and poured his fiery breath on his unsuspecting enemies. Those who were not instantly incinerated ran back into the cave, screaming. He roared and the sound was deafening as it was amplified by, and echoed off, the cave walls. He blasted fire far back into the cave. This entrance was huge, and he easily moved forward on his powerful legs, leaning forward and using his wings as front legs, much like a bat crawls. Again and again he blasted fire back into the cave. His preternatural hearing could detect screams and cries from deep within and he knew that his fire had reached much further back than he would be able to physically go. He could see that the rock walls were beginning to glow from the heat of his fiery breath. He gave a long, powerful blast of fire as he backed out of the cave.

Once Dave had cleared the entrance of the cave, he turned his fire to the rock walls. He blasted and blasted them. After a few moments, they were brightly glowing orange and the rock itself was beginning to melt. Dave took flight, backing from the mountain side but still blasting fire, again and again at the walls around the cave's entrance. Finally, the structural integrity could take no more and the mountain collapsed in, closing the cave forever.

Dave climbed into the night sky, silently soaring to the second cave entrance. It was easy to see, as hundreds of Afghanis were fleeing from this cave in abject terror. He swept down upon the furthest away first and rained dragon-fire upon them. Only the ones closest to the cave entrance had time to react. They turned to run back into the cave, in some desperate hope of shelter, but only a small few escaped the dragon's first pass. The others were burning and screaming on the mountain path.

The dragon wheeled and passed over them again, burning as he went. None, who had attempted to escape this way had made it to safety. He then turned again, landed, and blasted fire as deeply into the second cave as possible. This cave was much smaller and he could not enter, but it was much less structurally sound as well. After pouring fire into the cave for a few brief moments, he shattered the mountain-side with his powerful tail and collapsed this second cave, forever, as well.

He took to the sky, yet again. There was no sign of life as he came to the final and smallest cave entrance. Still, his fire seared the last cave, over and over. When he had finished, he collapsed this cave as well.

The dragon climbed into the night sky and searched the landscape. There was nothing moving; absolutely no sign of human life, whatsoever. He glided silently, high through the night sky, in ever widening circles, carefully scanning the ground below, but there was nothing. From start to finish, his attack on the cave complex had lasted less than thirty minutes, but he searched for survivors for about an hour after. There were none. All of his enemies had either been incinerated in dragon-fire, or buried alive, deep within the caves.

Dave turned and flew through the darkness to the mountain top were his Team was waiting.

. . . .

When Chris exited the aircraft with his team, he scanned the sky as he free-fell, looking for a flash in the darkness. After a few seconds, he saw what he had been waiting to see and knew that the dragon was now in flight. He and the Team safely deployed their parachutes and they landed very close to their intended position. They only had to walk about a half mile to the place where they would wait. Once they reached their destination, they set up a defensive perimeter and waited.

Chris made sure that he waited, facing the direction of Dave's attack. He thought that he could see flashes of light, and at the beginning thought he both heard and felt a low rumble, but the closest point where the dragon was wreaking his destruction was almost ten miles from their location, so Chris told himself that these things were all in this head.

They had waited, silently in the darkness on the mountain top, for just over an hour and a half. There was no sound or warning. The dragon simply came out of the night sky, absolutely silently, and landed in their midst. He made no signs of threat, but immediately lay upon the earth. In less than a minute, where the dragon had been was now Dave.

Chris radioed for the Seahawk and was told that they were ten minutes out. He and Diego quickly dressed Dave and got ready to leave, as Mike and James continued to scan for any signs of danger. They heard the Seahawk approach and all came together. When the helicopter touched down, they were all aboard in seconds; it was less than a minute from touchdown until they were again airborne. They were technically in enemy held territory, so the pilot flew the Seahawk at maximum speed. In about an hour, they landed at Bagram airbase.

Chris insisted that he be the one to carry Dave, and slung him over his back, holding an arm and a leg in front of him. They walked across a tarmac to another "modified" C-130, which was waiting to take them back. They walked up the rear gate and it closed behind them. Chris half expected to see the Crew-Chief from the plane they had jumped from approximately three hours before, but this was an entirely different plane, with an entirely different crew.

Chris lay Dave on one of the sling-like bench seats and turned to the Crew-Chief. "We're all set. Let's get out of here." The Crew-Chief nodded as the rear gate closed.

"You guys might want to buckle in during take-off, we climb pretty quick and pretty steep, so as to avoid enemy fire." The four

SEALs nodded, sat down and bucked in. The Crew-Chief went to the front of the plane. After a few moments they could hear the engines and the plane started to move. The take-off was steep but shortly they leveled off.

Diego spoke up. "You guys notice something kind of weird?"

"You mean the dragon we just saw," laughed James.

"Sort of," said Diego. "But the weird part is that we didn't see him."

"I'm pretty sure that I saw him," said James.

"After he landed and you took your goggles off," said Diego. "Did anyone else notice that you can't see the dragon with night-vision gear?"

"I thought that it was just my equipment," said Mike, "but I couldn't see him either. I tried infrared too. Nothing."

"You would think that he would give a pretty good heat signature," said Chris.

"You'd think it, but he didn't," said Mike. "I tried every setting we have, looking right at him, but there was exactly nothing there."

"So, the only way we can see him is with normal vision?" asked Chris.

"It would appear that way," said Diego.

"Can you guys do me a huge favor?" asked Chris. They all nodded. "Maybe leave that little piece of information out of the report that we give to Mr. Ezekiel."

"Sure, but why?" asked James.

"I'd just rather it be our little secret for the time-being, if that's ok," said Chris.

. . . . . .

They were all sitting around the table with Mr. Ezekiel, in the office in the first hangar, where the mission began. "Well, the Marines moved back in before you were off the ground in Bagram. They haven't met any resistance. They said that some of the rock at the main cave entrance looked like it was melted though."

"Yeah?" said Dave, disinterested.

"Well that's sort of a big deal, Dave," said Mr. Ezekiel. "To do that a fire has to be *at least* two thousand degrees Fahrenheit! So, yeah, that's sort of a big deal."

"Ok," said Dave.

"Anyway, it looks like you wiped them out," said Mr. Ezekiel.

"Except the ones that are buried alive," said Dave flatly.

"You sound like you're unhappy, Dave. What's wrong?" asked Mr. Ezekiel.

"What's wrong? Ok. I don't like doing Public Relations work because we have a President who wants to look good."

"Think about all of those Marines. How many lives do you think that you saved?" said Mr. Ezekiel with a smile.

"Yeah, I care about that, but you don't," said Dave. "People like you think of people in a uniform as expendable assets, not as people who have families that miss them. I understand the job, I do, but what we do needs to matter. What did we do today?"

"You secured an area of enemy territory and you did it without losing one American life," said Mr. Ezekiel. "Good job!"

"Did it maybe cross your mind that this was only enemy territory, after eight years of fighting, because it is a useless, mountainous, wasteland and there's no reason that any rational person would waste time, energy, or lives to get it?" asked Dave.

"It's held by the enemy. We kill the enemy. Doesn't seem too hard to figure out for me," said Mr. Ezekiel.

"Whatever," said Dave.

"Well, ok then," said Mr. Ezekiel, standing. "You gentlemen are all set. Just so you know, there are disagreements about how to use your team. I'm sure we'll figure it out eventually, though it might be a while before you hear from us again. But don't worry, we'll give you a call and send the chopper when we need you."

"And you *will* call first next time?" asked Chris.

"Of course!" said Mr. Ezekiel. "Alrighty, gentlemen. Your rides will be here shortly. Actually, Dave and Chris, it looks like yours is here now. Have a nice flight." Mr. Ezekiel walked out of the office.

Dave and Chris said good-bye to the other Team members, walked out to the black helicopter, and got in.

Dave sat back and took a deep breath. Chris quietly asked, "You ok?"

Dave took another slow, deep breath and quietly said, "Yeah, it's just … I don't know. A whole lot of people just died for a meaningless target. I know that right after 9/11 we wanted 'righteous vengeance' and I wouldn't have thought twice about this sort of thing, but, most – probably all – of those people had absolutely nothing to do with that attack. Yes, they are enemy combatants but the reality is that they are fighting us now because that's just what they do in this God-forsaken part of the world: they fight anyone and everyone. If it wasn't us, or the Russians, or whatever, they would be fighting each other."

"The first time I fought as the dragon, I took out people that were actively trying to kill us. Yes, there were a lot of them, but they were all trying to kill us. This was different; they had no idea I was coming and I just wiped them out."

"When we did what we did before this dragon-stuff, I always thought that our job was specifically good because we were taking out high value targets. We would kill the top guys and the other ones would – theoretically – eventually scatter; no longer having a plan or leaders to guide them. Thus, not only were we saving American lives, we were actually saving the lives of the 'little guys' on their side as well; who usually were kids that didn't really even know what was going on in the first place. Ultimately, what we were doing was preventing lots of innocent people from being killed by taking out a relatively small number of severely evil people. This time my job was the opposite of the surgical precision we used to have; I just killed them all. And it wasn't even a particularly important target, strategically or otherwise. I just killed them – horrifically – because they were there."

"I don't know, Chris. I just really feel like crap right now."

Chris knew that Dave wasn't looking for an answer, so he just nodded and said, "Sorry."

Dave smiled, "yeah. Me too." Then he leaned back in his chair, closed his eyes and waited for the Top Secret, black helicopter to land in the yard of his home in the forests of Maine.

Chapter 4

---

or

"Crisis"

2010

More than a year had passed since the dragon destroyed the cave complex in Afghanistan. The wedding was a beautiful event in late June. Everything went as planned. Yes, Sabrina was able to convince Dave to wear his uniform – with no real difficulty – and his compliance was rewarded with her use of the term 'sexy' many times throughout the day. After Chris and Gayle returned from their honeymoon, they looked for a house closer to the DA's office in Farmington. They found one, about a twenty minute drive from the Shepherds' house, and moved in September. Mary also began waking up with Anastasia on her days off, just as Christi continued to do on hers, and the now three-and-a-half-year-old Stasia, loved her alone time with 'Gramma' as much as she did with 'Aunt Christi'. Dave and Chris had not heard anything from Mr. Ezekiel and though they knew that it couldn't last, they were glad for it in the moment. They both helped out at the Campin' Store, and sometimes Dave brought Stasia along as well. Sabrina had picked up two regular shifts at the hospital – Tuesdays and Thursdays from eight to four – just for something different to do. She, Christi, and Mary all drove to work together and enjoyed working together as a team. Generally speaking, it had been a good fifteen months.

No one had seen the Queen of the Fae since she introduced herself to Dave and Sabrina, but her people had become much more visible. Stasia, Christi, and Mary would sometimes play with pixies during their adventures in the forest and had become particularly well acquainted with a naiad, named Yara, who lived in one of the streams that fed the lake. Also, Dave and Sabina became aware that there were many dryads along the paths they liked to walk, though the dryads typically kept to themselves. Of course, the gnomes continued to help in Mary's garden, and were considerably less grumpy than she had expected when Anastasia insisted on helping as well.

Generally, Friday nights were family get-togethers and this time of the year, that usually meant a campfire. Thus, on this crisp, early October evening Dave sat by the fire, with his arm around Sabrina as she cuddled close to his side. Anastasia was happily helping Mary and Christi bring out a bowl of hard, sour dough pretzels. Chris and Gayle were returning from a walk around the lake. John was sitting by the fire and puffing quietly on his pipe.

Dave was about to comment about how much he liked evenings like this, when his cell-phone rang. Sabrina shifted so he could answer it as she asked, "Who would be calling you now?" but she already knew. The only people with whom Dave spoke with any regularity were all here. There was only one logical guess as to who was calling.

Dave answered and Sabrina was sitting closely enough that she could hear the entire conversation. "Hello Dave, this is Mr. Ezekiel. It's been a long time since we have talked."

"Hello," said Dave flatly.

"Have you been well?" asked Mr. Ezekiel.

"I'm fine," said Dave.

"Good. Good. And Chris? How was the wedding?" They had not told Mr. Ezekiel about the wedding. But Dave knew that this was just a device for Mr. Ezekiel to show that he continued to be watching them.

"It was nice," said Dave.

"So, I'm calling because we have an extremely sensitive and important job for you boys. This one's going to take a little time, maybe upwards of over a week, so I thought we'd let you know with some advance notice."

"That was nice of you," said Dave, flatly

"We'll be picking you up at ten in the morning on Monday, you can sleep in."

"Thanks."

"You can tell Chris, ok." It wasn't a question. "Alrighty then. I'll see you on Monday. Have a fun weekend." And the line went dead.

Dave set the phone down. "I'm so glad that I have one of these things," he said sarcastically.

Sabrina held him closely and John asked, "Well. Was it them?"

"Yeah. They'll pick us up on Monday morning and we'll be gone for probably over a week this time."

"Any idea what you'll be doin'?" asked John.

"Probably something pretty bad, Dad. That's what we do." Dave replied, finishing his beer.

"Son, you gotta remember that you don't hold any blame for what you do in combat. You don't give orders; you follow 'em," said John.

"Yeah? Well, the last time I took about a thousand lives in thirty minutes, for an area of land no one cares about, so the people giving those orders can look good," said Dave.

Sabrina cuddled him softly. He usually didn't talk about what he did while he was away. She knew that Dave was very much motivated by an idealistic view of military action that seemed to be proving itself considerably less reality based as time passed. She could both see and feel the toll it took on him. She would never say it – because she wanted it to be his decision, and she knew her words would make it for him – but she deeply wished that Dave would retire from the Navy.

John puffed his pipe, thoughtfully, and then said, "Son, when I was back in Vietnam there was a lot of that sort of thing. It was really frustrating for us as well. I always tried to remember that I was fighting for the American people, not our government. That helped me stay focused."

"I get that Dad, and that's what I tell myself, every time. 'We're fighting them over there so we don't have to fight them over here.' All of that is true. The problem is that, for almost two years now, the focus is very different."

"Ezekiel called, didn't he?" said Chris, sitting down as Gayle stood behind him and put her hands on his shoulders.

"Yeah. Monday morning at ten." answered Dave.

"Did he say how long?" asked Chris.

"Maybe more than a week," said Dave.

Mary walked up to the fire with Anastasia, who was holding a large bowl of pretzels. "What's wrong?"

"The boys have to go away for a bit, on Monday," said John.

"Ok," she said. "Then we need to make this an especially nice weekend, don't we. Stasia, go get Aunt Christi from the kitchen, please."

"Ok, Gramma!" she said as she turned and ran to the house, her dark auburn pig-tails bouncing in the evening light as she ran.

Mary, bent to the cooler and grabbed two bottles of beer, handing them to Dave and Chris. "Boys, it is important to stay positive."

"Sure, Mama," said Dave taking the beer and twisting off the top.

"Why don't you just retire?" asked Chris.

"Because it's not that easy," answered Dave.

"You have clearly hated this for quite some time now. What, since you became the dragon, right?"

"That's when it got really bad, yeah, but — if I'm honest — it goes back a lot further."

"So, why do you stay in?" asked Chris.

"I don't know. What would you do if I left? You wouldn't have the set-up you have now."

"Don't stay because of me," said Chris. "And to answer your question, I'd probably leave too. We've been in twenty years. Full retirement benefit, and I got my sugar-mama," he tapped one of Gayle's hands, "so I'm good."

Gayle laughed. "I don't think anyone here is concerned about money. I think that you need to decide what you want to do, Dave. Since the two of you were kids, you talked about being Navy SEALs, but you've always taken things more seriously than Chris. He'll make things into a joke and you'll brood about them. That's why the way things are changing hits you harder. Chris will smile and think that they're idiots, but you feel like you have to fix it. Well, you can't fix it Dave. This is the way things are now. That's why I left too. If the way things are going is not consistent with your ideals — and it most certainly sounds like it isn't — you aren't going to be happy until you get out."

"That was nicely put, Babe," said Chris, smiling.

"You always said I was the smart one," she smiled back with a short laugh.

"What's going on?" said Christi, walking up to the fire. "Oh, Stasia will be right out. She decided that she had to put finishing touches on the picture she drew of the pixies."

"Dave got a call from work and they have to go back on Monday," said Mary. "Dave isn't happy about it."

"Well, are we telling him to retire yet?" asked Christi, crossing her arms, tilting her head, and looking directly at Dave.

Chris laughed, "Yeah, that's sort of where we were going with the conversation."

"Ok, so what's the problem?" Christi asked. "We can all see it, but no one wants to tell you, 'cause you'll get all broody."

"Well," said Dave, "I already sort of committed to this particular job, so I can't say no now."

"You could … it just might get loud," said Chris.

"I assure you that it will get considerably louder if I go," said Dave, with a hint of a smile.

"See? Now *that* was funny," said Gayle, smiling.

"So, whatever. You go on this one. Ok, then just walk away. You know that you want to; we all know you want to," said Christi.

Dave squeezed Sabrina softly. "What do you think about this?"

She took a slow, deep breath. "I think the same thing I think anytime that you ask me something like that: I think that it's your decision and no one else can make it for you. Obviously, I hate it when you're away and I hate that your job is probably the most dangerous job in the world. Here's the thing though, that's what you wanted to do, long before you met me. I love *you*, and that is part of you. No, it's not who you are, but it is one of the things that you do and have done for decades. I know that you love me so much that you would quit the instant I asked you to, whether or not it's what you truly wanted. And, Dave, I won't make that decision for you. When you believe that it is the right time to leave the Navy, you'll do it."

"I just hate the fact that everything has changed," said Dave. "I used to believe, so deeply, in what we were doing. I thought the cause was just; that we were acting in the defense of our people. But I feel less and less like that anymore. Now, especially with what I am always going to be doing as the dragon, I just feel this sense of culpability."

"But that's wrong, Dave," said Sabrina, gently. "If you were a pilot and had to drop bombs – if you're doing what you're told and you hit the target they tell you to hit – it isn't your fault when the bombs fall. You can't blame yourself when they pick stupid, or even horrible, targets."

"I guess," said Dave. "I don't know, maybe this mission will be better, or have some true tactical value, and I'll feel better."

"And when it doesn't?" asked Chris.

"I don't know," said Dave. "You do raise a good point though, we *have* actually been in for twenty years."

"Does that mean that you want to retire?" asked Chris.

"I'm thinking about it, ok," said Dave. "What about you, you want to retire?"

"Yeah," said Chris. "I'm just sort of trying to figure out when. Pretty soon though."

"When were you going to tell me?" asked Dave.

"I don't know … soon," said Chris. "I'm not the one having a crisis about it, Dave."

"I'm not having a crisis, I'm just not looking forward to being gone for more than a week," said Dave.

Everyone was quiet for a moment. The silence was broken by Anastasia running up and pulling on Sabrina's sleeve. "Mama, can I please have a pretzel."

"Since it's Friday night, I guess it's not too late," smiled Sabrina, caressing the little girl's cheek.

"Thank you Mama!" said Stasia, reaching into the bowl and then happily crunching.

Christi smiled, "what happened to that picture, Princess?"

"I gave it to Bastet," answered Stasia.

"Well let's go in and put it on the 'fridge so she doesn't lose it," smiled Christi, taking her hand and walking back to the house.

. . . .

The Team was sitting at a table in a conference room in a nondescript office building in Langley, Virginia. It was largely invisible to any eyes who did not know where to look, but Dave and Chris were very much aware of the powerful security presence in this building. No one who was not expected would be getting three steps in any entrance. This was obviously the headquarters of Mr. Ezekiel's organization.

A map of the Iran/Iraq boarder was projected on the screen as Mr. Ezekiel began to speak. "Good afternoon, gentlemen. I trust that you had a nice weekend. This operation is as profoundly important as it is risky. You will be hitting an Iranian nuclear research and development facility on the outskirts of Sanandaj. I will cover the details in a moment, but first, it is crucial that you understand how important it is that you get this right. Our government is trying to get the Iranians to come to the negotiation table regarding their nuclear program. We believe that if they have a catastrophic 'accident,' they will be more likely to talk to us. If you were waiting for a mission that has global significance, this is for you."

Dave leaned back, crossed his arms, and listened. Mr. Ezekiel continued. "You will be taking a brand new, top of the line, prototype, hypersonic jet from the Langley Air Base to Kirkuk, K1 Air Base. You'll be amazed how fast you get there. You'll be there in about three hours in this baby. It is so sweet!"

"Anyway, when you arrive, there will be people expecting you who will set you up with your gear and then get you on a Blackhawk to take you to your listening post, out near the Iranian border. Once you get situated at that position, you'll wait until about one or two in the morning. Dave, you'll make your transformation and fly out to the target."

"Now, this target is on the outskirts of a city, so there is a potential for you to be seen, but there will almost certainly be no one close by or awake, so the potential is small. However, even though it is the middle of the night, you still need to be super sneaky. Also, this has to look like an industrial accident. The plan that we want to go with," he clicked the projector to show a drawing of a building, like a blueprint, but obviously not drawn by a professional, "is this." He pointed at the "design". "The building is on the north side of town, so we want you to come in from the north. Smash through this wall and you should be in a very large room. There will be metal containers there, huge ones. Torch those and get out quickly. Fly as high and to the north as you can and wait to make sure that it doesn't need a second blast. It should take no more than a few seconds, if your fire is as hot as we think that it is. Then the entire building should explode. We don't think it will be an actual *nuclear* explosion, but you should get out of there when it goes, just in case. Once that explosion goes, you get back to your guys, they radio the Blackhawk – who will be expecting to hear from you – and you should be back on the plane, by or preferably before, their sunrise. Snip! Snap! About a twelve hour deal and all done. The time difference/turning of the globe thing makes this amazing."

"You said it would be maybe over a week, on Friday," said Dave.

"Yeah," said Mr. Ezekiel. "That was a dumb plan. In that one, you took a slow plane over and you walked from Kirkuk to outside Sanandaj, waited a few days, and then made the hit. Then you walked back and took another slow plane home. Dumb, right?"

"The writers of that one didn't know about the jet you're going to take and they were worried about a bunch of stupid things. For example, they though it would be a problem to drop a Team close to the Iranian border. But, we drop Spec Ops guys out there all the time, so it's nothing new. Also, they thought that the dragon couldn't fly that far – it takes three-and-a-half hours to drive there from the border, so maybe an hour flight – you can easily do that, right?"

"This is the only thing, we are balancing different dangers. It would be stupid to hike through Iran and hang-out for days; really good way to get caught. However, you really have to stay below radar and do your best not to get seen, Dave. We really don't need a video of a dragon, flying through the night – or worse, burning a building – going viral on YouTube."

"I'll do the best I can," said Dave, "but are you absolutely certain that hitting a facility in a city is a good idea? What about the other buildings?"

"The area appears to be industrial, so the workers should be home, asleep. That would mean no one to see you. And, if other buildings happen to go up, it's more reason for them to come to the table; not less. Win-win," said Mr. Ezekiel.

"Also, I know how much you hate to be away from home, your beautiful wife, and your pretty little daughter. I thought that any way to make it quicker would be appreciated."

"That's great, but this feels rushed. Do you have any actual photos of the building?" asked Dave.

"This one, of its north side," said Mr. Ezekiel, clicking the projector. It was a grainy photo, but Dave could see the distinct shape of the building, for which he would be looking. "I mean, it's Iran. Not like we can easily get a lot of access."

"Any other questions? No? Great," said Mr. Ezekiel. "The driver will take you directly to the jet and I'll see you all tonight at the hangar, when you get back."

The Team got up without speaking and left the room, walking to the front lobby where a driver was waiting. They all felt what Dave had said; this was very rushed. For the Team, it would be easy: spend a few hours in the mountains of the Iraqi border with Iran. But something felt wrong. They all could feel it. It was as if there was some small detail that Mr. Ezekiel had not mentioned and that they couldn't quite figure out.

. . . .

The ride to the Air Base was short. The car drove up to a side gate where the driver flashed identification and was let through with no questions. They drove into a hangar and stopped next to a futuristic looking black jet. They all got out. They were all wearing civilian clothing and carried no bags. A man in a black flight-suit with no identifying marks, ushered them onto the plane and got into the co-pilot seat. He reached back and shut the door to the cockpit.

The cabin was modest, with ten seats, dim lighting, and no windows. They felt the plane start to move and in a few moments they could feel the take-off. The plane quickly leveled. There was no sound of the engines but they could all feel a mild vibration.

"If it's under three hours, we'll be travelling well past Mach five," said Mike Zacchaeus.

"Let me guess," said Chris, with his crooked smile. "That's not possible."

James Morrison and Diego Wagner both laughed.

"No," said Mike, slightly embarrassed, but smiling. "But, it's way faster than anything that we're supposed to have developed as of yet."

"Then I'll be impressed," said James, "but I bet that Mr. Ezekiel exaggerated the time."

"The last plane was much faster than we expected," said Diego. "They said they had access to anything out there. Who knows, maybe they got some super-advanced technology from the aliens." Diego smiled.

"Sounds perfectly reasonable," laughed James.

"Hey Chris," said Diego, changing the subject, "that was a really nice wedding. Thanks for inviting us."

"It was my honor to have you guys," said Chris.

"That house," said Diego, "you guys really grow up there?"

"Yeah," said Chris smiling. "It's a really nice place."

"Where'd your family get the money for something like that set-up?" asked James.

"My grandfather was a dragon as well and he did some major stuff for the Allies in World War Two. They gave it to him afterwards," said Dave quietly.

"Major stuff? It must have been huge for that," said James with a laugh.

"I guess that he was a pretty major factor in winning the Battle of Brittan and gaining air superiority over Europe," said Dave. "You know … dragon, and all that sort of thing."

"What are they going to give you, then?" asked James.

"I think that I get the same deal as all of you," said Dave.

"How's that work?" asked James. "On these Ops, we sit around. You're the one who actually does stuff. We can be replaced, but you can't."

"I got what I asked for," said Dave.

"What was that?" asked James.

"I asked to be able to stay at home when we're not active. I didn't even think to mention money," answered Dave.

"Why the hell not?" asked James.

"Because it's not what I care about. And, to be honest, I'd trade all the money I have if they would give me what I really want from them," said Dave.

"What do you want from them?" asked Diego.

"I want them to leave me alone," said Dave, in almost a whisper.

"It's funny that you should say that," said Diego. "I have to tell you guys something. After this mission, I'm all done."

"What?!" said Mike.

"Yeah," said Diego. "I told Mr. Ezekiel before you guys got there. I'm not re-enlisting. I'm all done."

"What happened?" asked James. "To make you want to quit, I mean."

"Well, when they gave us the choice to continue working between these missions or to do something else. I took a long time to decide," said Diego. "But when I did, I decided to do some stuff in the civilian world. I don't want to go into any details about that, but while I was out there I met this girl. Her name is Bridget O'Shaughnessy. Dave, I think I finally understand you a little better, because I never want to be apart from her. Anyway, I don't want this life anymore. I want to have a simple life, and have a family with her."

Dave smiled, "Good luck, Brother. God Bless you both."

"What did Ezekiel say?" asked Chris.

"Nothing really," said Diego, "He shook my hand, said I had done good work, and then he wished me well. He didn't even ask for a reason."

"That's weird," said Chris.

"I don't think so," said James. "Maybe he knows that it doesn't take four of us to wait in the dark, get Dave dressed, and then hike to an LZ."

"That wasn't really the point of our job," said Chris. "We're supposed to be able to fight our way out, if things go badly. If that ever happens, four would be better than three. But, Diego, I totally get it."

"You're thinking of it as well, then?" asked Diego.

"I'm not gonna say that it hasn't been discussed," laughed Chris.

"See, isn't that just what I said, Mike?" said James. "These guys go inactive and then they lose the edge; the drive for this life. That's why when Mr. Ezekiel asked where we wanted to go, we stayed with our Team while you guys went home. No distractions that way. Keeps the fire in the belly."

"I'll say," laughed Mike. "Especially the way that you cook!"

James laughed. "But seriously, that's what happened."

"That might be one of the things that happened," Dave spoke up, "but it isn't the only thing. The Teams are changing, the whole military is functioning differently. Distraction is not the only reason that a lot of the older guys are leaving."

"Are you telling me that what we fight for – what you got in this for in the first place – doesn't exist anymore?" asked James.

"I don't know," said Dave. He paused and then said: "It's hard to see it that way when the mission is meaningless."

"Well then smile, Dave," said James. "It sounds to me like this one is a pretty big deal and could result in a much safer world … if they come to the table after."

"Maybe," said Dave. "I guess we'll see."

.   .   .   .

The black jet touched down at K1 Air Base at eleven-fifteen PM, local time; three hours and fifteen minutes from take-off. "See," said James to Mike, "more than three hours."

"But that's because we were moving with the rotation of the earth," said Mike. "On the way back, they'll probably make up that time 'cause our destination is moving towards us. Now my question is how high up we were, 'cause that'll change things too."

"Why didn't you go to school for science?" asked James.

"Maybe I did. And maybe I'd rather blow stuff up," smiled Mike.

"Right this way gentlemen, and we'll get your gear," said a Sergeant with a Special Forces patch on the arm of his field jacket. The Team was led into a building where they changed into the standard desert-camo fatigues and boots used by the US Army. They each had a M4, body armor, and ammunition. They had two radios – one carried by Diego and the other by Mike. They walked out to the tarmac, where a Blackhawk helicopter was waiting for them. They got in and Dave put on the headphones to talk with the pilot.

The rotors spun and the door was closed. The Blackhawk lifted off the ground and into the night Iraqi sky. "So, will you be the same one that picks us up?" asked Dave through the radio.

"That's correct. We'll be standing by," answered the pilot. "We shouldn't have more than a fifteen minute response time. About how long are you thinking?"

"If it goes according to plan," said Dave, "you should be able to pick us up in about two to two-and-a-half hours, but we'll radio."

"You guys are quick!"

"That's the plan," said Dave.

· · · · · · ·

The Sergeant who had met the Team as they got off the black jet stood on the tarmac and watched as the lights from the Blackhawk disappeared into the night sky. The door to a nearby building opened and a short, stout, grey-haired man with a grey beard and round glasses, who was wearing a tweed coat came out. He was followed by a much younger, taller and thinner man, also wearing odd civilian clothes. "Excuse me, Sergeant," said the older man – who was obviously out of breath – in a crisp British accent. "We are here to advise a team of five, who are to arrive on a non-military, black jet and who will be wearing civilian clothes when they arrive. Would you be so kind as to direct us to where we may wait for their arrival?"

The Sergeant thought to himself: "These Intel-guys can never get it right." He smiled and said: "You just missed them, Sir. But you can wait in that building, over there," he pointed to the building where the Team had changed clothes, "and you can discuss whatever business you have with them when they return in a few hours."

"Thank you, Sergeant," said the older man, who then took the younger man by the sleeve and walked into the building to which they had been directed.

When they got inside, Professor Jones turned to Tim and said, shaking his head: "Damn-it-all-to-hell, Tim. We are too late."

· · · · · · ·

The Blackhawk hovered inches above the ground of the landing-zone and the Team rapidly exited the helicopter. The Team ran and the helicopter lifted into the night. In a matter of moments, the Team was quietly walking through the night. When they had gotten approximately a half-mile from where they had been dropped, they set up a defensive listening post and Dave and Chris looked at the map one more time.

"It's just about one," said Chris. "You want to wait?"

"No," said Dave.

"How are you going to get through, the Iranians still have a pretty good defensive network out here?"

"Well, if what you told me after the last mission is right, they won't be able to see me."

"Any personal, visual gear won't be able to see you," corrected Chris. "We're not certain about radar."

"So, I'll fly, silent and fast. The moon is still a small crescent, so that'll help. And, worse-case scenario, I take out an Iranian defensive position."

"That would be a pretty big problem," said Chris.

"So, let's hope that doesn't happen."

"And when you get there?"

"I'll come in pretty hard and fast, the wall shouldn't hold up to that. Then I'll go as hot as I can and get out."

"You can control the heat?"

"I think so, it seemed like that with the caves," said Dave. "When I tried harder to melt the rocks, they melted like liquid. I feel like every time I do this, it's easier and I have more control. Last time I slept less, you said."

"I wonder if you can *make* yourself sleep less?" asked Chris.

"Well, they said that it was like resetting, but if there was nothing to reset, I suppose that it could be faster."

"Alright then," said Chris. "If you're sure you want to go now, I'll hold your clothes."

Dave started to quickly undress and Diego quietly laughed: "Watch. This'll be right when they walk up on us."

"Shut up, Dude," said Chris. "That'll jinx us!"

"Umm," said Mike. "There are no such things as jinxes."

"Yeah," said Dave walking into the night, wearing only boxer-shorts. "There are no such things as dragons either."

Dave raised his arms to the sky and tilted back his head. "I am the dragon and the dragon is me," he thought. There was a flash of light and heat, the pillar of fire blazed into the night sky, and a deafening roar echoed through the desolate landscape. The dragon then leapt into the night and was gone.

"Ok, displace and stay frosty," said Chris. "Anyone around, for miles, saw and heard that. Let's get under that cover on that ridge and stay out of sight until he gets back."

The Team moved swiftly and silently through the darkness. They found a position that could over-look their previous spot and three hundred and twenty degrees of the circle around them. Chris took a breath and settled in. "And now we wait," he thought.

. . . .

The dragon flew – fast, high, and silent – through the darkness. He was completely undetected. After about forty-five minutes, he could clearly see the lights of Sanandaj before him. He circled higher and to the north of the city. His preternatural vision made it easy to see his target, with perfect clarity, even in the darkness and at this height.

He saw the target building from the picture, but there was something else he hadn't seen in the briefing. On the south wall, there seemed to be another building. They were attached, that is to say they shared that wall in common, but they seemed to be distinct. The second building was boxy and four stories high. Interestingly, light was coming from many of its windows. He couldn't tell for sure what that building was or why it was attached to his target building. But then he remembered that Mr. Ezekiel had said his target was a research and development facility and that this area of the city was mostly industrial. He, therefore, guessed that this other building must have something to do with the production of whatever the other facility developed. It only made logical sense.

The dragon circled again, got into position and dove through the night sky towards his target. At the last minute, he pivoted his body sharply and crashed, feet-first, through the wall. The north wall of the building was reinforced concrete and much thicker than he had expected, but the force of his dive from so great a height was more than the wall could sustain. In fact, he was surprised that the force of the crash didn't bring down the entire building.

The room on the other side of the wall was exactly as Mr. Ezekiel had described: spacious and containing several large, metal containers and machines. He focused and unleashed the most intense flame burst he could produce. The fire engulfed the metal containers, which glowed red, and then white, in a matter of seconds. After ten seconds of blasting unearthly fire, the dragon backed out of the building and leapt into the sky.

With all the power and strength he could produce Dave surged up and away from the building at a forty-five degree angle, so as to simultaneously gain the maximum height and distance from the building. On powerful dragon wings, he rapidly climbed into the night. He was well away when the explosion occurred.

Over his years as a Navy SEAL, Dave had seen countless explosions, but never one quite like this. The building erupted in amazingly intense flames and he felt the initial blast-wave, even at this great height. The target building below, as well as the other attached building, were utterly devastated and now in a raging inferno. Other near-by structures had sustained significant damage and several were also now engulfed in flames. The target had clearly been annihilated.

The dragon turned and flew west, climbing higher and higher. He flew with the greatest possible speed to the extraction sight. He silently streaked through the night sky, away from the devastated Iranian facility.

. . . .

The Team had silently waited in the darkness for about two hours since the dragon had left. They had vigilantly scanned the night terrain for any sign of movement or danger, but had seen none. It was three in the morning, local time, but for them it felt like eight in the evening. They were not remotely tired and it was easy to pay attention to details. However, with no warning the dragon landed silently among them.

They all startled and Chris thought to himself, "I'll never get used to that." The dragon lay upon the earth and in just under a minute, it was Dave again.

Chris turned to Mike, "Radio for pick-up. I want to get out of here now. I just got a really bad feeling."

Mike radioed the Blackhawk and requested pickup, "ASAP!" "Yeah," he said to Chris, "I have that feeling too." He picked up his M4 and moved to a covering position with James.

Diego and Chris got Dave dressed. "I feel this ominous ... I don't know ... spookiness," said Diego. "It started right when he landed. Is something goin' on?"

"We need to get out of here," said Chris in a whisper. "That's what's going on."

"Blackhawk comin' in," said James. He paused and added: "And I feel it too."

"Stay frosty, boys," said Chris.

They circled Dave, M4's ready to fire at the slightest provocation. The Blackhawk came in close and hovered inches above the ground. Chris handed his M4 to Diego, who slung it over his shoulder. Chris bent and threw Dave over his shoulder. They moved as one and boarded the Blackhawk. A Crew-Chief slid the door closed and the helicopter rose. Chris lay Dave down on a sling-seat and put on head-phones. "Hey, can you guys punch it? Something doesn't feel right."

"Copy that," answered the pilot and the Blackhawk surged into the night sky increasing to its maximum speed.

Inside the cabin, the Team could feel the helicopter start to shake slightly and knew that the pilot was pushing it to its limit. "Thanks," said Chris leaning back next to Dave.

"You guys see something?"

"No, just a feeling," said Chris. "But we all had it and, when you do what we do, you learn to trust those feelings."

"Copy that," said the pilot. "At this rate, you should be on the ground somewhere between oh-four-hundred and oh-four-thirty."

"Thanks," said Chris, talking a slow breath to calm his nerves.

. . . .

The defensive position that the Team had occupied was under some light brush at the bottom of a steep slope. They had been able to see everything except what had been behind and above them on the slope.

The sound of the Blackhawk faded into the distance and there were no other sounds in that place for a few moments. Then, there was a slight crunch of stone-under-feet and small pebbles fell down the ridge. A large, dark shadow, with immense claws on its four feet slowly made its way down the ridge. It came to rest where the team had been waiting, only a short time ago. It was a darker patch of night, about ten feet in length, and was slowly waving a long, black tail behind it.

There was a harsh sound of sniffing as it moved amongst the places where each individual man had waited – slowly going from one to the other. It then moved to where the dragon had landed. Upon sniffing this spot, it made a low growling sound. It squatted down, in the middle of that spot, and there was a sound of liquid hitting the ground, which lasted for a few moments.

It then moved a few feet towards where the Blackhawk had picked them up and sat, looking out at the darkness in the direction the helicopter had gone. It sat for some time; silently motionless. Then it rose to its feet, tilted back its head and made a loud, horrible sound – something between a howl and a blood-curdling scream.

The dark creature then turned and quietly moved back up the slope. Silence returned to the area. The members of the Team would never forget the terrible feeling of dread that they had right before they were picked up by the Blackhawk – some nights it would wake them from a sound sleep. Though they would soon know that there had actually been a real danger attached to their fear, they would never know the true depths of the horrible danger in which they had actually been that night in the mountains near the border of Iraq and Iran.

. . . .

The Blackhawk touched down on the tarmac at K1 Airbase and the Team climbed out of the helicopter. It was just after four AM, local time.

Dave was awake. He had awoken just about an hour after he had transformed back. He was still slightly groggy, but he was back.

"That was the fastest turn-around yet," said Chris, as they walked towards the waiting Army Special Forces Sergeant.

"Yeah," said Dave. "I mentally tried some things right before I changed and it looks like it worked."

"Welcome back, Gentlemen," said the Sergeant as they approached. "Your English friends are waiting for you over there, where you will be changing."

"English friends?" asked Chris.

"Two guys who look like they're Intel; also dressed in civies."

"Well, let's go get changed and see," said Dave.

The Team walked into the room and found Professor Jones and Tim, sitting at a table, waiting for them. Professor Jones stood up and said: "Thank goodness that you're alright!"

"Why wouldn't we be?" asked James.

"Because we were late," said the professor. "We were delayed by odd circumstances and we arrived only after you had already left for the field. This was extremely unfortunate as there were two very important things we needed to tell you."

"You can tell us now," said Diego.

"I'm afraid that it will make little difference, at this point," said the professor, "but alright. The first was an important warning. The place where your Team was to wait – while Dave completed his mission – is deep within a territory that is prowled by a dread, black beast. He is horribly evil and filled with a dark rage. Had the dragon come upon him, of course there would have been no contest. However, had he come upon you alone, or while Dave was asleep, you would not have stood even the slightest chance. You boys are extremely lucky to be here. Was there any particular reason that you chose that specific location?"

"No," said Dave. "It's just where Mr. Ezekiel arranged for us to be dropped. It was a relatively straight path for me to the target and as close as we could get to the border."

"You're absolutely certain that Mr. Ezekiel arranged that location?" asked the professor.

"That was my understanding," said Dave.

"What are you sayin', Professor?" asked James.

"I'm not suggesting anything," he answered. "However, it does seem odd that he would not have known about the danger of the beast, or that he would have failed to account for it."

"But why would he set us up?" asked James.

"I'm not suggesting that he did," said Professor Jones. "I just feel that the situation does not make sense."

Dave had finished changing into his civilian clothes – as had Chris and Diego – while they were talking. "Guys, finish getting dressed. We need to get going. What was the other thing, Professor?"

"Dave, you probably want to have a seat," said Tim.

Dave didn't ask, but rather sat down at the table, as did the professor. James and Mike quickly began to change into their civilian clothes as well.

"David," said Professor Jones, slowly and delicately, "When you approached your target building, did you see anything unusual?"

"Yeah," said Dave, "since you mention it, there was something. There was a building, right up against the south wall of the facility, the opposite side from how I came in. Ezekiel hadn't mentioned it, but that whole meeting was rushed. He said that the area was mostly industrial, so I just figured that it was a factory, or something like that, where they would make whatever the facility developed."

"Did it look like a factory to you?" asked the professor.

"No, not really," said Dave. "But, I couldn't think of anything else that would make sense to have next to a nuclear research and development facility."

"That's because you do not think like the Iranian Regime," said the professor. "Tell me Dave, if the Iranians were trying to make nuclear weapons, what do you think would be their greatest fear?"

"I don't know," said Dave. "Maybe that they would blow themselves up. Or, that the Israelis … or we … would hit them in an airstrike, maybe."

"It is the second," said the professor. "Now, they have extensive anti-aircraft capabilities, but they had to find some way to deter the Americans and the Israelis from attacking in the first place. Can you think of the most effective way to do that?"

"I have no idea," said Dave.

"Do you know what a 'human shield' is, Dave?" asked Tim.

"Yeah, of course," said Dave. "They use them, over here, all the time. The bad guys find someone that they think that you won't shoot, or would be at least hesitant to shoot, and hide behind them to get the advantage. It usually works. … Why?"

"He asked you that to help you understand, Dave," said the professor. "That 'factory' attached to the target facility; what happened to it when the facility blew-up?"

"The factory exploded as well," said Dave. "And that was one hell of an explosion, just so you know. Both buildings were completely destroyed and they were in a raging inferno when I left."

Tim and the professor looked at each other and then slowly back at Dave. The professor gently placed his hand on Dave's and said, as softly as possible: "David … that wasn't a factory, attached to the target facility. … It was a children's hospital."

The room went utterly silent; no one even took a breath. Dave's head was spinning and he pulled his hand away from Professor Jones. He pushed himself away from the table and stood, both his hands still on the table steadying himself. He made direct eye-contact with the professor. "Are you saying that I just incinerated … a children's hospital?"

"I'm afraid so," said Professor Jones gently. "We tried to get here in time to stop you …"

"How many?"

"How many what?" asked the professor.

"How many children did I burn to death?" said Dave. His body was visibly shaking.

"Dave, don't do this to yourself," said Tim.

"How Many?!!!" shouted Dave.

"We think it was close to one-hundred and fifty. They weren't at capacity, but they were close," said the professor.

"Oh my God!" said Dave loudly. He pushed away from the table and took three steps towards the door. But then he stopped, dropped to his knees, put his face in his hands and began sobbing.

Chris knelt beside him and put his arm over his shoulders. Chris said nothing. He knew that anything that he would now say to comfort his brother would only make things worse. They sat together for over five minutes and then Dave looked up.

Tim had quietly walked over with a box of tissues and had sat on Dave's other side, about a minute before. He said nothing but reached out with the tissues. Dave took one and blew his nose. "Thanks," he said quietly.

Dave turned to Chris and said: "It's really ironic, you know."

"What's that?" asked Chris quietly.

"Do you remember how we met?"

"What, that fight with those older kids? Sure, how could I forget?"

"You remember why I started it?" asked Dave.

"Dave. Don't," said Chris.

"But, it's true," said Dave. "I'm a baby-killer."

"Dave, you need to stop it," said Chris. "You had no idea what that building was."

"No," he said, "but it doesn't change what I did." Dave got up, slowly, and turned to face Professor Jones. "Did Ezekiel know?"

"I don't see how it could be possible that he didn't," said the professor, plainly.

"Right." said Dave. "Everyone get on the plane, we're going home. I need to have a serious conversation with our boss, Mr. Ezekiel." Dave turned and walked out the door.

They watched him go and then Diego turned to Chris. "That was nuts! Sure cured me of any second thoughts of retirement."

"Yeah," said Chris giving a short laugh.

"Come on, Mike," said James. He looked at Chris and paused. Then he shook his head and quietly said, "Damn."

Mike, James, and Diego walked out of the room. Chris turned to the professor and Tim. Tim smiled and said, "at least he'll have the ride home to calm down a bit."

"Oh no," said Chris. "Dave having three hours, with nothing to do but sit and think about it? Yeah, that's much, much worse. You two coming?"

"I think we'll get back the same way we got here," said Professor Jones. "But, thank you, Chris."

"Ok," said Chris with a shrug. He turned and walked to the door.

"Oh. Chris," said the professor as Chris grabbed the door. Chris turned. "Please take good care of him and try not to let him do anything too … extreme."

Chris smiled his crooked smile "Sure," he said. "I'll hold back the dragon."

. . . . . .

After a silent three-hour flight, the team got off the black jet in a hangar at Langley Air Base. Diego waved as he walked away, "It's been a time, Brothers. See you guys when I see ya!"

Mike looked at James. "I don't think that you guys need us for this de-briefing, do you?"

"Nah," said Chris, "Why don't you two take off and get back to your Team."

"Take it easy," said James. "And Dave, none of that's on you, man."

"Thanks," said Dave quietly.

Mike and James walked away, leaving Dave and Chris alone, standing by the plane. "You think he's in that office?" asked Dave.

"Only one way to tell," answered Chris. "Dave, please try to stay cool."

"Stay cool about one hundred and fifty dead kids? Sure, Chris."

"Well what's the plan then?"

"I'm going to ask some questions, see what he says, and then I'm going to quit," said Dave. "I'm done."

"Ok," said Chris. "I'm with you, Brother."

They turned and walked to the office at the back of the hangar. Dave did not knock; he simply turned the knob and opened the door. Mr. Ezekiel was sitting in the dimly lit room, at the end of an oval conference room-style table, looking through some papers in a file folder. When the door opened, he looked up and said: "Oh, hi! Come in and sit down."

"I think we'll stand," said Dave, coldly.

"Suit yourself. Where are the others?" asked Mr. Ezekiel.

"This is the part where I'm supposed to say something about how we are the only ones who escaped some sort of black beast, right?" said Dave.

"Excuse me?" said Mr. Ezekiel, with a confused look. "A what? Are you saying that you lost three men from your Team, Dave?"

"No," said Dave, "They're fine. I understand that Diego is leaving the Navy and I'm not sure about the plans for the other two. But, you set us down in the middle of the territory of some sort of dark creature."

"Did you see a … creature, or beast, or whatever you are calling it?" asked Mr. Ezekiel.

"No," said Dave. "But it was out there, somewhere, and I know that you know about it."

"That's really weird, Dave," said Mr. Ezekiel.

"As weird as you sending me to incinerate a children's hospital?"

"I sent you to destroy an Iranian nuclear research and development facility," said Mr. Ezekiel, closing the file-folder and leaning back in his chair.

"Yup," said Dave, "a facility attached to a children's hospital. They used the kids as human shields so we, or the Israelis, wouldn't bomb the facility. That wouldn't 'look good,' would it? You wanted to send a message that nowhere and no one is safe or off-limits. But, you also needed it to not be directly traceable to you – at least not that anyone could prove – so, it had to look like a catastrophic accident. Maybe you wanted the kids dead too, or maybe it was just something extra. Tell me I'm wrong."

Mr. Ezekiel paused for a moment and then said: "You're not wrong."

"One hundred and fifty children were burned alive!" shouted Dave.

"The blast from the explosion killed most of them, almost instantly; only a few were burned alive, and they went really quickly," said Mr. Ezekiel with a small smile. "And actually, it was only one hundred and forty-three children who were in the hospital at the time."

Dave froze for a moment. Mr. Ezekiel knew every detail; he had planned this completely. "You're a son-of-a-bitch," said Dave quietly; fury building inside of him.

"Why would you say something like that?" asked Mr. Ezekiel. "We needed the Iranians to come to the table to negotiate away their nuclear program; the world needs it. I'm not the one who used the kids as a shield; who put them in harm's way. There needed to be a way to hit that facility and annihilate it, without the world being able to prove that it was us. We examined every imaginable possibility and the only one that worked was you. The only problem was that your childish, black-and-white ideas of chivalric 'right-and-wrong' would mean that there was no way you'd say yes. So, I gave you the plan with small omissions, which you would never notice and it was done."

"Is that what the black beast was for; to make sure that the secret died with us?" asked Dave.

"I don't know anything about this beast," smiled Mr. Ezekiel. "But if something did happen, out in those mountains, it certainly would have prevented a meaningless conversation about childish ideologies and overly simplistic notions of right and wrong, wouldn't it?"

"Killing women and children is always wrong!" said Dave, pure hatred emanating from his eyes.

"Oh, please," said Mr. Ezekiel. "Women and children always die in war. How many do you think were in those caves in Afghanistan? I could tell you, if you'd like." He smiled smugly.

Dave stepped forward with full intent of pummeling Mr. Ezekiel senseless, but Chris grabbed his arm to stop him. Chris whispered to Dave, "We need to go, right now, before things get any worse."

Dave nodded. He looked directly into Mr. Ezekiel's eyes, "You're a bastard-son-of-bitch and we're done."

"I'm a great hero of my nation," said Mr. Ezekiel, "and you'll never be done."

"You can die screaming and burn in Hell," said Dave. "We quit. Don't ever attempt to contact us again."

Dave turned and Chris followed him out the door. Mr. Ezekiel smiled and shook his head. "How do you think you're going to get back home, now that you've quit?"

Chris yelled back as they continued out of the hangar, "Maybe we'll walk."

. . . . . .

Chris quickly caught up with Dave, as he walked away from the hangar and across the airfield. He was headed in the direction of the nearest gate. Dave said nothing as they walked, so Chris did the same.

As they passed close to a nondescript building, one of its doors opened. Out of the doorway stepped Tim and Professor Jones. Dave and Chris stopped in their tracks, utterly surprised to see them. After all, they had left them on the other side of the world and traveled here at speeds that were supposed to be nearly physically impossible.

"How did you get here?" asked Chris.

"Like I told you, before we left, the same way that we got there," smiled Professor Jones. "We had a few stops, along the way, but I had high hopes that we would catch you. And so we have." He turned to Dave, "How are you, my boy?"

"I'm done," said Dave. "And now we have to find a way home."

"We thought that might be how this turned out," said Tim.

"You're welcome to come home the way we go," said the professor.

"How's that work?" asked Chris.

"Exactly how you'd expect," smiled Tim. "By magic."

"Right," said Professor Jones. "We'll take you back home and then we will be off to continue our role with Mr. Ezekiel."

"I'm done. Why would you still be working with him?" asked Dave.

"Just because your job with this office of the US government is at its end, does not mean that ours is as well," said Professor Jones. "Their activities still have a potential impact on our people, so we shall continue to operate as advisors, though our actual role will be more accurately classified as a monitoring, or early warning, of sorts."

"Great," said Dave, flatly.

"Right," said Professor Jones closing the door from which they had exited. "Now, when I open this door, follow Tim closely and only look forward. Ignore anything that you might see or hear and just follow Tim. I shall follow, last, to ensure that you make it through."

"Is this dangerous?" asked Chris.

"No," said the professor. "But, it could be extremely complicated if you went off on your own. Right. Here we go."

Professor Jones opened the door. Instead to the inside of a military building, they saw a long, very brightly lit hallway, with countless doors down each side. Tim entered, followed by Dave, then Chris, and finally the professor, who closed the door behind them. They walked down the hall quietly. Dave could hear Tim whispering to himself, but could not understand what he was saying. After walking for about two minutes, Tim turned to a door to his left. He opened it and entered and the others followed. It was a nearly identical hall, and they continued. They walked like this for nearly a half an hour – occasionally turning to a door on the right or the left. During their walk, they often heard strange sounds and occasionally a shadow would move past them, in the other direction. But, as they had been directed, they ignored all these things.

Finally, Tim turned to a door on the right. He opened it and they walked through. They were amazed to find themselves, not in another hallway, but rather they were walking through the front door of the Shepherd family home. It was right about sunrise on Tuesday morning. They had been gone slightly less than twenty-four hours. Dave and Chris looked first at each other and then at the professor and Tim, amazed.

"Not too shabby, right?" asked Tim.

"That was amazing," said Chris.

"Well," said the professor, "we mustn't linger. I'm sure your departure from the program will inspire many interesting meetings."

"Thank you," said Dave.

"It is our pleasure, David," said the professor. "We are always happy to see that you get home safely." The professor and Tim reopened the door, walked out, and closed it behind them.

Dave turned to Chris. "I guess we should see who's up."

. . . .

Dave and Chris walked into the kitchen to find Sabrina, Christi and Mary, dressed in scrubs, making a light breakfast, while Anastasia was with John in the sitting room, reading a story. "Hi," Dave said quietly.

They all looked up. Stasia ran to him yelling, "Daddy's home!" and Sabrina set down the apple she was cutting and quickly walked over to give her husband a soft kiss.

"We didn't expect you home so soon," said John standing up. "Everythin' ok?"

"Not really," said Dave, "But at least we're home."

"Mama, Christi, and I were going to go to work and 'Stasia was going to the Campin' Store with Granpa," smiled Sabrina, "but I can probably get out of my shift, if you want me to stay home."

"That'd be great, if you could," said Dave. "I sort of want to tell you a few things before I talk to everyone else."

"It won't be a problem on the floor," said Mary, who usually operated as their Charge Nurse. "I was probably going to have to draw straws to send someone home today, anyway. How about, John, you take Chris home, Stasia can still work with you today, and we all meet back here tonight and have a campfire?"

"Yay!" said Stasia.

They all agreed with Mary's plan and, in a short time, Dave and Sabrina were sitting alone, on the couch, in the room connected to the kitchen. That was, until Bastet came across the floor, on her soft paws. She eyed Dave, circling him and sniffing him for a few moments before hopping up on the couch and nuzzling his arm. He pet the cat as he looked at Sabrina.

She smiled, "What happened?"

Dave took a deep breath, "They changed the plan, dramatically. There was some pretty cutting edge, secret, technology involved – and I can't talk about that – but that's why we're back so soon. Well, that and some magic stuff at the end."

She laughed a little. "Some magic stuff?"

"I don't know, something to do with doors," said Dave. "Anyway, the thing I have to tell you happened on the mission, itself. It's all the highest level of secret, but, what happened will probably be on the news and you already know the biggest secret anyway."

"What's that?"

"That your husband is a dragon."

"Yes," she smiled, gently caressing his hand. "Yes, you are."

Dave, pulled his hand away. "Have you ever really thought about what that really means? Dragons aren't good, Sabrina. All we do is destroy and wreak havoc. We are unspeakably powerful monsters, who devastate anything before us; burning them in an unearthly inferno. How could you possibly want anything to do with that?"

Sabrina moved forward and took Dave's hand back in hers. He was looking down and she was certain that he was about to cry. She gently lifted his chin with her index finger and looked into his ice-blue eyes. "We've already talked about this, Dave. I will always love you. Now, tell me what happened."

"You need to understand that I truly didn't know," said Dave, quietly, starting to cry. "The target was a nuclear facility. The idea was to make it look like they had some terrible accident – which it does – so that they would negotiate to limit their nuclear program."

"That doesn't sound like a bad thing, Dave," said Sabrina, softly caressing his cheek.

"Yeah," said Dave, "I was ok with that. But there's more. They didn't tell me all the details. There was a building attached to the target that I wasn't told about. It was annihilated in the attack as well. Sabrina," he pause to catch his breath, "it was a hospital full of kids."

"Oh my God, Dave," she said as she pulled him close to her. "I'm so sorry!"

Dave half-heartedly tried to pull away as he cried. "Why are you comforting me? Don't you understand what I did?"

"I understand, baby," she said, petting his hair. "I understand that they told you a very different story to get you to do it. I understand that there is not a more noble, honorable, or heroic man whom I have ever heard of – let alone met – than you. I understand that they are to blame for this, not you. I understand perfectly."

"But … do you understand those things?" she asked. "And do you understand that I love you, more than any words can express? Do you understand that there is nothing in this world, or any other, that could make me stop loving you? You are my husband and I am your wife; we belong to each other forever!"

She pulled him closely to her, held him tightly, and kissed him passionately. Her hands were in his hair and around the back of his neck, and she would not let him go. She broke off the kiss, looked into his eyes as she wiped his tears away, and then she kissed him again. She leaned back on the couch, pulling him with her, holding him tightly, and kissing him with the utmost love.

Bastet softly jumped to the floor and padded to the glass French-doors to the outside. She sat up straight, with her back to the room. If one was not mislead by her kitten-like size and soft fluffy fur, one could almost believe that Bastet was standing guard.

.   .   .   .   .   .

"Well, what did you think he was going to do?" asked Professor Jones, sternly.

Mr. Ezekiel was leaning back in his chair with his hands calmly behind his head. "I thought he was going to find-out when and if the news reported it – which they have yet to do, by the way – and then I was going to go with 'who knew?,' and feign sadness at the tragic loss. I'd probably also throw in some of the 'finding the good in all this,' nonsense we tell people all the time. Why the hell would you tell him? And I know it was you, so don't bother lying."

"He deserved to have made his own choice," said the professor.

"More of that garbage, is it?" said Mr. Ezekiel. "This was too important to miss and we couldn't leave it up to a little boy who wants to be a knight instead of a dragon. And speaking of monsters, why would you tell him about the Beast?"

"He deserves to know that you set him up; they all do."

"I didn't set him up," laughed Mr. Ezekiel. "It was a calculated risk. The Beast has been taking out Spec Op patrols; it's gotten more active. I thought, 'two birds with one stone,' it'll catch their scent while he's gone and he'll probably show up just in time to see it approaching – or, worst case, he sees it fighting them – and he takes it out. Win-win!"

"But that isn't what happened, is it?" asked Professor Jones. "And now it has the scent of the dragon. Do you have any idea what that means?"

"Not really," said Mr. Ezekiel with a shrug.

"That Beast was safely in a very barren place, where the only things it had seen, in countless Centuries, were human warriors. He would hunt the strongest of them and was content with the sport. However, this is a creature who wants to be the top-of-the-food-chain, so to speak. There is no question in my mind that it has now seen a dragon and also has seen that dragon turn into a man. It will not be content to remain in its territory thereafter. Because of your foolishness this creature will be unleashed on an unsuspecting world. Who knows where it will go?"

"You do," Mr. Ezekiel smiled, arrogantly. "You just said that it will try to find the dragon. Maybe that will clear Dave's head and get him back to work."

"It is unlikely that the Beast could track him all that way; given a number of things," said the professor. "And you should put David Shepherd out of your mind. He and his brother have retired from the Navy and are no longer your concern."

"Sure," said Mr. Ezekiel. "Whatever you say. Dave is the only one of that Team I specifically needed to keep, and I don't have another mission for him right now so, he can pretend that he's retired if it makes him happy ... for the moment, at least."

"Mr. Ezekiel, I strongly advise that you leave David alone."

"And I strongly advise that you not worry about it, Professor," smiled Mr. Ezekiel. "I'd contact you first, anyway. So, why don't you go and meet your partner at the restaurant before he eats all their cheese."

Professor Jones shook his head and turned to the door. "Good day, Mr. Ezekiel."

Chapter 5

or

"The End of Everything"

A beautiful autumn drifted gently into a sparkling Maine winter and life began to feel slightly less chaotic for the Shepherd family. Shortly before Thanksgiving, Sabrina happily discovered that she was pregnant again and this news was received with great joy by all. After having formally retired from the Navy, Dave and Chris now often helped at the Campin' Store; Chris more so than Dave. Dave would generally stay home on the days Sabrina did not work at the hospital. Anastasia loved the adventures that the three of them had together with the pixies in the forest. Christi and Mary also continued to be very much involved with Anastasia, who loved the attention they poured on her. Gayle was having great success as the Franklin County Assistant District Attorney and it was generally assumed that she would easily become the District Attorney when her boss retired next year. Everything had been going well.

When the snow came, they saw less of the pixies but more of the gnomes, who would deliver cut and aged wood to the house at least once a week. Mary laughed when Dave asked, "have they always been doing this?"

"Well, Darling, how often have you split the wood for our fires?" she laughed.

The winter was cold and snowy, as it ought to be, but it went by without event. A sense of calm, as if a storm had passed, settled in on them all. As the spring of 2011 approached, there was a generally optimistic sense of hope in the air.

. . . .

"Come in," said Mr. Ezekiel, as Professor Jones opened the door. "Sit down. We have a lot to talk about."

Professor Jones and Tim walked into Mr. Ezekiel's opulent office. On the way there, they had noticed that the usually hidden security presence had been replaced by several heavily armed, paramilitary guards. They sat down in the leather chairs facing Mr. Ezekiel's desk. He was smiling broadly and steepled his fingers as he leaned back in his chair.

"Is there a reason for the extremely visible, armed presence?" asked Professor Jones.

"You can never have too much security," said Mr. Ezekiel.

"You said that you had some very important news," said the Professor. He had never liked, nor trusted Mr. Ezekiel, but after the events of October, this had turned into an absolute loathing. They had, thankfully, had minimal contact since that time. However, now the professor had a dark feeling that this meeting would not be a good one.

"Yes," said Mr. Ezekiel. "We found him."

"Whom did you find?" asked the professor.

"Bin Laden," smiled Mr. Ezekiel. "We found Osama Bin Laden in Pakistan."

"Oh," said Tim, "that's good news. But what does this news have to do with your office?"

"Because of where he is," said Mr. Ezekiel, "they are having a difficult time figuring out how to take him out. There are a few plans circulating, but mine is getting a lot of traction."

"I'm sure you plan on getting to your point, Mr. Ezekiel," said Professor Jones, starting to become annoyed.

"Well," said Mr. Ezekiel, ignoring the professor's impatience, "the problem is that the location is a compound near a town. It is hard to get there without drawing attention. So, I thought, if the people had their attention suddenly drawn to something else, say … like a massive fire … our guys could get in with no problem."

"Absolutely not," said Professor Jones firmly.

"I haven't even asked a question," laughed Mr. Ezekiel.

"David Shepherd is retired," said the professor.

"We would just need the dragon for a little fly-by. You know, so it doesn't look like we blew-up the town to get Bin Laden."

"There is absolutely no way that he will even entertain the idea," said the professor.

"It's Osama Bin Laden!" said Mr. Ezekiel. "This is the most valuable target we have. You're saying that he won't even listen to you when you ask?"

"There we are, Professor Jones," said Tim, "that's why he called us. He wants *us* to ask Dave."

"And why wouldn't you?" asked Mr. Ezekiel. "This is an important mission and … well … he likes you."

"He likes us precisely because we respect him and would never ask him to do this kind of work," said Professor Jones.

"What kind of work?" asked Mr. Ezekiel. "He'd just make a distraction. Snip. Snap. The people look away, our guys take out the bad guy, no problem."

"You are asking him to burn a populated town," said Professor Jones.

"Not the whole town."

"This is ridiculous. We are absolutely not asking him," said Professor Jones.

"Well," said Mr. Ezekiel, "then I guess I'll have to ask him myself."

"That would appear to be the case," said the professor.

"You understand that this will mean that I might have to convince him … because, as you say, he'll probably say no."

"I don't see any way that you'll be able to convince him," said Tim.

"Oh, I'm not so sure about that," smiled Mr. Ezekiel. "Sure, he probably won't go for the story. And the money probably won't work either. So, I'll probably have to use threats or actual force."

The professor stared at him with a combination of silent disgust and anger, but Tim spoke, saying: "So, you think that you can use force on a dragon?"

"His family aren't dragons, are they?" smiled Mr. Ezekiel. "And, there's nothing he cares about more. So, you see, even the dragon has a weakness."

"You wouldn't threaten Dave's family!" said Tim, disgusted. "Not even *you* would do that!"

"Well, that sort of depends on him."

"I think that you are a very sick man, Mr. Ezekiel," said the professor. "But I warn you, this will not end well for you."

"You have no idea what resources I can bring to this," smiled Mr. Ezekiel. "Oh, trust me. He'll do it or that'll be the end of our dragon problem."

"Come, Mr. Smith," said the professor standing. "We are leaving."

Tim stood and they both walked to the door. "Where do you think you're going?" said Mr. Ezekiel. "You're not leaving. There's no way you make it down the hall. Now, sit down."

"Good day, Mr. Ezekiel," said Professor Jones as he opened the door. "You shall not see us again."

The professor and Tim walked through the door and closed it behind them. "Damn fool." said Mr. Ezekiel, standing.

He walked to the door and opened it. The only people in the hall were two of his guards. "Where are the two who just left my office?" he asked.

"No one left your office, Sir," said one of the guards. "This is the first time that door opened since you let those men in."

"Damn it!" yelled Mr. Ezekiel, slamming the door.

. . . .

It was Saturday, the nineteenth of March, 2011. There was still wet snow on the ground and the trees were bare, but the temperature was above freezing and it was partially sunny. The hope of the new spring hung in the air.

They all had the day off, so John closed the Campin' Store for the day and Mary had planned that they all would make a day of working with the maple trees they had tapped to make syrup. It was still perfect weather, as the nights were below and the days were above freezing. They had all got up and had a nice pancake breakfast. It was now after ten. They had just finished getting dressed, and were in the yard, ready to go out into the forest and have their work-party.

Queen Maeve appeared among them. In her hair was a small wreath of bare twigs and she was clothed in a robe of light-colored fur. John and Chris made no indication that they could see or hear her. The others silently listened as she spoke.

"Saraph!" she said with urgency, "Something of great evil is coming. Somehow, my sight is clouded, but I know it comes. The first who will come is a man, but one whom you must not trust. It is hard to see what follows, but it is not good. You must take your family and run."

"Thank you for the warning, Your Grace," said Dave. "I wondered how long it would be. Tell your people to stay out of danger."

"Dave, who are you talking to?" asked Chris.

"Shhh!" said Gayle. "He is speaking with the Queen of the Fae. She's warning us of danger."

"I'll say," said Chris, as a black BMW pulled onto the large gravel parking area next to the house.

The Queen of the Fae immediately vanished. The door of the BMW opened and Mr. Ezekiel got out. He was alone. He wore his expensive clothes, designer sunglasses and a long navy blue, wool overcoat. "That's one heck of a road from the main highway! You drive that all winter? Hi Dave, how have you been? Is this you're lovely family?"

Dave walked towards Mr. Ezekiel. He spoke to the family, not looking away from the intruder: "Dad, get everyone in the house."

John nodded to Mary, "You heard him, Babe."

Mary led all the women, and Anastasia, into the house. "Keep your coats on," she said, smiling. "Let's just be prepared for anything."

Chris followed, with John. They approached behind Dave, to offer support. They stood behind him with their arms crossed.

"What do you want?" asked Dave flatly.

Mr. Ezekiel smiled broadly. "What? No 'hello, how have you been?' That's not very friendly Dave."

"Because we're not friends," said Dave plainly. "What do you want?"

"And who's this fine gentleman?" Mr. Ezekiel continued. "I mean, I know Chris. Hi, Chris! But, I don't know the other guy."

"How long are you going to continue trying to schmooze me to get me to let my guard down?" asked Dave. "Cut the crap. What do you want?"

"Well, gee Dave," Mr. Ezekiel continued to smile, "I was just trying to be friendly."

"How about you just get to the point," said Dave.

"Ok, Dave. If that's how you want it." Mr. Ezekiel paused. "I have a little job for you. You're gonna love it. It's the chance of a lifetime."

"I'm retired," said Dave. "Go away."

"But you don't understand, Dave!" continued Mr. Ezekiel. "This job is more important than anything you've ever done. You will be part of a historic event!"

"I don't care," said Dave. "I told you that I'm done and I meant it."

"Dave, just hear me out."

"No. Go away!"

"Dave ..."

"The last time we spoke I told you never to attempt to contact me again. Get the hell out of here." Dave could feel the anger rising.

"We have a chance to get Bin Laden, Dave," said Mr. Ezekiel, calmly.

Dave paused for a moment and then said, sarcastically: "Let me guess, you want me to incinerate him while he reads a book to some kids, on live TV."

"No, no, no," said Mr. Ezekiel with a laugh, "but that's pretty funny. We just want you to make a distraction so they can get him without being seen. Snip. Snap. Easy as pie."

"What kind of distraction?" asked Dave.

"Just a small fire," said Mr. Ezekiel, smiling. "One short pass and you're out. That will draw the attention of everyone in the town. Then, the boys do their business."

"You really are a piece of work," said Dave. "You thought that you could come up here and convince me to burn a town ... a town with people in it? After last time? Hell no."

"Dave, this is nothing like that."

"You know what? Go to Hell! I'm done." Dave turned to walk away.

"Dave, stop," said Mr. Ezekiel.

"Alright, that's about enough," said John, in his deep Texas drawl. "Dave told you no, so it's time that you leave."

"Well, I'm afraid that he doesn't get a choice, John," said Mr. Ezekiel smiling. "It is John, right? Dave's father. US Marine Corps, Force Recon, Vietnam. Wounded in the Tet Offensive. Then you met your wife, Mary – a Navy nurse out of Da Nang. You want me to continue?"

John was caught by surprise but quickly recovered. "What do you mean that he doesn't get a choice?"

"He doesn't. This is way too important," said Mr. Ezekiel. "Dave, I told you at the beginning that if you say no, I'll have to try to convince you. That's what I'm doing now. Eventually, I *will* convince you. I'd prefer it if we kept things friendly and did this the nice way. But then there is always the other way."

Dave turned and took a step closer to Mr. Ezekiel. "And what, exactly, do you think that way would be?"

"Now, Dave," said Mr. Ezekiel smiling, "nobody wants that kind of thing. After all, you have such a lovely place here. A nice house, with all those lovely ladies. What are their names again? Oh, yes: Mary, and Gayle, and Christi, and of course who could ever forget the exceptionally beautiful Sabr-"

Dave punched Mr. Ezekiel with all of his strength, square in the face. The force of the blow lifted Mr. Ezekiel completely off the ground and threw him back into the side of the BMW. "Don't you *ever* say my wife's name again!" he shouted. "You think that you can threaten me and my family and that this will get me to do what you want, you stupid, arrogant ass?! Let me make this very easy for you to understand! The next time I see you, I will send you straight to Hell, myself!"

Dave turned and walked away. Chris followed him, laughing lightly under his breath and whispering, "Jesus, Dave."

John reached down to give Mr. Ezekiel a hand up, but it was slapped away. Mr. Ezekiel shook his head to stop the spinning. He pulled himself up, holding his nose, stumbled a bit, and then opened the door of the BMW. "Just remember that you did this to yourself, Dave!" he shouted after Dave. "You're in the goddamn Hotel California, you little bitch! You can check out anytime you like, but you'll never, *ever* leave!"

Mr. Ezekiel got in and started the BMW. It spun, throwing gravel as he turned and drove down the access road. At the sound of the car, everyone else came out of the house. Dave walked to Sabrina. He embraced and kissed her. "What is it?" she asked.

Dave took off his wedding ring and handed it to her. "I love you, Sabrina. It looks like the fight has finally come here."

Dave turned to John who was walking back to them, "They'll be coming. It'll be soon and a lot of them. Get the guns and get everyone as deep into the forest as you can. I'll find you after." He took off his coat and handed it to Sabrina. "Go with them and don't worry about me."

Anastasia said, "Why is Daddy taking off his coat?"

"Never mind, Baby," said Christi. "Come on, we're going to have an adventure."

Everyone quickly and silently went into the house, by the French-doors next to the lawn. Sabrina lingered and took Dave's hand. "Is everything going to be ok?"

Dave took a slow, deep breath. "Stay together, listen to Dad and Chris and you'll be alright. I'll do everything I can to stop them here. But, Sabrina … they are going to be coming at us as hard as they possibly can. Just keep moving and don't look back. I'll catch up with you as soon as …"

"I love you, Dave," she said, stopping him from saying any more. "I'll love you forever." She gave him a soft kiss, a small smile, and then she turned and went into the house.

"I love you, Sabrina," Dave whispered as she walked away.

. . . .

Inside the house, Mary had opened a hidden cabinet in the sitting room. Decades ago, John had purchased six AR-15's – one for each family member – along with enough thirty-round magazines and ammunition to last through a significant fire-fight. Recently, he had also purchased body-armor for everyone but Anastasia – there wasn't a 3-4 child's size. Mary was busily handing these out as Sabrina came in.

"I haven't fired a round since basic training" said Gayle.

"And if you're lucky, you won't fire one today," said Chris, throwing a small pack with clothes and boots – for Dave – over his shoulder.

Many questions were racing through all their minds, but no one spoke. Their vests were adjusted over coats and Sabrina and Christi slung their rifles so they had hands free to help Anastasia.

"I'm scared, Mama," said the four-year-old little girl.

"I know Sweetie," said Sabrina with a small smile. "Daddy will protect us."

Bastet ran across the room and brushed past Stasia's leg. "Now come on," smiled Sabrina. "Be brave for our little kitty."

Anastasia reached down to pick up the cat, but Bastet dodged her grasp. However, as they began to walk, Bastet followed them.

"Follow me," said John, leading the way into the forest. "We've left so many tracks in the snow taking care of the maples that they won't know which ones to follow. Stay close and stay low. Chris, cover our six."

"You got it, Da," said Chris.

They moved quickly into the forest. What had begun as a bright, late-winter morning full of promise had completely changed in a matter of less than an hour.

· · · · · · ·

Dave stepped out to the edge of the deck and stood, looking out over the lake. Maeve appeared next to him. She was quiet, and pensive. Neither of them spoke for about two minutes. It was the Queen of the Fae who broke the silence.

"Saraph, you shall not be fighting them alone. This is our home as well, and we shall be fighting along with you."

"Thank you, Your Grace."

"It is time, Saraph. They are coming."

The Queen took several steps away from Dave, to give him room for the transformation. Dave looked back at the house that had been his home since he was born. He then looked back out to the lake and the surrounding forest. He took a deep breath and thought "This is the end of everything." A single tear came to his eye. He pushed these thoughts away and focused his mind on what he must do next. "I am the dragon and the dragon is me!"

.   .   .   .

They were making their way up the side of a hill that was covered with wet snow and bare trees when an earth-shaking roar echoed through the forest. Sabrina's pupils involuntarily dilated in abject horror and she whispered: "Christ have mercy!"

They all knew, before Chris could say anything: that sound could only be the dragon. Sabrina looked back at Chris and he nodded: "That's him. Da, we better pick up the pace."

The pace of the small group quickened. Mary was the first to notice the trees, but soon all the women saw it as well. It seemed that the trees were parting to make an easier path in front of them, but closing in behind to make them harder to follow. "The dryads," she whispered to Sabrina, "They are with us."

Sabrina nodded. Christi, walking close by them added, in a whisper, "You won't believe this, but so is Bastet!"

The three women turned and saw. The small fluffy cat was bounding through the snow along-side them, easily keeping their pace. "That is the best cat that has ever lived," smiled Christi.

.   .   .   .

The dragon leapt into the sky and flew, fast and low, over the icy water of the lake. He blasted fire into the icy-cold water, sending up wave upon wave of thick fog. The mists grew and grew over the water and he vanished from the Queen's view; a shadow, silently slipping out of sight.

Maeve, Queen of the Fae, shrugged her shoulders and her robe fell to the wooden deck. Naked, she slowly spread her long, thin dragon-fly-like wings, which had been folded across her back and hidden under her robe. Her wings began to beat and she gently lifted into the air above the water. Her arms spread to the sky and she loudly called out in a language that no human ears had before heard. She was chanting loudly, hovering over the water.

Dark clouds quickly gathered in the once clear sky. Winds began to howl through the trees. Thunder rumbled and a bolt of lightning tore through the sky. The Queen had called a storm, and with the storm, the forest and streams were awakening. The water in the streams was roaring and the trees seemed to be awake and angry. Seeing her work, Maeve smiled. She fluttered to the ground, folded her wings, and picked up her robe – gracefully slipping it back on her body. Quietly she said: "We wouldn't want to make them blush like that, again. Especially not at a time like this." She laughed, and then, she vanished.

. . . . . .

John finally reached the location he had been aiming for. Years and years ago, John and his best friend Pete had made a plan. They prepared a defensive position about a quarter-mile from the house. They had excellent cover but what's more, they were able to have a view, both of the house and out over the lake, without being visible themselves. They had spent months, making it just exactly the way they wanted it. Perhaps it had been paranoia, perhaps it had just been something to do, or perhaps it had been guided by the hand of Providence. Whatever it had been, they were now in an excellent defensive position, exactly when they most needed it.

. . . . . .

Mr. Ezekiel was on a highway, driving south at well over eighty miles per hour. He wasn't sure exactly what highway he was on, only that the pink line on the GPS said that he was going the right way to get to the private airstrip where his plane was waiting.

His head was still swimming, his ears ringing, and his nose was throbbing and dripping blood. He had to breathe through his mouth. His broken glasses were on the passenger seat, beside him. "That little bastard broke my nose," he said out loud. He activated his Bluetooth earpiece, connected to the phone in his jacket pocket. "This is Ezekiel."

"Go ahead, Sir."

"The operation is a go. When we are underway, I want to have full communication with all pilots, and the officer on the ground."

"Yes, Sir. It's all set up. Your call-sign is … um … 'god' … as you requested.

"Excellent! When I give the order to go, how soon can they get there?"

"That just got a little dicey, Sir. It looks like some sort of weather anomaly – lightning and high winds, and a thick mist over the lake – has sprung up at that location. It's very strange, because everything around it is only partly cloudy. Anyway, our satellite can't really see anything down there anymore, just so you know. But, the helicopters can probably be on target in fifteen minutes and the Humvees will be a few minutes after that."

"Great. Have the satellite switch to infrared, that'll probably give a clearer picture. I should be wheels up in five, so tell them to be ready to go by then."

"Copy that, Sir. Have a nice flight."

Mr. Ezekiel pulled onto the small airstrip, where a black jet was waiting for him with the engines running. He got out of the BMW, without shutting off the engine, and stumbled to the crew-member standing by the door.

"Hello, Sir," said the crew-member, "we are ready to go."

"Great. How fast can we get there?"

"I'm sorry, Sir, but we'll be in US airspace. We'll have to use the standard engines. Probably, it'll be about two to three hours."

"If that's the best we can do. Have a medical team meet me when we land."

"You look pretty rough, Sir."

"Yeah, well you should see how the other guy's gonna look in about a half hour or so."

"Sir?"

"Never mind. Let's go."

Mr. Ezekiel got in his seat, strapped in, and tilted the seat back slightly. He felt the engines kick up and the jet start to move. He smiled as it climbed into the sky. "Everything'll start to get better in just a few minutes," he thought. "They can do the Bin Laden mission without the distraction; they're SEAL's. And if the dragon doesn't want to work for me ... there doesn't need to *be* a dragon."

When he felt the jet level off, he activated his Bluetooth. "All teams, all teams. This is god. The mission is a go, repeat the mission is a go. Immediately deploy! Get out there and kick ass!"

．　．　．　．　．　．　．

Two AH-64 Apache attack helicopters flew through the storm clouds and made a pass over the lake. The mist was dissipating and they were in a standard formation, with one taking point and the other acting as a wing-man. They quickly made a circle around the lake and then hovered, over the water, facing the house; rain streaming down their windshields.

"God, this is Eagle-one," the pilot of the front Apache spoke over the radio. "We have no sign of the target on any spectrum. There is a small heat signature on one of the hills, but it is way too small to be the target. What do you want us to do?"

"Eagle-one, Eagle-two, this is god. He's hiding somewhere. You need to draw him out so that you can engage. Ground will be on location in a few minutes and you need to get him down before they arrive. Hit the house."

"Sir?"

"Fire all missiles and rockets on the house, Eagle-one! Raze it to the ground. Expend all ordinance; you are making a statement. That should draw him out."

"Copy that, god. Firing all."

The Apaches increased altitude, tilted their noses down and unleashed a full barrage of Hellfire missiles and Hydra rockets. It was an impressive display of fire-power. Missiles and rockets slammed into the structure, for close to a minute, utterly devastating the Shepherd family home. Explosions and fire burst forth and the house was reduced to a heap of burning rubble.

Eagle-one muttered to himself, "Talk about overkill." Then he spoke over the radio: "God, this is Eagle-one. Target destroyed."

There was no time for Mr. Ezekiel to reply. The retaliation was brutal and immediate.

. . . .

The dragon had flown to a hillside by the side of the lake after he had created the mist. He landed amongst the trees and waited, admiring the storm the Queen had brought. It was not very long – though longer than he had expected – before two Apache attack helicopters flew over the lake. He watched as they circled, no doubt looking for him. They then hovered for a few moments, facing his family's home. He wondered what they planned to do and quietly waited.

When they began firing on the house, he was initially in shock. He could not believe his eyes as his home was brutally destroyed in a matter of seconds. However, his shock quickly turned to rage. He leapt from the hillside and flew, as fast and as hard as he could on his powerful wings, directly at the Apaches.

The dragon slammed into the side of the second helicopter. His huge, powerful feet and razor sharp, talon-like claws grasped and crushed the canopy; tearing through and utterly shredding the bodies of the pilot and gunner before they knew they had been hit. The rotor blades slammed into the dragon, but broke off on impact and fell like twigs, doing no harm to him.

The front Apache spun to get in firing position. The pilot was screaming over the radio: "Contact right! Contact right! Eagle-two's down!" The gunner attempted to engage the thirty millimeter chain-gun, but he never got the chance.

The dragon released the first of his prey and the devastated Apache fell from the sky. As the helicopter plunged into the waters of the icy lake below, the dragon blasted the unquenchable wrath of his fiery breath directly at the canopy of the turning Apache. An unearthly inferno engulfed the entire front two-thirds of the helicopter. The metal hull, itself, was burning in the intensity of the heat. The Apache exploded as it fell from the sky.

The dragon, beat his wings and hovered over the broken and burning helicopters sinking into the water below him. He blasted his fire upon them, once more. Fuel and oil had gushed from the first of the shattered vessels and floated on the surface of the water. The dragon-fire and second burning Apache ignited this and flames burst from the surface of the lake. The dragon threw back his head and roared to the sky in both rage and triumph.

. . . .

When Mr. Ezekiel heard the panicked cry from Eagle-one come over the radio he smiled broadly. He said to himself: "I got you, you little bastard." Then he spoke over the Bluetooth: "Shadow-one, shadow-two, this is god. Target the heat source above the lake and terminate the target utilizing all, repeat *all*, of your Hellfire missiles."

"Copy, god."

Mr. Ezekiel continued to smile broadly. The Hellfire missile was designed to penetrate heavily armored tanks and each of the two remaining Apaches was carrying eight of the amazingly lethal weapons. "You want to be done? Oh you're done now, you little bastard!" he said to himself.

. . . .

Another set of two Apaches rose into the sky from behind the rolling hills. They were positioned, one on either side of the lake, in a pincer-type maneuver. Through their infrared sensors, they could see immeasurable heat pouring from the sky into the icy water below, but it was with their naked eyes that saw the dragon unleashing his wrath and roaring in triumph.

Both Apaches targeted and fired. Sixteen Hellfire missiles streaked through the sky and found their target; slamming into the flanks of the dragon from both sides.

The dragon was caught completely by surprise. He had not noticed the warning of his preternatural senses, being instead focused on his rage and wrath. As he roared in triumph over the shattered, burning helicopters, all sixteen Hellfire missiles slammed into him. As the dragon, Dave had been hit by enemy fire before and nothing had ever hurt him. This was different. The repeated force of the exploding missiles – coming from both sides simultaneously – pounded his ribs. Though the missiles easily penetrated man-made armor, they failed to pierce the dragon's hide. However, he was hit over and over by powerful weapons, and though what Dave felt wasn't exactly what he would call pain, he nonetheless realized that he could no longer breathe. His eyes went dark and he could feel himself falling.

As the dragon fell from the sky and hit the water, the pilot of one of the Apaches spoke over his radio. "God, this is Shadow-one. Target is down. We got him."

. . . .

As the dragon sank into the deep, icy water of the lake, three large Humvees rolled onto the gravel area next to the burning rubble that had once been a large and beautiful house. Men poured out of the vehicles and quickly took tactical positions; their weapons ready. They were all armed with M4 carbines and dressed in winter woodland camouflage. It was a full platoon, separated in three squads.

The platoon leader spoke. "First squad, you're taking the left flank. Sweep the forest in that direction. Third squad, head up the right flank. God says that there is a small heat source on that hill. Second squad, stay with me and the Hummers while we wait for further orders. Oh, and men, no matter what you think you see out there, shoot to kill. We're not taking prisoners back; shoot everything that moves and don't stop until it doesn't."

The men of squads one and three quickly moved out and the second squad formed a quick defensive position. The platoon leader spoke into his radio: "God, god, this is Yankee-leader. Yankee team is on location and deployed. The house is toast and the target is swimmin' with the fishes. We're gonna sweep and mop up."

"Yankee-leader, this is god. Good. Air support will stay until you're done. And remember, absolutely no survivors."

"Copy, god."

. . . . . .

Chris had watched as the first flight of Apaches flew over their position. He flashed a hand-sign to John, who whispered for everyone to stay down. Sabrina and Christi were in the center of the defensive position with Anastasia. "Shh," whispered Sabrina, her index finger to her lips. "We must be very still and quiet so that the bad men don't find us."

"Ok, Mama," said Anastasia looking terrified.

The others had taken position in a semi-circle, John and Mary were close together and facing what used to be the path to their position – before the dryads had obscured it. Chris looked out over the water and towards the house. Gayle was nearby him, to his left.

When the missiles and rockets pounded the house, they were all silent as the sound and fury of the explosions echoed in their ears. A sea of emotions washed over them as they watched the destruction of their home. And it was then that the dragon fell upon the attackers.

They were breathless. None, other than Chris, had before seen Dave as the dragon, much less the abject brutality of his attack. Anastasia jumped to her feet when the dragon came into view. She pointed, jumping up and down and yelling: "That's Daddy, Mama! Daddy's the dragon!" Sabrina tried to hold her daughter still. She couldn't grasp how it was possible that the little girl could know, but she didn't have time to think about it.

The missiles crashed into the dragon and he fell. Sabrina's hands went to her face and she cried out in a combination of pain and terror at the sight of the dragon – that was her husband – falling from the sky. But the sound of her cry was immediately eclipsed by her daughter. "Daddy!!!" Anastasia shrieked, as she pulled away from Sabrina. Christi grabbed for her arm, but the pig-tailed four-year-old girl wriggled free screaming, "No!!! My Daddy needs me!!!"

She fell forward to all fours and crawled with a speed none of them would have imagined possible. They all moved to grab her, but froze when it happened.

There was no flash of light or heat. There was no pillar of fire. There was no roar. It was a smooth and seamless motion. As the little girl wriggled forward, she fluidly transformed into a dragon.

Her form was very different than Dave's. Her skin was a smooth cerulean blue, rather than his rough black with red highlighting. She had four legs rather than two, and her sleek blue wings emerged from slightly behind her shoulders. She also had a long, snake-like neck and her eyes were the same as her father's. Her movements, however, were faster and more fluid than his; wriggling like a salamander. She had fangs and claws, like her father, but they were considerably smaller. As a whole, she was much smaller – only about ten feet in length, not counting her wildly thrashing tail.

She sprung forward, with a cry that sounded more like a loud yip or a sharp bark than a roar, as she charged down the hill. Sabrina screamed after her: "Stasia!!!" But there was no stopping her; she was a dragon.

"Damn it!" said Chris as he leapt up following her. "Troops on the ground and headed this way!" He quickly moved, with expert tactical agility, from tree to tree, as he chased after the blue dragon.

She came through the trees upon the unsuspecting men of third squad with unspeakable fury. They were well past the tree-line and starting up the slope to their target area when she savagely fell upon them. One would have expected that a blue dragon, tearing down a hillside through leafless trees, on snowy ground, would have been seen or heard. She was not. The storm had raged with more fury when the dragon fell from the sky. Now, it was practically as dark as night and the wind was howling through the trees, bringing with it a cold, stinging rain. So, when the blue dragon burst forth upon the men, they were utterly unprepared.

She leapt upon the first man and tore out his throat before he could scream. She spit fire at the two behind him, engulfing them in flame. Her fiery breath could not compare to her father's, but it was enough to burn flesh and bone. The men fell, screaming as they died in fire. The six other men opened fire on the dragon. Their bullets struck her, to no avail.

Chris was not far behind the blue dragon. He came around a tree to her left and squeezed his trigger. A perfectly aimed round struck the squad-leader directly between the eyes and he fell; dead before he hit the ground. One of the remaining men, pivoted to engage Chris, but Chris quickly squeezed the trigger three times and dropped him before he could get off a shot.

The dragon turned left and bathed another two of the men from the third squad in fire. They fell and the other two turned to run. Chris squeezed his trigger and the one on the right, fell on his face, while the dragon leapt upon the other and tore him to pieces as he screamed in both terror and agony.

When she was finished, the dragon turned and looked at Chris. She moved quickly, and almost playfully, towards him. He stood still as she brushed her head against his chest, nearly knocking him over. He stroked his hand down the side of her head and said, "Good girl, Stasia." He smiled his crooked smile and thought to himself: "You'd think that I'd get used to it. Nope, that'll never, ever happen."

. . . .

John and Mary were desperately trying to follow Chris with their eyes down the sights of their rifles, but had lost him before they heard the sound of gunfire. Gayle had moved closer to her parents to aid in covering Chris, but had lost sight of him as well.

Christi was sitting and holding Sabrina, who was silently rocking, her body shaking and tears on her cheeks. Dave's wedding ring was clenched in her hand and held tightly to her chest. Bastet placed her front paws on Sabrina's leg and starred at her face. Sabrina took a shuttering breath and smiled at the small, fluffy cat. It was then that a sudden and inexplicable wave of dread washed over all who were left in the position on the hill.

The first sounds they heard, over the howling wind, was the crunch of large feet on the snow from behind them. Christi looked up and cried out loudly, "Daddy!!!" They all turned and saw it: a huge, black Beast, moving through the trees directly towards them. It seemed to be looking directly at Christi and Sabrina; pure evil and hate glinting in its red eyes.

As it moved towards them, John, Mary and Gayle aimed their rifles and fired in unison, to no avail. It came to the edge of the clearing and they could hear it growling. Bastet's fur was standing on end. She hissed at it loudly and slowly moved from Sabrina and Chrsiti's side, crouching between them and the Beast, as if to defend them.

The Beast crouched as well, preparing to spring. It leapt into the air, towards its prey. But, just as it leapt forward, so did Bastet. With a fierce yowl, she leapt from the ground. In less than the blink of an eye, where once there had been an extremely fluffy, kitten-sized, very brave, cat, there was now and enormous light grey and black stripped tiger. Her yowl became a loud and savage roar as she slammed into the beast – in mid-air – driving it back and slamming its body into the trees behind them.

They all stopped firing and starred in disbelief as the fierce tiger tore into the dread black Beast. The Beast uttered horrible, blood-curdling screams as the tiger-that-was-Bastet tore through its body with claws and fangs. They fought, smashing into tree after tree, Bastet clearly dominating the Beast. Roars, and howls, and crashing, and screams echoed through the forest trees, until Bastet tore out the throat of the black Beast and allowed its life-less body to fall to the ground.

Bastet starred at the dead Beast and they all watched as its body slowly melted into a thick, black liquid. When she saw that, the huge tiger turned and calmly walked directly towards Sabrina and Christi. The women were very still, and would later say that they were very surprised to find that they had absolutely no fear as the tiger approached them. She stopped when she reached them and waited. Both Christi and Sabrina placed a hand on the Great Cat. Christi placed her face against the tiger's neck and nuzzled her, saying, "Thank you, Bastet. We love you!"

The tiger made a sound that might have been a deep purr. She then turned and walked silently off into the forest.

. . . .

Squad one was carefully but rapidly sweeping through the trees when they came upon a clearing. The squad-leader looked, but could see nothing through the darkness and the pouring rain. He gave hand-signals for the team to proceed with caution.

When they were about half-way across the clearing, the squad-leader noticed strange shapes in the snow. He signaled the men to halt and slowly crept forward to investigate.

There appeared to be close to fifty, large garden-gnome statues, standing in some sort of formation. However, they were not wearing the usual pointy, red hats. Their beards had braids in them and they all carried either ornate double-headed axes or three-foot-long spears. The squad-leader smiled as he looked at the odd little statues. He stood up straight, and turned to his men. He laughed as he called out, "Nothing to worry about; they're just gnomes!" Unfortunately for first squad, their leader was wrong. These weren't statues.

The gnome in the front of the formation raised his axe and cried out in a deep voice: "Die Königin will es!"

The others raised their weapons and gave a battle cry. The men of the squad stumbled back in confusion as the gnomes charged into battle. They swept over the terrified men and utterly vanquished them in seconds.

The gnomes orderly got back into formation and the leader again raised his now-bloody axe, saying: "Weiter!" as he gestured forward with his axe and the gnomes began to march toward the lake.

· · · · · · ·

Dave opened his eyes. He was in his human-form. He knew this cave. He sat up but was extremely surprised by what he saw. He had expected a small fire and the friendly girl, with whom he had before spoken. Instead, there was a raging fire. Standing behind it was a majestic female figure, towering over him. She had a shining black armor breast-plate, greaves, and vambraces. She wore a black leather skirt, which fell to her knees. Her flowing black hair was loose and wild, and her huge black-feathered wings were spread wide. In her right hand was a flaming sword and her blue eyes flashed fiercely. Though she was very different, Dave knew that this was the Angel of Death.

"So, that's it. I'm dead." Dave said plainly.

Her voice was recognizably the same as what he remembered, but with much more force and severity than he had before experienced. "In the name of all that is Holy, we don't have time for this right now! Saraph, you will get up this instant! Your family needs you! Now get up, Saraph! Get up and fight!"

The world spun and went dark. He opened his eyes. He was the dragon again. He was under icy-cold water. He moved his body and surged; powerfully swimming upward.

. . . . . .

The Apache, Shadow-one, was hovering over where the dragon and the other helicopters had crashed and burned in the lake. There had been no movement or signs of life from the water in some time, so now he was standing by to support the ground forces. Shadow-two was hovering some way off, behind him and to his left in a wing-man position.

The platoon-leader was with the Humvees in a defensive position with squad two, waiting for word from the teams in the forest.

. . . . . .

After the defeat of the black Beast, John decided that they needed to move forward, the way Chris and the blue dragon had gone, in the hope of linking back up. "Together, we might have a better chance, and I'm not riskin' that no one heard anythin' that just happened."

They stayed close and moved silently, rifles at the ready. It wasn't long before they found Chris and the dragon, crouched by the tree-line, looking out at what used to be their yard. The dragon turned and quickly walked – in a slinky, wriggling way – up to Sabrina. She tentatively placed her hand on the dragon's large head and asked Chris, "can she understand me?"

"Dave always seemed to, and – if anything – Stasia seems to be way more like herself in dragon-form than Dave ever was."

Sabrina, turned to face the dragon and said, quietly but sternly, "You can't run off like that again, we need to stick together."

Afterwards, no one could agree, but Chris always said that the dragon seemed to nod, in agreement."

"So, what do we have out there, Son?" asked John.

"It looks like three Hummers, but only one squad is with them. We took out a full squad, so I'm betting that there's another one out in the woods, somewhere. None of that should be too big of a deal, with our little friend here to help us. The problem is that there are two Apaches providing air-support. I don't think she's ready for that, so I'm not really sure what to do next."

John paused, but before he could answer, events exploded into action. The squad of men by the Humvees, started wildly firing into the woods in the opposite direction from where they were hiding. They could hear a loud commotion and then the men started to fall. What neither John, nor Chris could see, was that a horde of gnomes, brandishing axes and spears, had fallen upon the men of the squad and were in the process of wiping them out. Christi laughed out loud, "Gnomes!"

Christi, Sabrina, Mary and Gayle could see the battle, because they had "The Sight". The men could not. The men of the ground forces, however, could see the attacking gnomes because the gnomes wished it to be so – driving the greatest possible amount of fear into their enemies.

The platoon-leader was screaming wildly for the Apache to fire into the trees. Shadow-one pivoted his Apache to fire, but he never got the chance. An enormous black dragon burst from the lake below him. The dragon practically wrapped himself around the Apache attack helicopter – wings, legs and tail encircling it. His powerful jaws crashed through the canopy and as the crew screamed in terror, he unleashed unearthly dragon-fire upon them. They fell, burning, into the icy water, the dragon dragging them down.

They watched from the trees as light flashed below the surface of the lake. There was a brighter flash, and water sprayed into the sky as the Apache exploded beneath the water. They waited breathlessly. In a few moments, the dragon burst from the surface of the water and climbed into the sky, with an earth-shaking roar.

The last Apache spun and desperately tried to fly away from the dragon. "God, god! Shadow-two! Ground team gone! Air team gone!

We're pullin' out hot! Givin' her everything we-" and the radio went dead.

The dragon did not come directly after the fleeing Apache. Rather he climbed high into the sky. Then he tuned and dove, crashing down upon them from above, unleashing the absolute fury of his fire. The burning helicopter crashed into the far-side of the lake and sank below the surface.

. . . .

After their victory the gnomes, faded into the forest. The winds began to die-down, the rain stopped, and the clouds started to dissipate. The enormous black dragon swept from the sky and incinerated the three Humvees. He then circled over the lake for a final time before landing on what had once been their lawn.

The small blue dragon ran – slinky and wriggly – from the tree-line and stood on her hind legs in front of the black dragon. She let out three yelping noises and then, returned to all fours. The family was walking from the tree-line behind her. She turned around and scampered back to Sabrina. The blue dragon gave a shake – like an animal shaking water from its fur – and an ash cloud fell from her, leaving a very dirty, naked, four-year-old little girl on her hands and knees. She got up and walked the few steps to Sabrina, yawning. "Mama," she said, "I'm sleepy and need a bath."

Sabrina gave her a hug and fluffed her hair. Christi walked over, took off her coat and wrapped her niece in it. Anastasia smiled and snuggled close to Christi.

The black dragon looked at them – tilting his head from one side to the other – as if he were confused. He moved as if he was coming forward, but as he did, ash fell in an enormous cloud. The cloud cleared and Sabrina saw Dave, slowly walking towards her. She ran to him and threw her arms around her husband. He smiled but his legs started to give-out beneath him. Sabrina gently lowered him to the ground. Still holding him, she knelt and gently kissed his lips. "You made it!" she said softly. "I love you, so much!"

Dave's eyes fluttered and he gave a weak smile. His eyes were half-closed but he looked into Sabrina's grey-blue eyes and whispered:

"I love you, Sabrina." Then his eyes closed, he slowly exhaled, and he went completely limp.

Sabrina's nursing training and instincts over-powered the wave of fear that swept through her. She moved quickly, laying her husband back and feeling for a pulse. There was none. She immediately began chest-compressions as she called out to the others, "Help! He's coding!"

Mary rushed to Sabrina's side. Christi handed the now-sleeping Stasia to Gayle and joined them. Sabrina pushed hard and fast in the center of Dave's chest, quietly saying: "Come on, Baby! Don't you dare give-up!"

. . . .

Dave slowly opened his eyes. He was, again, lying on the floor of an all-too-familiar cave. Only this time, the fire was again small and the other occupant of the cave again appeared as she had the previous times: unintimidating and wearing her black "Don't Fear the Reaper" t-shirt.

"Hi Saraph, I'm sorry if I scared you before, but you really needed to get back in that fight."

"It's ok," said Dave, sitting up.

"So, you're back," she smiled. "I'm kind of surprised."

"What do you mean?" asked Dave. "Didn't you call me here?"

"Not this time. This is all you, Saraph. What's going on?"

"I don't really know. I suppose that I have to be here … because of the other dragon."

"Why do you think that?" she asked.

"Well, that's the way it works, right?"

She laughed softly. "No. That's not how things work at all. Let me guess, the 'guardians' told you that there can only ever be one dragon at a time, right? I really wish they would stop filling the holes in what they know with things they made-up or guessed to be true. So, no, you don't *have* to die because your daughter is also a dragon."

"The fact that your little *girl* is a dragon should cause you to question what they told you, anyway," she continued. "Isn't it supposed to be impossible for a girl to have the trait or to pass it on? What a lot of nonsense."

She smiled. "The reality is that they have the whole 'origin of the dragons' story wrong. I do enjoy the Ragnarok tie-in, but that's not what happened, at all."

"So, there were no Asgardians, then?" asked Dave.

"Oh no, of course they were around … quite a long time ago. But there was no 'Odin magic' that made warriors into dragons. The Asgardians didn't make your kind, though a warrior like you did fight along-side them, from time to time. But, no, Ragnarok was about totally different issues and dragons were not involved."

"Some of the history they told you was correct, but the Fae kept completely to themselves until the time you would call the Early Middle Ages. That means that some of their stories that take place before that time are a little sketchy, at best."

"So, how did we come to be, then?"

"You were created, like everything else He created. Creatures in this world change; sometimes through natural processes and sometimes because He changes them. For reasons that only He knows, He changed *this* about your people. It isn't all that complicated; divine intervention never is. He willed it to be and that's what happened. The history of what happened after is about what your ancestors chose to do with that reality."

"Did my grandfather really live for five-hundred years?"

"Yes, he was special, too."

"But if there can be more than one dragon, why did he die when I was born?"

"That's not your story to know, Saraph. At least not right now. All that I will say is that it had nothing to do with you being born."

"So, I guess I'm confused, then. If I don't have to die because there is another dragon in the world, and you didn't call me here, why am I here?"

"It was the choice that you made. I'm not sure why you made it, but you did."

"But, I don't want to die."

She smiled. "Right now, your wife is pushing on your chest, with your wedding ring in one of her hands as she does, desperately trying to get you back. Your mother and your sister are ready to step in to help, the second she gets too tired to continue. And your father, brother and other sister are standing by, terrified and praying. None of them want you to die either."

"What do I do?"

"If you want to go back? Don't die. The conversation that we are having has two possible endings. One is that you stand, take my hand, and we leave. The other is we finish talking and then you go back and live. I certainly have a preference, but it isn't really up to me."

"Well, then who is it up to?"

"It's up to you, Silly. I'm here to help you. I do that with everyone, but you are different. You are special. I know that you still don't understand, but we have a special connection."

"Is it because of all the people that I have killed?"

"No, Silly," she laughed. "And you're not all that prolific, anyway. There are many, many others who are responsible for the deaths of profoundly more than you have been. No, we have a special connection because I'm your Guardian Angel."

"My Guardian Angel is the Angel of Death?" Dave asked. "Don't you have kind of a lot to do? Why would you also be a Guardian Angel?"

"My work is not a problem. I'm an angel, we don't really operate with the same rules of space and time – not having any matter and all that sort of thing. And I'm your Guardian Angel because I picked you. That's how it works. He presents us options and we make choices. I thought that you were special, so I picked you and I do my best to help you … when I can. That's what we do, you know. He made us to serve, not Himself, but you. That's why the others fell; they refused to serve, not Him, but you. But, that's another story."

She smiled brightly. "So, Saraph, you need to make your choice. Do you want to take my hand, or do you want to go back?"

Dave smiled, "I want to go back."

"Ok. Remember that I'm always here if you need me," she smiled. "Now, close your eyes and go back to them."

Dave closed his eyes. He felt a rush, like coming up to the surface from deep under water, and opened his eyes. He started coughing.

Sabrina, stopped chest compressions and pulled him up, close to her. She was crying. Dave lifted his arms to hold her and whispered: "Sorry."

Sabrina laughed and held his face, tears still wet on her cheeks. "Sorry? ... *Sorry?* ... I love you, Dave!" And she held him and kissed him like she would never, ever let him go as she gently slipped his wedding ring back on his finger.

· · · · · · ·

They had moved back into the forest, at least a mile away from the lake and the still burning ruin of what was once their home. They had built a small fire, to keep warm and were sitting around it, trying to figure out what to do next. Some pixies had brought them blankets and clothes for Anastasia – they didn't ask where the pixies got these things, they just thanked them for the gifts. They all took the time to tell the parts of the story that others had missed and Christi was just finishing telling Dave about Bastet, when Queen Maeve appeared amongst them, by the fire.

"I'm glad that you survived, Saraph," she said.

"Thank you, Your Grace," said Dave, "and for everything that you and your people did to help us."

"Is he talking to a faerie, again," Chris asked Gayle.

She made an irritated face at him and turned to the Queen. "Your Grace, is there any way that you can fix it so that they can see what we see?"

"This is a great gift, but, yes." Maeve lifted her right hand into the air, closed her eyes, and spoke: "John. Chris. Let that which your kind may not see, now and forever be seen by thee!"

The two men felt a sharp pain in their eyes and blinked hard. The pain faded in moments, and when they opened their eyes, they had "The Sight."

The world was brighter, clearer, and there were things they had never before seen. "Thank you, Ma'am," said John to the Queen.

Chris said, "Is this how you all see all the time?"

Dave introduced Queen Maeve to the others. And she smiled, saying: "It is nice to meet the whole family. Now, Christi, please finish telling the story of your friend, Bastet."

"Oh, she *was* a friend! She was also the best cat *ever!*" said Christi.

"My dear," smiled Maeve, "she is so much more than that. Bastet is the type of being that people once incorrectly called a goddess. She is no more a deity than I, but she is certainly not a part of what one might call the 'natural world,' either. She must have a great love for your family to have stayed with you this long."

"We all love her, too. I really wish she would come back home," said Christi sadly.

"You wish it?" asked Maeve with a smile. She stood and spoke with authority. "Lady Bastet, I, Maeve, Queen of the Fae, call to you and ask you to come amongst us and speak with us."

There was a rustling in the trees, and then she walked out into the fire-light. It was Bastet, but not as they had ever before seen her. She was a beautiful woman, about five feet, four inches tall. She had long black hair and was naked, except that her body was covered with thin, soft, light grey and black striped fur, with a patch of white fur on her chest, above her breasts and under her chin. It was strange, but no one reacted as if she was actually naked – though she certainly was. At some instinctive level they thought of her as a cat – no one would expect a cat to wear clothes. She had the pointed ears of a cat on the top of her head and a long cat's tail. Her eyes were the same grey-blue cat's eyes they had always known. She was wearing a red leather band around her neck with a small golden medallion. "Hello," she said in a soft but rich voice.

"Bastet?" said Dave.

"Yes, Saraph," she smiled. "It is so good to see you."

"Were you always really like this ... all this time?" he asked.

"I am always all of my forms, but I choose to show the most appropriate form at the most appropriate time."

"Yeah, Ma probably wouldn't have let her sleep on your bed if she had showed up like this," laughed Chris.

She smiled with a cat-like seductiveness, "His teen-years would certainly have been ... much different." She then turned quickly, yet almost shyly, to Sabrina. "I mean no disrespect to you, my Lady. From the first time you came home with Christi, I knew that you and Saraph were meant to be as one."

"Thanks," smiled Sabrina. "So, you can really be the same as you were, before – the small cat, or the huge tiger?"

"I can."

"If you did … if you were our kitten again … you could come with us … wherever we end up going," said Christi, shyly.

"If you all wish me to stay as part of your family, it would give me great joy to join you," she smiled. Then she blinked and where Bastet the woman had been Bastet the small kitten-like, fluffy cat now sat, purring loudly.

Anastasia stirred from her sleep and sat up, yawning. She moved close to Christi, snuggled down next to her and quietly listened.

"That does raise a complicated problem. Where do we go now?" asked John. "I mean I get the whole 'the government giveth and now they can taketh away', but …"

"The government did not give you that house," said Maeve. "When Vinterlogen came here, he asked for the land, the lake, and a cabin. That's what they gave him: a small, log cabin. My people made the home that you all knew. We made it before and we can easily make it again; I could make it so in a matter of minutes. But not here; that would not be safe."

"You're right. It's not safe," said Dave. "Ezekiel will come back. There is no doubt about that in my mind. He … and with him the US government … has declared war on our family."

Other than speaking to the Queen of the Fae and to the Lady Bastet, just moments ago, Dave had been very quiet since he had awoken. He had been thinking about everything that had happened and a silent rage had been building within him. "If the US government wants to go to war with a dragon, then that's what they're going to get. After all, it won't be the first time that a dragon has razed a city."

Sabrina interrupted him. "You will do absolutely nothing of the kind." She spoke softly, but with an irresistible firmness.

"They destroyed our home and tried to kill our family. I think that a brutal retaliation is absolutely merited," said Dave.

"The men who did that are all dead. Cities are full of innocents, who know nothing about what happen today. I know you're angry – I think we all are – but this isn't you. Dave, you spent your whole life fighting with honor, being a knight who truly lived the code of chivalry. You swore to defend the innocent, not to annihilate them," answered Sabina.

"Ezekiel isn't dead," said Dave.

"Do you understand what I'm trying to say, Dave?" she asked, taking his hand. "You can't let yourself turn into him, no matter what he has done to us. Everything you've ever stood for would be lost the moment you unleashed dragon-fire on the cities you swore to protect."

Dave looked down but Sabrina pulled him close to her. "It's going to be ok. You don't have to fight anymore. Dave, I'm asking you to stop. Let this war be over."

Dave could feel both the firmness and the gentleness in her words. He could feel the love that was behind them as well. With crystal clarity, he could see that she was trying to save him – as much now as when she fought to bring him back, earlier that day. And it was then that he made the choice not to succumb to his rage. He would stay with Sabrina, and he would fight no more.

"I love you, Sabrina," he said. "You're right." He took a slow, deep breath and quietly said, "Ok … I'm done with them."

Queen Maeve smiled. "Problems like Ezekiel often have a way of finding their own solutions. Let us speak of another, more immediate problem you all face: you need a home."

"There is a place, very much like this, where we could have a new home and land for you all. It is not in this country, it is in Canada; in a place called British Columbia, near a city called Vancouver. The forest is very similar and there is a nice, deep, lake. The hills are mountains, actually, but other than that, you will find things the same. The land will be yours, and no one will question it. It has always been that way, of course."

"In your house – the same as before, but updated to fit your family as it is now and shall be in the future – you will find all your clothes and things as you left them this morning. You will also find that all of your papers are Canadian, as if you lived there all your life. You will also be untraceable from here; it will be like this never existed. I can get you there in the blink of an eye. Would you like this new world?"

"What about everyone's jobs: the hospital, Gayle's work, and the Campin' Store?" asked Dave, quietly.

"The Campin' Store will be there – and more profitable, as there are several parks close by – as is a small hospital, where you all have the same jobs as you had here. Gayle has a comparable job as a Canadian version of her work here – don't worry, you already know all the differences in the laws, if you concentrate. As far as anyone knows," Maeve smiled, "this is no different than it ever was."

"I hate to be the one to ask about money," said Chris.

"Anything you have here will be there," said Maeve, "with the exception of the specifics of government pensions, though I doubt you'll even notice to miss them.

"Also, you will find that you remember everything that you need to know – like how to get to the grocery store, for example. The people you will be working with won't think that you're new, and you'll remember them as well."

"This is all done by magic," smiled Maeve. "Once you step through the doorway I open, those things will all be real."

"Isn't there always some sort of dreadful price for this sort of thing," asked Dave. "That's the way it always works out in every story I have ever read."

Maeve laughed brightly. "Those stories were written by human hands, from human minds full of fear of me and my people. Neither you, nor any member of your family ever needs fear us. There is no price for gifts that I give freely ... other than your continued friendship and good will, of course."

"Also," she continued, "my people will move with you to this new land. You shall loose nothing and we shall continue to be with you. What is your answer?"

They were all quiet for a moment. The silence was broken by Anastasia. She yawned and said: "Mama, I want to go where the nice Queen is talking about. Can we?"

Dave laughed, "I'm okay with this plan."

Sabrina kissed him, "Me too."

"Unless anyone has a good reason to say no," said Mary, "I think we're moving."

Maeve raised her arms and sang in a language none of them knew. A point of light appeared in the forest and grew. It was like a growing ring of fire in the air. It grew to be big enough for several people to walk through together and the space inside the ring looked like the rippling surface of the lake. "All you need to do is say good-bye and walk through to your new home," smiled Maeve. "You'll find that the lights are on and a nice dinner is waiting."

Dave took Sabrina's hand and then he took Anastasia's as well. He looked around at the forest he had known since childhood and smiled a sad smile. He hated to leave this place, but he knew that this was how it had to be. "Come on," he said, as he walked to join the Queen by the door in the air.

The others stood and followed and Bastet bounded up to Stasia's side. The Queen of the Fae smiled, "Alright. Follow me."

With that, she turned and led them through the door.

. . . .

"Come in and have a seat," said the older man, seated at the center of the table, flanked by the other four, important looking people – two on each side of him.

Mr. Ezekiel sat down in the chair on the other side of the broad table, facing them. His broken nose was bandaged and he had on a different very-expensive suit. Two days had passed since the battle and he was surprised *The Committee* had waited this long to summon him.

Very few people knew about Mr. Ezekiel's organization, but all who did believed that he was ultimately in control of it, with vague supervision and consent given exclusively by the President of the United States of America. A similar situation was thought to have existed since the organization's inception in Nazi Germany, only with Hitler acting as the President was thought to act now. To all appearances, this was the way the organization was run, but this was not correct.

This organization was run by a Committee of five. *The Five* powerfully and secretly controlled many different things from the shadows, this organization was only one small piece in their game. Mr. Ezekiel was only one of a handful of people who were aware of their existence. He knew enough to fear them, but not much more … other than that – though they appeared to be – The Five were not, in fact, human beings.

Mr. Ezekiel sat and waited for them to speak; fear freely flowing through him.

"We sent people to examine the site you discussed in your report. The only thing that they found was what had once been a small log cabin, burnt to the ground. There were no bodies. There was no wreckage of any kind – on land or in the water. There were no signs that the battle you described ever occurred."

Mr. Ezekiel was shocked, "That can't be! I know it happened!"

"Yes," said an older woman to the left of the man in the center, "we're sure that you do."

The man in the center continued, "A most unfortunate business, Ezekiel. Most unfortunate. That brings us to our next item. We are shutting down this agency. Too much money for too little return and the mission is ultimately unnecessary. Also, I'm sure you can imagine how the press would react to the fact that the current administration continued to fund one of Hitler's personal favorite projects, if this ever were, in fact, discovered. No. No. It is to be no more."

Mr. Ezekiel was exasperated. "What am *I* going to do?!"

"That would bring us to our last point, Ezekiel," said the man in the center. "You played an extremely dangerous game. You thought that you could control an asset, who had a particularly intense … skill set, and through your own misjudgment and arrogance you lost that asset. Then you thought that it was a good idea to go to his home and threaten him about participation in an extremely secret mission – for which we have no need whatsoever of his skills – and after he refused, you destroyed his home, attempted to kill both him and his family, lost an elite platoon of men, not to mention three Humvees, and four Apaches, with their crews. Is there any limit to your profound misjudgment?"

"Sir …" said Mr. Ezekiel.

"I am not finished," said the man in the center, sternly. "The possible consequences of your actions are too horrible to imagine. Had you succeeded at killing a member of this man's family – God forbid his wife or daughter – American cities would be an inferno as we speak! We can only hope that we are not now merely in the calm before a fiery storm! You, Sir, are an extreme danger to national ... no ... *global* security, for a great many reasons. Because of that, Ezekiel, we see no other choice than to immediately terminate you."

Mr. Ezekiel opened his mouth to protest, but a hood went over his head from behind. He felt his hands grabbed and pulled back, from behind, and his head firmly jerked back. He tried to struggle but the ones holding him we far stronger. He wildly screamed in terror, but his scream turned into a wet, gurgling sound as the ice-cold, razor-sharp blade deeply sliced his throat. His blood spilt down the front of his very-expensive suit and onto the floor. Then, Mr. Ezekiel's head slumped forward and he was dead.

"Yes. Yes. Very nicely done," said the man at the center of the table. "Have a team clean up this mess." He stood, "Well, shall we all get some lunch?"

. . . . . .

It was a warm summer day in 2012, next to a beautiful blue lake, surrounded by a thick forest, in the mountains north of Vancouver, British Columbia. In the shade, on a wooden deck that extended out over the water, Dave Shepherd was lying on a double chaise lounge, peacefully sleeping with his arm around his beautiful wife Sabrina. Sabrina was quietly watching their five-year-old daughter, Anastasia, happily playing with Bastet – a soft, fluffy, kitten-sized cat – on the lawn. Aunt Christi was sitting nearby, on a blanket on the warm grass, gently playing with Stasia's one-year-old baby sister, Sadie.

John and Mary Shepherd walked out of the house with some trays of snacks. Chris and Gayle emerged from a trail, holding hands. Gayle was obviously at least five months pregnant. They reached the deck together and Chris reached into the cooler, coming up with a cold bottle of Moosehead Lager. He took a drink and laughed, "Da, you used to this one yet?"

"It's not my 'Cowboy Beer', but it's cold. I'll take one of those," he replied.

Chris handed John a bottle and Dave stirred. "Mmm. Hi Sweetie," said Sabrina and she fuzzed his beard and kissed him gently. Did you have a nice nap?"

"I did. It certainly is a nice day," said Dave, stretching and sitting up. Chris handed Dave a bottle of beer and he took a sip. "You know what?" said Dave smiling and putting his free arm around Sabrina. "Maybe tonight I'll make a fire."

Epilogue

or

"Another Amazing Cheese."

Constable Gordon Summersbey, of the Royal Canadian Mounted Police, lay in a trauma bed in Vancouver General Hospital. He was very lucky to be alive. After the helicopter crash, he had been in the snow, on the mountainside, for two days before the rescue-team had found him. Both his legs were broken and he had almost succumb to hypothermia, but he was alive. The doctors said that he was now stable and could be interviewed by his Inspector, for whom he was now waiting.

The nurse knocked at his door and stuck her head in: "Are you up for some visitors, Constable?"

"Visitors?" he thought to himself. But he answered, "My Inspector, you mean?"

"No," she smiled, "These men said that they work for a Special Office in Ottawa. They said that it is urgent they speak with you as soon as possible."

"Well, let them in then," he said.

The nurse smiled and opened the door for the gentlemen from Ottawa. The first was a stout older man with short cropped hair and a well-trimmed beard; both grey bordering on white. The second was a tall and thin much younger man with slightly bushy hair. The nurse left and they both pulled up chairs to the bedside.

"Hello, Constable Summersbey, my name is Professor Jones and this is my colleague, Mr. Smith," the older man spoke in a crisp Oxford accent. "We work for a Special Intelligence Office for the government in Ottawa. We would like to talk to you about your accident."

"Why don't you just read the report? Inspector Campbell is coming soon. I'll give him all the information," said Gordon.

"Oh, we would much rather talk to you in person, Gordon," smiled the professor. "Isn't that correct, Mr. Smith?"

"It is, indeed, Professor Jones," said the younger man, in an almost sinister tone.

"Right then," said the professor. "Tell us what happened."

The young Constable took a breath. "Alright. Well, we were at our station, near Garibaldi Provincial Park, when we got word that a private plane had gone down in the higher mountains, somewhere to the northwest of us. We were to take the AS350 helicopter and join in the search effort. I was in the back with the rescue team. We knew it would be getting bad – a storm was coming in off the Ocean – but we had to find those people. There were other teams out there, of course."

"We flew around the vicinity of where they said the crash had been, but we found nothing. The weather was getting pretty bad – wind and snow – and it was getting close to when it would be dark. One by one, the other teams were going back in to wait-out the storm. Our pilot wanted to take another pass through a more secluded valley."

"I really don't know what happened, but I knew we were in trouble. Lights were flashing and alarms were going off. The helicopter lurched all over the place and then it just felt like we were falling. There was crashing and screaming and pain and then everything just went dark."

"When I woke up, it was day and we were on the mountain-side, I have no idea how I had been thrown from the helicopter, but I was tens of meters away from the rest of the crash. The helicopter had burned and, from where I was, it didn't look like there could have been any survivors. I tried to move, but my legs were obviously broken and throbbing in pain. I managed to drag myself to the side of a huge red cedar and prop myself into an almost-sitting position. There was no way that I could signal for help, so, I just waited and hoped for the best."

"All day and all night, no one came. I was so hungry and so cold. I was sure that I had lost a lot of blood in the breaking of my legs. I started to think that I wasn't going to make it."

The next morning, though, was just mad. I saw something out there. You know, people talk about seeing the Sasquatch, eh? Well, I saw something even crazier than that."

"What did you see?" asked Professor Jones, leaning forward.

The young Constable smiled. "I saw dragons. There were two of 'em. A huge black one and a small blue one. It looked like the big one might have been teaching the smaller one something about flying – the way they were maneuvering, you know. Anyway, the little one saw me and made a loud yipping-bark sound. The bigger one looked at me and circled around. Then it was sort of like he led the little one away. And they were gone."

"That evening, and I was pretty out of it by that point, they found me. I guess some hikers saw the helicopter – though why hikers would be way out there I don't know – and called it in. And that's the whole story."

"That is fascinating, don't you agree Mr. Smith?" said the professor.

"It most surely is, Professor Jones," he replied.

"For sure. For sure," said the Constable. "But there's no way I'm giving that story in an official report. I'm not even sure why I told you, to be honest – maybe my head's still not right. But we're just chatting, right now, so I guess there's no harm. Just so you know though, there's no way I'll ever admit that I said this if you report it."

"Why ever not?" asked the professor with a smile.

"Well, you guys seem friendly enough … for the most part," he eyed Mr. Smith, suspiciously. "But Inspector Campbell is a complete hard-ass. No way I'd tell him a story about dragons. I'd have to be crazy, 'eh?"

"Crazy, indeed," smiled the professor.

"Anyway," continued the Constable, "it was probably the hypothermia, the blood-loss and the hit from the crash. There's no such thing as dragons. Everyone knows that. If I started spouting off about that sort of thing, they'd all laugh at me. Or even lock me up!"

"Probably throw away the key," said Mr. Smith, the sinister tone in his voice gone.

"We wouldn't want that, would we, Mr. Smith," smiled the professor.

"Wouldn't want it one bit, Professor Jones," smiled Mr. Smith.

"Well, I'm too smart for that," smiled the young Constable. "Only short, boring reports for Gordon Summersbey."

"I say, Gordon," said Mr. Smith, now falling completely into his regular Cockney accent. "What's that basket you got over there?"

"Oh that? My Mum dropped of some stuff – wrapped sausages and chesses, mostly. The Doc says that I'm not supposed to eat that sort of stuff yet. Too bad really, Mum likes the gourmet stuff, so it's probably really good. You can take some if you like."

Mr. Smith smiled brightly, "Really?"

Professor Jones frowned at Mr. Smith but Gordon said, "Sure, take what you like. There should be a small cutting board and a small knife in there. Try it out to see if you like it and then take the best one. No one else is going to eat it anytime soon."

Mr. Smith moved with great excitement and selected a "Black Diamond Cheddar", aged five years, which said "Vintage Reserve Cheddar" on the label. He gently, carefully opened it and sliced off a small piece. He lifted it to his mouth and took a small bite. His eyes lit up: "This cheese is amazing! Mature tones, an intense bite, those little crunchy, salty bits: this cheese is simply marvelous!"

Gordon laughed, "I'm glad you like it. Take it with you."

"Oh, thank you! Thank you! You can call me Tim, by the way."

"Alright, Mr. Smith, that is quiet enough. What would Her Grace think if she saw you like that?" said Professor Jones in a very grumpy tone.

"You two know the Queen?" asked Gordon, surprised.

Tim and the Professor looked at each other for a moment; the slip had been unintentional. "Yes, quite right," said the professor. "Our Office reports to her, upon occasion."

"She's amazingly spunky, for her age," said Gordon.

"You have no idea," muttered Professor Jones. "Right then, off we go."

"Feel better, Gordon," said Tim. "And thanks for the cheese!"

Tim and the professor were walking out the door and a rather portly and overly serious-looking RCMP Inspector, with a large handle-bar mustache, was walking in. "Good day," said the professor, continuing on.

Inspector Campbell shut the door behind him. "Who were those people, Summersbey?"

"Just some friends," smiled Gordon, "stopping by to wish me well."

"Alright," said the inspector, sitting down and taking out an official looking folder and a pen. "Now, tell me what happened."

"I don't really remember much," began Gordon. "I must have hit my head in the crash, I had hypothermia, and I had a lot of blood loss. It was just a bad helicopter crash and I got lucky."

. . . . . .

Tim and the professor walked out of the hospital and down the street. "Is it absolutely necessary for you to eat all the cheese you see?" asked the professor.

"This is really good cheese, you should try some."

"Perhaps later. But why do you always gravitate to the cheese?"

"Don't know," said Tim. "Perhaps I'm part mouse."

"That would explain a lot, actually," said the professor. "Well, he did our job for us; that story won't be told."

"He's a nice lad," said Tim, thinking about the re-wrapped piece of cheese in his pocket.

"Rather," agreed the professor. "Well, we should go and let them know that all is well: the boy is alright and he won't be talking. It was nice of them to call in his location, but we shall have to urge them to be more careful about being seen while he is teaching her."

"The mountains are quite remote," said Tim. "It's probably safer here than most places."

"Quite right," said the professor. "And if they do just get seen, it does give us a chance to get out and do something."

"And if they hadn't, Gordon would have died ... and not that it's the same thing, by any means, but ... we also would not have discovered another amazing cheese!" said Tim with a smile.

"Oh, you can share it with them all tonight, when we go over for dinner," laughed Professor Jones. "Now come on, Tim, let's be on our way."